CAPTIVES

SHAUN HUTSON

CAPTIVES

Macdonald

A Macdonald Book

First published in Great Britain in 1991 by
Macdonald & Co (Publishers) Ltd,
London & Sydney

Copyright © Shaun Hutson 1991

The right of Shaun Hutson to be identified as
author of this work has been asserted by him
in accordance with the Copyright, Designs and Patents Act
1988.

A CIP catalogue record for this book
is available from the British Library.

ISBN 0 356 19576 7

Printed and bound in Great Britain by
Hazell Books Ltd, Aylesbury, Bucks

Macdonald & Co (Publishers) Ltd
165 Great Dover Street
London SE1 4YA

A member of Maxwell Macmillan Publishing Corporation

Dedicated to Mr Wally Grove.
My most valued friend.
From one unsociable bastard
to another.

Acknowledgements

As with all my books, there now follows a list of everyone or everything that contributed to the writing and beyond. Even if it was only to try and keep yours truly something approaching sane. To everyone mentioned you have either my thanks or my admiration (some even have both).

Extra special thanks to Gary Farrow, my manager, for his continuing efforts to ensure that anyone but *us* pays for expenses (and, no, I'm still not wearing a bloody suit). Thanks, mate. Thanks also to Chris Page at 'the office' (despite his taste in football teams). Many thanks to Mr Damian Pulle, the Houdini of the VAT returns.

Very special thanks to Nick Webb for his faith and his matchless ability to find gut-busting restaurants. To John O'Connor, Don Hughes, Bob Macdonald, Terry Jackson and Dave Kent and, especially, *all* my sales team for hammering everyone into submission. You don't release this lot, you *unleash* them. Thanks also to everyone in publicity and marketing. Extra special thanks to Caroline Bishop who put up with me 'on the road' (I promise to wear a vest next time, C.B. . . .). But to everyone who contributed to a superb campaign, I thank you. To Barbara Boote and to John 'I know that one' Jarrold, many thanks. In fact, to everyone at Macdonald/Futura/Sphere I extend my thanks.

Special thanks, as ever, to Peter Williams and Ray Mudie.

To Tom Jones (no, not *that* one) and UCI. To Steve Hobbs at Bletchley Library for his help and interest.

Very special thanks to Mr James 'this is how this one is going to end' Hale, editor *par excellence* (have I spelt that right, James?).

To Brian 'I've got two tickets here and by the way there's another one arriving soon' Pithers. To Graham Rogers at 'Late Night Late' (I always wanted to be on TV, Graham). Thanks also to 'Mad' Malcolm Dome and Phil Alexandar at *RAW*, to Jerry Ewing at *METAL FORCES* and to Krusher at *KERRANG!* (and GLR of course . . .). Thanks to Gareth James, John Gullidge, Nick Cairns and John Martin. To John Phillips, or should I say Rikki . . .

Massive, immeasurable thanks to David Galbraith (and to *ROCK POWER*) for the meat pie and the day of a lifetime and also to Dave 'can I have your autograph Mr Gilliam' Evans.

Extra special thanks to the phenomenal Margaret Daly who tried to kill me in Dublin, but in the nicest possible way. Thank you for your amazing work.

Many thanks, as ever, to Broomhills Pistol Club, particularly to Bert and Anita. To Dave Holmes who sat and talked to me without giving a toss I'd only end up with three hours sleep. Thanks, mate . . . Keep the sick jokes coming.

Special thanks to all the staff and Management at The Holiday Inn, Mayfair, for their continued friendliness and kindness. Thanks also to everyone at Dromoland Castle in Ireland, to the Mandarin Oriental in Hong Kong, the Barbados Hilton and to Bertorelli's in Notting Hill Gate.

Thanks are due, as ever, to Steve, Bruce, Dave, Nicko and Janick for allowing me to share their stage and re-live more dreams. I am eternally grateful. Thanks also to Rod Smallwood, Andy Taylor, everyone at Sanctuary Music and to Mr Merck 'sliced into fifteen pieces by lunchtime' Mercuriadis.

Many thanks to Mr Jack Taylor, Mr Amin Saleh and Mr Lewis Bloch for all their help and advice. Thanks also to Mr Brian Howard at Russells for removing a rather annoying stone from my boot.

Thanks, for different reasons, to Alison at EMI, Shonadh at Polydor, Georgie and Zena.

Many thanks to Ian Austin who deserves a line on his own and who, in fact, deserves much more. The man whose ability to talk is surpassed only by his value as a friend. Thanks.

Indirect thanks to Queensrÿche, Nevada Beach, Thunder, Harlow, Black Sabbath and Great White. Also to Oliver Stone, Martin Scorsese, Walter Hill and Michael Mann.

This novel was, as ever, written on Croxley Typing Paper, wearing Wrangler Jeans and Puma Trainers (I don't give up easily you know . . .). Also many thanks to Yamaha Drums, Zildjian cymbals and Pro-Mark sticks for helping me clear numerous mental blocks . . . (come on, if I can try for some jeans I can try for a cymbal or two . . .).

My greatest thanks, as always, go to my Mum and Dad for everything they've done and continue to do and for my long suffering, ever-patient wife, Belinda. For putting up with me through this and other novels and for enduring the ups and downs of yet another season of me worshipping Liverpool FC, you have, and always will have, my thanks and my love.

And to you, my readers, for still being there, for sticking with me, thanks. To those of you joining the ride for the first time, welcome. Thank you all.

Shaun Hutson

Revenge is a kind of wild justice.
Francis Bacon

PART ONE

What is good? All that heightens the feeling of power, the will to power, power itself in man.

Nietzsche

I don't believe in Love,
I never have, I never will.
I don't believe in Love.
It's never worth the pain that you feel.

Queensrÿche

One

He knew he was going to die.

Knew it.

He didn't *think* he might. Didn't *wonder* if he would.

Brian Ellis *knew* he was going to die.

The barrel of the shotgun was less than a foot from his face. It poked through the shattered remains of the safety glass partition, so close he could smell the oil and cordite from the yawning muzzle.

From that muzzle seconds earlier had come a thunderous blast which had ripped through the toughened glass as if it had been spun sugar.

It had been at that point that Brian Ellis had filled his pants. He stood there now, reeking. Standing there with a dark stain spreading across the front and back of his trousers. He couldn't think, couldn't move. All he was aware of was the sickening warmth around his lower body coated in his own excreta.

And he was aware that he would die.

He wanted to scream. Wanted to be sick. Wanted to pray. Wanted to bellow at the top of his lungs that he was only twenty-three and he didn't want to die. *Please don't kill me. Please, Jesus Christ, God Almighty for fuck's sake don't make me die.*

The barrel of the Spas wavered closer to him and he began shaking uncontrollably.

Alarm bells were ringing; somewhere else in the bank a

child was crying. A baby. Someone was sobbing. Someone was moaning.

Brian heard the sounds but none registered in his mind.

All that registered was the sure and certain conviction that he would soon be dead.

The alarm had gone off automatically as soon as the safety glass had been blasted away. There had been no furtive attempts by one of the other cashiers to find the alarm button that linked the bank directly with Vine Street police station. There'd been no need. Besides, this wasn't a film where the cashiers and customers stood around calmly (if somewhat worried) while tills were rifled, lives were threatened and then masked men ran from the bank into the arms of the law, who had arrived in the nick of time after being alerted by that single, secret alarm. *How comforting was fiction.*

The man who stood in front of Brian Ellis wasn't wearing a mask; he hadn't warned everyone to be quiet, hadn't told them that if they did as they were told no one would be hurt.

He had walked straight through the door of the Midland Bank in the Haymarket, pulled a Spas automatic shotgun from inside his coat and opened fire. First he shot a woman who had been standing close to the door counting money before she pushed it into her purse. She now lay in a bloodied heap, her limbs tangled like those of a puppet with cut strings. Her handbag and its contents were strewn across the marbled floor, some five pound notes having come to rest in a puddle of her blood.

Scarcely had the sound of the first shot died away than the gunman had fired again, into the counter glass. It had exploded inwards, showering those behind it with fragments of needle-sharp crystal. One of the other cashiers had suffered a badly cut face. It was her moans that Brian could hear as she tried to pull a thin fragment of glass from one corner of her eye.

The child he could hear crying was in a pram at the other end of the counter. The mother was crying softly too.

Don't make me die.

His mind shrieked it again.

The gunman was looking at him, as if he had recognised him. A vague recollection of a face seen in a crowd. *His* face was calm, his eyes narrowed. These were not the staring eyes of a madman. There was deliberation in his movements. He appeared unfazed by the strident ringing of the alarm bells that continued to fill the bank.

'Give me the money,' the man said calmly, his eyes never leaving Brian's.

But Brian couldn't move.

'Now!' the man snapped, pushing the barrel of the shotgun closer to the cashier's face.

Despite its earlier lapse, his bladder managed to bring forth more. Brian felt more fluid running down his leg, soaking into his trousers.

Please don't kill me.

He could feel the tears welling up in his eyes.

Dear merciful Christ, not now.

'The money,' rasped the gunman through clenched teeth.

The child was still crying.

'Shut that fucking kid up,' snarled the man without turning his head. He actually poked the barrel of the Spas against Brian's cheek.

Sirens.

Oh sweet fucking Jesus. Lord God in Heaven please . . .

The sirens were blaring from the direction of Piccadilly. They would be here in a matter of moments.

Please, make him go. Please God, make him go now.

5

The alarms continued to screech. The baby was still crying. And the sirens came closer.

A look of mild annoyance passed fleetingly across the gunman's face. He took a step back.

Not now. Don't make me die now, please God, don't . . .

He fired once, the barrel only six inches away from Brian's face. The report was massive, drowning out all the other sounds for a moment as the discharge tore most of the cashier's head off. He remained upright for a second, blood spouting from what remained of his cranium, then he pitched forward, sprawling over the counter.

If God had heard Brian's prayers he had chosen to ignore them.

The gunman turned and headed for the door. As he reached it he paused and looked at the woman with the pram.

The child was still crying.

He looked at her, then at the pram, then he fired twice.

Both blasts struck the pram, ripping through it.

He pushed the door and walked out into the street.

Those passing saw the shotgun; some screamed, some ran. Some just froze.

A police car, blue lights spinning madly, sirens screaming, came roaring around the corner into the Haymarket. The gunman gritted his teeth and looked behind him. The traffic lights were on red.

The traffic was at a halt.

He tossed the Spas to one side, digging inside his jacket for a pistol. Pulling the Smith and Wesson 9mm automatic free, he ran towards a motorcyclist who was idly revving his engine, watching the lights, waiting for them to change. Exhaust fumes poured from the pipe of the 850cc Bonneville.

The lights were still on red.

The police car drew closer.

The gunman shot the motorcyclist once in the back of the neck, pushing his body from the bike, gripping the powerful machine by the handlebars to prevent it toppling over. He swung himself onto the seat, twisted the throttle and roared off, the back wheel spinning madly on the slippery road before gaining purchase.

He swung left into Panton Street.

The police car followed.

Two

As the Bonneville rounded the corner into Panton Street its rider found himself faced with an oncoming car.

The driver of the car blasted on his hooter as much in surprise as annoyance, looking on in bewilderment as the bike shot up onto the pavement and sped off.

A second later the police car skidded round in pursuit, slamming into the front of the car as it passed, shattering one headlamp.

Inside the police car Constable Norman Davies was speaking rapidly into the two-way radio, giving the location of the unit and also attempting a description of the man they were pursuing. He gave the number plate, forced to squint to read it as the bike hurtled back and forth from pavement to road, swerving past both parked and moving cars alike. Davies also called for assistance and for an ambulance to go to the bank in the Haymarket; although he had not seen the carnage inside, it was standard procedure.

Besides, he and his companion, Ralph Foster, now hunched over the wheel in concentration, had seen the motorcyclist shot. Davies winced as he remembered the police car inadvertently running over one of the dying man's outstretched legs.

He was informed that other mobile units were in the area and closing in on the bike, and that routes were being shut off. The man, he was assured, wouldn't get far.

Foster spun the wheel to avoid an oncoming car, jolting the Rover up onto the kerb. The driver of the other car also struggled to guide his vehicle out of the way. The blue lights and the wailing sirens were remarkably effective in clearing a path through even the most densely packed traffic, thought Davies, still gripping the handset, one eye on the fleeing gunman.

'Heading for Leicester Square,' Davies observed as the bike roared on.

Fragmented phrases floated to him across the airwaves as the Rover hurtled on in pursuit.

'. . . closing in from Coventry Street . . .'

'. . . three dead . . . Haymarket . . .'

'. . . in pursuit . . . identity unknown . . .'

'. . . armed . . . dangerous . . .'

Davies couldn't agree more with the assessment of their quarry.

The bike was heading towards the junction of Panton Street and Whitcomb Street. Leicester Square lay just beyond.

From an underground car park ahead a van emerged, reversing in front of the bike. The rider didn't hesitate, merely gunned the engine and sent the Bonneville rocketing up onto the pavement once more, ignoring the two people who had just emerged from the Pizzaland on the corner. He struck one. The other managed to jump back but hit the window of the restaurant and the glass gave way. There was a loud crash as he fell backwards through the clear partition, sprawling across a table as glass rained down on him.

'Oh Christ,' murmured Davies.

The bike spun to the left again, up Whitcomb Street, still against the traffic.

Foster twisted the wheel and the rear of the Rover skidded on the wet ground, spinning round to slam into the side of the van. A jarring thud seemed to run the length of the vehicle, and both policemen winced, but Foster floored the accelerator and sped after the bike.

The rider did not once afford them even the most cursory glance. He was hunched over the handlebars, gripping the throttle, seemingly oblivious to the cars he sped past in the wrong direction. The wind streamed into his face, sending his shoulder-length hair flapping out behind him as he rode.

The street seemed to be filled with a cacophony of blaring hooters and shouts or screams as pedestrians found themselves forced to leap from the pavements as the Bonneville surged along, its rider oblivious to those he struck.

Ahead he saw a man snatch a child up into his arms and duck down beside a parked car, shaking as the police car also passed within a whisker of them.

Another police car was approaching from the left, lights and sirens joining its companion in a discordant melody.

The motorcyclist paused for a moment then sped off up Wardour Street, past the Swiss Centre, pursued now by two police cars.

'Units covering from Shaftesbury Avenue,' a metallic voice informed Davies. 'Give your position.'

He did just that, almost dropping the handset as Foster sent the car slamming into the side of a passing transit, sparks

9

spraying into the air as metal grated on metal. A hub-cap came free, Davies didn't know from which vehicle, and went spinning across the road.

Many pedestrians had now stopped on the roadside and were watching the chase. Others walked on, ignoring it. More than one tourist hurried to take photos.

The Bonneville was speeding towards the traffic lights at the top of the street, leading into Shaftesbury Avenue.

They were on red.

'Right, you bastard,' snarled Davies.

The rider worked the throttle and gathered speed.

Still red.

The needle on the speedo of the motorbike touched sixty. The bike shot across the lights as if fired from a cannon.

'Keep going,' yelled Davies, watching the bike speed past an oncoming Sierra, causing the driver to brake suddenly. There was a loud crash as a Cortina close behind slammed into the back of the other car. The Sierra was shunted forward, rolling towards the onrushing police car.

Foster swung the car round and paint ripped from the rear of the vehicle as it scraped the front bumper of the Sierra. But they were clear of the crossroads, heading up Wardour Street now, the motorbike still trailing exhaust fumes, the police sirens still wailing. Behind them the second car had narrowly missed the pile up in Shaftesbury Avenue and it, too, was in pursuit. From a side street Foster glimpsed another motorbike, a white one.

A police bike.

One second was all it took.

One second of broken concentration, then he heard Davies screaming a warning.

As he looked back through the windscreen he saw a man step in front of him.

10

Three

The police car was doing fifty when it hit the pedestrian.

The impact catapulted the man into the air where he seemed to hang, as if magically supported, for several seconds before crashing back to earth, bones splintered and blood pouring from several ragged gashes. He rolled over in the gutter and lay still.

Davies looked back over his shoulder to see that the second police car had pulled up and one of the officers was getting out to look at the luckless soul.

'Jesus, Jesus fucking Christ,' shouted Foster, his face a mask of horror and revulsion. 'I couldn't stop. I couldn't . . .' He was breathing heavily, his face as white as milk. Davies said nothing; he merely gripped the handset and watched as the motorcycle policeman cruised up closer to the fleeing Bonneville.

He was almost level with his quarry when the rider reached inside his jacket and pulled out the automatic.

'No!' shouted Davies, as if in warning.

He saw the pistol being raised, pointed at the head of the motorcycle policeman.

The rider of the Bonneville fired once.

The high velocity round powered into the face of the other rider, blasting through the right cheek, pulverising the zygoma. At such close range the lethal bullet exploded from the policeman's skull through the left occipital bone, even

11

blasting through his helmet, which filled with blood. Portions of bone and smashed helmet flew into the air, carried on a geyser of crimson.

The bike merely flopped hopelessly to one side, colliding with a stationary car. The policeman was hurled from the seat, sprawling across the bonnet, blood spattering the windscreen.

The Rover sped past the body.

'Lima Six come in.'

The voice on the two-way startled Davies and he jerked in his seat, hesitating a moment before answering.

'Lima Six, go ahead, over,' he said breathlessly, still watching the escaping motorcyclist up ahead.

'Lima Six, be advised that Oxford Street and all roads leading off it are now closed by other units,' the voice told him.

Now there's nowhere for him to go, Davies thought triumphantly. *Nowhere else to run, you bastard.*

'Lima Six, do you read? Over.'

'Understood, we will continue pursuit. Over and out.' He jammed the handset back onto its clip on the dashboard and leant forward slightly. 'Let's get this fucker,' he hissed.

The rider had still not looked behind him. Only when he reached Oxford Street did he glance over his shoulder, to see that the Rover was gaining on him. He looked right and left and noticed that there were two police cars moving towards him from the direction of Charing Cross Road. Ahead of him Berners Street was blocked; he could see police cars and uniformed men moving about on the pavement. Half a dozen of them moved towards him.

He turned the bike to the left, revved the engine and sped off down Oxford Street towards Oxford Circus.

The Rover came hurtling out of Wardour Street, wheels squealing on the tarmac as Foster struggled to keep it under

12

control. He succeeded and the car roared off after its prey like a predatory animal in search of its next meal.

Traffic on both sides of the road had been halted; the only vehicles moving were the motorbike and the pursuing Rover.

Pedestrians stood, immobilised by shock, staring. From the safety of their own vehicles other drivers watched the chase, some with amusement, some with irritation. Always bloody traffic hold-ups in Central London.

A thought suddenly struck Davies.

He snatched up the two-way.

Ahead of them the Bonneville was slowing down, the rider swinging it round so that it was facing the shops. Onlookers scattered in terror as he revved up, looking towards the oncoming Rover.

'Is Ramillies Place sealed off?' Davies asked urgently.

'Negative. It isn't possible to get a car . . .'

The voice trailed off.

No, not a car.

The narrow walkway that led from Oxford Street to Ramillies Place wasn't wide enough to get a car through, but it *would* accommodate a bike.

Just wide enough for a bike.

The bike appeared to be aimed at the narrow alley next to Marks and Spencer but, as the police car drew nearer, Davies saw that it was not.

'What the hell is he playing at?' muttered Foster.

The motorcyclist revved his engine for what seemed like an eternity, the back wheel spinning, leaving great rubber slicks on the road as he held the power in check. He might have been daring the uniformed men to come closer.

The car was within fifty yards.

Exhaust fumes poured into the air around the bike, so thick that it appeared the machine was on fire.

13

Thirty yards.

He looked to his left and right and saw cars converging from both sides.

Fifteen yards.

He released the throttle and the bike rocketed forward.

The gap that would take him to freedom beckoned.

He was less than twenty feet from it when he turned the bike towards the window of Next.

The Bonneville hit it doing sixty, erupting through the thick glass, which exploded in a dense shower. Several shop window dummies were carried into the store by the impact, one trailing along, tangled in the front wheel of the bike by the garments it was dressed in.

The bike cartwheeled but the rider held on, like a rodeo rider anxious not to lose his mount, his face hideously cut by the glass.

Even when the bike exploded.

The blast shook the building, blowing out what remained of the front window, a searing ball of flame enveloping the machine and the rider. As he hit the ground his skull seemed to fold in on itself, the bone crumbling as he struck the floor with incredible force, sticky portions of brain bursting through the riven skull.

He lay beneath the remains of the bike, the flames devouring his flesh, stripping skin from his bones. Blisters rose, burst and then blackened as the fire engulfed him, turning him into a human torch.

Those who'd been in the store when he crashed through the window fought to escape the scene of devastation. Members of staff fled past fire extinguishers in their haste to flee what could rapidly become an inferno.

Uniformed men now forced their way in, held back by the flames that had engulfed the Bonneville and its rider, who now

14

lay beside two blazing mannequins. As the fire destroyed them they dissolved, their false limbs melting in the ferocity of the inferno. One, still wearing the remains of a silk camisole and knickers, its false hair scorched off, seemed to roll over onto him, the heat twisting its plastic limbs into grotesque shapes, bending and moulding its arms so that they seemed to close around the dead man in a final fiery embrace.

Four: 29 December 1976

They had pulled three bodies from the wreckage.

The fourth they had found at the roadside, obviously thrown clear when the Metro first crashed.

The car was on its roof, a tangled mass of metal that looked as if it had been attacked by a gang of thugs wielding sledgehammers. The field in which it had finally come to rest was strewn with pieces of metal that had been torn from the chassis as the car had cartwheeled into oblivion. Other objects were also scattered around.

A high heeled shoe.

A handbag.

A couple of cassette tapes.

A watch.

A severed hand.

Wally Hughes gathered them all up, moving slowly round the wreckage, dropping the personal effects into a plastic bag. They might help with identification when the time came. The occupants of the car certainly couldn't. So bad were their injuries it was even difficult, at first glance, to tell which were male and which female. The driver had been impaled on the steering column. It had taken Wally and two of his companions over twenty minutes to remove the corpse, one of them vomiting when the body came in half at the waist as the torso was finally freed. Whoever had been in the passenger seat had fared no better. The head had been practically severed by broken glass when the windscreen had shattered. Portions of skin still hung from the obliterated screen like bizarre decorations.

Christmas decorations?

Wally shook his head and sighed, stooping to pick up a blood-flecked wallet. Death at any time of the year was a terrible thing, but at Christmas it seemed even more intrusive. In his twelve years as an ambulanceman he had noticed how the public seemed to take on an almost lemming-like mentality. Despite warnings every year not to drink and drive, to take more care in dangerous road conditions, men and women (sometimes children too) were pulled or cut or lifted piece by piece from car smashes. Huge pile-ups or single-vehicle accidents. What did it matter? Death was death, whether it happened to one or twenty at a time.

This time there had been four.

The car had come off the road at speed, obviously, hit a grassy bank, ploughed through a low stone wall, cartwheeled and ended up on its roof. How had it happened?

That was always the first question that came into Wally's mind as he approached the scene of an accident. He didn't even consider things such as, 'Will the victim be alive? If so, how bad will the injuries be?' Besides, it was usually simple to tell, on first glance at the scene of carnage, how likely it was that there would be any survivors. In this particular case he had taken one look at the wreck and decided that the ambulance would be driving straight to the morgue, not the emergency wing of the hospital.

He picked up a glove, dropped it into his plastic bag and straightened up, wincing slightly at the pain from his lower back. Rheumatism. The cold weather always exacerbated it and tonight was cold. There was a thick coating of frost on the grass and the road was icy, especially on the bend.

Perhaps that was what had happened. The driver had lost control on the slippery road. Perhaps he'd been going too fast. Perhaps he'd been drunk. Perhaps he'd been showing off.

Perhaps. Perhaps.

None of that seemed to matter now. They wouldn't know why it had happened, not for a few days. In the intervening period, Wally and his companions would have countless other accidents to deal with. At Christmas time the ambulance service in Greater London alone dealt with upwards of 3000 emergency calls a day.

Merry Christmas.

By the roadside two ambulances stood with their rear doors open, the blue lights turning silently. The glare of their headlamps cut through the blackness of the night, one set pointing at the wrecked Metro. In the gloom Wally continued with his task of recovering personal effects. He noticed that blood had sprayed over a wide area around the car; it glistened on the frosted grass, appearing quite black in the blinding whiteness of the headlights. There was little talk among the other men as they went about their tasks. There was a weary familiarity about the whole thing. It wasn't the first time they'd seen it and Christ alone knew it wouldn't be the last.

The head of one of the passengers in the rear of the car had hit the back of the driver's seat so hard they had found three teeth embedded in the upholstery. Now, as he flicked on his torch and shone it over the ground, Wally found two more teeth. He picked them up and dropped them into the bag.

A police car was also parked close to the bend, and one of the officers was making notes. As soon as identification of the victims was made it would be the job of the police to notify the next of kin. Wally was glad he didn't have to do *that* job. It was one thing to pull a man from a car, a man who was still screaming despite the fact that he had no face, but it was something else to sit calmly opposite a mother and inform her that her son was dead. To tell a father his daughter had been crushed beneath a lorry, that it had taken twenty minutes to scrape her brains up off the road.

Wally shone the torch over the ground once more, then headed back towards the wall, stepping through the gap the car had made on its fateful passage.

He was heading towards the closest ambulance, glancing across at two of his companions lifting the fourth body on a stretcher, when he heard the shout.

'This one's still alive.'

Five

'We drew the short straw again.'

Detective Sergeant Stuart Finn fumbled in his jacket pocket for his Zippo, flipped the lighter open and lit the Marlboro jammed between his lips.

As the lift slowly descended he glanced across at his companion who was gazing distractedly at the far wall.

'I said . . .'

'I heard you,' Detective Inspector Frank Gregson told him, his eyes still fixed on a point on the wall.

Finn looked at his companion then across to where his gaze seemed fixed. He noticed a fly on the wall, sitting there cleaning its wings.

The lift bumped to a halt and Gregson glanced up to reassure himself that they were at the right floor. As he stepped towards the door he swung the manila file he held, squashing the fly against the wall, where it left a red smudge.

'I know how he feels,' murmured Finn as he stepped from the lift. The doors slid shut behind him. 'Flies eat shit, don't they?'

Gregson didn't answer.

'I *certainly* know how he feels,' the DS added wearily. 'Well, come on, Frank. Any ideas who this joker might have been?'

'How the hell am I supposed to know?' Gregson said. 'They drag the bloke out of a fire after he's been chased halfway across the West End. By the time they get him out he's so badly burned his fucking mother wouldn't even know him. If he's got one.'

Their footsteps echoed dully in the long corridor as they approached New Scotland Yard's forensic labs. Signs proclaimed: PATHOLOGY. Gregson looked down at the file again, glancing at the number in the top right-hand corner. That was all the man was to them at the moment. A number. No name and *certainly* no face. That had been burned away along with most of the rest of him. But he had to be identified and that job was to be done by the Yard's forensic pathologists. Once identification had been made it was the task of Gregson and Finn to find out why the man had run amok.

Finn took a drag on his cigarette and swept a hand through his thinning hair. He was twenty-nine, a year younger than his

19

superior but his bald patch (which worried him) made him look older. Gregson was greying at the temples but, he told himself, the light hairs were the result of stress and not the onset of more mature years. Both men were thick-set, Finn perhaps a little slimmer, although his belly strained unattractively against his shirt. He'd put the weight on a few months ago when he first tried to give up smoking.

Gregson opened the door of the pathology lab. The two men walked in.

'Where's Barclay?' the DI asked a man in a lab. coat who was fiddling with a microscope slide.

The man nodded in the direction of a door marked PRIVATE: NO ENTRY BY UNAUTHORISED PERSONNEL.

Both policemen made for the door. Gregson knocked and walked in without waiting for an invitation.

It was cold inside the pathology lab.

The cold and the smell were two of the things that always struck him. The acrid stench of death and sometimes decay. He had seen things inside this room that others only saw in nightmares. *Call it an occupational hazard.*

The chief pathologist, Phillip Barclay, had his back to the men as they entered. He glanced over his shoulder and nodded a greeting. Behind him banks of cold cabinets stood like huge filing drawers. A storehouse for sightless eyes. Freezers containing bodies or awaiting them. On one of six dissecting tables lay a body covered by a sheet. It was towards this table that the two policemen walked, their footsteps echoing even more loudly in the high-ceilinged room.

'If you've come looking for answers I'm going to have to disappoint you,' said Barclay, turning to face them.

Gregson looked challengingly at him, watching as the pathologist swung himself off the stool on which he'd been sitting. He walked across to the dissection tables and pulled the sheet back.

'Shit,' murmured Finn.

The shape beneath the sheet was little more than a blackened skeleton. Flesh, crisped and blackened by the fire, still clung to the bones but it looked more like a coating of thick ash ready to fall off at the slightest touch. A few teeth gleamed whitely through the blackened mess, but much of the skull had been pulverised on initial impact. Finn could see tiny fragments of brain, also blackened, welded to the inside of the shattered skull.

'I've examined what there is of him, obviously,' said Barclay, pulling the sheet further back and stepping back, arms folded. 'But it's going to be a long job identifying him.'

'What about dental records?' Gregson wanted to know, his eyes never leaving the corpse.

'As you can see, most of the head is gone. Obliterated. He hit the window head first when he went through it. Actually, that's the strange thing. From the extent of the damage to the head and upper body I'd say he was leaning forward when he hit that window.'

'Meaning?' Gregson wanted to know.

'He intended to do it. He was making *sure* he killed himself.'

'Looks like he did a pretty good job,' Finn remarked, sucking on his cigarette.

Barclay looked disdainfully at him.

'Don't smoke in here, please,' he said.

Finn looked aggrieved.

'Why? It's not going to bother *him*,' he said, nodding towards the corpse.

'It bothers *me*,' the pathologist said, watching as Finn nipped out the cigarette, burning his fingers in the process. He dropped the butt into his jacket pocket.

21

'You *could* identify him from dental records, though,' said Gregson.

'Like I said, it won't be easy. It'll take time but it's not impossible.' There was a long silence, broken again by Barclay. 'How many did he kill?'

'Including the baby, five. Six more are in hospital, one on the critical list. It doesn't make sense,' Gregson observed, shaking his head. 'The whole thing was clumsy. He robbed a bank, but he left with no money and in a way which almost guaranteed he'd be caught. Then, when he *could* have escaped, he killed himself.'

'Bit elaborate for a suicide, isn't it?' Finn mused.

'Couldn't you take any prints from the guns?' Gregson asked.

Barclay shook his head.

'He was wearing gloves.'

The DI chuckled sardonically.

'Gloves but no mask. He didn't care if we got a look at his face but he didn't want us identifying him by his fingerprints.'

Again the silence.

'Can you get a report to me as soon as possible, Phil?' Gregson asked.

'I told you, it will take time.'

'Just do it,' the DI snapped.

'If he isn't in our records it's going to take even longer,' Barclay reminded the policeman.

'You're the expert,' Gregson remarked and headed for the door, followed by Finn.

As soon as they'd left the lab, the DS lit up another Marlboro. They headed back towards the lift.

'Why did he kill himself?' Finn muttered, sucking on the cigarette.

Gregson could only shake his head.

'Perhaps when we know who he is, we might know *why*?'

'You don't sound too hopeful.'

Gregson jabbed the 'Call' button on the lift.

'You saw the body. Would *you* be?'

It was probably part of the motorbike.

Perhaps even a fragment of the shop floor. The dead man had certainly hit the floor hard enough. Barclay didn't rule out the possibility that part of it had been embedded in the pulped skull upon impact.

The pathologist held in his tweezers the small piece of melted matter he had taken from the pulverised remnants of the killer's head. He gazed at the tiny melted fragment gripped between the prongs.

The intense heat had melted it, leading him to believe that part of it was some kind of plastic – incredibly hard plastic.

Barclay considered the fragment a moment longer, then dropped it into a petrie dish.

It would need closer analysis.

He reached for the phone on his desk.

Six: 14 March 1977

The room was small.

Less than fifteen feet square, its full extent was slowly revealed as lights were turned on one by one. Puddles of light

23

filled the gloom, each one scarcely strong enough to fight off the blackness that shrouded the six occupants.

Dr Robert Dexter stroked his chin thoughtfully as the light above him came on, bathing him in its cold white glow. He scanned the faces of the others in the room, listening to the soft click as each successive spot lamp was illuminated.

He was joined a moment later by a slightly older man who cleared his throat self-consciously, aware of the silence and apparently anxious not to disturb it. He pulled a chair closer to Dexter, wincing when it scraped the wooden floor noisily. He sat down and pulled nervously at the sleeve of his jacket.

The room was windowless, the only brightness inside provided by the spotlamps set in the high ceiling. Each one was aimed at the four other occupants of the room who sat in a line facing Dexter and his companion.

He looked along the line, pausing for a moment on each face as if trying to commit it to memory. In fact he knew each one well. Like a painter trying to decide on a subject, he moved his glance carefully from face to face, met only once by eyes that held his gaze.

And it was always those eyes.

Every day during the session they would begin the same way, in darkness. Then Dr Andrew Colston would switch the lights on one by one and Dexter would look at those same four faces.

And, always, he would be met by *those* eyes.

Dexter held the gaze for a moment longer, then glanced down at the clipboard on his lap. He matched each name to the four faces before him.

Colston shuffled his feet, as if anxious to begin. He too was eyeing the other occupants of the room but it wasn't their faces he was looking at.

It was the stout leather restraining straps that kept each of them firmly secured to the heavy wooden chairs.

24

Dexter glanced once more at the line of faces, aware, again, of the last of them and the incessant stare that seemed to bore into him. Once more he met those eyes and found himself unable to hold the stare.

Was that a sign of weakness?

Or fear?

'Who's going to start today?' he asked, his voice muted and flat inside the small room.

Silence.

There was no response from any of them.

Just that unflinching stare.

Dexter shuffled in his seat and smiled. His practised smile. His comforting smile. His reassuring smile.

'I'm sure one of you has something to say,' he continued, looking at the first of the four seated before him. 'Charles. Will you start today?'

The man looked at him, his eyes rheumy and red-rimmed. He looked as if he'd been crying. He held Dexter's gaze for a moment, then shook his head crisply.

The doctor sighed with exaggerated weariness. He raised his hands as if in surrender then looked at each face once more.

Those eyes still watched him.

Leave me alone. I don't want to talk.

'If you won't speak to me voluntarily then I'll have to ask you questions,' he told them all.

There was a thud and Colston looked across in alarm.

One of them had brought a fist thudding down on the arm of the chair.

Colston was grateful for the restraining straps.

'Silence is bad,' Dexter said. 'You shouldn't bottle up your feelings. Let them out. Imagine they're a river. Let your thoughts flow out. Speak.'

The rivers have dried up, thought Colston, using one hand to hide the slight smile which flickered on his lips. It vanished as he saw *those* eyes gazing momentarily at *him*.

'Very well,' said Dexter, turning over a sheet on the clipboard. 'We'll begin with Jonathan.' He sat forward in his chair. 'Tell us why you cut off your mother's head.'

Seven

It looked like a puddle of vomit.

James Scott looked at the remains of the pizza, now cold in the bottom of the box, and shook his head. His stomach rumbled noisily. He'd managed to force down half the pizza but that was all he'd eaten since eight o'clock in the morning. He glanced at his watch and saw that the time was nearly 9.30 p.m.

Beyond the confines of his office Scott could hear music thudding away and the occasional shout. He sighed and ran a hand through his brown hair, pausing to stretch his shoulders, hearing the joints pop. He muttered something under his breath and peered round the office.

Framed photos of girls, some of them performers at the club, stared back at him, pouting, smiling, licking their lips. Scott regarded them indifferently, his gaze flickering around the room to the calendar. That also featured girls, naked and half-naked. All shapes, all sizes, he thought, smiling humourlessly. Beneath the calendar, tacked to a bright red notice-board, was the rota. On it he had written, in his neatest script, the working hours for the barmen, the doormen and the hostesses. He had eleven people working for him, although one of the girls was only part-time. They were pretty reliable, most of his staff. They did their work, did what they were paid for and didn't cause him much trouble.

He'd been manager of 'Loveshow' for over three years now. The club was in Great Windmill Street, almost opposite the old Raymond Revue Bar. From his office window Scott could see into the street below, out onto the flashing neon and the rubbish that littered the road, some of it stacked up in large plastic bags and dumped on the pavements. He watched as pedestrians walked round it as if it were some massive dog turd. Others wandered in and out of the other clubs and bookshops that clogged the thoroughfare, each of them peddling the same merchandise. Books, magazines. Live shows. Scott remained at the window for a moment longer, then returned to his desk. He glanced at the portable TV set perched on one corner of it, thought about turning it on, then realised there was still work to be done.

He reached into his desk drawer for the drinks inventory. Time to re-order. Scott pulled off his jacket and hung it carefully on the back of his chair, rolling up the sleeves of his shirt to reveal thick, hairy forearms. Despite a life spent behind desks (or at least the last six years) Scott was stocky and bore only the smallest of unwanted podges. He looked down for a moment at the flesh straining just that little bit too tightly against his shirt and shook his head. He sucked in a deep breath and held it, watching his stomach retract, smiling briefly before he released the breath and his belly flopped back into place. *Flopped*. He was hardly obese, he told himself. A few weeks working out in a gym would turn that irritating flab into muscle again. It wasn't too late. It was too early for middle-age spread. He was only thirty-two, for Christ's sake.

Forget your figure and get on with your fucking work, a voice inside his head told him. He nodded as if in answer to the silent beration and picked up his pen.

The office door opened and he looked up in surprise.

The girl was naked apart from a pair of stockings, a tiny pair of G-string knickers and a black basque.

'Fucking bastard,' hissed the girl, striding towards Scott's desk and lifting one leg onto it. 'Look,' she snapped.

'What's the matter, Zena?' he said wearily, inspecting her leg but seeing nothing untoward.

'Useless bastard shot his load all over my new stockings,' Zena Murray told him angrily. 'Look.' She jabbed a false fingernail towards a slick of slippery fluid on her thigh. 'Now he won't pay,' she continued.

'What happened?' asked Scott, getting to his feet.

'He bought a drink, bought *me* a drink. We talked, well, *I* talked for a few minutes then he pulled it out and asked me to wank him. I told him it'd cost him extra but he said that was okay.' She shook her head indignantly. 'So, what happens, I put one finger on it and he shoots, doesn't he? All over my . . .'

'New stockings,' Scott said, completing the sentence. 'So what's the problem?'

'They were new!' she yelled at him.

'Jesus Christ, take some money out of petty cash for another pair. They're only fucking stockings,' Scott said, exasperated.

'It's not just that. He says he won't pay now.'

'So what are you bothering *me* for? Get Rick to throw him out,' Scott told her.

'Rick's not here,' she told him scornfully.

'All right, come on,' Scott said, pushing her in front of him.

They left his office and walked along a short corridor, passing two doors marked 'Private' and another which bore the word LADIES in white plastic letters. Beneath that someone had blue-tacked a piece of paper which bore the legend: NO PISSING ON THE TOILET SEATS.

The corridor smelt of stale urine and cheap perfume. It was a smell Scott had come to know well in the last few years.

'Where the fuck is Rick, anyway?' Scott wanted to know. 'This is the second time this week he hasn't come in. I've got better things to do than argue the toss with punters.' He smiled at his unintentional joke. Zena didn't see the humour in the remark. She raised her eyebrows indignantly and pushed open the door which led into the main area of 'Loveshow' and stalked in, Scott following.

The music that had been a dull thud in his office now enveloped him, roaring from the speakers mounted on the wall.

'. . . *Our love is a bed of nails.*

Love hurts good on a bed of nails.

I'll lay you down and when all else fails,

I'll drive you like a hammer on a bed of nails . . .'

Zena grabbed Scott's arm and pointed with one long finger towards a balding man sitting in a corner, hidden for the most part by shadows.

'That's him,' she snarled.

'Okay,' murmured Scott, nodding. 'I'll handle it now.'

'Don't forget about my stockings!' Zena bellowed after him, shouting to make herself heard above the roar of the music.

What are you going to do, sunshine? thought Scott as he approached the balding man. *Get mouthy? Get scared?*

Let's see.

Eight

The floor show in the club couldn't have been more aptly named.

It consisted of a large double bed raised up slightly on a platform no more than six inches high. On two sides of the bed were nine or ten armchairs, each one faded and, in places, threadbare on the arms. Facing the bed, three sofas had been placed end to end. One was leather but the material was so cracked and worn it might as well have been draylon like the others. There were low coffee tables in front of each seat. The carpet, also worn, was dark brown to hide stains more easily. The walls were only slightly lighter and these were decorated with more framed pictures of girls, older than the ones in Scott's office. One or two were yellowed at the corners; one had even come free of the frame and a corner was turning up slowly. Customers were presumably supposed to be excited by the prospect that the girls in the pictures would actually be performing for them but, as one of the pictures featured Marilyn Monroe, that wish was at least a little vain.

The balding man was sitting in an armchair beneath a photograph of a girl holding a kitten. He didn't seem to notice Scott approaching him; he was too busy looking around.

There were about six other customers dotted around the place, drinking the warm beer and the grossly overpriced shorts. One man was in conversation with a hostess; she talked animatedly to him while sipping a Coke cradled in one hand and, with her other hand, trying to free the material of her knickers from the cleft of her backside.

On the bed in the centre of the room two young women writhed in the throes of practised pleasure, chatting to each other as they rubbed vibrators across each other's breasts, their voices drowned by the music.

A man in his early twenties, a cigarette dangling from one corner of his mouth, sat staring raptly at the two girls on the bed, his right hand, jammed into the pocket of his jeans, moving beneath the material.

Scott glanced across at the goings-on for a second then turned his full attention to the balding man, who had finally spotted him. Zena sat down beside the man and glared at him.

'You owe the lady some money,' said Scott, his face expressionless.

'Why?' said the man, looking first at Zena then at Scott.

'Because you bought me a drink, then you did *that*,' she rasped, jabbing her nail in the direction of the semen.

'I paid for the drink,' the man protested.

'You didn't pay for my conversation, or for anything else,' Zena told him.

'*Conversation*? What are you talking about?' the man said indignantly.

Scott snatched up one of the menus that lay on the coffee table and flipped it open.

'Buying the hostess a drink signifies agreement to pay the hostess fee,' he quoted, as if he were reading some point of law. Then he dropped the menu back on the table. 'You owe her sixty pounds.'

'Sixty pounds?' the man said, getting to his feet. 'Forget it.'

He tried to step around Scott but Zena pushed the table with her foot, blocking his way.

'Come on, pay up,' Scott demanded sharply.

The man raised a hand to push past him. Scott grabbed him by the wrist and shoved him away.

'Sixty,' he hissed, a glint in his eye visible even in the dull light of the room.

'I haven't got it,' said the man, swallowing hard.

Scared, eh?

'Well, fucking find it,' hissed Scott through clenched teeth.

The man tried to push past him again.

Scott pressed a large hand into the man's chest and shoved him back.

'You find that fucking money now. Sixty quid.'

He could see the fear on the man's face. Flabby white face, glasses. Suit, tie. *A respectable type.*

'You think you can walk in here and do what you fucking like.' Scott was breathing heavily now, the knot of muscles at the side of his jaw throbbing angrily. 'Get your money out.'

'Don't hurt me. Please.'

Scott almost smiled.

There was the fear again. Christ, he was beginning to enjoy this.

The balding man tried once more to get past.

'I told you not to push me,' Scott snapped.

'I didn't push you.'

His voice was wavering. He looked as if he was ready to burst into tears.

'Sixty quid or I'll push your fucking teeth so far down your throat you'll have to eat through your arsehole.'

The man fumbled for his wallet, pulled out three twenties and shoved them into Scott's hand. This time, when he tried to pass, the younger man let him. The man made for the narrow flight of stairs that would take him up out of the viewing area. As he was leaving another man was about to take a seat. The balding man muttered something to him and glared at Zena.

32

She immediately scurried across and aimed a kick at the back of his legs.

'Fuck off!' she yelled at him as he disappeared up the steps.

Scott shoved the sixty into his pocket and headed back to the door marked STAFF ONLY.

'What about my stockings?' Zena said. He dug in his trousers and found a couple of pound coins. He tossed them to her. She caught them and smiled at him.

'You're a real charmer, Scotty,' she said.

He made his way back to the office, his breathing gradually slowing down. The sort of incident with the balding man wasn't unusual in clip-joints like 'Loveshow' but Scott didn't think it was his job to deal with them. He'd done enough of that when he worked as a bouncer. Eight years ago. Ten. It seemed like an eternity. The scar on his left forearm was a reminder of it. At a disco one night he'd been ejecting a couple of piss-heads when one of them had cut him with a sharpened steel comb, opening his arm almost to the bone with the razor-sharp prongs. Scott had broken his jaw and three of his ribs before tossing him into the street.

Now he closed the door of his office, relegating the music behind him once again to nothing but a dull thud. He walked across to the window and peered out again into the street. It was raining heavily now; the street and pavements were wet. The sparkling neon reflected up off the slick concrete. It looked as if someone had spilled fluorescent paint on the thoroughfare. Across the street, in the doorway of an empty shop, a man was sitting, wrapped in a dirty coat, sipping from a bottle of spirits. When it was empty he hurled it into the street, where it shattered in front of a passing car. The driver slammed on the brakes, leapt out and ran across to the man, kicking him twice as he shouted his annoyance.

Scott returned to his desk and sat down, pulling the drinks inventory towards him, scanning the columns of figures.

They bought in bottles of whisky and vodka for about three pounds each. They sold them for seventy. He had one of the menus on his desk and he flipped it open, looking at the prices.

Five pounds for a coke. Ten pounds for a pint of lager. Then there was the list of cocktails. A screwdriver was thirty pounds. It went as high as eighty for a Tequila Sunrise.

Beneath the list was a line which read: ALL COCKTAILS ARE DE-ALCOHOLISED.

You didn't get drunk but you pissed a lot.

If you chose to have the company of a hostess it cost you thirty pounds for a conversation with her. Anything beyond conversation was negotiable, but Scott knew the girls had their own price list for their services. Thirty for a hand job. Fifty for a straight fuck. Eighty for one without a rubber. One hundred quid could even get you a blow job without a rubber. Risky, these days, but then money was money, wasn't it? The entrepreneur always had to take a few risks.

He would take a trip down to the cash-and-carry in the morning, after he'd checked his stock of drink. He'd give Don, the barman, a call in a minute. He doubted if they needed much. The vodka was three parts water, as were most of the spirits. Scott sat back in his seat for a moment, his hands clasped on his lap. At least Don was reliable; he always turned in, no matter what. Not like that fucker Rick. He should have been there tonight.

I shouldn't have to throw punters out. It's not good for my image. The manager is here to manage, not get mixed up in rough stuff.

When and if Rick ever came back he'd find his cards waiting for him. Cunt.

34

Scott returned his attention to the inventory.

He was about to start work when there was a knock on the office door.

'Who is it? I'm trying to bloody work,' he called.

The frown on his face rapidly disappeared as the door opened.

Nine

'Sorry if I'm disturbing you, Jim,' Carol Jackson said apologetically.

Scott got to his feet.

'You're not,' he told her. 'Come in.' He smiled at her, relieved to see the gesture reciprocated.

She closed the door behind her and moved towards him, pausing as she looked down at the remains of the pizza. She wrinkled her nose and smiled again.

'Dinner,' he announced almost ashamedly. Then he took her in his arms and kissed her. Carol draped one arm around his shoulders perfunctorily and broke the kiss first. She perched on a corner of his desk and Scott looked at her appraisingly.

She was about three years younger than him. About five-two but slim. Blonde hair framed her face and cascaded just past her shoulder blades. As she stood close to him she toyed distractedly with the ring on her right middle finger. It was gold and held a small onyx.

One of Scott's gifts to her.

The metal was going black in places.

35

They had been seeing each other for almost fourteen months; the relationship could be called erratic. She worked at the club. Scott worked at the club. They saw each other almost every day during work. They had been seeing each other *out* of work for nearly as long.

She was wearing jeans and a baggy sweatshirt, a red one. Another gift from Scott. He liked to see her wearing things he had bought her. Now he looked at her and smiled.

You're beautiful.

He didn't even attempt to *say* it.

'I heard that Zena had a bit of trouble earlier on,' she said.

'It was nothing,' he told her. 'I sorted it out.'

'Manager's duty?'

He nodded.

'Do you want a drink?' Scott asked.

'I should go and get changed, I . . .'

'A quick one,' he insisted, smiling.

She agreed and he reached into the bottom drawer of his desk and pulled out a bottle of Southern Comfort and two glasses. She watched as he poured.

'Don't you ever get sick of this job, Jim?' she wanted to know.

Scott handed her the drink, looking bemused.

'It's a living,' he told her.

'I hate it,' she said, venomously. 'I hate what I do. I hate the people who come in here to watch me.' She took a long swallow of the drink and closed her eyes.

'Are you all right?'

'I'm okay. I'm just pissed off. Everyone has the right to be pissed off with their job, don't they? It just surprises me you don't get pissed off with *yours*.'

'Like I said, it's a living. I don't hate it.'

It sounded like an apology. As if he should hate it and himself for doing it.

'You never used to be like this about it,' Scott said.

'I didn't think it would go on as long as this,' she snapped. 'I've been working clip-joints since I was nineteen. That's nearly ten years, Jim. It's a long time. I wanted more out of life. I *want* more. More than being stared at by men with nowhere else to go. Fucking perverts. You know some of the ones we get in here. I hate them. And I'm beginning to hate myself for *performing* for them.' She took another long swallow and gazed across the room at the wall.

Scott got to his feet and moved closer to her, putting his arm around her, pulling her close.

'Do you want to talk about it later?' he asked, kissing the top of her head.

'What good is talking going to do?'

'I didn't know you felt the way you did. Perhaps if you spoke to me about it . . .'

'You don't understand,' she interrupted.

'*Make* me understand,' Scott asked.

She drained what was left in her glass and handed him the empty receptacle.

'Can I see you after work?' he asked.

She shrugged.

'Walk out and watch the show,' she said bitterly. 'You can see as much of me as you want.'

'You know what I mean,' Scott said, irritably. *Why do you make it so hard for me?*

'Can I see you later?'

She kissed his cheek and turned to pull away but he caught her by the wrist and pulled her close to him. This time she responded with a little more passion, actually allowing his tongue to probe past the hard white edges of her teeth and into the moistness beyond. She touched his cheek as they parted in a gesture that was almost maternal. It wasn't the touch of a lover. He held on to her other hand, to the hand that bore the onyx ring.

The metal was turning black in places.

They were still holding hands when the office door opened.

'Can't you fucking knock?' Scott called.

The newcomer stuck his head around the door and looked first at Scott, then at Carol.

'Very cosy,' he said, noticing that they were holding hands. 'Sorry if I'm disturbing you.' He entered.

Scott swallowed hard as the door was pushed shut.

Ten

In all the years he had worked for Ray Plummer, Scott had never been sure whether or not to believe the rumours that his boss wore a wig. If it was a hairpiece, whoever had made it was to be complimented. There was even a patch of thinning hair at the crown to add authenticity.

Now, as the older man entered the room, pulling a cigarette from the gold monogrammed case he'd removed from his pocket, Scott glanced quickly at the lustrous black hair that covered Plummer's head.

Toupee or not toupee, that was the question.

Scott smiled a greeting, hoping it would mask his amusement at his quip.

Watch it.

Carol stepped away from him slightly and also smiled at Plummer, who walked across the room and peered out of the window into the street below, puffing slowly on his Menthol cigarette. He hated the taste of the bloody things but his doctor had told him that if he didn't cut down from his usual forty Rothmans a day he'd be in line for lung and heart trouble before he was forty-five. And, with just seven years to go to that deadline, Plummer was taking no chances. He'd cut down on his intake of cholesterol, too. He'd even started jogging. He hadn't quite got to the stage of popping sunflower seeds but, if it made him healthier, he'd be quite prepared to start on all the organic shit, maybe even become a vegetarian. Although the thought of doing his weekly shop at a fucking garden centre instead of a supermarket made him wonder if he wanted to be *that* healthy.

He turned and smiled, a crooked smile exaggerated by the scar on his left cheek that reached from the corner of his mouth to the ridge of the bone.

'I was passing by,' he said. 'Thought I'd drop in and see how business was.'

Scott offered him a drink but Plummer declined.

'Got to watch the old liver, James,' he said, holding up his hands. *And the heart. And the lungs.*

'I'd better go,' said Carol. 'I'm due on in ten minutes.' She smiled thinly at Plummer then at Scott.

'I'll see you later,' he said softly, but she had already gone.

'Nice girl,' Plummer said. 'Lovely arse.' He blew out a stream of smoke.

'Is this a social call?' Scott said, changing the subject.

'You sound suspicious, Jim. Think I'm checking up on you?'

'I only asked.'

'Like I said, I was in the area, thought I'd pop in and see how business was.'

'It's good. We took over two grand last night. Mostly on drink, of course.'

Plummer smiled.

'Of course,' he echoed. 'I wish all my bloody joints were doing as well as this one. Old Benny, you know Benny Fox runs one of my places over in Dean Street, he's lucky if he sees two grand in a fucking *week*.' Plummer shook his head. 'It's the quality of the girls, you know. I mean, some of them in the other places, they're not top quality, if you know what I mean. There's one bird over at Benny's I swear to Christ he got her from Smithfield. Arse like a fifty-dollar cow. Face to match.' He shook his head. 'We need more girls like that Carol. She's tasty.'

Scott eyed his boss warily for a moment, anxious to change the subject again.

Plummer sat down at Scott's desk and glanced at the remains of the pizza.

'Not exactly *haute cuisine*, is it?' he said, wrinkling his nose.

'If I had as much money as you, Ray, I'd eat better,' Scott told his boss.

'Perhaps you could do with a raise. I can afford it. Most of the shops and clubs turned a profit last year and my other *business* concerns are ticking over nicely.' He took a final puff on the cigarette, then ground it out in the middle of the pizza. He smiled that crooked smile again.

Plummer owned six clubs in Soho, most of them providing live sex shows. Four also showed imported films and sold a range of soft and hardcore magazines. The shop upstairs at 'Loveshow' dealt in that kind of literature. It came in on containers three times a month, carried in by lorry drivers paid to smuggle the banned material in the cabs of their trucks. He also owned a couple of gaming clubs in Kensington (the more respectable side of his business) and he had just bought into a syndicate responsible for opening a large outdoor sports arena in Fulham. With an annual profit of over ten million pounds, Plummer was one of the underworld's wealthier barons. He disliked being compared to a criminal gang boss, though. He had men working for him, some of them armed, but he wouldn't have called them a gang. Associates was a word he preferred. He didn't own clip-joints, he operated adult entertainment emporia. To Plummer this wasn't a lie. He saw himself as a businessman, not a crook. There were those on the other side of the law who would disagree.

He had a criminal record, but the most he'd ever been charged with was possession of cannabis. That had been ten years ago. Now he made sure he went nowhere near the cocaine and heroin that had formed the bedrock of his little 'empire'. The passage of time had made him wiser, more cautious. More manipulative. Ray Plummer, in his own eyes, was an upstanding member of the community. For Christ's sake, he even had a firearms certificate for the Beretta automatic he carried in his car. It wasn't wise to cross the law.

Besides, it cost too much to pay the bastards off.

He ran a hand over his hair, smoothing down a piece that was sticking up.

Be careful or you'll have the whole lot in your lap, thought Scott.

Plummer got to his feet.

'I've got to go, Jim,' he said. 'Other calls to make.' He shook hands with the younger man. A firm grip.

'I'll walk out with you,' Scott said.

'No problem; you stay here, finish your work. I might have a look at the show on the way out.' He smiled. 'Maybe that Carol, or whatever her name is, will be on.' He winked and was gone.

Scott glared at the closed door, then pulled the bottle of

Southern Comfort towards him and poured a large measure. He downed it in one, bringing the glass down so hard on the table it almost cracked.

Beyond the closed door the thud of the music continued.

Eleven

Zena Murray pulled off her stockings and balled them up, tossing them into the waste-bin nearby. Then she took off her basque and G-string and sat naked in front of the mirror, taking her make-up off. Beside her, Carol Jackson was busy applying hers. The two women sat in front of the mirror which stretched the length of the wall in the dressing room. The term was rather grand for what was little more than an enlarged cupboard with lights and a mirror. Clothes were hung on hangers and suspended from hooks on the peeling walls. The light bulbs which surrounded the mirror were flickering in places; some had blown completely. A drawer beneath the dressing table contained the girls' props, a selection of vibrators and dildos. There was a pay phone on the wall. One of the other girls had stuck a postcard of Mel Gibson on the side of it. There were other pictures sellotaped to the wall by the phone, cut from magazines. One of Jon Bon Jovi, another of Mickey Rourke.

'I'll be glad to get home tonight,' said Zena, wiping eye-shadow from her top lid with a cotton ball. 'Did you hear what happened with that bastard earlier on? Ruined my stockings, then didn't want to pay.'

'I heard,' Carol affirmed.

'Scotty gave me the money for another pair. He's a nice bloke.'

Carol smiled into the mirror. The gesture looked strained, artificial.

'Are you still seeing him?' Zena wanted to know.

'Sort of,' Carol said, applying the thick red lipstick she always wore when she worked.

'Either you are or you aren't. You've been going out with him for a while now, haven't you?'

Too long.

'It's not like it used to be between us, but I don't think Jim realises that,' said Carol.

'Then don't you think you ought to tell him?' Zena said, looking at her companion in the mirror.

'Tell him what? That I don't want to see him any more? It's going to be a bit difficult while we're working together.'

'So you're going to keep the poor bastard hanging on? Thinking that you still feel something for him, just because it's not convenient for you to split up with him. Is that it?'

'It's not as simple as that, Zena. I like him. He's a nice guy. But he's going nowhere and he doesn't even realise it.'

'And where are *you* going, Carol?' She looked at her companion. 'Out in front of another audience, just like you do most nights. Just like you *will* be doing until your tits sag and your bum drops and you get fat and no one wants to come and see you anymore. Then you'll probably start working the hotels and the streets full-time. Just like the rest of us.'

'Are you telling me I'm wrong to want more out of life?' Carol snapped. 'Do you honestly *enjoy* what you do here, Zena?'

'No, but it pays the rent, and that's all that matters to me at the moment. Look, Carol, it might not be much of a life but it's all we've got.'

'That's shit, there's more to it than that. There has to be.'

Zena wiped some foundation from her cheeks with a moist tissue.

'So, Scotty's only crime is that he's going nowhere. Is that it?' she said.

'I don't know how to tell him it's over. I don't know how he'll react. I know he thinks a lot of me. He's told me he loves me. I don't want to hurt him, Zena.'

'Well, you're going to hurt him a fucking sight more the longer you leave it,' Zena snapped. She got to her feet and started to dress, pulling on jeans and a T-shirt, stepping into a pair of ankle boots.

'Am I wrong to want more out of life?' Carol asked the other girl again.

'No, but I think you're dreaming, Carol. I'm not sure there *is* that much more. And if there is, it wasn't meant for the likes of you and me.' She smiled thinly, then opened the door of the dressing room. The sound of the music was suddenly louder as Zena paused there.

'*. . . skin tight leather on satin sheets . . .*'

'*Don't hurt him, Carol. He doesn't deserve it,*' Zena said, smiling.

'*. . . Now she's got me surrounded . . .*'

Zena said goodbye and closed the door, shutting out the music once more.

Carol turned back to the mirror and studied her own reflection. She ran both hands over her breasts.

Starting to sag yet?

She reached for a cigarette and lit it, sucking hard, allowing the smoke to burn its way to her lungs.

There is more. There has to be.

The clock on the wall ticked soundlessly, the hands crawling around inexorably. *Showtime.*

44

She would tell Scott it was over. Zena was right. She shouldn't hurt him. She would tell him.

Eventually.

The phone rang.

For a moment Carol was startled by the ringing, then she turned and picked up the receiver.

She recognised the voice immediately.

'Hi. I'm just about to go on,' she said.

'I know,' the caller said. 'Where shall I pick you up tonight?'

'Same place as before.'

'Same time?'

'Yes. Look, I'd better go.'

'See you later.'

She hung up.

In the back of his Mercedes Ray Plummer was smiling as he replaced the car phone.

Twelve

Scott was still in his office when 'Loveshow' closed. He had some paperwork to finish but decided it could wait until tomorrow. He glanced at his watch, saw it was just after 11.30 and rubbed his eyes. He had to take the money from the bar and the hostesses round to the night safe and deposit it before he went home. The money taken at the door and that collected from the sale of books and videos upstairs in the shop was kept in the building until the next morning. Best not to bank the whole lot at once.

The bar takings were laid out before him, as was the money taken by the hostesses. Over eight hundred pounds in cash, all neatly arranged in piles according to denomination. Scott wound the piles securely with elastic bands and put them into the bag intended for the night safe.

Don Lloyd, the barman, stuck his head around the door and said goodnight. Scott waved and smiled, then looked at his watch again. After a moment or two he got to his feet and wandered down the corridor from his office towards the dressing room.

He knocked and waited.

'Come in,' a voice from the other side called and he poked his head in.

One of the other girls, a tall dark-haired young woman he knew as Lynn Fraser, smiled at him. She was completely naked, unconcerned by his presence. Scott was similarly uninterested in her state of undress; his attention was drawn towards Carol, who was removing her make-up.

'How did it go tonight?' he asked.

Carol shrugged. 'Same as usual,' she said flatly.

'Well, my Rob's going to be overjoyed when *I* get home,' said Lynn, reaching for a tissue from the box nearby. 'I'm as horny as hell.' She wiped some of the moisture from her vagina with the tissue. 'Gets you like that some nights, doesn't it?' she continued, looking at Carol.

'I suppose so,' she replied unenthusiastically.

'Half an hour with a vibrator stuck up you,' Lynn cooed. 'I can think of worse ways to pass the time.' She giggled and began to dress. 'I hope Rob isn't banking on a good night's sleep.'

'Can I have a word with you when you're ready, Carol, please?' said Scott. 'In my office.' He smiled at Lynn and retreated from the dressing room before Carol could answer him. Behind him he could hear the dark-haired girl still giggling.

Scott went around flicking off lights. He waved goodnight to Lynn as she left hurriedly, chuckling. Then he made his way back to his office.

He sat down on the edge of his desk and waited.

Come on. Come on.

Carol finally appeared, looking a little pale.

Scott smiled broadly at her.

'Ready?' he said happily.

'For what?' she said, somewhat bemused.

'I thought we could get something to eat. You said we could talk . . .'

She cut him short.

'I didn't say that, Jim,' Carol sighed. 'I don't feel too good. Maybe it's the time of the month.'

'Are you coming back to my place tonight? If it is the time of the month we don't have to . . .'

'I just want to get home.'

Tell him. For Christ's sake, put him out of his misery.

'I'm very tired, Jim.'

He clasped his hands together and nodded, the smile fading but still flickering on his lips.

'Maybe another night,' he said. 'Tomorrow, perhaps?'

She nodded.

That's it, just keep him dangling.

'I'm sorry,' she said. 'I just feel a bit rough.'

Lying bitch.

'You go home and get some rest. I'll see you tomorrow,' he said. 'You'll feel better then and we can talk.'

About what? About how it's all over?

She turned to leave but he crossed to her, put one hand on her shoulder and made her turn around. He bent forward and

47

kissed her, aware once again that she was keeping her arms by her sides. He took one arm and draped it over his shoulder, then repeated the action with her other.

'Not too painful, is it?' he smiled.

She smiled back.

Don't hurt him.

They finally parted and she said goodnight. He told her he would see her tomorrow, he had some things to do before he left.

Carol closed the office door and made her way down the corridor. As she drew level with the dressing room the pay phone inside began to ring. She opened the door, walked in and picked up the receiver.

'Hello,' she said wearily.

Silence. Only the odd pop and hiss of static.

'Hello,' she said again. 'Can I help you?'

'Carol Jackson.' It was a statement rather than a question.

'Yes,' she said after a short pause. 'Who's this?'

'I'm watching you.'

She held the receiver away from her ear for a moment and glared at it, as if her anger could somehow be transmitted down the line to the caller. When she pressed the receiver to her ear again she could hear soft breathing.

'If you're going to do it then do it properly, you useless bastard,' she hissed. '*Heavy* breathing, it's supposed to be.'

'I'm watching you.'

'Then what am I doing?' she asked.

'You're about to leave and I'll be waiting for you.'

This time her response wasn't quite so swift.

Other girls had received calls like this. It was almost an occupational hazard. She was about to speak again but the caller got there first.

'I'm waiting.'

There was a click as the phone was hung up and she was left with just the buzz of a dead line in her ear. Slowly she replaced the receiver. Then, wrapping her coat around her, she climbed the steps to street level and stepped out onto the pavement.

It was still raining, a thin, miserable mist of drizzle.

High up in his office, Scott watched her scuttle off towards Shaftesbury Avenue.

But his were not the only eyes that watched her.

Thirteen

It was almost 1.30 a.m. by the time Scott finally got home.

He trudged into the main entrance of the block of flats where he lived, heading towards the lifts. Behind him he left wet footprints on the tiled floor. As he reached the lifts he noticed that a sign had been affixed to the door: OUT OF ORDER. Beneath it, in biro, someone had scribbled: THEY ALWAYS FUCKING ARE.

Scott sighed and made for the stairs. Fortunately his flat was on the sixth floor; it wasn't too much of a trek. He wondered, briefly, how those on the fifteenth and sixteenth floors were managing. The block where he lived, like many others in Brent, was home to a wide variety of people. One-parent families, those in temporary accommodation, the usual ethnic mixture and, of course, long-term residents like himself. As he climbed the stairs he glanced at some of the graffiti sprayed or drawn on the green painted walls.

TORIES OUT
ARSENAL FC ARE CUNTS

As he reached each landing he glanced out of the large glass windows looking across to the other blocks that thrust upwards into the sodden night sky like pointing fingers. He saw the anti-collision lights of a plane high above in the blackness. It was leaving London, heading north. Scott wondered where its passengers were bound for.

He finally reached the sixth floor and rummaged in his jacket pocket for his key. As he stood in the corridor trying to find it he heard shouting from the flat next door. A man's voice, then a woman's, swapping obscenities and insults. Further down the corridor behind him a baby was crying.

Scott finally found the key and let himself in, shutting the door behind him, slipping the bolts across. There had been a spate of burglaries in the block lately. He didn't want to take any chances. He was, however, better prepared for intruders than most of the residents of the block. Locked away in the cabinet beside his bed was a 9mm Beretta automatic 92S.

He pulled off his jacket and trousers and hung them on a hanger over a radiator to dry off, then stripped down to his underpants and padded through into the kitchen to make a cup of tea.

From next door he could hear the couple still rowing. Scott didn't know their names, despite the fact that they'd lived next to him for more than five years. He'd never taken the trouble to get to know them or any of the other residents. He didn't *want* to know them, he wasn't interested in their lives and he was damn sure they weren't interested in *his*. He filled the electric kettle and pressed the 'play' button on the radio-cassette that stood beside it, adjusting the volume so that he could no longer hear the rantings from next door. *Noisy fuckers.*

 '*. . . All alone now, except for the memories.*
 Of what we had and what we knew.
 Everytime I try to leave it behind me,
 I see something that reminds me of you . . .'

He stood staring at the kettle as if willing it to boil. Then he pulled open a cupboard and searched for the tea bags, dropping one into his mug.

He thought about Carol.

The image of her floated into his mind unbidden. He savoured it for a moment, his thoughts interrupted by the clouds of steam that began to billow from the kettle.

Carol.

He wished she was with him now. She seemed to be on his mind constantly, whether he wanted it that way or not.

Couldn't he do anything without thinking about her?

That's what it's like when you're in love.

He grunted.

Love. What the fuck did he know about love?

His father had told him that many times.

His father . . .

He pushed the thoughts to the back of his mind and wandered through into the sitting room, switching off the cassette first. He drank his tea then decided to have a shower before retiring. He was tired and his body ached; he wouldn't need much coaxing to sleep but he felt as if he needed to cleanse himself.

He passed through the sitting room, through another door past his own bedroom. Past the other bedroom.

The one he kept locked now.

The one where his father . . .

Fuck it.

51

The memories were there; they always would be. No amount of time was going to make them disappear. Perhaps the years would make them less potent but they would not easily be excised from his consciousness. He paused by the door to his father's room, or what had once been his father's room. Then he twisted the key and walked in.

It was bare, completely empty but for the single bed, now stripped, which stood beneath the window. His father had lived with him for three years prior to his death ten months ago. A stroke and then a gradual decline into senility, followed by a second devastating brain haemorrhage, had seen the old man off. It was the time after the first stroke that Scott had found so trying. His father, then seventy-two, had been rendered more or less helpless, housebound and unable to do anything but sit and stare at the television or out of the window all day. Scott's mother had left home when he was fourteen; he had no brothers or sisters to help him care for his father. The burden had fallen squarely on his shoulders. At first it hadn't been too bad. The old man could feed himself at least, but then he began to suspect that Scott was trying to poison him. He refused to eat. His weight dropped from twelve to seven stone. Scott had felt pity for him but, as the old man refused to eat, pity had given way to anger and then to hatred. He had seen his father wasting away but Scott had known that it could have been avoided. He lowered his head as he thought of the hatred he had felt for the man sometimes.

Was this shame?

Scott had brought him food only to see it hurled across the kitchen.

More than once he'd come close to hitting the old man.

Old bastard.

Now, now; he couldn't help himself.

52

Scott had wanted to believe that but it didn't alleviate the frustration he felt.

Don't you mean hatred?

At times it had become almost impossible for him to distinguish where he drew the line between his loathing of his father or his hatred of the illness that had transformed him.

'You bloody fool,' his father would repeat, glaring at him venomously. 'I can't eat that.' Then the tray or the plate would be hurled across the kitchen once again.

Just die, you old fucker. Do us both a favour and fucking die.

How easy it would have been to place the Beretta against the old man's head and blast what was left of his brains all over the wall.

And when the second stroke had taken him Scott had felt something akin to relief, until he visited him in hospital only hours before he died. He had walked into the room at the side of the ward and found his father's shrivelled form in an oxygen tent, tubes attached to his arms and nose. Scott had sat beside him, his mind blank, as if he had no pity, no hatred, no emotion of any kind left inside him. It was unsettling. His own indifference towards his father's impending death was infinitely more disturbing than any emotional outburst he may have been prone to.

Should have been prone to?

The hospital staff had told him it was just a matter of time; all he could do now was wait for the end. He might as well sit outside. But Scott had remained at the bedside, watching his father's sunken features, still unable to feel anything, still frightened by his own lack of emotion.

Why hang on? Just let go.

The father Scott had known and (*had he loved him? Truly*

loved him, ever?) lived with for so many years had been dead long before this second stroke. The man he had (*loved?*) known had ceased to exist after the first haemorrhage. The soul was gone, he was watching the decay of the husk now. Scott had been preparing to leave when his father's eyes had flickered open and, instead of a glassy stare, Scott had seen recognition. It had shocked him, brought all his feelings flooding back. In a moment of horrible clarity, it was as if his father knew and understood that he was going to die, and in his eyes that realisation was reflected. He knew he was going to die and he wept at the inevitability of it.

Then, just as quickly, the glazed look had returned and he had slipped back into coma and then beyond to death.

Scott stepped back and slammed the door, as if shutting out the sight of the room would close away the memories.

It didn't.

He couldn't sleep.

Scott had lain awake for over an hour listening to the wind whistling outside the window. Thinking.

He thought about his father.

He thought about Carol.

Finally he swung himself out of bed and crossed to the window.

Rain spattered against it like wind-blown tears.

He felt very alone and he didn't like the feeling. Not much frightened him but loneliness scared the hell out of him.

I don't want to die alone.

He thought of Carol.

His hope. His salvation.

She would be with him; he wouldn't be alone.

He glanced at the phone beside the bed, thought about

calling her. He just wanted to hear her voice.

Maybe in a little while.

The wind continued to howl.

Fourteen: 3 April 1977

The man came hurtling across the room, mouth open, arms outstretched, his eyes bulging wide with rage.

Dr Robert Dexter took a step back from the observation slit in the door, relieved that three inches of solid steel separated him from the patient beyond. Inside the room, the man continued to fling himself at the door, banging his head against the metal partition, finally spitting on the glass of the observation window, the thick mucus obscuring Dexter's view of him.

'Increase his medication,' Dexter said, glancing down at the clipboard he held.

'He's on 50mg of Thorazine twice a day already,' Andrew Colston told him.

'Well, it doesn't seem to be working, does it? Up the dosage.'

Their footsteps echoed through the high ceilinged corridor as they approached the next door. Dexter slid back the observation panel and looked in.

The occupant of the cell was sitting cross-legged on his bed in a meditative pose, his head bowed. He was naked.

Dexter fumbled with the bunch of keys that dangled from his belt, inserted one in the lock and walked in. Colston followed.

55

The man looked up and smiled, then lowered his head once more.

'How are you this morning, Roger?' asked Dexter, sitting on one end of the bed. Colston stayed behind him.

Roger Lacey looked up and smiled broadly, revealing a row of off-white teeth. His hair was cropped short, so short in fact that it was little more than stubble at his temples and the nape of his neck. His body was slender, heavily muscled, his hands resting one on each of his knees. As the two men watched he gently lifted his right hand and gripped the massive erection he sported. He began moving his hand up and down his shaft.

'It's time,' he said quietly.

'Roger, stop that for a moment,' said Dexter, his eyes fixed on the man's face.

Colston found his own gaze riveted to Lacey's busy right hand.

'Where are they, Roger?' Dexter asked.

'Under the bed.'

Dexter nodded and Colston knelt down and reached beneath the bed. His hand closed over a thin plastic tray. He slid it out into view and passed it to his colleague who set it down on the bed in front of Lacey who had slowed the pace of his masturbating now.

On the tray were twelve watches, not one of which was working. The hands were frozen, all stopped at different times. Dexter lifted one and turned it over. The back had been clumsily but effectively opened then wedged back into position again.

With his breath coming in gasps, Lacey watched as Dexter pulled a pair of surgical gloves from the pocket of his jacket, lifted one of the time-pieces and, after slipping the gloves on, flipped the back of the watch off.

The inner workings of the mechanism were coated and clogged by a thick, congealed substance Colston recognised as semen.

The other eleven time-pieces carried a similar cargo within them.

'You're not going to take them, are you?' asked Lacey, his face losing its colour, his hand now slack on his penis.

'What do you think would happen if we did?' Dexter asked.

Lacey shook his head agitatedly looking first at one doctor then the other. He licked his lips and tried to swallow but his throat was too dry.

'Roger,' Dexter repeated. 'What do you think would happen if we took the watches away? Do you *know*?'

Lacey shook his head even more vigorously.

'Did your wife take the watches away from you?' the doctor asked.

'Yes.'

'Is that why you killed her?'

'Yes.'

'So what do you think is going to happen if we take them away now? Can you tell me?'

'There have to be some survivors,' said Lacey falteringly.

'Survivors from what?' Dexter wanted to know.

'The war. When the war comes, everyone will die except those who are prepared.'

'Like you?'

'Yes.' He smiled.

'Why do you keep semen in the back of these watches, Roger?'

'They will be the survivors. They will grow. When the time comes.' He chuckled at his own pun. 'The time will come.' He began masturbating again. 'Every male discharge contains approximately two hundred million sperm. I have created

57

enough to re-populate the world after the war. From each of them a person will grow.'

Dexter replaced the watch and got to his feet. Followed by Colston he headed for the door.

Behind them Lacey quickened the speed of his strokes, his breathing now harsher.

On the other side of the locked door Dexter pulled off the surgical gloves and shoved them into his pocket.

'How did he kill his wife? Stabbed her, didn't he?' the doctor mused.

Colston nodded.

'Apparently the police found traces of semen in every wound. All twenty-eight of them.' Colston looked through the observation slit to see Lacey reach his climax, thick white fluid pumping from his penis onto his hand. The doctor watched as the patient tried to scoop it up, desperate not to waste any of the precious ejaculate. He snapped the slide across and looked at Dexter.

'Do you think he's ready to be moved?' he asked.

'Not yet,' the other man proclaimed. 'Even though he killed his wife he didn't and still doesn't display any latent homicidal or psychopathic tendencies.' Dexter shook his head. 'He's not right for us.'

They moved further down the corridor, past other cells.

Past a young woman who had systematically torn out every finger– and toe-nail to prevent dirt settling unseen on her body. (The interns called her Lady Macbeth.) Past a man in his early thirties who had killed both his mother and father with a garden fork because they refused to attend the baptism of his half-caste daughter. He had covered their bodies in axle grease to 'blacken' them, anxious that they should know what it felt like to be 'coloured'.

Dexter looked in on the man, checking his name. Colin Wells.

'Does he have any family?' the doctor wanted to know.

'A sister,' Colston informed him.

'What about his wife?'

'She ran away after the killing of his parents, took the baby with her.'

'Where's the sister?'

'She lives nearby. She still visits occasionally.'

'Damn,' murmured Dexter under his breath.

There were two doors left.

Dexter crossed to the first of them and peered inside.

The occupant was kneeling in the centre of the room wearing only a pair of boxer shorts. His body was thin and wasted, his face pallid. He was bald except for some snow-white hair over his ears. Even the hair on his chest and the thick strands that curled from his nostrils were as white as milk.

Thomas Walsh had been institutionalised for nearly thirty of his seventy-three years.

As he heard the key turn in the lock he turned, still kneeling, to face his visitors.

Dexter and Colston watched as he rose imperiously then pressed his palms together, touched his fingertips to his chin and bowed.

'Good morning, Tom,' said Dexter, peering around the room.

Hardly an inch of the wall was untouched, barely a fraction of the white paint showing through the mass of scribblings which had been completed with crayon, marker pen. Even blood.

The pattern was uniform, duplicated hundreds, thousands of times over and over again on the walls.

It looked like two musical notes joined together but the lines were harsher, drawn with quick flourishes.

It meant 'power'.

Tom Walsh had been captured by the Japanese in Burma in 1940, forced for five years to work on the infamous Burma Railway, subject to the whims of brutal guards, starved and tortured. He had returned to England after the war a broken man both physically and mentally. Ten years in and out of hospital being treated for diseases he had picked up in the Malaysian jungles had seen his mental state deteriorate even further, his hatred of the Japanese grow ever stronger.

He'd been working in a car factory when a Japanese delegation had visited one day back in 1958.

Tom had managed to kill two of them and blind another with a soldering iron before he was stopped.

He'd been committed. He was the asylum's oldest patient.

Dexter exchanged a few words with him, then watched as he bowed ceremoniously when the two doctors left.

That left the last cell.

'*I* can check it if you like,' Colston said quietly.

Dexter thought a moment and shook his head. He took a step towards the final door, fumbling with his keys, his mouth dry. He didn't look through the observation slot first.

As he lifted the key to the lock, his hand was shaking.

Fifteen

The lift doors slid open with a muted whirr and DI Frank Gregson stepped out into the corridor.

He moved quickly but unhurriedly, his footsteps rattling out a tempo in the quiet corridor. At such a late hour every noise seemed amplified, too. Not that New Scotland Yard was run by the clock. Crime and criminals didn't hold regular hours, murderers didn't clock on and off.

By God, my dear Holmes, I should say not.

Gregson found the door to the pathology labs locked, as he'd expected, but he had a key and let himself in, walking through the outer lab. into the autopsy room itself. He paused in the doorway, recoiling slightly from the pungent odour of chemicals and death that greeted him like a long-lost friend. Reaching round he slapped at the panel of switches. Seconds later, the room was bathed in cold white light as the banks of fluorescents in the ceiling cast their luminosity over the dissecting tables. The light was reflected in their polished, stainless steel surfaces and Gregson caught a glimpse of his own distorted image in one as he passed.

The tables were empty, their occupants removed and stored in the cabinets that lined the walls. So many puzzles lay within those boxes. So many unanswered questions.

Gregson stood looking at them for a moment, the silence inside the lab. quite overpowering. It was like a living organism, so complete it was almost palpable. It surrounded him. He felt as if it were penetrating his very pores, seeping into his bloodstream and circulating around his body.

He could hear the thud of his own heart in the solitude and its pace quickened as he found the locker he sought. He slid it out.

The body was covered by the familiar plastic sheet and the DI pulled it back to reveal the charred corpse beneath.

He stood gazing, for what seemed like an eternity, at the crushed skull, the wisps of hair that still clung to the blackened remains of the scalp. The scorched bones still covered, in places, by burned flesh.

He reached out and touched what was left of the face.

A piece of black flesh came away on his fingertip. He looked

61

at it for a moment then rubbed it away between his index finger and thumb. It crumbled like ash.

He looked at the body once more, his forehead deeply lined.

When he spoke, his gaze never leaving the charred body, his words echoed around the silent laboratory:

'Who *are* you?'

Sixteen: 15 April 1977

The new patient was due to arrive in a week.

At present he was still under guard inside Wandsworth, but according to the letters Dexter held in his hand – one from the Governor of that prison, the other rubber-stamped by the Home Secretary – he was to be receiving into his care a man by the name of Howard Townly.

Townly had, over a period of two months, kidnapped, tortured and finally murdered two men and three women, all of whom he had picked up while they were hitching lifts. He had made home movies of their deaths, replaying the videos over and over again for his enjoyment.

Townly was thirty-six.

About the right age.

Dexter checked through his notes on the man and saw that he had been unmarried. He was an only child.

This looked hopeful.

His mother had given evidence on his behalf during the trial.

Dexter shook his head.

No good.

Dexter sat back in his seat, massaging the bridge of his nose between thumb and forefinger. He had the psychological evaluation of Townly before him, too. The police psychiatrist who had interviewed him had noted that the man had tendencies towards schizophrenia, paranoid delusions and sociopathic leanings. A hopeless case? That was probably the reason he was being sent to Bishopsgate. The institution, which Dexter had been in charge of for the past eleven years, had over three hundred patients within its antiquated walls. They ranged from those who visited on a daily basis through to the voluntarily committed, graduating to the criminally insane. In fact almost a third of the inmates were of that latter category. Prisons, unable to cope with them, shunted them off to Bishopsgate, Broadmoor or Rampton. Dexter often wondered if this was a genuine attempt to put them in the hands of those better equipped to deal with their mental instability or merely a way of relieving the pressure on an already overcrowded prison system which sometimes packed men three to a cell.

Perhaps the very fact that these men were insane had ensured they at least enjoyed a little more privacy for the period of their incarceration.

Insane.

It was a word he heard nearly every working day. One which he had been hearing for as long as he could remember in connection with the wildly aberrant behaviour and attitudes of some of his wards. What the hell was insanity? And who had the right to define it as such?

Dexter had come to see, with some individuals he'd treated, that insanity was not a disintegration of the mind but rather a re-building. Madness was sometimes displayed in a startling clarity of thought which apparently 'normal' mortals could never hope to understand. There was a relentless logicality to the way a madman thought. That madness sometimes proved to be so

63

single-minded, so obsessively consuming, that Dexter found himself not fearing or hating these murderers he had charge of but admiring them.

Ted Bundy, an American mass-murderer convicted of killing more than twenty young women, was once quoted as saying, 'What's one less person on the face of the earth, anyway?' When war, usually started and controlled by supposedly sane men, took the lives of millions, Dexter found it easy to subscribe to Bundy's observation. Who was madder, the solitary individual who killed a dozen for his *own* reasons? Or the soldier, trained to kill hundreds in the name of a cause he could not even understand?

His philosophical musings were interrupted by a knock on his office door.

'Come in,' he called.

Colston practically stumbled in, his face drained of colour.

'What's wrong?' Dexter asked, noticing his colleague's expression.

'One of the patients,' Colston said agitatedly. 'You must come now.'

'Is it *that* important?'

'It's in Ward 5.'

Dexter was on his feet in a second. He and Colston moved with great haste along the corridors, Dexter almost breaking into a run as they drew closer. His mind was in turmoil, ideas and visions flooding through it like a raging torrent through a broken dam. He didn't even think to ask Colston what had happened.

Ward 5.

He swallowed hard.

They turned a corner and came upon two interns standing beside a heavy steel door. It was firmly locked and secured.

The entrance to Ward 5.

The ward was in the East Wing of the institution and accessible only to half a dozen interns, Colston and Dexter himself. The two doctors watched as one of the interns, Baker, unlocked the door and stepped back to allow them through. He and another man called Bradley followed.

'Where?' Dexter said. 'Which cell?'

Colston led him past four doors, grey-painted and nondescript but for an observation slot and a small square hatch for pushing food through. Colston paused at the fifth and nodded towards Bradley, who unlocked the door and stepped back, allowing Dexter to enter the room.

The smell of excrement hit him immediately, but he was able to ignore the stench; his attention was riveted to the body of the man slumped against the far wall of the cell.

He was in his thirties, Dexter knew, but a stranger would have found it impossible to guess at his age.

His face looked as though someone had been across it in all directions with a cheese-grater. His skin hung in bloodied ribbons from bones which were visible in places through the crimson mess. The front of the grey overall he wore was soaked with gore and, as Dexter moved closer to kneel beside the man, he noticed a thick, reddish-pink piece of matter lying in the man's lap. A glance at his open mouth revealed that the reddish-pink lump was the end of his tongue. He'd bitten through it, severing it. His teeth, visible because what remained of his shredded lips was stretched back in a rictus, were also coated with crimson. It looked as if he'd been using scarlet mouthwash. One eye, torn from its socket, dangled by the slender thread of the optic nerve. It rested neatly on his mangled cheek, the orb fixing Dexter in a sightless stare.

The doctor looked down at the man's hands and saw that the fingers were drenched with blood, strips of flesh, some two inches long, stuck beneath the nails. He had used his

65

fingernails like claws on his own face, gouged his own eye from its socket.

Colston, standing in the doorway, was aware almost for the first time of the uncanny silence that reigned over the rest of the ward. It was as if the other occupants were in silent mourning.

'The same as the others,' he said quietly.

Dexter nodded and got to his feet, the expression on his face one not of sadness but of anger. He looked at Colston.

'I want a report on my desk by the morning,' he said. Then he looked back at the shredded features of the man, blood beginning to congeal in the wounds. 'We have to know.'

Seventeen

He gripped the headboard and thrust harder into her, each motion of his hips accompanied by a grunt.

Ray Plummer smiled down at her as he penetrated her, gritting his teeth in concentration, his efforts enlivened when he saw the look of pleasure on Carol Jackson's face.

She gasped and raised her legs, hooking them around the small of his back, raising her buttocks to allow him deeper penetration. She began to rotate her hips gently, coaxing him towards the climax she knew was close.

Come on, for Christ's sake get it over with.

She moaned loudly, knowing that the sounds she made, coupled with the clenching of her vaginal muscles around his penis, would, as ever, bring him to climax quickly.

He was sweating profusely; as she ran her fingers up and

down his back she felt their tips sliding through a sheen of perspiration.

Come on, Ray. You can't hold out much longer.

'That feels so good,' she cooed expertly. 'Do it faster.'

'Faster, slower,' he panted, trying to keep up his rhythm. 'Harder, softer. How do you want it?'

'All those ways,' she breathed.

Only just get a bloody move on and finish, will you?

She reached over and began to squeeze his testicles, stroking them gently, breathing ever more deeply, her exaggerated show of pleasure becoming more pronounced.

She felt him stiffen, felt his body tense.

'Oh yes,' she gasped with relief, knowing the time had arrived.

He thrust into her with one final, deep lunge and she felt his hot seed filling her, seeping from her vagina as he continued to pound away, his breath rasping in his throat.

She reached up to stroke his hair but he pushed her hand away, content that she should run her fingers up and down his back.

Get off me for Christ's sake.

He remained on top of her, his breathing gradually slowing.

'Jesus, that was good,' she gasped, her own breath coming in practised gasps.

He touched her cheek with his fingers and smiled a smile of accomplishment before finally rolling off her and lying exhausted on the bed, wiping perspiration from his forehead. Immediately she reached for the tissues beside the bed and began mopping up the warm fluid seeping from between her legs.

'Leave it,' he said breathlessly, watching as his semen trickled through her pubic hair.

She rolled onto her side and began stroking his chest.

'It's all right for you,' she said. 'You don't have to sleep in the wet patch.'

He laughed humourlessly.

'You should be used to it by now,' he muttered, holding her chin between his thumb and forefinger.

I've done it to you enough times.

She moved away from him slightly and laid her head on his chest, listening to his heart pounding, closing her eyes in relief that it was over for another night.

'Felt good, didn't it?' he said, his tone self-congratulatory.

'Yes,' she lied.

She could feel his semen oozing uncomfortably over her thighs but she tried to ignore it, knowing that he would be asleep soon. Then, as she usually did, she would slip out of bed while he was snoring like a fog-horn and take a shower. Wash it all away. For now she lay where she was, aware that he was twisting her long hair around his fingers. Occasionally he would tug a little too hard and she would wince but she said nothing, content to let him play his little games.

It was warm inside the flat. In contrast, her own place was like a fridge. All she had to keep her warm was a two-bar electric fire close to the bed. Plummer's penthouse apartment was fully central-heated. In the large sitting room he even had an open fireplace full of mock logs. She would often sit gazing into the gas flames late at night while he slept, tracing shapes in them, wondering if some of those shapes were the shape of her future.

The flat itself was one of a group of four in Kensington, not too far from Kensington High Street. She knew that the other people who lived as Plummer's neighbours were well off. One was a lawyer, another a judge. She wasn't sure what the woman who owned the bottom flat did. Something in the City, she thought. It was ironic that a man of Plummer's means should be sharing the building with two people who, effectively, worked on the opposite side of the law to him. The apartment was worth, Plummer had told her (repeatedly), around three quarters of a million. He owned two houses in Belgravia as well, both of which were in the process of being converted into flats. He fancied himself as a landlord.

He reached across and picked up his glass of Jack Daniels, tiring of his game with Carol's hair. She heard the sound of his expensive ring clinking against expensive crystal as he picked the glass up. He took a sip and then swung himself out of bed.

'Where are you going?' she wanted to know.

'Don't be so nosey,' he told her, disappearing into the en suite bathroom. He emerged a moment later carrying a small rectangular box which he held out to her. As she took it from him she noticed that the lid of the box bore the legend: GARRARDS JEWELLERS.

He sat down on the edge of the bed and watched her open it.

The pendant was solid gold, twice the size of a thumbnail. The light from the bedside lamp caught it and sent golden beams radiating from it.

Carol opened her mouth in awe as much as surprise.

'It's beautiful,' she said, not taking her eyes from the velvet-lined box and its costly contents.

'Put it on,' said Plummer, watching as she took it from the box and fastened it around her neck. It hung invitingly between her breasts. 'Do you like it?'

'Thank you, Ray. It's gorgeous,' she told him, touching his cheek with her fingertips. She stroked his hair, but again Plummer pushed her hand away.

'I got it today,' he said, reclining on the bed, not bothering to cover his flaccid penis. 'Probably cost more than you earn in a year.' He smiled.

'You pay me,' she reminded him. 'You could do something about that.'

'I don't pay you. Scott does.'

'He pays me what you *tell* him to pay me.'

Plummer brushed a hand across the front of his hair.

'You still seeing him?' he wanted to know. 'Or should I say are you still fucking him?'

'I see him occasionally,' she confessed. 'It's all over between us, though; it's just that I can't seem to get around to telling him.'

'Does he know about you and me?' Plummer wanted to know. For a moment she saw a flicker of uncertainty on the older man's face.

'Would it matter if he did?' she asked.

It would make it easier for me, splitting up with him, if he did.

'I suppose not,' Plummer said. 'It's just that he's a bit unpredictable. Flies off the handle a bit quick, sometimes.'

You're scared of him.

The realisation brought a slight smile to her lips and she touched the locket almost unconsciously. It wasn't the first gift he'd bought her. She had a solid gold Cartier watch at home, endless amounts of silk underwear. He'd even taken her to Paris for a weekend about six weeks ago (she'd told Scott she'd been visiting relatives in the North). Of course she couldn't wear any of the things to work, Scott would want to know where they had come from.

'You shouldn't spend your money on me, Ray,' she said, looking at the pendant again.

'It's only money,' he said. Plummer enjoyed spending, enjoyed buying her things. He enjoyed impressing her with his wealth. Besides, she was a very good-looking young woman; he liked being seen with her. A number of his friends had remarked on her good looks, good figure. They envied him and he liked that. It was a good enough reason to hang on to her.

For the time being.

'Someone's got to look after you,' he said, stroking her hair.

'You're going to look after me?' she asked, smiling.

You're going to help me escape the life I hate?

He smiled.

'Who else is going to do it?' he wanted to know.

No one. She knew that. He was her only way out and she didn't intend to let him go. Whatever she had to do to keep him happy, she would do it.

Happy, was that the word? Perhaps satisfied was more apt.

'Take care of me, Ray,' she said softly, her eyes filling with tears. She leant forward and put her head on his chest.

Be careful, the mask is slipping.

He put his arm around her shoulders and pulled her closer.

'Don't worry, darling,' he said, his face impassive. 'I'm here.'

So make the most of it while you can.

The phone rang.

'What the fuck . . .' Plummer hissed, looking at his watch and then across at the bedside clock, as if to reassure himself of the time.

2.36 a.m.

The ringing continued.

'Shit,' he grunted and reached for the phone, picking up the receiver. 'Hello.'

'Ray Plummer.'

He didn't recognise the voice.

'Yeah. Do you know what fucking time it is?' he snapped.

'Shut up.'

'Who the fuck are you talking to . . .'

'Shut up and listen.'

'Who are you? Give me one good reason why I shouldn't hang up.'

'Because I've got something to tell you, you cunt. Something to your advantage. Now shut the fuck up and listen.'

71

Eighteen

Plummer sat up, the receiver pressed tightly to his ear, his eyes narrowed.

'Listening?' the voice chided.

'Yeah, go on,' he rasped.

Carol looked at him and mouthed 'Who is it?' but he raised a hand to keep her quiet.

He concentrated on the voice, listening to every syllable in an effort to work out his caller's identity. If it was somebody pissing about he'd have their fucking head.

'You're probably wondering why I called,' said the voice.

'Just get on with it. What do you want?'

'Patience is a virtue, Plummer. Now, do you want to hear what I've got to say, or shall we stop now?'

'You couldn't tell me anything I wanted to know anyway.'

'Oh ye of little faith.'

'Are you going to get to the fucking point, or what?' Plummer's initial bewilderment had turned to anger. He felt tempted to slam the receiver down.

'The point is you are about to be shat on from a great height,' the voice told him.

'By who?'

'Ah, now that's why I called. Interested *now*?'

He was about to shout something down the phone when the caller continued.

'Whoever has the most money controls London, right?

Whether it's you or one of your . . . associates. You all own property, clubs, gambling places. You own people. I'm right, aren't I? The one with most money stays in control.'

'Yeah,' Plummer said slowly.

'Ralph Connelly is about to receive a shipment.'

'Of what?'

'Cocaine.'

'That's bollocks. Connelly doesn't deal in drugs. He makes all his cash by laundering other people's money. He does some of mine, for fuck's sake. I knew you were full of shit. Get off the fucking line . . .'

'Cocaine worth twenty million pounds. The shipment's coming in six days from now.'

Plummer hesitated.

Twenty million.

'Why should I believe you?' he asked.

'*Don't.* It makes no odds to me but twenty million, you'll agree, is a lot of money. By my reckoning that should make Connelly top dog.'

'How did you find out about this cocaine?'

'That's my business.'

'Then why make it mine too?'

'Just call it personal reasons.'

'You want a cut,' Plummer said, smiling thinly.

'I said it was personal.'

'Look, any arsehole could ring me and tell me something like this. There's still no reason why I should believe you.'

'Connelly bought a warehouse in Tilbury about a week ago, didn't he?'

Plummer paused for a moment.

'Yeah, he did.'

'What would he want with a fucking warehouse? Like you said, laundering is his business.'

'And business is good. Why would he want to start up with drugs?'

'Like I said, twenty million is a lot of money. Would *you* turn it down? He was offered the shipment by some people in France.'

Plummer stroked his chin thoughtfully.

'How do you know all this?' he asked, even his anger receding now.

'That's not important. What I *do* need to know is, are you interested in the cocaine?'

'Yeah, I am. Twenty million.

The caller cut him short.

'I'll be in touch soon.'

He hung up.

'Wait,' snarled Plummer. Then, hearing the buzz of a dead line, he slammed the receiver down. 'Cunt,' he hissed. Watched by Carol he clambered out of bed and padded through into the sitting room to pour himself another drink. Who the fuck had called him? he wondered. His interest had been aroused. Twenty million notes. Jesus. That *was* interesting. He smiled.

He might not have smiled so broadly had he realised his flat was being watched.

Nineteen

Scott replaced the receiver and sat staring at it for a moment.

He would ring again in five or ten minutes.

Outside, the wind had dropped slightly but the rain had

intensified. It slapped against his window, the constant spattering like a thousand birds pecking at the glass.

Try again now.

He reached towards the phone.

No. Leave it.

Instead he hauled himself out of bed, angry that he'd been denied the welcome oblivion of sleep. He crossed the small bedroom to the dressing table, which bore a motley selection of after-shave bottles and deodorant cans, some empty. There were wage slips, too, piled up in order and weighed down with an ashtray still full of dog-ends.

There was a framed photo of himself and Carol.

He picked it up and ran his glance over it, his eyes pausing every so often to look at her face.

The picture had been taken about eight months earlier. They had managed to get out of London one night and spent two days in Brighton. The weather had been good and the picture showed Carol in a bikini, her arm around his shoulder. He'd asked some bloke sitting near them to take the picture, relieved when it had come out so well.

Christ, she was lovely.

He touched the photo with one index finger, as if to feel the smoothness of her skin. The warmth of that day seemed a million years ago as he stood listening to the rain hammering against the windows. He put the photo back and wandered through into the kitchen, where he retrieved a bottle of vodka from one of the kitchen cupboards. He took a glass from the draining board, then returned to the bedroom, sat on the edge of the bed and poured himself a large measure.

He used to give his father a drink. After the first stroke, a couple of shots seemed to put the old bastard in a better frame of mind. After the second one, dropping him in a vat of the stuff wouldn't have helped.

Fuck him. Forget about him.

He'd tried, but it had proved surprisingly difficult. When he remembered his father it wasn't as the wasted, comatose figure he'd watched over in hospital or the cantankerous sod he'd been forced to put up with for ten months. He remembered him as the sometimes abrupt, sometimes lonely but often funny man he'd shared his flat with for two years and eight months *before* the first stroke. Prior to that the old boy had lived in a flat of his own in Muswell Hill. He'd been forced to move out when it had been taken over by a new landlord.

Why the fuck had this particular spectre returned to haunt him, he wondered? Why was he thinking about his old man when the only person he truly cared for was Carol?

Perhaps it was the loneliness that made him think.

He felt lonely now, sitting on the edge of his bed, the drink cradled in his hand, listening to the rain. He thought how his father had once confided to him what *he* felt. And it was fear of that feeling which remained firmly embedded in his mind. Scott needed someone. No, not *someone*; he needed Carol.

He reached for the phone and jabbed out the digits of her number, just as he'd been doing for the past half-hour.

He just wanted to hear her voice.

The phone went on ringing.

Just let me hear her.

Perhaps she'd pulled the connection from the socket so she wouldn't be disturbed.

Pick it up.

Maybe she'd put the phone under a stack of pillows to muffle the ringing so it didn't wake her up.

Come on. Come on.

The ringing continued until he slammed the receiver down in frustration.

Perhaps she was ill.

76

Perhaps she wasn't there. She might have been hurt on her way home. She could be in hospital now.

What if. . .?

He downed what was left in the glass and poured himself another, gulping half of it down in one swallow.

She was not there. He knew it. *Felt it.*

Then where?

He gritted his teeth, his breath coming in short gasps.

Where was she?

He looked across at the photo on the dressing table. She smiled back at him.

Scott shouted and hurled the glass across the room. It hit the wall and shattered, spraying shards of crystal in all directions. Vodka dripped from the wet patch on the paper.

He wondered how long it took for loneliness to become despair.

Twenty: 16 April 1977

The tumour was as large as a man's fist.

Dexter looked at it lying in the metal dish, a huge collection of dead cells, darkish brown in colour, tinged a rusty red from the congealed blood which coated it. It had been taken that morning, from the skull of the dead man they had found in Ward 5 the previous day.

Now Dexter observed the tumour and tapped a pen gently against his chin, his thoughts running pell-mell through his mind.

'What about the others?' he asked.

Colston sighed and shrugged his shoulders, pulling up a chair beside the desk.

'Four out of the five are exhibiting similar symptoms to those of Baker,' he said. 'I checked them over this morning before I did the autopsy.'

'Damn,' snapped Dexter, getting to his feet. He crossed to the window of his office and looked out over the well-manicured lawns and the tall trees that swayed in the wind.

'Is there anything we can do?' he asked, without looking at his companion.

'If the tumours are developing at the same rate then I could operate, try to remove them. We'd at least save their lives,' Colston told him.

Dexter watched as an intern led two patients across the lawn, one of them kicking a football ahead of him like an excited child.

'You said four out of the five were exhibiting similar symptoms,' he said quietly. He turned to face Colston. 'What about . . .'

The other doctor shook his head, cutting him short.

'So far no change,' he said.

A slight smile creased Dexter's lips.

'Then we're doing *something* right,' he said, clutching this small piece of optimism as a drowning man clutches the proverbial straw.

Colston sucked in a deep breath.

'And we're also doing something very *wrong*,' he said. 'That's the third death in as many months. If the tumours in the other four continue to develop . . .' He allowed the sentence to trail off.

Dexter returned to his desk and tapped the five files stacked in front of him.

Each one bore the note WARD 5 in its top right-hand corner.

Below that was the name of the patient.

'What do we do?' Colston wanted to know. 'Stop?'

'Certainly not,' said the other man indignantly. 'It *will* work, Andrew. I'm *sure* of it.'

'Then at least modify the process until we see the progress of the other five.'

Dexter shook his head again.

'The other *four*,' he interjected. 'You said one of them was still all right.'

'It might just be a matter of time before a tumour develops there too . . .'

Dexter interrupted again.

'No,' he said with conviction. 'It *won't*. I just believe it won't.'

'Because it's what you *want* to believe.'

'Do you blame me?' he snapped.

There was a long silence, finally broken by Colston.

'No, I don't blame you,' he murmured. 'And don't worry, I'm not going to back out on you. Not now.'

Dexter smiled appreciatively and picked up the files marked Ward 5.

He flicked through the first four relatively quickly.

It was the last of them that interested him.

Twenty-one

The needle, almost six inches long, had been pushed through the girl's nipple, inserted with clinical efficiency through the fleshy bud.

George Kinsellar turned the page of the magazine and proudly displayed another double spread, this time of a young girl with several metal rings through her vaginal lips.

'What about that?' Kinsellar said. 'Be like shagging a scrap-metal yard, wouldn't it?' He chuckled his throaty laugh which ended as usual, with him hawking loudly, chewing thoughtfully on the mucus for a moment and then swallowing it again.

Kinsellar was a thick-set man in his early fifties, his face pitted, his hair thinning.

'How can anybody get their rocks off to something like that?' said Scott, shaking his head, taking the magazine from the older man and flipping through it. He finally dropped it into the supermarket trolley he was pushing and continued walking up the long aisle between the high shelves.

The warehouse was in Holloway and Kinsellar had owned it for the last six years. The bulk of his business was done with Ray Plummer's organisation, although he supplied a number of the other firms in the capital with videos, books, 8mm films and appliances. Fifty per cent of what he sold was illegal but business was booming. He followed Scott around, making notes on his pad of what the younger man was ordering.

The magazines were stacked up to three feet high on shelves that reached almost to the tall ceiling of the warehouse. Light struggled to penetrate a skylight which was so filthy it was nearly opaque. Inside, the place smelt of newsprint. As he pushed the trolley, Scott couldn't help but smile to himself. Whenever he visited this place (usually once a month to check up on new stock and place his order) he couldn't shake the feeling that, pushing his trolley around amidst shelves piled high with books featuring every kind of sexual perversion, he was like a shopper in some depraved branch of Sainsbury's.

'Some of this new stuff that's been coming in is fucking ace,

I tell you,' Kinsellar said, making another note. 'Especially the German stuff. The krauts certainly know what they're doing when it comes to porn.' He chuckled, hawked and swallowed. 'I got a load of videos in the other day. You've never seen anything like it. Birds eating each other's shit. I was fucking amazed.' He smiled. 'I just kept thinking, "I hope they got it right on the first take". I mean, it's difficult enough getting an actress to cry on cue, isn't it? But to shit on cue.' The sentence disappeared beneath that mucoid chuckle.

Scott continued pushing the trolley, his mind elsewhere.

Carol wouldn't be in until eight that night.

He had another nine hours before he could ask her where she'd been last night when he was trying to call her.

They rounded a corner and began down another aisle.

'You're quiet today, Jim,' Kinsellar noticed at last.

They don't call you flash for nothing, George, do they? thought the younger man.

'Business bad, is it?'

'Business is fine.'

It's me that's fucked up.

'You still seeing that bird that works at the club?' Kinsellar wanted to know. 'Whatsername . . .'

'Carol,' Scott said, reaching for another magazine and flipping it open. He studied the first few pages, looking at the girls lying on a bed, their fingers thrust deep into their vaginas, their labia spread wide for the prying camera. He dropped the magazine into the trolley and walked on.

'Yeah, I'm still seeing her,' Scott said wearily.

'You don't sound very enthusiastic.'

Scott rounded on him.

'What do you want, a fucking blow-by-blow of the last two months?' he snapped.

81

'All right,' Kinsellar said, taking a step back. 'No need to bite my fucking head off. I just wondered if I could help. If you wanted to talk about it.'

'Stick to selling the mags, George. Being an agony aunt doesn't suit you,' Scott rasped.

'You young blokes are all the same. Think you know it all when it comes to women, don't you?'

'I wish I knew something. *Anything*. I don't understand them.'

'You and every other bloke around, my son,' Kinsellar told him. 'I've been married twice, lived with two other birds, the last one for fifteen years, and I'm still none the wiser. But I've seen more of them than most.'

'Are we talking crotches now, George?' Scott said acidly. 'Well, come on, let me have it. Let's hear some advice from the world's number one cunt expert.'

'Somebody really did rattle your cage this morning, didn't they?' Kinsellar said. 'You had a row with her, is that it?'

Scott shook his head.

'No, I haven't had a row with her,' he said. 'That's the trouble. We've hardly spoken in the last couple of weeks.' He suddenly became aware that he was opening up to Kinsellar. 'Fuck it, why am I telling you?'

'A trouble shared . . .'

'Fucks up two people instead of one. I know,' snapped Scott. 'Now can you stop asking me questions about Carol?' He glared at the older man.

Kinsellar shrugged and followed him in silence for a few paces.

'You still shagging her?' he asked at last.

Scott spun round, his eyes blazing. He grabbed the older man by the lapels of his jacket and hurled him up against one of the bookshelves, his face only inches away from Kinsellar's.

'No more questions,' he hissed through clenched teeth.

Kinsellar tried to nod but Scott's fists beneath his chin prevented that gesture.

'All right,' he croaked.

Scott held him a moment longer then pushed him away.

A large figure appeared at the end of the aisle. Six-four and over sixteen stone, he was Kinsellar's nephew, biceps and chest hardly covered by the T-shirt he wore, muscles pumped up by years of loading and unloading lorries and generally helping with the older man's business. He looked at his uncle then at Scott.

'It's all right,' Kinsellar called to him. 'Go back to work, Bernie. There's no bother.'

Bernie hesitated a moment, his gaze held by Scott.

You want some, too? Come on then, you big fucker.

Scott could feel the vein at his temple pulsing angrily.

The big man disappeared again.

Scott pushed the trolley on.

'You're bloody crazy,' Kinsellar said, catching up to him. 'I was only asking a question.'

'You ask too many questions, George. It's my problem, so *I'll* sort it out, right?' He looked unblinking at the older man, who nodded.

'You ought to watch that temper of yours, son. It's going to get you into bother one day.'

Scott looked at him impassively.

'What about the videos?' he asked.

The ordering took less than half an hour. Scott sat in Kinsellar's office gazing into space, a mug of tea gripped in one hand. He didn't seem to notice that it was burning his fingers. He finally looked across at the older man and got to his feet.

'I'd better go,' he said, glancing at his watch.

Another eight hours before he could see Carol.

'I've got some good stuff coming in next week,' Kinsellar told him. 'German again. Some bird in a video having toothpicks shoved through her cunt lips.'

'Just send some over, eh?' He headed towards the door.

'Are you seeing Carol tonight?' the older man asked.

Scott turned slowly to look at him, his face darkening.

'I told you not to ask me any more questions about her, George,' he rasped.

'Just curious,' he said, a slight grin on his face. 'Maybe it comes with age.' He cackled his mucoid giggle.

'And I told you, you ask too many questions.'

'I've got one more,' Kinsellar said, reaching for a magazine that lay on his desk. He flipped it open to the centre spread where a girl with her legs spread wide and fingers parting her moist vagina was smiling into the camera.

'What is it?' asked Scott.

Kinsellar held up the centre spread.

'Where do you reckon *she* lives?'

Twenty-two

Detective Inspector Frank Gregson leaned back on the two rear legs of his chair and began rocking gently, his gaze riveted to the sheets of paper on his desk.

They were statements taken from witnesses to the shooting in the Haymarket two days ago. Jesus, it seemed longer than two days. It seemed like a fucking eternity. Maybe it *would* be an eternity before they identified the mysterious killer. Once that was done they might at least have a chance of figuring out why, when escape had been possible, he had chosen to kill himself.

No word had come up from the pathology labs. from Barclay as yet. He was still working on the remains of the corpse, trying to find some clue in the twisted, blackened remnants of humanity that might give them a lead on the individual who had, for no apparent reason, taken six lives (one of the victims on the critical list had died late the previous night) and then killed himself, all in the space of about five minutes.

Where did he come from?

Where did he get hold of the weapons?

Why did he choose to strike where he did?

Fuck it, thought Gregson, it was all questions and no answers so far.

The statements didn't help much, either.

'One says he was blond, another says he was ginger,' the DI muttered, flipping through the neatly typed sheets. 'One says short hair, another says tied in a pony-tail. It's a wonder they all managed to agree he was the same fucking colour.'

On the other side of the desk, DS Stuart Finn pulled a Marlboro from the packet and jammed it between his lips. He lit up, blowing a long stream of blue smoke into the air.

The DS was holding a photo-fit picture on his lap. It was held firmly in place by a bulldog clip at the top and bottom.

'That's the artist's impression,' he said, handing the sketch to Gregson. 'Based on the witnesses' statements.'

Gregson ran his gaze over the picture, his face expressionless. He tossed it onto his desk contemptuously.

'Does it match up with anything in our files?' he asked, clasping his hands across his stomach. He was staring down at his desk as if trying to see through the wood, through the floors to the pathology labs. below.

'There's only one way to find out and that's to go through every one. One by one.' Finn shrugged. 'Want to toss for it?' He smiled thinly.

'If there were two bloody statements which said the same thing about him then we might have a chance. As it is . . .' Gregson stopped in mid-sentence and flipped open the first file of statements. He leafed through them, pulling one out. It had been made by a cashier in the bank the man had entered. He looked hurriedly through the others until he found what he sought. The other statement was that of a motorist who had nearly collided with the killer when he'd been escaping on the motorbike.

'Staring eyes,' said Gregson, running his index finger over the words in both statements. 'Two of them *do* agree on *one* thing,' he said. 'The killer had staring eyes.'

Finn shrugged.

'Have I missed something?' he said. 'Perhaps he had thyroid. I'm not with you.'

'We nicked a guy about six years ago, he'd done a series of bank blags, never got away with much; he seemed more interested in hurting people than the money. He hit four banks all in Central London, same method every time. He walked in, blew out the cashier's window and took the dosh. He always carried a shotgun and an automatic.'

Finn nodded slowly, the recollection gradually coming to him.

'The most striking thing about him, most of the witnesses at the time said,' Gregson continued, 'were his eyes. His staring eyes.' He tapped the two newest statements. 'Staring eyes.'

'Lawton,' the DS said, a faint smile on his lips. 'Peter Lawton. Shit, I remember him now.' The smile faded rapidly.

'It's a coincidence, though, Frank; somebody imitating Lawton's methods, that's all. He's been inside for six years, still got another five to do before he even comes up for parole.'

Gregson nodded slowly.

'Weird, though, isn't it?' he muttered. 'Copy-cat killers, maybe, but copy-cat bank robbers?'

'What are you saying?'

The DI shrugged.

'I don't know what the fuck I'm saying,' he snapped. 'We know Lawton couldn't have done it because he's inside. So what do we make of these statements? The man had staring eyes,' he read aloud.

'Twin brother?' Finn offered somewhat lamely.

'Do me a favour,' said Gregson, getting to his feet. 'At the moment, though, I'm willing to consider anything. Let's check his file.'

Finn looked at his watch.

7.20 p.m.

He stubbed out his cigarette in the ashtray which was already overflowing with butts. A couple spilled over onto Gregson's desk and he swept them into his hand hastily before his superior noticed.

'Another fucking blank,' said Gregson, looking at the file on Peter Lawton. 'No family, no living relatives.' He looked at Finn. 'No twin brothers.'

'So what do we do next?' the DS wanted to know.

'You tell me.'

'Well, I fancy a drink. Join me?' Finn said, getting to his feet.

'No, I'm going to stay here for a while, try and think this through.'

'Frank, we're banging our heads on a fucking wall until pathology comes up with something concrete to identify the bloke. What's the point?' Finn asked, exasperated.

'You go, I'll see you in the morning,' the DI said, flipping open Lawton's file once again.

Finn hesitated, then said goodnight and left. Gregson heard his footsteps receding down the corridor.

Peter Lawton, sentenced to fifteen years for armed robbery and murder. Term being served in Whitely Maximum Security Prison, Derbyshire.

Term being served.

Gregson rubbed both hands over his face, exhaling deeply.

Another ten or fifteen minutes and he would leave. It was time to go home.

But first there was something he had to do.

Twenty-three

The wound was big enough to push two fists through. Portions of ribcage, shattered by the shotgun blast, protruded through the mess of pulped flesh gleaming whitely amidst the crimson.

Gregson looked long and hard at the photo, then slipped it carefully, almost reverently, on top of the others.

The baby had been practically cut in two by the blasts that had ripped through its pram.

Gregson looked at the tiny form, his face expressionless. There was another shot of it from a different angle. The angle made no difference to the massive damage that had been inflicted on the tiny child.

The DI took a swig from the glass of whisky he held in his other hand and pulled another photo from the pile on the table.

Before leaving New Scotland Yard he had collected the files on all of the victims of the gunman whose identity still remained a mystery.

There was a picture of the head of the motorcyclist the man had shot outside the bank.

The wound in the base of the skull looked relatively small, no larger than a ten pence coin. It was the other photo that showed the exit wound which caused Gregson to drain, a little more quickly than he would normally, the last dregs in his glass.

The bullet had exited just below the motorcyclist's right eye, shattering the cheekbone and dislodging the eye from its socket.

Although, Gregson reasoned, it hadn't been the shell itself that had blasted the orb free but the gases, released from the high velocity round as it had powered through the man's head. The eye was intact, still attached to the skull by the optic nerve.

Gregson dropped the picture down with the others and got to his feet, crossing the room to the sideboard. He opened it and took out the bottle of Teacher's. He poured himself a large measure, thought about adding some soda then decided against it. For long moments he stood by the sideboard, his breath coming in low, deep gasps, as if he'd just run a great distance. He rolled the glass across his forehead, his back still to the sitting-room door.

He heard the door open but did not turn as his wife entered the room.

Julie Gregson was wiping her hands on a dishcloth. She muttered something about the diamond in her engagement ring coming loose and gazed across the room at her husband.

'Dinner's ready,' she said.

'I'm not hungry,' Gregson said flatly, his back still to her. He took a swig from his glass.

'Did you have any lunch?' she wanted to know.

He shook his head.

She moved towards him, passing the table where the photos were spread out.

'Jesus Christ,' she muttered, noticing the topmost of them. She moved a step away, her eyes still fixed on it, mesmerised for a moment.

Gregson finally turned to look at her.

No. Not at her. At the table. The photos.

'What are they?' she said, the colour draining from her face.

'Isn't that obvious?' he said acidly, sitting down and looking at the photos again.

'*Who* are they?' Julie enquired, still keeping away from the table.

'Is it important?'

She moved the dishcloth from one hand to another, gazing at her husband then looking swiftly at the pictures once more.

She was a couple of years younger than him, her face etched with lines a little deeper than a woman in her late twenties would expect. She was slim, almost thin, her small breasts hardly visible even beneath the tight T-shirt she wore. Her jeans were faded, one knee threadbare, her skin showing through the narrow rent in the material.

'Why did you bring those home?' she wanted to know.

'It's part of my job,' he told her without looking up.

She balled up the dishcloth and dropped it onto the table beside the pictures. Then she sat down on the edge of the chair opposite him.

'Your bloody job,' she said quietly, but with anger. 'Everything is part of your bloody job, isn't it?'

'It pays the mortgage. Perhaps you should remember that.' He looked at her impassively.

'I work, too, Frank, in case you hadn't noticed. I do my bit towards the running of this house.'

'But it's my *bloody* job,' he said contemptuously, 'that pays the bills, isn't it? Perhaps you should think about that before you start moaning. What do you want me to do, give it up? Find something else to do?'

'When you're like this I wish you'd never joined the force,' she told him. 'Especially not the murder squad.'

'When I'm like what?' he said, that note of contempt still in his voice.

'You know what I'm talking about. *This* case, the last *few* cases, they've been getting you down *badly*.'

'Bullshit,' he sneered.

'It's *not* bullshit,' she rasped. 'It's true.' She glanced down at the photos briefly, revolted by them. 'Look at yourself, Frank, dwelling on what this man's done even when you're at home.'

'Do you think I can just wipe it clean when I leave my office?' he said, with scathing contempt. 'Do you think my mind is like a fucking blackboard? You scratch things on it, words, sights, you scratch those on it during the day, then at night I just forget about them? Is that what you think?' He picked up the next picture. It showed what was left of the skul of the cashier who had taken a blast from the Spas in the face. Gregson shoved the picture towards Julie angrily. 'Can you expect me to wipe something like *that* from my mind so easily?'

She looked away from the picture, feeling her stomach churn.

'I see things like that every day and every night,' he continued vehemently. 'And you expect me to forget them? Have you any idea what goes through my mind? What thoughts are in here?'

He prodded his temple with his index finger. 'No, you haven't. You could never understand.'

'Then *make* me understand,' she said, tears welling in her eyes.

'You really want to know? You really want to hear about my work?' His eyes were blazing now, fixing her in an unflinching stare.

'You should talk about it more often. You bottle things up too much, Frank.'

'Okay, where would you like me to start?' he said, glaring at her. 'Would you like me to tell you what the inside of that bank looked like after that fucking maniac had finished using the shotgun? How there were brains spread over the road when he shot the motorcyclist? Or perhaps you'd be more interested in another case. The one where the woman killed her husband with a carving knife because she'd found out he was having an affair. There were so many knife wounds in him it took us over an hour to count them all. And blood. You want to hear how much blood there was? She severed both his carotid arteries, you see. The ones in the neck. Nearly cut his fucking head off, in fact. She said later that all the time she was stabbing him he kept saying he was sorry. He kept saying he didn't want to die.'

Gregson was sucking in breath through clenched teeth now.

'What else would you like to hear?' he taunted. 'About the four-year-old who'd been sexually abused by her stepfather? He'd used a bottle on her. A beer bottle. Shoved it up her arse. The only problem was he didn't expect it to break. He didn't expect her to scream quite so loudly, so he jammed the rest of the bottle into her face until she shut up. That would have been bad enough but she'd been dead for three days when we found her. He'd put her in the attic. She was blue where she'd lost so much blood, apart from the bits of her that had turned gangrenous. Jesus, it stank in that fucking attic.'

Tears were rolling down Julie's cheeks now as she looked at her husband, the words pouring forth from him with a kind of monstrous glee.

'Is this what you want to hear?' he chided. 'Is this what you want to know about my job? What about the drunk that was mugged in Piccadilly the other night? I mean, there was nothing for them to take so they just beat him to death. They used his head like a football, took runs at him. Two would hold him down while the other one kicked him. Kicked him so hard that three of his front teeth were driven up into the roof of his mouth.'

She got to her feet.

'That's enough,' she sobbed, wiping her eyes.

'I've hardly started,' he said, looking at her. 'I thought you wanted to hear all about my work.' He smiled humourlessly.

'I wanted to help you,' she told him, sniffing.

'How can *you* help?'

'You should talk to me more.'

'I've just been talking to you and you can't fucking take it. You ask me what I do, you ask me to tell you what goes through my mind, and when I do you can't take it.'

She wiped more tears from her face.

'Can't you see what it's doing to you, Frank?' she asked.

'That's *my* problem, not yours.'

'It's not just *yours*. I can't stand to see what this job is doing to you.'

'Why?'

'Because I love you,' she snapped, a note of anger joining the despair in her voice. 'Christ knows why, but I do. Let me help.'

He shrugged.

'You want to help me? Leave me alone. That would be a great help. Get off my fucking back.' The words were spoken without a flicker of emotion.

She turned and headed for the door, turning as she reached it to look angrily at him.

'I tried. Don't ever say I didn't try to help you,' she said tearfully.

'Who asked you to help? *Me*? No.' He shook his head.

'Frank, please . . .'

He cut her short.

'You want to help? Then leave me alone.' He looked away from her. He didn't see her leave the room, only heard the door slam.

Gregson took another swallow from the glass. Then he picked the photos up and carefully began to go through them again, one by one.

Twenty-four

He watched her writhing on the bed, hardly aware of the music that roared out of the speaker above his head.

'. . . *Lady Red light, rock me tonight . . .*'

James Scott leant against the doorframe, peering through the gloom towards the bed where Carol Jackson was naked, a vibrator clutched in one hand. She was running the gleaming phallus up and down her body, pausing occasionally to look at the members of the audience.

There were two men dressed in suits sitting in chairs on one side of the bed, both of them chuckling as they watched Carol's rehearsed gyrations. Every few moments one of them would rub the erection he sported. They continued laughing,

94

nodding towards Carol as she turned to face them, the vibrator between her legs.

Scott sighed as he watched the display.

He'd tried to talk to her when she arrived but she'd been late and she'd had to hurry off and change. She said she'd talk to him later. It offered some ray of hope, at least. He had so much to ask her. Before she'd arrived he had been angry, had told himself he would be firmer with her; but as soon as he'd seen her the anger had evaporated. She was here, that was all that mattered. She was near him.

He watched the display for a moment longer, glaring at one of the customers who whistled appreciatively when she took the vibrator from her vagina and kissed the tip.

As Zena joined her on the bed, Scott turned and headed back towards his office.

He wanted to ask her if she was all right, wanted to know why she hadn't answered the phone when he'd tried her number the previous night. And yet, strong as his curiosity was, something told him that he should *not* ask. He didn't own her. She wasn't accountable to him.

Yet he felt he had a right to know. After all, they had been seeing one another for over a year.

He sat in his office listening to the dull thud of the music, thinking about Carol and Zena lying on the bed together, performing their usual act.

Where had she been last night?

He sat forward in his seat, angry with himself for dwelling on the matter. He pulled the bottle of Southern Comfort from the drawer in his desk and poured himself a measure, swallowing half in one gulp.

Don't ask her, it's not important now.

He turned the glass in his hand, gazing into the dark fluid for a second before downing more of it. He refilled his glass,

95

the thud of the music diminishing slightly. They must have finished.

Scott got to his feet and headed for the office door, the drink still in his hand. He walked down the corridor which led to the changing room, knocked and walked in.

Zena sat on one of the stools in front of the mirror, peering at her reflection. She smiled as she saw Scott standing there.

'It's a good job I'm not shy, isn't it?' she laughed, allowing the silk basque she wore to hang open, revealing her breasts. She noticed his drink.

'Whatever it is I'll have a swig, Scotty,' she said. 'I'm parched.'

He handed her the glass and she sipped from it as she slipped off first the basque then her panties. Naked, she sat on the stool.

'Where's Carol?' he asked.

'One of the punters called her over, I think she's having a drink with him.' Zena shrugged. 'It's another thirty quid, isn't it?'

Scott nodded and turned to leave.

'I'll nip back later,' he said.

'Scotty, wait a minute.'

She swivelled round on the stool to face him, completely unconcerned by her nakedness. It seemed not to bother Scott either.

'What is it?' he asked.

'You think a lot of her, don't you?' Zena said, cradling the drink.

'Is it that obvious?' he said, smiling humourlessly.

She nodded.

If only you knew, you poor sod.

Zena smiled at him, wondering if she should drop a hint of some kind, let him know that his feelings for Carol weren't

96

reciprocated. But she decided it wasn't her business. They had to sort their own lives out. As she sat there, naked, Zena realised for the first time that she found Scott attractive. She enjoyed the thought of him looking at her and reddened slightly as she felt her nipples begin to stiffen.

Forget it.

'I'm sure she won't be long,' she told him, swallowing what was left in the glass. 'Do you want me to tell her you were looking for her?'

He shook his head.

'I'll come back later,' he said. Then he was gone, the door closing behind him.

Zena turned back to the mirror, studying her reflection for a moment longer. Then she began to take off her make-up. The dressing room door opened and Carol entered, still carrying the vibrator. She put it down on the dressing table, and exhaled wearily.

'What did that bloke want?' Zena enquired.

'A blow job,' Carol said. 'I told him to piss off.'

'You can afford to turn down a hundred quid, can you, Carol? You're lucky.'

Carol didn't answer; she just looked at Zena as the two women faced the mirror.

'Scotty was looking for you,' Zena said.

'What did he want?' Carol enquired.

'He didn't say. Are you going to tell him tonight?'

'Tell him what?'

'That's it's all over between you. How much longer are you going to keep him hanging on, Carol?'

'Look, Zena, it isn't really your business, is it?' Carol snapped.

'He's a nice bloke. I like him and I don't like to see him get hurt.'

'Then *you* go out with him.'

'Maybe I should. Maybe he's more my type than yours. I mean, according to you he's going nowhere. Well, I'm happy the way I am, too. Perhaps you get used to being a nobody after a while. We're not all like you, Carol. Some of us make do with our lives, make the best of what we've got instead of moaning about what we *haven't* got.'

'Thanks for the lecture,' Carol said, acidly.

'Why don't you stop being such a bitch and tell the poor bastard?'

Carol got to her feet, pulling a towelling robe around her.

'Drop it, will you?' she snapped.

'You're seeing someone else, aren't you?' Zena said, flatly.

Carol looked anxious for a moment.

'What makes you say that?'

She raised her eyebrows in mock surprise.

'I've done it myself, Carol, I know the signs,' she said. 'Want to tell me who he is?' She smiled. 'He must be well off if you can afford to turn down hundred-quid tricks.'

Carol didn't answer.

Well off. He was rolling in it.

'Is he going to be the one who's going to take you away from all this?' There was a note of scorn in Zena's voice.

'I told you, Zena, just drop it, will you?' Carol said irritably. 'It's my business, not yours.'

Their argument was interrupted by the ringing of the phone.

While Carol went to answer it Zena finished dressing, checking that she had all her bits and pieces before picking up her handbag. She paused to light a cigarette, watching Carol cradling the phone between her ear and shoulder.

On the other end of the line Ray Plummer was apologetic.

He couldn't pick her up tonight.

'It's okay,' said Carol. 'What's wrong?'

98

Nothing, he assured her. He just had some business to attend to.

'Will I see you tomorrow?' she wanted to know.

He said she could bank on it. He'd take her out for a meal.

'Great,' she said, her tone not exactly jubilant.

Zena waved goodbye and slipped out. Carol raised a hand in farewell and then she was alone in the dressing room with just Plummer's voice for company.

'Where are you ringing from?' she asked him.

He said he was at one of his gaming clubs in Kensington. He said he was sorry she was going to be alone tonight. He told her he wanted her.

'I want you, too,' she lied.

He said goodbye.

'See you tomorrow.'

He'd already hung up.

She put down the phone, stood gazing at it for a moment and banged the receiver.

'Damn,' she hissed. When she turned back to look in the mirror there were tears in her eyes.

Twenty-five

They didn't speak all evening.

Julie Gregson had sat looking at the television, not really comprehending what she saw, while Gregson himself had continued drinking, flicking through the photos.

She'd looked over at him a couple of times, the expression on her face a combination of sorrow and anger.

Only when the hands of the clock crawled round to midnight did she speak. She asked him if he wanted a hot drink, tea or coffee, before she went to bed.

He shook his head and finished off the Teacher's instead.

'Are you coming to bed?' she asked.

'Soon,' he murmured, without looking up.

She paused in the doorway and ran a hand through her hair, watching as he flicked through the photos again.

'What do you think you're going to find, Frank?' she asked him. 'You've been looking at those damned things all night.'

'Just call it homework,' he said flatly.

'What are you trying to find?'

'Answers. It's my job.' He finally afforded her a glance she would have preferred he'd kept to himself. It was icy as he glared at her. 'But you didn't want to hear too much about my job, did you?'

'Don't start again, Frank,' she said wearily. 'Are you coming to bed? Yes or no?'

'You go,' he told her. 'I'll be up in a while.'

'How many whiskies later?'

He smiled thinly.

'Just go to bed, Julie. I'll handle it.'

'That's just the trouble, Frank,' she told him. 'I'm beginning to wonder if you *can* handle it anymore.'

She left him alone. Gregson heard her footfalls on the stairs, heard her moving about in the bedroom above him. He listened to the sounds for a moment longer then got up and crossed to the sideboard where he retrieved another bottle of whisky. He poured himself a measure and sat down on the sofa once more.

He returned his attention to the photos.

Twenty-six

A thin film of condensation covered everything in the small bathroom, even the clock on the wall. Behind the veil of dewy moisture the hands had reached 1.15 a.m.

Water dripped from one of the taps. Carol Jackson watched the droplets falling for a moment, occasionally raising her toe to prevent the constant *plink*.

She ran both hands through her hair and put her head back, closing her eyes, enjoying the feel of the water lapping around her neck. The flesh on her fingertips was already beginning to prune but she felt as if she needed to stay in the water to wash away more than just the grime of the day and the evening. If only it could wash away her problems as easily.

Before she left 'Loveshow' that night Scott had spoken to her, asked her if she was okay, told her how nice she looked.

Christ, his attempts at small-talk had been so clumsy she almost felt sorry for him. It had taken him a seemingly endless time and a barrage of aimless chatter before he finally asked her why he couldn't reach her the previous night when he'd called. She had the lie ready and told him she'd unplugged the phone from the wall because she didn't want to be disturbed. As if she was regularly pestered in the early hours of the morning by social calls.

But Scott had merely smiled, nodded and said he understood. He'd been worried about her. She'd felt like telling him not to worry about her, that she didn't *want* him to

101

worry about her. But she had not been able to find the words.

Lies were simpler.

He'd asked her to come for a meal with him when the club shut, but she'd found that another lie had been preferable. She'd told him she had to get home. Her sister was going to call her from America. She hadn't spoken to her for months. She would see him another night.

Maybe.

Carol dipped her hands into the water again and rubbed her face, catching a distorted view of herself in the mist-shrouded bathroom mirror opposite. She wondered what had made her think of the excuse she had used to Scott. Her sister was going to ring her? They hadn't spoken for months. That part at least was true. Carol hadn't spoken to any of her family for some time. She wrote occasionally, when she could be bothered, and her mother sometimes replied.

Sometimes.

The last time she had spoken to her sister, Fiona, had been on her birthday. Fiona was five years younger and worked for a record company in the West End. It was a well-paid job and she had her own flat in Hammersmith. Carol had never even seen the place but she knew that it must be an improvement on her own humble dwelling in the basement flat of a large house in Dollis Hill. There were four other flats above her and she was on nodding terms with the other residents. She even spoke to one of the women who lived on the top floor.

Carol should have hated Fiona. She had often thought that. Fiona had everything she didn't: a good job, a nice place. More than that, she had a future.

There were times, many times, when Carol could see herself this same way in ten years' time, lying in the bath regretting her wasted life. *And yet how was she to change it?* She sighed, knowing that it was not in her own power to do so. Her fate lay, to a large degree, with men like Plummer. He had wealth, power and influence. He commanded respect. He was her escape route.

And then there was Scott.

She closed her eyes more tightly, as if trying to blot him out of her thoughts. If only it were so easy to remove him from her life. She knew deep down she was afraid to tell him their relationship was over, not because she couldn't bear to speak those words but because she genuinely feared how he would react.

Feared? A little melodramatic, wasn't it?

He'd be hurt for a while but he'd get over it.

Wouldn't he?

Perhaps Zena had been right. She *was* a bitch.

She pulled herself out of the water and reached for a towel, wrapping it around herself, using another to dry her hair. She padded through into the sitting room and switched on the television. There was a black and white film on one channel, a discussion programme on another. She switched the set off and started drying herself, standing close to the two-bar electric fire that was the only form of heating in the room. She had an electric fire in her bedroom but the radiators on each wall were merely eyesores; they didn't provide the central heating she craved on cold nights like this.

As she was drying her hands she looked at the gold ring Scott had given her, the metal black in places. She ought to clean it.

It could wait.

She finished drying herself and pulled on a long sweater to cover her nakedness, then wandered into the kitchen to make herself a warm drink before she went to bed.

At first she didn't hear the phone ring.

The water was gushing from the tap into the kettle, obliterating all other sounds.

Then she heard it and turned towards the sound coming from the sitting room.

Who the hell was calling her at 1.30 in the morning?

She sighed. Scott. Checking that she was okay.

Why can't you leave me alone?

She put down the kettle and walked back into the sitting room, picking up the receiver.

'Hello,' she said resignedly.

Silence.

'Hello.'

Still no sound.

She felt her heart beat faster.

'I'm watching you.'

The voice cut through her as surely as if it had been cold steel.

She gripped the receiver until her knuckles turned white.

'How did you get this number?' she said quietly, trying to control the fear in her voice.

Silence.

'I know your sort,' she said, her show of bravado fooling neither herself nor the caller.

Only silence greeted her remark.

Slam the phone down.

'I know all about you,' the caller said, and now Carol was certain that it was the same voice as the other night. Not that she'd had much doubt in the first place.

Now she *did* slam the phone down.

For long seconds she stood looking at it, her eyes fixed to it as if it were some kind of venomous reptile that was about to bite her.

Take it off the hook.

She actually had her hand on the receiver when the phone rang again.

She snatched it up and pressed it to her ear but this time she didn't speak.

She heard a sound at the other end. A wet sound. Like someone licking their lips.

'I'm still watching you,' said the caller. Then he hung up.

Carol stared at the receiver, but all she heard was the dull monotone of a disconnected line.

She didn't put it back on its cradle.

She simply dropped it.

Twenty-seven: 10 May 1977

The explosion had been massive.

It had torn away the roof of the kitchen area, sending slates and lumps of stone hurtling skyward like shrapnel. The remains of the structure had simply collapsed in upon itself as if the walls had been made of paper. Tongues of flames thirty feet high had erupted from the wreckage, the pieces of burning debris showering down on the roof of the asylum like fragments of comet, some actually tearing through, others bursting again, causing more havoc, spreading the fire more rapidly than anyone could have imagined.

It took less than six minutes from the initial blast to transform Bishopsgate Institution into a blazing inferno.

The whisper was gas leak, the result was devastation.

The fire brigade had been called and ambulances were outside the building ready to ferry the dead and injured away. The air was alive with a cacophony of sirens and the roaring of flames. Firemen directed jets of water at the flames while their companions struggled to help the staff of the institution evacuate patients.

Smoke, belching from the burning building, hung like a thick black shroud over the blazing asylum. The air was filled with millions of tiny cinders, as if a plague of small flies had infested the air.

Inside his office Dr Robert Dexter pulled on his jacket and ran out into the corridor. An intern hurtled past him, his white jacket smoke-stained, his hair singed. Dexter could hear screams of rage and fear as he started along the corridor, aware of the acrid stench of burning.

He saw two more interns running towards him, both sweating profusely, their faces dark, their uniforms dirty.

The West Wing is clear,' said one of them. 'We managed to get everyone out.'

'The firemen are evacuating the rest of the building,' said his companion.

Dexter nodded.

It was then that he saw Colston round the corner.

Dexter ran towards his colleague, his face pale.

'We've got to get out,' said Colston, his breathing rapid. 'The whole place is coming down around us.'

As if to emphasise his words there was a loud creaking noise, a wrenching timber. A shower of sparks burst from the ceiling and covered the two men, who both ducked down. The smell of smoke was stronger now and Dexter could actually see the first wisps of it curling round into the corridor.

'We've got to get to Ward 5,' said Dexter.

'Let the fire brigade take care of it,' Colston said agitatedly, coughing now as more smoke filled the corridor.

Dexter grabbed him by the shoulders.

'And let them find what's in there?' he hissed, his gaze firmly on his colleague.

The realisation seemed to hit Colston and he nodded. Together they hurried up the corridor, relieved that the smoke wasn't too dense as yet. Even so, both men found that the acrid fumes stung their throats as they ran on through the clouds of smoke.

They passed a window and Dexter glanced sideways to see the firemen outside spraying the building with water. A number of people were being helped into ambulances, some supported by uniformed men.

The two doctors ran on, reaching a closed door. It led through into another corridor and Dexter snatched at the handle. He cursed at the heat of the metal in his grip but he pulled the door open, standing back as he did so.

A searing blast of flame swept through the open door and as Colston pushed himself back against the wall the fire scorched his sleeve. Dexter waited a moment then ran on.

The smoke was dense inside the corridor, tongues of flame flaring from both sides.

Doors of cells stood open, some of them blazing infernos. The incessant clanging of fire bells, curiously redundant in the blaze, filled their ears. Colston hesitated, but when Dexter bellowed at him he followed, shielding his face from the heat with one smoking arm. He could smell the burned hair on his arm. His eyes were watering, the back of his throat felt as if someone had turned a blow-torch on it. Dexter seemed unconcerned by the blistering heat; his only desire was to reach Ward 5.

They had two more corridors to pass through.

The first was clear.

The second was an inferno.

The roof had been holed by a lump of falling debris and the grey sky was visible through the clouds of smoke spewing through it. To the right Dexter saw something twisted and blackened, still ablaze, lying in the doorway of a cell.

It took him a second or two to realise it was a body.

'Leave them,' shouted Colston, forced to shout to make himself heard above the roaring of flames and the clanging of firebells.

Dexter turned to look at his companion, his watery eyes narrowed.

'We can't,' he roared back, ducking as a piece of the ceiling crashed down only feet from him. 'If the fire brigade reach Ward 5 before us . . .' He allowed the sentence to trail off, then shook his head.

Both men sucked in deep breaths and ran on. Colston thought his lungs were on fire too.

Another door and they would reach their goal.

It was ahead of them at the end of the corridor and, as he ran, Dexter pulled a bunch of keys from his pocket. As he reached the door he could feel an incredible heat from beyond, even through the thick steel.

He turned the key and wrestled with the handle, ignoring the blisters that rose on his hands. He tugged the door open. The two of them dashed in.

The ceiling was ablaze.

From one end of the corridor to the other the area above them was one writhing, twisting mass of fire. Lumps of blackened plaster and wood fell around them, some striking them.

Dexter moved towards the first door and selected a key.

From inside there were screams. Wild, almost animalistic yells of fear and rage.

'We can't!' shouted Colston, shielding his head as more of the burning masonry showered down.

'We have no choice,' Dexter told him. Another piece of the ceiling fell inwards, driving them back, the flames rearing up, snatching at them like venomous reptiles. Colston shielded his face, raising his voice again to make it heard above the raging inferno that now threatened to engulf them.

'We can't get them all out,' he shouted, staring wide-eyed at Dexter.

The older man realised he was right.

He headed for the last cell.

'No!' shouted Colston in horror. 'You can't.' He tried to prevent Dexter opening the door but the other man already had the key in the lock. He pushed Colston away.

The door swung open.

Dexter thrust the bunch of keys into his colleague's hand.

'Open that door!' he bellowed, the heat now almost unbearable. He nodded to the door at the end of the corridor and Colston did as he was told, pushing the key in, straining to turn it, to release the lock.

More sparks showered him; the ceiling seemed to hover, as if suspended on invisible wires.

It was a matter of moments before the entire thing caved in.

Colston twisted the key helplessly in the lock, afraid that the heat might have warped it out of shape.

Inside the cell Dexter took a cautious step towards the occupant. As ever he found that he was shaking slightly as he drew nearer.

'We have to go,' he said, his voice calm and measured, his eyes never leaving the inhabitant of the room. He could feel how dry his throat was. Not all of it, he realised, was due to the fire. When he tried to swallow it felt as if somebody had filled his mouth with chalk.

'Come on!' screamed Colston.

'We must go now,' Dexter said, his tone more forceful.

'Dexter, for God's sake!' Colston bellowed, looking up at the ceiling.

Inside the cell the single occupant moved towards Dexter.

It was then that the ceiling collapsed.

Twenty-eight: Exile

The figure moved slowly in the darkness, treading carefully in the gloom, cursing the lack of light but welcoming the cover the blackness brought.

The only sound was the crunch of footsteps on the gravel of the driveway.

An owl sat in the lower branches of a nearby tree, unable to hunt as efficiently without the presence of the moon. It watched the figure that moved from the house to the car repeatedly.

More than once the figure would stand still beside the car as if listening to the stillness of the night, ears attuned to the slightest sound or movement. Then, satisfied that no one else was around, the dark shape would move stealthily about its business once again.

There was rain in the air, the odd gust of wind bringing with it the first droplets that threatened a storm. Banks of cloud were gathering to the west, blown ever closer by the rising wind. It rattled the branches of the trees and ruffled the feathers of the owl, which finally tired of watching the furtive movement and flew off, its wings beating quietly in the darkness.

The figure looked up, following the bird as it soared high into the night sky in search of prey.

After a moment longer spent listening to the stillness the shape returned to the house.

There were no lights burning within the building; the darkness inside was as total as that of the tenebrous gloom without. But the figure moved more assuredly within the confines of the house, scurrying back and forth from room to room, sometimes pausing in one room, glancing around as if to check that everything was in place.

Finally, the figure ascended the stairs, slowly but purposefully.

The rain began to fall more rapidly now, the wind propelling the droplets like handfuls of cold gravel.

When the figure emerged from the house again it turned its face to the rain as if in welcome, standing there for a moment before turning to another dark shape which accompanied it.

Had the owl still been perched in the tree it would have seen a second figure join the first in the blackness.

The first of them opened the passenger door and ensured that the second was comfortably seated, then closed the door and locked it from the outside.

That task completed, the first figure walked unhurriedly around to the other side of the car and slid behind the wheel.

The silence was broken by the noise of the engine, which idled for a moment. Then the car was driven away from the front of the house, the wheels crushing gravel as the tyres rolled.

It began to pick up speed along the short driveway then turned into the road.

There was no traffic about at such a late hour. The occupants of the car may as well have been the last two people on earth.

The car disappeared into the night.

Twenty-nine

He'd stolen the car an hour earlier.

The automatic transmission on the Datsun had taken a bit of getting used to and when he'd first slipped behind the steering wheel he'd cursed his luck. But, fuck it, he needed a car. He'd manage. Now Mathew Bryce slowed up as he approached the traffic lights in Shaftesbury Avenue, his eyes scanning the hordes of people that filled the bustling thoroughfare. So intently was he studying the throng that he didn't notice the lights slip onto green. The blast of a hooter behind alerted him to the situation.

Bryce swung the car right, peering round at the driver behind, raising two fingers. The man mouthed his own insult back and drove past.

'Cunt,' muttered Bryce, his eyes still flicking back and forth. He saw couples. Old, young. Girls in groups. Sometimes alone. Some people hurried along, others strolled through the night. A young man was running along, trying to stop a taxi before it pulled away, but he was unsuccessful and stood, hands on hips, glaring at the vehicle as it moved off. Bryce passed him and grinned out at the man.

All around the neon signs from clubs, pubs and restaurants filled the night, creating a kind of artificial twilight. With the window wound down, Bryce could hear the crackle of so much static electricity. He slowed down as he saw a woman crossing the road ahead of him, watching her breasts bouncing

112

in her tight-fitting top. Her silver-coloured hair trailed over her shoulders, blown by the wind that whipped through the narrow streets. It also disturbed the litter that lay in the gutters and on the pavements. An empty can was sent rattling across the concrete like a kind of bizarre tumbleweed. A youth passing by took a kick at it and sent it skittering into the road. Further along an old man, bundled up in a thick overcoat, was sorting through one of the overflowing dustbins, picking out portions of half-eaten food and carefully dropping them into the plastic bag he carried, making his choice as fastidiously as any gourmet at a buffet table.

Bryce swung the car right again, then sharp left into Rupert Street. Again he slowed down, peering at a young woman standing in a doorway talking to a tall man in a suit. Bryce stared at her with interest. She couldn't have been more than twenty, her shapely legs revealed by the short mini-skirt she wore. She was puffing contentedly on a cigarette as she spoke. Bryce stopped the car, the engine idling.

It was a couple of minutes before the man finally noticed and looked questioningly across at Bryce, who was now leaning on the windowframe, looking more closely at the girl.

'You lost, mate?' the man in the faded suit called.

Bryce didn't answer.

The girl also turned to face him now, brushing a stray hair from her mouth.

He looked at her features, his own face expressionless.

'What do you want?' the man called.

A car turned into the road behind Bryce, the driver braking to avoid a collision.

The man in the faded suit moved towards the car.

'You got a fucking problem, or what?' he said, irritably.

Bryce pressed down on the accelerator and the car moved off, leaving the girl to stare after him. He turned another corner and saw a car pulling out of a parking space. Bryce guided the Datsun into it, cursing when it juddered slightly. He switched off the engine and sat there for a moment, his window down, the noises of the night filling his ears. He leant forward, his forehead resting on the steering wheel. From across the street he could hear music and, all around him, voices and the ever-present crackle of neon. He put both hands over his ears as if to shut out the noise. Then, slowly, he sat up again, looking around him, catching a glimpse of his own reflection in the rear-view mirror. It stared back at him accusingly. His face was pale, the dark rings beneath his eyes all the more prominent because of his pallor. His hair was thick but combed back severely from his prominent forehead. As he ran a hand over his chin he heard the rasp of his bristles against his fingertips.

Bryce grunted, gripped the rear-view mirror and tore it off.

He hurled it onto the back seat and sat there, panting. Then he turned slowly and looked at the blanket that lay across the rear seat.

The blanket had belonged to the owner of the car.

The can of petrol and the hunting knife it concealed belonged to Bryce.

Thirty

For a moment she thought he was going to fall over. Paula Wilson stood rigid as she watched Mark Eaton lurch from the doorway of the pub in Cambridge Circus. He shot out a hand

and steadied himself, smiling stupidly at her.

The gesture only made her more angry.

'You never know when to stop, do you?' she snapped angrily, looking first at him then at the night sky. The first drops of rain were beginning to fall. Paula pulled up the collar of her suede jacket. A large droplet of rain fell onto it and she sighed. Grey suede. It would be ruined in the downpour.

'I'll be okay,' said Eaton, stumbling towards her, bumping into a dustbin. Some of its contents spilled out onto the pavement and he stooped to pick them up as if he were tidying his own house. Passers-by looked quickly at the young couple, particularly at the young woman in the grey suede suit who was shouting so vehemently.

'You probably can't even remember where you left the car, can you?' she rasped.

'I just need some fresh air, that's all,' he told her, none too convincingly. 'I'll be fine.' He sucked in several deep lungfuls of the night air. The odour of burning hot-dogs came wafting to him and he noticed a street vendor cooking the blackened frankfurters a few yards away. The smell made him want to vomit. He saw Paula turn away and made a grab for her arm. 'Where are you going?' he wanted to know.

'I'm going home,' she told him, shaking free of his grip and setting off towards Romilly Street.

Eaton followed her.

'I'll drive you,' he said.

'I'm not getting in a car with *you* in *that* state,' she said angrily. 'I'll get a taxi.' She continued walking, Eaton now almost running to keep up with her. Her high heels clicked on the pavement, beating out a furious tattoo.

As she reached the side of the Prince Charles Theatre he grabbed her again and pushed her into one of the sheltered doorways marked 'Exit'. The theatre had been closed for more than forty minutes now; they weren't likely to be disturbed.

'I'm not letting you go,' he told her, standing in front of her to block her way.

'Get out of my way, Mark,' she said, glaring at him.

'I told you, just let me clear my head and I'll drive you.'

'It's going to take more than fresh air to clear your head tonight. Maybe you should try dynamite.' She thought about pushing past him again, but as she saw the rain beginning to fall more swiftly she realised that perhaps, for the time being, sheltering in this doorway was more prudent. She looked up at him, her eyes still full of anger. 'Why did you have to spoil it, Mark?' she said, her voice quieter.

'I don't know what you're talking about,' he told her. 'Look, I had more to drink than I should have done. I'm sorry about that.'

'Well, it's too bloody late now, isn't it? You can't drive in your condition.'

He smiled that stupid grin again. It only served to make her more irritable.

'It's always the same when you get together with Dean and Richard, isn't it? They keep drinking and you have to keep up with them, don't you?'

'Don't speak to me as if I'm a child, Paula,' he said, wiping his mouth with the back of his hand.

'When you're with *them* you act like one,' she chided. 'Why did you tell them we were going to be in that pub tonight, anyway?'

'I didn't *tell* them,' he protested. 'That's where they usually go for a drink. It wasn't *my* fault they happened to come in while we were there. It's a free country, you know. What was I supposed to say? "Sorry, lads, but it's Paula's birthday, we're out celebrating, so would you mind pissing off and leaving us alone?" I work with them, for Christ's sake. They're mates.'

116

'Well, then, get one of them to drive you home,' she said bitterly.

'We were supposed to be spending the night together,' he said, touching her cheek with one hand. He grinned again.

'A celebratory fuck, is that what you mean?'

'I wouldn't have put it quite like that,' he chuckled, and the chuckle soon became a fully-fledged laugh.

Paula decided she'd rather get her grey suede suit wet than endure any more of his drunken ramblings. She pushed past him and out into the downpour. He tried to stop her but she pushed him away.

'I'm sorry, Paula,' he called after her.

'So am I!' she yelled back, pushing past a couple of young men who eyed her approvingly, one of them whistling as she swept along the road.

The bastard, she thought. The stupid, unfeeling, childish bastard. For a bloke of twenty-six he acted like a twelve-year-old sometimes, she thought, trying to ignore the rain. If his two idiot friends hadn't turned up then everything would have been all right. She *would* have gone back to his flat, she *would* have spent the night. A celebratory fuck had been high on her list of priorities to mark her twenty-third birthday. But now there would be none of that. Perhaps this was the excuse she had been looking for to stop seeing him. Over the past four months she had come to realise more and more that Mark Eaton wasn't the type of man she wanted a relationship with. She wasn't sure if she wanted a relationship with any man yet. Not a long term one, anyway. She was twenty-three, for Christ's sake. Her whole life was in front of her; the last thing she wanted was to be tied to one man.

The rain was easing up slightly, she noted with relief, but it had still fallen with sufficient ferocity to soak her jacket and skirt. She cursed to herself, looking up the street for a taxi.

One was just dropping off at Wheeler's restaurant ahead of her. She hurried towards it but the driver pulled away, switching his light off as he did so.

She turned and watched him go then trudged on, passing a club called Maxims. There were two men standing in the doorway, both of them foreign, she guessed, from a quick glance at them.

'You want to come inside, darling?' asked one, smiling at her, revealing a mouthful of yellowed teeth.

She ignored him and walked on.

'You've got a nice arse,' the other one shouted after her and she heard their laughter. She felt her cheeks burning but she also afforded herself a brief smile.

Yes, you bastards, she told herself, I have got a nice arse. It's for sure you'll never see it.

You or Mark Eaton.

She'd ring him at work tomorrow, tell him she didn't want to see him again, she decided. Time to be decisive, she told herself. Ahead of her was Dean Street, the lights from the McDonald's at the Shaftesbury Avenue end bathing the street round about. She'd be able to get a taxi outside there without any trouble. They were often dropping off at the hotel round the corner.

Ahead of her some construction work was being done behind the Shaftesbury Hotel. Even in the darkness she could see the outline of a crane nudging upwards towards the rain-sodden sky. The yellow shape of a JCB was also unmistakeable, even in the gloom. Safety lights had been placed at the entrance to the small site as a warning to motorists. She passed by the high boards that separated the site from the pavement, muttering to herself as she stepped in something soft. She hoped it was mud.

Balancing on one foot she reached into her handbag and took out a tissue, wiping the mess from her shoe.

She noticed a taxi pass and saw, with relief, that it was dropping off at the end of the street. She slipped her shoe back on and prepared to sprint after the vehicle.

'Don't pull away,' she murmured to herself, almost slipping over in more of the mud, her eyes fixed on the cab.

From behind her, from the darkness of the site, one hand clamped around her mouth, another tugged at her hair.

She was pulled off her feet.

Swallowed by the blackness.

There wasn't even time to scream.

Thirty-one

Her mind went blank.

There were no thoughts at all, only emptiness. No flood of fearful imaginings as she was pulled to the ground. No terror at what fate befell her.

Paula Wilson's mind had been wiped clean as surely as if it had been a blackboard swept clear of chalk. All she was aware of was the pressure on her face and hair, which suddenly slackened as she was thrown down into the mud. The glutinous muck seemed to close around her, holding her motionless; but what stopped her moving was the absolute terror of her situation. The only thing that seemed to respond was her bladder. She wet herself, urine running warmly down the inside of her thigh.

She felt those hands on her again, tugging at her hair, clamping her jaw shut. She was being pulled behind the partition that separated the street from the construction site, out of sight of any passers-by.

Out of sight, out of mind.

A handful of her hair was torn from her scalp and she felt searing pain. Blood ran in a thin trickle down the side of her face, but even the pain wasn't sufficient to galvanise her into action. Her body and her mind remained as frozen as if they'd been injected with Novocaine.

She felt a great weight pressing down on her chest and stomach and realised that her attacker had knelt on her midriff, driving one knee into her solar plexus. The air in her lungs was expelled rapidly. She felt light-headed, as if she were about to faint, but the coldness of the mud on her face and legs kept her conscious.

Then she saw the knife.

The desire to survive suddenly became uppermost in her mind. Her muscles unlocked and she struck out at her assailant.

Mathew Bryce kept his weight on her torso and slashed at her hand as she struck him.

The blade sliced effortlessly through her palm, opening it in a wide and bloody wound, the edges of which slid back like an open mouth. Blood splashed him, its warmth a marked contrast to the chill of the night.

With one hand still fixed over her mouth he drove the blade forward again.

It punctured Paula's left cheek, grating against teeth as he pulled it free, ripping a molar away with it. The tooth, still fixed to a portion of gum, fell into the mud. She raised her hands to protect herself once more and his next thrust cut through the fleshy part of her thumb. He felt her breath against his hand as she tried to scream in pain and terror. He sliced through the fingers of her right hand, severing the tendons.

120

She was writhing beneath him now, finding reserves of strength he had not anticipated. He turned the knife in his hand and brought it down in a stabbing action, the blade shearing through her left breast and cracking two ribs. He tugged it free and brought it down again, this time breaking her left collarbone. Blood was pumping from the wounds, some of it spraying onto his face as she waved her hands about in a vain attempt to ward off the killing strikes.

Bryce finally rolled off her, grunting as she lashed out with her foot and kicked him in the side. She tried to scream but the gash in the side of her cheek had caused blood to run back into her throat and all she could do was to retch as the coppery liquid clogged her windpipe. She tried to raise herself up, mud sticking to her clothes and hair.

Bryce stabbed her again, just above the right kidney, and she pitched forward, trying to crawl now through the mud, tears of pain and fear streaming down her cheeks. He got to his feet and drove a powerful kick into her side, smiling as he heard a rib crack. He kicked again. And again. He stamped on the back of her head as hard as he could, twisting on his shoe to grind her face further into the mud.

Further into the mud.

He put all his weight on that foot, pressing with all his strength and weight, watching her trying to wriggle free, trying to raise her face from the mud which was suffocating her. Her movements gradually became less frantic, her bloodied hands clutching backwards ever more feebly at his leg.

She wasn't quite dead when he dropped to his knees in the mud beside her, grabbed her matted hair and tugged her face up so that he could look at her.

The initial impact with the ground, despite its softness, had broken her nose. Her face was a mask of blood and sticky mud. Both her lips were split, crimson fluid running over her chin.

121

Bryce rolled her onto her back and began tugging her clothes off, hurling them aside as he reached her underwear, tearing frenziedly at her bra, exposing her breasts, ripping her flimsy knickers off to expose her pubic bush.

He spread her legs wide, using his stained finger tips to part her vaginal lips. For long moments he knelt there gazing at her genitalia, then he reached behind him towards some crumpled, mud-soaked cellophane.

Balling it up he pushed it into her vagina, using his first two fingers to shove it deeper inside her. He found an empty crisp packet, the wrapper from a bar of chocolate. These he also pushed into the swollen orifice, jamming it with such force that he tore one of her vaginal lips. Fresh blood spurted onto the mud.

The ring pull from a can. He drove that into her as well, the metal tearing more of the delicate flesh.

She was still moving, still trying to scream with this fresh pain, this unbearable perversion he was committing. Her jaw was broken; she could not open it to vent her cry of agony.

He used the tip of the knife to force a piece of stone into her riven orifice, the razor-sharp edge gashing her badly.

Mercifully, Paula Wilson passed out.

Bryce crawled over her and looked into her face, pulling open her eyelids as if suspecting she was merely pretending to be unconscious. He stabbed her again, this time in the throat, leaving the knife there, driven with incredible force through her until the tip actually punctured the wet earth and left her pinned there like some exhibit in a museum.

He got to his feet and walked towards the partition, his hands reaching assuredly in the blackness for the can of petrol. He unscrewed the cap and walked back towards Paula. The powerful smell of the fuel filled his nostrils as he tossed the cap away, raising the can into the air.

He tipped it up, feeling the thick fluid cascading down over him, soaking through his clothes, some of it trickling into his mouth. It made him retch, but he stood there until the can was empty and the golden cascade had finished. Then he tossed it to one side and stood there, hands by his sides, looking down at her corpse.

He reached into the pocket of his jacket and pulled out a lighter, holding it before him for long seconds, petrol dripping from his hand. He flicked it, looking at the flame which glowed dully before him, fluttering in the breeze.

Bryce smiled, feeling the petrol soaking through his clothes, feeling the cold clamminess on his skin. The smell was almost overpowering.

He lit the lighter once more, then, with a slow, deliberate movement, he pressed the flame to his petrol-sodden clothes.

They ignited immediately.

Thirty-two

'What is this? Guy Fawkes week?'

Detective Sergeant Stuart Finn took a drag on his cigarette and looked down at the body of Mathew Bryce.

The corpse had been burned beyond recognition, the flesh stripped from the bones, his clothes simply vaporised by the ferocity of the fire. Finn noticed that the stud on Bryce's jeans had melted in the heat, the molten metal having dribbled into the dead man's navel. The air reeked of the sickly-sweet smell of burned flesh.

Detective Inspector Frank Gregson knelt beside the body, his eyes fixed on the face. The mouth was open, stretched wide in an incinerated rictus. A couple of white teeth gleamed in the smoking hole that passed for a mouth but, as Gregson himself looked more closely, he saw that some fillings in the man's mouth had also melted. He prodded the remains with the end of his pen, watching as a sizeable chunk of burned flesh fell away. He got to his feet and motioned for the ambulanceman to replace the blanket over the body, hiding it from view once more.

About a yard from the remains of Bryce lay another blanket-shrouded shape.

The remains of Paula Wilson.

Gregson and Finn wandered across to the second body, both men looking around them.

The building site was a hive of activity now, despite the lateness of the hour. Both uniformed and plain-clothes officers were moving about. Men from forensics were picking their way slowly and carefully over the site, their search aided by several powerful arc lights that had been set up around the perimeter. The cold white glow of the lamps illuminated the murder scene.

Elsewhere on the site men moved around taking photos of the place and of the bodies. Outside in the street, would-be onlookers were kept away by uniformed men. A couple of ambulances stood at the entrance to the site, along with a police car. Unmarked cars were parked opposite. The officers who'd arrived in them were taking statements from those who had seen or heard anything, hoping that there would be some lead to the case, some clue as to why Paula Wilson had been murdered. Perhaps some clue as well to who had killed her.

The bodies had been found by the owner of a record shop in Dean Street. He'd been working late in the office above his shop and had caught sight of the flames coming from behind the partition as he'd been walking down the street towards Shaftesbury Avenue. The man had been taken to hospital suffering from shock. He was now under sedation. He'd managed to burble something about a burned body to a uniformed man who'd been on foot patrol nearby. The uniformed man had called through to New Scotland Yard.

Gregson and Finn had been there within fifteen minutes.

By 12.36 a.m. the area had been sealed off and was swarming with policemen.

'Where the hell is Barclay?' said Gregson as the two men approached the second body.

'He's been called, he's on his way,' Finn said, taking another drag on his cigarette.

Gregson dropped to his haunches and pulled back the blanket that covered Paula Wilson.

His face was expressionless as he studied the body, pulling the cover further down until he revealed the full extent of her injuries. He stroked his chin, his gaze focused on the rubbish stuffed into her vagina. Finn noticed it too and raised his eyebrows.

'Keep Britain tidy, eh?' he murmured quietly.

Gregson ignored his remark, his gaze fixed on the girl's torn and mutilated genital area.

He stuffed her full of rubbish.

Gregson looked at her other injuries, at the wounds in her chest and throat. The cuts on her face and hands. He pointed to the bad gash across her palm and the lesser ones on her fingers.

'Defence cuts,' he noted. 'She was trying to fight him off.'

'I'll tell you what puzzles me,' said Finn, looking down at the body. 'Why didn't he burn *her* as well as himself?'

Gregson could only shrug.

'Why did he burn *himself?*' the DI mused.

'Was there any ID on him?' Finn wanted to know.

'If there was, it went up in smoke with him. What about the girl?'

'Paula Wilson, twenty-three years old. Single. She lived with her parents.'

'Have they been told yet?'

Finn nodded.

'They've got to come in and identify the body, poor sods,' he said.

'What was she carrying when he attacked her?' Gregson wanted to know.

'Just a handbag.'

'Anything taken?'

'She had credit cards and fifty-seven quid on her. As far as I can tell he didn't even *look* in the bag.'

'Because he didn't intend stealing anything,' Gregson said flatly, pulling the cover back over the body and getting to his feet. His knees cracked loudly as he straightened up. 'He got what he wanted.'

'And then torched himself? It doesn't make much sense, does it?' said Finn.

'Just like the other one didn't,' the DI reminded his partner. Both men looked at each other. 'Hell of a coincidence, isn't it? One man robs a bank, doesn't take any money, kills six people then burns himself up. A few days later another man mugs a young woman, but he doesn't want her money; all he wants to do is kill her then, when he's finished, he sets fire to himself. Like you said, perhaps Guy Fawkes night has come a bit early this year.'

'You think they're linked?'

'What the fuck do *you* think?' snapped Gregson irritably. 'Two murderers commit motiveless crimes then burn them-selves to death within one mile of each other in the space of

126

a week. You're telling me there's no connection?' He shook his head. 'What we've got to find out is who they were and what the hell that connection *is*, because I've got a bad feeling about this.'

'Like what?'

'Like, they might not be the only two.'

Thirty-three

He paused before the mirror and adjusted the knot in his tie, finally satisfied that it was straight. Then Jim Scott took a last look around the room, checking that everything was tidy.

He'd been up since 7.30 that morning, dusting, picking up any stray pieces of paper from the floor. He even managed to force himself into doing the washing-up, which had been lying in the sink for a couple of days.

Scott polished the handle of the door to the room which used to be his father's. He didn't go inside. There was no need. There was nothing to tidy up in there.

He had rung Carol at 8.30 that morning and asked her if she would see him after work. Would she come back to his flat? They could get a take-away and eat it when they got back. He had found himself gripping the receiver tightly.

Please say yes.

She had agreed without her customary reticence. Scott had put the phone down and shouted triumphantly, punching the air as if he'd just been informed he'd won the pools or come into a vast inheritance. All the anger and disappointment of the past few days was forgotten. She was going to spend the night with him. That was all that mattered.

She'd been to the flat on a number of occasions before, usually staying the night. When they'd first started seeing each other it had been almost every night. He studied his reflection in the mirror again, noticing that his smile had faded slightly. He wished that things could be as they were in the beginning. There had been passion between them then. There had never been any excuses about not being able to see him then.

Not like now.

Scott crossed the bedroom to the cabinet beside the bed.

So much they had to talk about.

He slid open the top drawer.

The Beretta 92S automatic lay beside a pile of handkerchiefs.

He looked at the weapon for long moments.

So much they had to talk about.

Scott slid the drawer shut once more.

Carol rolled over in bed and sighed, gazing at the poster of James Dean on her bedroom wall.

Beneath the picture of the film idol were the words: BOULEVARD OF BROKEN DREAMS.

They were the only kind of dreams she knew.

Broken. Wrecked.

Ray Plummer had rung about twenty minutes before Scott to apologise that, again, he couldn't see her. He'd make it up to her, though, he had said. He'd get her something nice. Something expensive.

When Scott had rung she'd said yes to him almost without thinking. Now she began to realise what she had agreed to do. To spend the night with him. By agreeing to spend the night, had she also agreed to sleep with him? They had been lovers, after all, still were occasionally; although the term lovers was redundant as far as Carol was concerned. *They had sex occasionally.* That was it. In her mind, there was no involvement, nothing other than physical contact.

She knew it was different for Scott.

But she knew that there were other reasons why she must see him tonight. She had no doubt that he was becoming suspicious of her. Of her excuses. She needed to spend time with him to allay those suspicions for a while.

Until when?

Until it was time to tell him that it was all over between them?

Until it was time to move in with Plummer?

Time for the final escape.

Carol rubbed her face with both hands and thought about getting out of bed.

For some reason she looked across at the phone, perhaps expecting it to ring again.

Only this time it might not be either Scott or Plummer.

When it had rung earlier that morning she had hesitated for interminable seconds before picking it up, remembering the call of the previous night. It had taken a monumental effort of will and courage finally to snatch up the receiver. Even in the light of day she felt the fear pricking her as she pressed it to her ear and spoke into it. She had been hugely relieved to hear Plummer's voice.

Should she tell *him* about the calls?

Perhaps she should tell Scott.

Tell someone, for God's sake. Don't keep it to yourself.

And if she did tell them? What could they do? She herself had no idea who was making them. Or why.

Carol swung herself out of bed and headed towards the toilet, glancing at the phone as she passed. She paused in the doorway, looking down apprehensively at the phone.

He wouldn't ring, she told herself. Whoever he was, he wouldn't ring now. Not so early. He seemed to prefer the hours of darkness.

Whoever he was.

She suddenly reached for the jack plug and pulled it from the socket in the wall.

She was safe from his calls now.

At least for the time being.

Thirty-four

The stench was appalling.

DS Finn pulled his handkerchief from his pocket and held it close to his nose as he peered down at the body.

'He's not as badly burned as the first one,' said Phillip Barclay, prodding the remains of the dead man's face with a probe. A piece of blackened skin came away from the cheek, exposing the bone beneath.

'Will that make identification easier?' Gregson wanted to know, his eyes never leaving the corpse.

'Theoretically,' the coroner told him. 'But his hands are very badly burned; that rules out finding him by his prints. It looks like it's going to be dental records again.'

'Provided he's in the files,' Finn added, his voice muffled through the handkerchief.

Gregson looked at his companion as if contemptuous of the fact that he found the stench of burned flesh so repellent. Then he returned his attention to the body.

'Any further progress on the first one?' he asked.

Barclay could only shake his head. He seemed more interested in his new subject. He used a probe to force the jaws open a little wider, peering into the black maw that was Bryce's mouth. Even the tongue was burned, black and swollen by the ferocity of the heat. Two fillings in the dead man's rear teeth had indeed melted and Barclay chipped away at the molten matter with one end of the probe, cursing when a whole tooth came free of the scorched gums. He retrieved it from the back of Bryce's throat with a pair of tweezers, dropping it with a dull clink into a small kidney dish.

'See the hands,' he said, lifting the first two digits of the dead man's left hand, indicating how the fire had stripped away the flesh and bone as far as the first knuckle. What remained resembled ash and Gregson feared it would simply blow away should a strong breeze fill the room.

All around them the steady hum of the air conditioning, keeping the room at an even sixty-five degrees, was the only sound apart from their voices.

'What about the girl?' said Gregson, moving to the metal table next to Bryce.

Laid out on it, her nakedness exposed for all to see, was Paula Wilson. Her skin was already tinged blue in places from loss of blood. The savage gashes made by Bryce's blade stood out even more vividly against the paleness of her flesh. Gregson stared down at the corpse, into the open eyes. He allowed his gaze to wander over the slashed throat, past the punctured chest. He looked briefly at the cuts on her hands, at the dark bruises which covered her torso and upper thighs like ink stains on blotting paper. The flesh of her vagina was torn and swollen. Her pubic hair had been shaved off during the course of the autopsy. The Y-shaped incision from pelvis to throat had also been made by Barclay in his quest to discover more about the

131

nature of the girl's death. It may have seemed obvious from the state of the wounds in her throat and chest, but he had to follow procedure.

Gregson saw that her entire body was a mass of cuts and bruises, some small, some huge. The fatal cuts.

'Cause of death, as you can see, was stabbing,' said Barclay. 'Although I found petechiae which would seem to indicate he . . .'

'What the hell is that?' snapped Gregson.

'Small haemorrhages in the blood vessels of the eyes, usually associated with strangulation or suffocation.' He pointed to her battered face. 'That would have happened when he pushed her face into the mud.

'The wound in the throat was the death wound,' the pathologist continued. 'She lost an enormous amount of blood.'

'What about the things he stuffed inside her?' Finn wanted to know, glancing at the ravaged vaginal area, the flesh around it blackened with bruises.

Barclay shrugged his shoulders and turned to the work-top behind him. He picked up a small plastic bag and laid it beside the dead girl's body.

'I took eight separate articles from inside her vagina,' he said, indicating the contents of the bag. The stone. The ring pull.

'Sick fucker,' hissed Finn. 'What the hell would he want to do that for?'

'Was she raped?' Gregson asked.

Barclay shook his head.

'The vaginal swabs showed evidence of urine, but that was hers. The killer left no bodily secretions of any kind. Rape wasn't his motive. He just wanted to kill her.'

'Well, he made a fucking good job of it,' Finn said flatly. He nodded towards the defence cuts on her hands. 'Looks like she put up quite a fight.'

132

Barclay nodded slowly.

Gregson, one hand cupping his chin, stood staring down at the body.

Vagina stuffed with rubbish.

He had seen something like this before.

Coincidence?

'Was she dead when he did it?' Finn asked. 'When he shoved those things inside her?'

'No,' Barclay said matter of factly. 'The amount of bleeding from the vagina would indicate she was still alive. Aware of what he was doing. My guess is, if she'd been dead he wouldn't have bothered.'

'Like I said to you earlier,' Finn began. 'Why not torch *her* as well as himself?' He looked at Gregson, who had wandered back to look at the incinerated corpse of Bryce.

The DI stood as if mesmerised by the body before him.

The stillness of the pathology lab. was beginning to make Finn uneasy and the infernal stench of burned flesh was repulsive. He waved a hand as if to dispel the odour. He thought about lighting up a cigarette, even reached for the packet, but Barclay's disapproving glance finally dissuaded him.

'Is your report finished?' Gregson asked the pathologist.

'Almost.'

'I want it as soon as it is.'

He turned and headed for the door, followed by Finn.

'I want to know who those two fucking blokes are,' he said sharply. 'And I want to know fast. There's two now. There might be three soon.' He opened the door and walked out.

Finn scuttled after him.

'Frank, do you know something I *don't?*' he said irritably as they walked towards the lift, their footsteps echoing through

133

the corridor. 'You said something back at the murder site about the two suicides being linked.'

Gregson nodded.

'What makes you say that?' Finn demanded.

'I just think it's a hell of a coincidence that two killers should both burn themselves up after committing a crime, especially when both could have escaped.'

They reached the lift and Gregson jabbed the button to call.

Finn lit up a cigarette and puffed on it, glancing up at the numbers that lit up in turn as the lift descended towards them.

'So what do you make of it?' the DS wanted to know. 'The way you're talking, you make it sound like some kind of fucking conspiracy.'

'Look, I don't know what the hell is going on, right?' snapped Gregson as the lift bumped to a halt at their floor. He stepped inside. 'All I know is there's something fucking weird happening.'

'Ten out of ten for observation, Frank,' said Finn, smiling thinly. 'I think I'd have to agree with you there.'

Gregson glared at his companion.

'If you've got something on your mind you should tell me,' the DS said irritably.

'I'll tell you what's on my mind. That you should go home now and leave me to check a few things out. Got it?'

'Like what?'

'Go home, Stuart. Leave it to me. If it checks out then I'll tell you. If it doesn't, it's only *my* time that's been wasted, right?'

'We're supposed to be working *together* on this,' Finn reminded him.

The lift came to a halt and the doors slid open but Finn shot out a hand and closed them once more, his finger pressed on the 'DOOR CLOSE' button.

'What the fuck are you doing?' snapped Gregson.

'Level with me, Frank. Tell me what you're thinking,' the DS said, looking his partner in the eye.

Gregson looked down at Finn's hand, his finger still on the button.

'I'm thinking that if you don't move your fucking arm I'm going to break it,' he hissed.

Finn released the button and the doors slid open. Gregson stepped out, looking back at his partner.

'Leave this to me for the time being,' he said. Then, as the doors slid shut, he turned and walked away.

The MO was the same.

Gregson had suspected it from the first time he'd seen Paula Wilson's body.

Now he was sure.

Multiple stab wounds, no rape, but the vagina of the victim stuffed with rubbish.

He flipped through the file before him, checking the photos, comparing them to those he had of Paula Wilson. The photos in the file were eighteen months old.

Three different girls, but each one had been killed the same way. Each one had been mutilated, each one had been defiled.

Gregson ran a hand through his hair and sat back in his chair. He reached for his mug of coffee and took a sip, wincing when it was cold on his lips and tongue. He put the mug down, his gaze skipping over the pictures laid out before him.

Three girls, murdered eighteen months ago. Stabbed and beaten, their vaginas stuffed with rubbish.

And now, four hours ago, Paula Wilson, stabbed and beaten, her vagina stuffed with rubbish.

135

The DI reached for his phone, picked it up and jabbed the extension number for the Records Office. He waited as the phone rang.

Waited.

Finally it was picked up and he heard Steve Houghton's voice.

Gregson didn't bother to announce himself.

'Steve, have you got a file down there on a bloke called Mathew Bryce?' he said, drumming his fingertips on his desk.

Houghton said that he had.

'When you've got a minute, I'd like to see it,' the DI told him.

It was there again.

He'd found it in more or less the same place as before. Removed it from the shattered, burned remains of the second killer's head.

Barclay looked at the blackened piece of matter in the dish; it was smaller than his thumb nail. Next to it was the portion of the mysterious substance he'd taken from the first body.

Both were blackened by the fire, both melted.

He frowned as he prodded first one, then the other with the end of his pen.

Analysis of the two pieces had shown that they were indeed composed of plastic and a number of other elements. Silicon had been found in both.

He exhaled deeply, wondering if he should include this piece of knowledge in his report, wondering if he should mention his findings to Gregson. He decided to withhold the information for the time being. Until he knew more. Until he had some idea, however vague, what these strange, melted objects were.

So far, he was clueless. And that worried him.

Thirty-five

'I think we've got trouble.'

The door to Jim Scott's office had been flung open without a knock and Zena Murray was standing before him, her face pale.

'What sort of trouble?' he asked, getting to his feet and following her out of the office.

'Two fucking drunks,' she said, her tone a mixture of annoyance and anxiety.

'Where the fuck is Rick?' Scott demanded. 'He's paid to keep things running smoothly. What kind of bouncer is he?'

'Rick's watching them but they've got some friends with them, too.'

Scott nodded and followed Zena out into the main floorshow area of 'Loveshow'.

He glanced across at the bed and saw Carol lying on it, her basque open to reveal her breasts, her tiny G-string barely concealing the tight curls of her pubic bush. On either side of the bed the seats were full. He counted five men, all in their thirties, watching the tableau before them.

Close by him Rick Calder leant against the wall, hands dug in the pockets of his jeans.

Scott jerked his head towards the bouncer, a gesture designed to bring him closer. When Scott spoke he had to raise his voice to make himself heard above the loud music accompanying Carol's act.

'. . . I see you walking by,
You got that faraway look in your eye . . .'
Calder, a couple of years younger than Scott, kept his eyes on the five men as he listened.

'What's going on?' Scott shouted.

'Those fuckers over there,' Calder said, nodding in their direction. 'A couple of them are pissed.'

'Then why the hell did you let them in in the first place?' Scott demanded.

'I was having a squirt. I didn't see them come in,' Calder said defensively.

One of the men was on his feet, swaying in time to the music and also to Carol's gyrations on the bed. He took a stumbling step towards her, then seemed to sway and fall backwards into his chair. The other men laughed.

Scott looked on, his eyes blazing.

Carol continued with her act, trying to ignore the men close by.

'Show us everything!' shouted one of the men, his voice audible even above the thunderous music.

'Show us your cunt,' another called.

Carol ignored his remarks, her eyes closed momentarily as if she were concentrating on some complex choreographed movement. She slipped the silk from her shoulders and pulled the flimsy garment off, rubbing it against her breasts.

'Do it, you fucking whore!' shouted one of the men, laughing. His companions laughed too.

The music roared on.

'. . . I don't need your dirty love.
I don't want you touching me . . .'
Scott stood still, his breath coming in gasps.

Carol ran her index finger over the slinky material of her G-string.

138

One of the men got to his feet again and lurched towards the bed.

Keep away from her.

Scott also took a step forward but halted as the first man's companion pulled him back.

'Get on with it!' another shouted, holding up his glass in salute.

Carol stood up on the bed, hooking her fingers into the top of the G-string. The five men began clapping in unison as she started to ease it over her hips, gradually revealing her pubic hair.

'. . . There's a name for girls like you.

You belong in the gutter I know you do . . .'

She finally pulled it free, allowing it to drop to her feet. Naked she stood before them, caressing her body with both hands as the music roared on around her and the shouts of the men grew louder. She tried not to look into their eyes, tried to concentrate on the dark outline of Scott, who stood close to the bottom of the steps to her left.

'Suck this!' shouted another of the men, fumbling with the zip of his trousers. Another moment and he had pulled his penis free. He staggered drunkenly towards Carol, his throbbing organ protruding from his zip.

'That's it,' snapped Scott and both he and Calder moved forward.

The man actually had his foot on the edge of the bed when Scott grabbed him by the shoulder.

'Sit down,' he rasped, and threw the man backwards. He landed squarely in his seat, his penis still sticking through his flies.

'What the fuck is this?' another of the men shouted, glaring at Scott.

'I think it's time you gentlemen left,' said Scott.

139

The first man was busy doing up his flies, yelping in pain as he caught a pubic hair in his zip.

'We paid our fucking money, we want to see the show,' another protested.

'Go and find another show,' Scott told them. He turned towards Carol. 'Get dressed.'

She nodded and moved away from the bed.

As she did, the youngest of the five men grabbed her around the waist and lifted her into the air, laughing as he did.

'We only came in for some fun,' he said, chuckling.

Scott turned furiously on the man, his body shaking as he saw the other man holding Carol.

Get your hands off her.

'At least let us have our money's worth,' said the man holding Carol.

'Let go of her,' snarled Scott through clenched teeth.

'You charge enough in here,' the man protested.

Let go of her.

Scott grabbed the man's hand and prized open his grip, squeezing his wrist in a vice-like hold that threatened to break the bones.

Don't you dare put your hands on her.

Scott pulled the man close to him, his eyes blazing.

'What the fuck is wrong with you?' the man said, trying to shake free.

Scott glared at him a second longer then drove his head forward sharply, slamming his forehead into the bridge of the man's nose, hearing the sharp crack of bone with satisfaction. The man fell backwards, blood spurting from the shattered cartilage.

Immediately the other four men were on their feet. Two turned and ran for the stairs, but the others flung themselves at Scott.

140

He parried a clumsy blow and struck out with his left foot, driving it hard into the man's groin. As he crumpled up, Scott grabbed his hair to pull his head upright then he sent a powerful punch into his face, splitting the top lip.

Carol, still naked, stood close by, her arms around Zena, watching the fight.

The music roared on as an accompaniment.

'. . . *You've been outta my life so long,*

There's no way I'll stay . . .'

Calder struck another of the men in the stomach, hurling him over one of the sofas, aiming a kick at him as he scrambled to his feet and ran for the stairs.

The first man, blood streaming from his broken nose, struggled to his feet, his hand closing around a glass. He hurled it at Scott but missed. Scott turned to face him, dragging him upright by his lapels. He looked into the man's eyes, then across at Carol.

Scott brought his knee up into the man's groin so hard he felt it connect with his pelvis.

The man uttered a strangled cry and tried to clutch at his injured testicles.

Scott looked across at Carol again, still not releasing his grip on the man.

He drove his head forward again.

And again.

His own forehead was red now as he slammed it against the man's face. He opened a gash above his eye, another on his cheek. Blood from the injured man had spilled onto Scott's face and speckled his shirt. Scott hardly noticed that his adversary's eyes were closed. Instead he smiled across crookedly at Carol, holding him as if he were some kind of limp, blood-spattered rag doll. He grabbed a handful of the man's hair and yanked his head back hard, finally throwing him against the wall, watching

141

with satisfaction as he slid down to the floor, his shirt a mass of blood, his face cut and bruised by the onslaught. The man's companion stumbled across and helped him to his feet.

'Get out,' hissed Scott. 'Next time I'll kill you.'

The men made their way up the stairs, one of them slipping half-way, almost falling.

Scott felt something warm and wet on his face and realised it was blood. He wiped it away with the back of his hand then looked at Calder.

'Make sure they don't come back in here,' he snarled.

The bouncer nodded and followed the men upstairs.

The music roared on.

'. . . I don't need your dirty love . . .'

Scott looked at Carol, who met his gaze impassively.

'You all right?' he asked.

She nodded.

'Go and get dressed,' he told her, smiling thinly. He looked down and noticed that there was blood on his hands too. He pulled a handkerchief from his trouser pocket and slowly wiped the crimson stains away.

Carol and Zena disappeared through the door marked 'Private'. Scott finished wiping the blood from his hands then stuffed the stained cloth back into his pocket.

There was more blood on the carpet.

He smiled.

Thirty-six

Before he switched off the engine he glanced at the clock on the dashboard.

12.36 a.m.

Frank Gregson swung himself out of the Escort and slammed the door, fumbling in his pocket for his front-door key. He finally found it and let himself in, careful not to drop the thick manila file he had cradled under one arm. As he moved through the house he switched on lights, finally ending up in the sitting room. There he dropped the file onto the coffee table, crossed to the drinks cabinet, took out a bottle of Teacher's and poured himself a large measure. As he stood drinking the fiery liquid he heard movement from above him, soft padding footfalls on the stairs.

He sighed and finished his drink, filling the glass again.

'I couldn't wait up any longer.'

The voice came from behind him as Julie moved into the room. He didn't bother to turn; he knew where she was. He heard the creak of springs as she perched on the edge of the armchair.

'You could have phoned,' she said. 'I was worried.'

'If anything had happened to me you'd have heard about it soon enough.'

'I'd cooked you some dinner; I had to throw it out.'

'My loss is the dustbin's gain,' he said, finally turning to face her.

She wore just a short housecoat. He knew she was naked beneath it.

Naked, like Paula Wilson had been on that slab.

'Do you want me to get you something?' she asked, curling her legs under her.

'I'll manage with this,' he said, raising the glass. He crossed to his seat and sat down, gazing at the file before him. 'Sorry I disturbed you,' he added, as an afterthought.

'I wasn't asleep. I was waiting for you to get in,' she told him.

He smiled thinly.

'Well, something came up at the office, dear,' he said acidly, taking a sip of his drink. 'That's why I'm late.'

'If you mean that girl, I saw it on the news.'

'Yes, I *do* mean that girl. Paula Wilson, aged twenty-three.' He raised the glass in salute. 'Rest in peace.'

'They said the man who killed her committed suicide.'

Gregson nodded.

'Went out in a blaze of glory, you could say,' he added.

'Do you want to talk about it?' she asked.

He shook his head and chuckled softly.

'We tried talking about it last time, if you remember rightly. It wasn't a raging success, was it?' he said flatly.

'Frank, don't start.'

'Well, what exactly do you want to know? What details interest you about *this* case?'

She pulled her housecoat tightly around her and met his gaze.

'Do you want to know how many times he stabbed her? Or how many pieces of rubbish he'd shoved inside her?'

'What do you mean?'

'He stuffed pieces of rubbish between her legs. Inside her vagina. He filled her cunt with garbage.' Gregson hissed the

144

last sentence through clenched teeth. Julie swallowed hard and lowered her head slightly.

'Have you any idea who he was?' she said finally.

Gregson shrugged, got to his feet and poured himself another drink. He turned and looked at his wife for a moment before returning to his seat.

'Strangely enough I have,' he said. 'The only problem is, it doesn't make sense. My theory holds water about as well as a fucking colander.'

She looked at him questioningly, relieved at least that he was talking to her.

'The MO he used matches one of a murderer we put away eighteen months ago,' said Gregson.

'I'm not with you, Frank,' she said.

'No, you're not, are you?' he said cryptically. 'You're not with me.' He downed a large measure of the whisky. 'Perhaps it's better that you're not. I told you before that it isn't your problem.'

'And I told you that it was,' she snapped. 'You think I enjoy seeing you like this? Wrapped up in yourself, punishing yourself? There's no need for it, Frank. Not when *I'm* here, you don't have to keep your problems or your thoughts to yourself. I *want* to help. I'm worried about you.' Her tone softened slightly. 'It's you I want to help because it's you I love. Please don't shut me out, Frank.'

'You want to be a part of *my* world?' he asked sardonically. 'And everything in it?'

'Yes.'

He opened the file and pulled out one of the photos of Paula Wilson, holding it up for Julie to see, ensuring she had a good view of the knife wounds and the pulped face.

'Say hello to reality,' he said.

Julie glanced at the picture and lowered her head again.

'You wanted to look, then look,' he snapped, throwing the photo towards her. It floated to the floor. 'Perhaps you like this one better.' He flicked a picture of Bryce's burned body in her direction. 'How many more do you want to see?' He picked up the file and dumped it on the table in front of her, standing over her challengingly. 'Go on, look at them. Look at the fucking photos.'

He knelt down beside her and pulled another from the file, holding it up against her face as she tried to pull away from him.

Paula Wilson just before the autopsy.

'Look at it!' he shouted.

Bryce after they found him on the building site.

'Come on, I want to know what you think.'

She finally shook loose of his grip and struggled to her feet.

'I think you're crazy,' she said, fighting back the tears. 'I think this job is dragging you down and you don't even know it. Either that or you don't even *care*.'

'It isn't a nine-to-five job, Julie. You don't clock in and out. At least you don't clock your *mind* in and out,' he said. 'You carry it with you every fucking hour of the day and night. I carry those images and those sounds and smells in my mind, all the time.'

He took another gulp of whisky, wiping his mouth with the back of his hand.

Julie bent down and picked up one of the photos. She held it for a moment then dropped it in front of her husband.

When she spoke, her voice was low, strained.

'I'll leave you alone with your work,' she said.

Thirty-seven

'Something on your mind?'

Jim Scott looked down at Carol Jackson, raising himself up on one elbow.

She was gazing at the ceiling, tracing the outline of a crack in the plaster, holding his hand lightly as they lay naked side by side.

Tell the truth, shame the devil.

It had been one of her mother's sayings. Now she wondered if she should put it into practice.

Tell him. Put him out of his misery.

She glanced up at him and smiled.

No. Now wasn't the time.

He squeezed her hand and asked again what was on her mind.

'Nothing,' she told him. 'Why?'

'It looks as if there is,' he said, his own smile broader.

'So you're a mind-reader now, are you?' She looked into his eyes.

I'd be in trouble if you were.

He swung himself out of bed and wandered through into the kitchen, returning with two glasses and a bottle of Southern Comfort. He poured them both measures then got back into bed, watching as Carol shifted position, sitting up slightly to avoid spilling the drink. She looked at Scott as he drank, his eyes fixed on something across the dark bedroom.

Their lovemaking hadn't exactly been of the wild abandoned variety. Scott had barely been able to sustain his erection, due to Carol's relative passivity; it was as if his own ardour had been dampened by her perfunctory attempts to please him. But she had faked it enough times before with him and with Plummer. As far as she knew, neither man was aware of her disinterest.

Scott was just glad that she was with him. She was *his* tonight. They hadn't spoken about the incident in the club earlier when he'd fought to protect her. Scott smiled to himself as he remembered the sight of the man's bloodied face. It had been so easy to hurt him, to break his nose. To split his face open. He'd bled a lot. Scott downed his drink and poured himself another. A celebration, perhaps? He lay down beside her again, the drink resting on his chest.

'I've been thinking about getting a bigger place,' he told her finally.

'Why? This is enough for you, isn't it?' she said.

'Well, I won't be on my own forever, will I?'

It could have been a plea.

Carol didn't look at him.

'I mean,' he continued, 'if someone was to move in with me, it wouldn't be big enough.'

She smiled thinly.

'I'd worry about that when the time comes, Jim,' she said, sipping her drink.

'Have you thought of moving?' he wanted to know.

'I'm happy where I am, I suppose,' she lied. 'Although perhaps happy is the wrong word. It's just that I'm stuck with it.' She turned her head away from him for a moment.

No way out. Except perhaps through Plummer.

'I miss you when I can't see you at nights,' he confessed.

'You see me every night.'

148

'You know what I mean.' He took a long swallow of liquor. 'Seeing you at work, that doesn't count. Any bastard who pays can see you like that.' He began running his finger around the rim of the glass.

'If it's any consolation, I hate earning my money that way too,' she told him.

'I don't blame you for what you do. You've got a good body, why not use it to your advantage?'

'I don't do it out of choice, Jim,' she said, her tone hardening. 'I do it because I've got no bloody option. Do you realise how much I hate that job? Do you know what I'd do to get out of there? What I'd do to change my lifestyle?'

He shook his head.

'Anything,' she said. 'And I mean *anything*.'

'I didn't realise. I'm sorry.'

She took a swig of her drink.

'I've been doing it for over ten years now,' she told him. 'I've had enough.'

'But what else could you do? There isn't any way out.' He smiled. 'I'll probably still be working there in ten years' time.'

'Yes,' she said, with scarcely disguised contempt. 'You probably will.'

They regarded each other impassively for a moment.

'Maybe a rich Arab would walk in one night and whisk me off to a life of luxury,' she said bitterly.

'I hope not,' said Scott, his face set in hard lines. 'I wouldn't want to see you with anyone else.'

She swallowed hard.

Did he know?

'Why not? Things change, Jim. People change,' she said.

'Not people like you and me,' he said adamantly.

They lay in silence for long moments before she looked at

149

him again.

'You said you wouldn't want to see me with anyone else,' she murmured. 'What would you do if there *was* someone else?'

He looked at her, his eyes blazing.

'I'm curious,' she said, qualifying the statement.

Christ, if only he knew.

Scott swung himself out of bed once more and pulled open the drawer of the cabinet. He took out the Beretta 92S and grasped it, pulling back the slide. The metallic click filled the room. Carol moved away inches involuntarily at the sight of the pistol.

'I'd kill him,' said Scott flatly.

He squeezed the trigger and the hammer slammed down on an empty chamber, the click amplified by the silence in the room.

'And what about me?' she asked.

Scott smiled, the pistol still gripped in his fist.

'I'd probably kill you too.'

Thirty-eight

He was gone when she awoke.

Carol rolled over sleepily and felt for Scott but found that she was alone in bed. She blinked myopically, trying to clear her vision. There was a piece of paper lying on his pillow; she reached for it, running one hand through her hair.

SEE YOU TONIGHT. LOVE, JIM.

Love.

She sighed and lay down on her stomach, the note resting on the pillow in front of her.

She knew now that it was going to be difficult, if not impossible, to break from Scott. Especially after what he'd said the previous night. He obviously felt more deeply for her than she had even imagined. That not only troubled her, it frightened her. Carol pulled herself across the bed to the cabinet and slid open the top drawer.

The Beretta was inside, underneath some notepads.

She took the pistol out and hefted it.

Would he really kill her if he found out she was seeing Plummer?

Common sense told her it had been a somewhat theatrical threat, but her knowledge of Scott told her otherwise. She had little doubt he would use the gun if he had to. Carol pulled back the slide, the weapon feeling heavy in her hand. She sat up in bed, the sheet falling away from her body to reveal her nakedness. Lifting the pistol she gripped it in both hands and aimed it at the mirror on the dressing table across the room, drawing a bead on her own reflection. She squeezed the trigger and the hammer slammed down.

She lowered the gun again and sat back against the headboard. Scott would never let her go. No matter how she told him, no matter how gently she broke it to him, no matter what explanation she gave.

She was trapped.

She should tell Plummer. But what good would that do? For a moment she gazed at her reflection, feeling as lost and alone as she ever had in her life. The mirror-image gazed back impassively. Carol put the gun back in the drawer and caught sight of a small box with a green lid. She took off the lid and found fifty 9mm rounds, all neatly arranged in rows of five. She lifted out one of the brass-jacketed rounds and held it between her thumb and forefinger, feeling the sleek lines, looking with bewilderment at the hollow tip of the bullet. Finally she put it back, closed the lid of the box and slammed the drawer shut.

Was she being unfair to Scott?

It was a question she had asked a dozen times in the past week.

She was seeing another man behind his back. She was giving him the impression she still cared for him, if somewhat guardedly. Yet all the time she knew she had to get away from him – not that she disliked him or hated him. Their relationship had run its course. It was as simple as that.

Simple?

She almost smiled.

It was anything *but* simple.

She realised that the longer she played out the charade the more damage it would do to Scott when the game finally ended. But after what he had said the previous night, how could she end it? Carol rubbed her face with both hands and shook her head.

No way out.

She glanced at the drawer and its lethal contents.

Perhaps there *was* a way.

Perhaps.

The journey back to her own flat seemed to take an eternity.

She sat on the tube staring absently at her fellow passengers, who either returned her gaze uncomfortably or gazed around, reading the advertisements over the seats. When there was no one opposite her Carol found herself confronted by her own image again. At one station a couple of youths got in and sat opposite her, the taller of the two eyeing her constantly as she crossed and uncrossed her legs. As they got out, the tall one leant close to her and muttered something about a blow job. They disappeared along the platform as the train moved off.

Carol walked from the station to her home, fumbling in her handbag for the key, finally letting herself in.

The room smelled of yesterday's food and she went around opening windows to dispel the odour. She'd taken a bath at Scott's place so, with a few hours left before she had to get ready for work, she made herself a cup of tea and sat down in front of the television.

It was then that the phone rang.

'Hello,' she said, putting down her mug, hissing as she burned her fingers on the hot china.

'Welcome home.'

She recognised the voice immediately.

'What do you want?' she said, her voice catching.

'Just to let you know I'm still watching.'

'What do you want?' she shouted, fear and anger now rearing up within her.

'You'll find out.'

The line went dead.

Carol slammed the receiver down and sat staring at it for interminable seconds, as if expecting it to ring again. Her hands were shaking so violently that she slopped hot tea onto her skin. The pain made her drop the cup which promptly sent the warm fluid soaking into the carpet. Carol watched as it spilled, unable or unwilling to do anything about it.

She lowered her head, cradling it in her hands.

Tears trickled down her cheeks as she began to cry softly.

Thirty-nine

The man had vomited, a reaction neither Gregson nor Barclay had observed before.

When relatives came to identify the bodies of their loved ones they usually fainted, burst into tears or just silently acknowledged the fact that it was their kin lying on the slab. Clive Wilson had taken one look at the pulped features of his daughter and doubled over, vomiting copiously on the floor of the pathology lab.

'Do we take that as a positive identification?' Gregson said as the man was helped from the room by two uniformed men.

Barclay was unamused by the DI's quip.

He merely pulled the plastic sheet back over the dead girl's face and motioned for two of his assistants to replace the body in its cold locker.

'Wait,' Gregson said. He took hold of the cover and pulled it down again, studying the cuts, bruises and patchwork of contusions that had disfigured the girl.

'Shouldn't you be taking care of Mr Wilson?' said Barclay.

'Finn's up there. He'll deal with it. Besides, I'm a policeman, not a fucking social worker,' Gregson said flatly, his eyes never leaving the body. Finally he pulled the sheet back and motioned for Barclay's assistants to continue. They lifted the body and slid it back into the locker, where it would be kept for the next two days until funeral arrangements had been made. Those final forty-eight hours would also give Barclay the opportunity to check the corpse once more for anything he may have missed, such as fibres, prints or anything else that might give a clue to the identity of her murderer. After that the body would be handed over to an undertaker and New Scotland Yard's responsibility would be discharged.

Paula Wilson's clothes had been put into a plastic bag, each item removed from the sealed forensic bags, along with what little jewellery she'd been wearing at the time of her death. These would be returned to her family.

Gregson stood beside one of the slabs, glancing down at the puddle of vomit left by Clive Wilson. The acrid smell permeated the air.

'You'd better get that cleaned up,' he said to the pathologist, who regarded him irritably, as if the thought hadn't occurred to him.

'Have you finished in here now?' Barclay wanted to know.

'No. I want to see the two bodies. The killers,' the DI told him.

'Why, for Christ's sake?'

'Humour me, will you?'

Barclay crossed to one of the lockers and slid it open. Encased in a rubber bag like some kind of monstrous pupal life-form, the body appeared. Barclay undid the zip far enough to reveal the blackened remains of the features. Gregson stared at the charred corpse then glanced at Barclay and nodded, indicating that he wanted to look at the second corpse. The pathologist repeated the procedure so that both incinerated bodies were in view.

'Still no progress with identifying them?' the DI asked.

'Not with the first one; he was burned as badly as anything I've ever seen,' Barclay confessed. 'The second one,

155

though . . .' He allowed the sentence to hang in the chill air. 'I found part of a thumb print on the inside of Paula Wilson's left thigh.'

'Why the hell didn't you say something earlier?'

'Because I wasn't sure.' He sighed. 'I'm still not one hundred per cent sure but I thought that ninety-five was better than nothing. I sent the print down to photographic, they're going to work it up.'

The pathologist stood looking at his companion, watching how intently he gazed at the scorched remains of the two dead men.

'What is it about them, Frank?' he said, finally. 'Why the fascination?'

'Because they're mysteries to me, and I don't like mysteries or unanswered questions. But there's something else, too. I've got something nagging away at the back of my mind. Something to do with these two men. They both used MO's I've seen before.'

'That's not so unusual, is it? Copy-cat killings are nothing new,' Barclay said.

Gregson didn't shift his gaze.

'Does Finn know your theory?' the pathologist asked.

Gregson shook his head.

'It's best he doesn't.'

'Why?'

'Because if he knew what I was thinking, he'd probably suggest I was locked up.'

Forty

'. . . Police stated that there were anywhere between five hundred and a thousand protesters but that the march was peaceful . . .'

Jim Scott sat in his office, feet propped up on the desk, his eyes fixed on the TV screen. It flickered every now and then but not enough to bother him or to break his concentration. The black and white images were of a large group of people moving through Central London, most of them carrying placards that the cameras managed to pick out.

STOP OVERCROWDING
PRISONS NOT ZOOS

Scott looked on impassively.

'. . . The march was led by the Right Honourable Bernard Clinton, MP for Buxton, whose constituency houses Whitely Prison . . .'

There was a close-up of a man in his late forties, dressed in a grey jacket and a large overcoat. The fur of the hood matched the white of his own hair. The man was chatting to people on either side of him and looking at the cameras every now and then. Reporters stepped in front of him, thrusting microphones forward.

'What do you hope this march will achieve, Mr Clinton?' asked one.

'Prisons in this country have been overcrowded for too long,'

157

the MP replied. 'Whitely is probably the worst example. It just so happens that it is in my power to do something about it, or at least to make the Government aware of the problem.'

'What is your main complaint with the system as it is at present?' another reporter asked.

'In Whitely, as in many other gaols, remand prisoners are kept in the same sections of the prison, in some cases in the same *cells*, as convicted men, occasionally even murderers. This is intolerable.'

Scott sipped his drink and continued gazing at the screen.

'. . . *The movement for prison reform has gained momentum in the last three months, ever since the murder of a remand prisoner in Whitely by a convicted killer. Mr Clinton took up the case after relatives of the dead man approached him . . .*'

There was a shot of Trafalgar Square and Scott could see the protesters milling around the fountains. Clinton stood at the top of the steps and was addressing them but the camera panned across to the reporter standing in the foreground who was addressing his remarks direct to camera.

'. . . *Officials from the Home Office are expected to visit Whitely Prison and a number of other maximum security gaols throughout the country in the next few weeks, to see at close hand how bad overcrowding has become. Mr Clinton himself will lead a delegation to Whitely before the end of the week and a motion to discuss the possible reform of the penal system has been tabled in the Commons.*'

The reporter signed off and the pictures of the rally were replaced by the newsreader in the studio. Scott listened for a moment to a story about yet another famine in Africa, to someone appealing for people to send money for food, and then switched off.

Send them money for food, next thing they'll be wanting money for clothes, he chuckled to himself. He pulled the phone

158

towards him and jabbed the digits of Carol's number.

It rang.

And rang.

He glanced at his watch, sure that she wouldn't have left yet. He allowed the phone to ring another five times then tried his own flat, wondering if she might have stayed there until it was time to come in.

There was no answer there either.

He tried her flat once more, and still all he heard was the insistent ringing tone. He pressed down on the cradle and replaced the receiver.

She should be at work soon, anyway.

Ask her where she was.

He decided against that. He just hoped she was all right. Perhaps she'd slipped out for something. Or to see someone.

To see someone? Like who?

Why had she asked him the previous night about what he'd do if he found out she was seeing someone else?

He dismissed the thought. There was no need to be suspicious, she was merely asking out of curiosity. He suspected she'd been surprised by his answer. Scott smiled. Perhaps it would make her realise just how much he felt for her.

He crossed to the window of his office and looked out. It was raining again; the pavements and road were slick with water. The neon signs all around were reflected in the moisture, as if they themselves lit the concrete from the inside.

Scott always thought of London as existing in two different times. There were those who lived and worked by day and those who did so by night. Worlds apart.

The time of darkness had come again.

He smiled.

PART TWO

Now hatred is by far the longest pleasure;
Men love in haste but they detest at leisure . . .
Lord Byron

They have the morals of alley cats and minds like
sewers . . .
Neville Heath, convicted murderer, on women.

Forty-one

The door crashed open and slammed back against the wall with such force it seemed it would come off the hinges.

Michael Robinson blinked and sat up, staring blearily in the direction of the noise. He rubbed his eyes and peered down from the top bunk.

The uniformed figure stood in the doorway, eyeing the occupants of the cell impassively.

'Move it,' said the figure. 'Slop out.'

Robinson yawned and swung his feet over the side of the bunk.

'I think this is our alarm call, Rod,' he said, stretching.

From the bunk below him Rod Porter grunted and turned over, as if to resume the peaceful sleep from which he'd just been disturbed.

'Move yourself, Porter,' said the uniformed figure brusquely.

'Fuck you,' murmured Porter under his breath.

Robinson jumped down from the top bunk.

'You interrupted my dream, Mr Swain,' said Porter, hauling himself out of bed. 'I was just getting a blow job from Michelle Pfeiffer.'

'The only blow job you're likely to get is a bike pump up your arse. Now move yourselves, both of you,' snapped the uniformed man.

Robinson and Porter both retrieved the small plastic buckets from one corner of the cell and wandered out onto the landing. Robinson smiled as he lifted the plastic cover from the slop bucket to reveal a lump of excrement. He shoved it at the uniformed man's face, watching with pleasure as he recoiled from the stench.

'I think mine is a little bit underdone. Perhaps you ought to have a word with the kitchen staff,' he said, smiling.

In front of him, Porter grinned. The uniformed officer didn't appreciate the joke and pushed Robinson out onto the landing where, already, a steady file of men were spilling from their cells, joining the long line on either side of the landing as they made their way to the toilets.

Whitely Prison was coming to life.

On landings above and below them the same routine was in practice. They had followed it every morning and would continue to follow it until their sentences were up. Men shuffled along over the cold floors, some dressed in grey prison-issue pyjamas, others bare-chested or in boxer shorts. Each of them held a small bucket. Most were filled with excrement. Slopping out was as much a part of prison life as exercise, work and, for the fortunate ones, visits. Robinson and Porter knew it well enough. They'd been sharing a cell for the last two years. Robinson was in for ten years for armed robbery, while his companion was half-way through a twelve-year stretch for a similar crime. His extra two years had come about because he'd shot a security guard in the leg with a twelve-bore.

Both men were in their mid-thirties, and both had spent most of their lives in and out of institutions. Porter had been raised in a children's home from the time he was two years old. He'd run away repeatedly as he'd got older, never with anywhere to go but just anxious to be free of the confining walls and restrictive atmosphere. As the years had progressed a series

164

of petty crimes had seen him in remand homes, borstals and finally prison. It was usually robbery.

Robinson had experienced a more stable upbringing. He was married with a couple of kids. Stealing had come more as a necessity than anything else. His wife had expensive tastes and the kids always wanted new clothes or bikes or games. Both men had come to Whitely from other prisons, Robinson from Strangeways, Porter from Wandsworth.

A large proportion of Whitely's inmates had also come via other gaols throughout the country; prisons where they couldn't be handled adequately. In many cases Whitely was a last resort. Or a dumping ground, whichever way you chose to look at it. It was like a drain where the dregs and filth exuded from all the other prisons in the land had been gathered together; the human refuse brushed aside and locked up in an institution that was a dustbin for the unwanted and unmanageable.

Located in the heart of the Derbyshire countryside, surrounded on four sides by hills, it was a monument to the backwardness of penal reform. A massive, grey stone Victorian building, it housed over 1600 inmates, twice its allotted amount. Remand and convicted prisoners lived side by side.

Robinson nudged the man in front of him and nodded a greeting as the man turned.

The uniformed man noticed the movement and stepped close to Robinson.

'No talking,' he said.

Robinson shrugged and smiled innocently.

'Cunt,' he whispered, stifling the word with a yawn.

Across the landing an identical procession was filing towards their own latrine. Men who had emptied their slop buckets were returning to their cells. There were the odd murmurings, the sounds echoing throughout the large building, but they were quickly quelled by warders anxious to maintain silence.

165

Porter peered over the landing rail, through the steel netting that was strung from one side to the other, and noticed that, on the landing below, prisoners who had finished slopping out had not in fact returned to their cells but were standing outside, their attempts at entry barred by warders. He frowned, wondering what was going on. His musings were interrupted as he reached the latrine. He and Robinson emptied their slop buckets into the waste chutes provided, rinsed them with boiling water and then made their way back to their cell.

The door was closed, the entrance blocked by another warder, Raymond Douglas. He was a red-faced man with a pitted complexion who always looked exhausted, as if he'd just completed a marathon.

'Stay there,' he said, toying with his key chain, holding up his free hand to add weight to his instructions.

Further down the landing, other prisoners also stood outside their cells. Irritated mutterings grew louder.

'. . . What's going on? . . .'

'. . . Why are we being kept outside? . . .'

'What's the deal, Mr Douglas?' Porter asked.

'You'll find out,' said the warder. 'For now, just shut it.'

Porter eyed the uniformed man malevolently, then exchanged puzzled glances with his cell-mate.

'Cell search?' Robinson murmured. 'Someone been smoking whacky baccy again?'

'I said shut it,' Douglas snapped.

'Just curious,' said Robinson, gazing around him.

On all the landings men now stood outside their cells, increasingly frustrated and increasingly cold. It wasn't exactly warm inside Whitely and many of them were dressed only in shorts. The babble of discontent grew more insistent, to the point where even the warders couldn't quell it.

'What the hell is going on?' Porter wanted to know.

166

'SHUT UP.'

The voice boomed around the inside of the building, bouncing off the walls with its ferocity and power.

All heads turned in one direction, peering upwards to find its source.

'Shut up and listen,' the voice continued, and now the inmates could see where the thunderous exhortation came from.

On the uppermost landing, flanked by warders, stood a tall, powerfully-built figure in a dark blue suit, his greying hair slicked back so severely it appeared that he was bald. He gripped the landing rail with hands as large as ham-hocks. He regarded the men beneath him impassively, his eyes flicking back and forth as they looked up at him.

Peter Nicholson, the Governor of Whitely Prison, began to speak.

Forty-two

You could have been forgiven for imagining that Peter Nicholson had undergone surgery to replace his vocal chords with a megaphone. His words boomed out, spoken with clarity and in a tone that suggested that he was keeping his words simple for the less intelligent inmates of the prison. On either side of him the warders looked down onto the other landings, watching for any signs of unrest amongst those below. Warders on each of the individual landings also ensured that silence prevailed as he spoke.

167

'As you may have heard,' the Governor said, smoothing his hair back with one hand, 'Whitely has been in the news lately. The media are obviously hard up for stories because they seem interested in what they refer to as our overcrowding problems here. Also, the local MP has taken it upon himself to look personally into what goes on in this prison.'

Robinson looked at Porter and raised his eyebrows quizzically.

'To that end,' Nicholson continued, 'a Home Office delegation will be visiting this prison tomorrow to see how it runs and to see how well you're all cared for.' He smiled sardonically.

A murmur rose that was quickly silenced.

Nicholson paused for a moment theatrically.

'The members of this delegation will be speaking to a number of prisoners. Asking about conditions, etcetera.' He looked around the upturned faces. 'You may speak to them if you wish. Help them with their questions. You may have some questions for *them*. If you have any problems or grievances, you're quite free to tell them.'

'Yeah,' murmured Porter. 'And get our fucking heads busted by the screws when they've gone.'

Swain took a step towards him, shooting him a warning glance.

'If any of you have any problems, at any time, you know you are free to speak to the officers in charge of your landing or to me personally,' Nicholson continued.

There was another babble of chatter, and this time it took longer to quieten.

Nicholson looked around once more. His green eyes, like chips of emerald, caught the light and reflected it coldly. He brushed a speck of dust from his sleeve as he waited for the silence he required. Finally satisfied, he continued.

'I want this prison running perfectly for these visitors,' he said. 'I want co-operation between you and the officers. I want the cells spotless. I want them to be impressed by what they see. I don't like people meddling in the way I run this prison and that's what they're doing. Meddling. I want them to leave here knowing that this prison is well run and that its inmates are being adequately dealt with. I don't expect them to leave here with a catalogue of stories about what a terrible place Whitely is. As I said, you may speak to them if you wish. That is your prerogative. But bear in mind that if they hear too many bad reports, they'll disrupt the way I run this prison. And I don't like disruptions. I hope that's understood.' He looked around him, then smoothed his hair back once more. 'That's all.'

Nicholson and his officers turned and moved away from the landing rail, out of sight of the other prisoners.

On all the landings the inmates were allowed back inside their cells.

'Breakfast in twenty minutes, get a move on,' said Warden Swain, slamming the door shut behind Robinson and Porter.

'Suck this,' rasped Porter, holding his penis in one fist. 'Fucking cunt.'

Both men started to dress, taking it in turns to wash as best they could in the small sink perched on the cell wall.

'I wonder if anyone will be stupid enough to tell this bunch of do-gooders the truth?' Robinson mused, drying his face.

'Are you joking?' Porter muttered, fastening his grey overall. 'Even the screws wouldn't tell them anything. They're more frightened of Nicholson than most of the cons in here.'

Robinson nodded in agreement.

'A tour of the prison, eh?' he said, smiling. 'I wonder what they'll make of our humble little home.'

'Probably want to move in with us,' Porter quipped. He crossed to his locker and took out a comb, running it through

169

his short black hair. The inside of the locker was a mosaic of photos: naked women, a team picture of Liverpool FC and a couple of postcards all vied for attention. He blew a kiss to one of the women, then closed the locker again.

Robinson was sitting on the edge of the upper bunk.

'I'll tell you one thing, Rod,' he said, 'and I'll bet money on it. There's at least *one* part of this nick they won't see. Nicholson will make sure of that.'

Forty-three

The office was large, functional rather than welcoming. Efficiency was the keyword. It was a place of work, after all, thought Peter Nicholson, and it had been *his* place of work for the last sixteen years. He'd seen many changes in the penal system as a whole and Whitely in particular during his days as Governor at the prison. The changes since he first began working in the service had been radical, to say the least. He'd begun back in the fifties as a prison officer. He'd served his early years in Wandsworth. In fact, he'd been one of two warders who had escorted Derek Bentley from the condemned cell to the hangman on 28 January 1953. Bentley had been sentenced to hang because his accomplice, Christopher Craig, despite having fired the shot that killed a policeman, had been too young for the rope.

After Wandsworth Nicholson had moved around from prison to prison, serving his time as surely as any of the inmates in those institutions. The difference was that he could go home at the end of every shift. He had an increasingly long key chain to show for his years of service.

His enthusiasm for his work and his intelligence had led to his being appointed Assistant Governor at Wormwood Scrubs. From there it had been only a matter of time until he was given his own prison.

Whitely was all he knew and had known for the last sixteen years.

The penal system he worked in was not the only thing that had changed during Nicholson's time. His own attitude had hardened, too. He'd originally joined the service after his mother had been attacked and beaten almost to death in 1950. He felt that he was acting, by proxy, for her and all victims of crime like her in his role as gaoler. And that was exactly how he viewed his job. He didn't see his task as correcting the ways of men who had strayed into crime and needed help; he and his warders existed to protect society from the kind of human garbage locked within the walls of Whitely.

He stood up, glancing across at the photograph of his wife on the desk. The image smiled back at him as he straightened the frame. He moved over to the window of his office and looked out.

He could see into the empty exercise yard. Beyond it, protected by a high stone wall, was a small chapel in the grounds of which were a number of graves, each one marked by a simple marble marker; some were actually decorated by headstones or crosses. They bore the names of prisoners who had died at Whitely. Men who, with no family on the outside, had nowhere else to rest. Even in death they were confined within the walls of the prison.

A couple of inmates were picking up leaves from around the graves, sweeping them into a large black sack. The skeletal trees that grew close to the chapel rattled their

171

branches in the wind, which whipped across the open ground.

The closest town of any size to the prison was over twelve miles away, across barren land now unfit even for farming. The remains of an open-cast mine, shut down over a decade earlier, lay to the west.

A single road, holed and pockmarked, connected the prison's main gates to a small tarmac road which wound through the hills and moors like a dry tongue in search of water.

The wind rattled the window in its frame but Nicholson remained where he was, keeping vigil, gazing out over his empire.

The buzzer on his intercom interrupted his thoughts.

He turned and flipped a switch.

'The warders you asked to see are here, Mr Nicholson,' his secretary told him.

'Send them in,' he instructed her.

A moment later the door opened and five men in uniform trooped in. Nicholson motioned to them to take a seat. He leant on his desk top, waiting until the last of them was seated, then stood upright again, pulling himself up to his full six feet. He looked an imposing figure.

'You know what this is about,' he said curtly. 'I want to be sure that everything runs smoothly when this blasted delegation gets here tomorrow. Any hint of trouble, I want it stamped on.' He looked at each man in turn.

'Will you be showing them round yourself, sir?' asked John Niles.

Nicholson nodded.

'How many are there?' Raymond Douglas wanted to know.

'Four. One woman.'

172

'That should please the men,' said Niles, smiling. The other officers chuckled but Nicholson didn't see the joke.

'If any of those bastards finds out that one of them is going to be a woman, there could be trouble,' Nicholson said flatly. 'Take care of it.' He smoothed his hair back with one hand. 'I want them in and out of here as quickly as possible. I don't like the idea of people investigating my prison.'

'Why are they coming to Whitely, anyway?' Paul Swain enquired. 'We're not the only prison in the country that's overcrowded.'

'That's perfectly correct. Unfortunately, however, we *are* the only prison where a remand prisoner was murdered by a lifer recently.' He held up his hands in a dismissive gesture.

'I hope they're not too disappointed by what they see,' said Gareth Warton.

Nicholson looked at him unblinkingly.

'Meaning what?' he said irritably.

'You have to agree, sir, conditions *are* below standard.'

'Standard for what? This is a prison, in case you'd forgotten. The men here are here because they broke the law. Most of those in Whitely are here because they're too unruly or dangerous even for other jails to cope with.' He fixed Warton in his gaze. 'We, Mr Warton, have the scum of the earth under this roof.'

'They still deserve better conditions,' Warton persisted.

'They deserve nothing,' Nicholson hissed. 'They're here to be punished. We're here to ensure that punishment is carried out.'

'Isn't it our job to help them too, sir?' Warton said.

'*Yours*, perhaps, if that's how you feel. I don't see it as my job to help them. It's my job to help the people on

173

the *outside* and I do that by making sure the scum in here *stay* in here.' He fixed Warton in the unrelenting stare of his cold green eyes. 'Do you know what we are, Mr Warton? We're zoo keepers, paid to keep animals behind bars.'

Warton coloured and lowered his gaze.

Nicholson sucked in an angry breath and turned back to look out of his office window.

'When the delegation arrives I want them brought here,' he said. 'I'll show them round the prison, round the recreation rooms and cells. If they want to speak to any of the prisoners they can. But I want at least two men present at all times.'

'Will you be taking them to the maximum security wing, sir?' Swain asked.

'Yes, and the solitary cells,' the Governor told them.

'What about the hospital wing?' asked Niles.

'No,' snapped Nicholson, turning to face the officer. 'The infirmary, perhaps, but there's no need to show them anything else.' He looked up and down the line of faces. 'Are there any questions?'

There weren't. Nicholson dismissed the warders, returning to the window for a moment as if searching for something out in the windswept yard.

From where he stood he couldn't see the hospital wing.

The thought suddenly spurred him into action.

He turned back to his desk, picked up the phone and jabbed an extension number.

As he waited for it to be answered he drummed lightly on the desk top. The phone was finally answered.

'We have to talk,' said Nicholson. 'Come over to my office. It's important.'

Forty-four

Ray Plummer filled the Waterford crystal tumbler with soda and ice and handed it to John Hitch, and then repeated the procedure, passing the other brandy and soda to Terry Morton.

Morton thanked him, interrupted in his appraisal of a pair of Armani statues.

'And this stuff is worth money, is it, Ray?' Morton said, motioning towards the figurines.

'Of course it's worth money, you prat. Why do you think I bought it?' Plummer said. 'Fuck me, I'm surrounded by Philistines.'

He took a sip of his own drink and sat down in the leather chair closest to the fireplace, looking into the authentic fake gas flames as he sipped his drink. He touched his hair self-consciously, worried that the high wind outside might have disturbed it.

Morton remained on his feet, swaying backwards and forwards from the balls to the heels of his shoes. The delicate tumbler was out of place in his heavy hand; he looked as if he would have been more comfortable carrying a bottle of beer. Or a cosh.

'Sit down, Terry, you make the place look untidy,' Plummer told him, smiling at Hitch, who grinned back as his companion sat down hurriedly.

Both Hitch and Morton had worked for Plummer for more than ten years and he trusted them as much as anyone in his organisation. Hence their privileged presence in his penthouse flat. They were two of only a handful of his employees allowed to enter this most private of havens.

Hitch was a couple of years younger than his boss but his long blond hair and perpetual sun tan (the product of a solarium) made him look closer to thirty than thirty-six. Morton was the opposite, dark-haired, squat, almost brutish in appearance. He'd been a successful amateur boxer before he joined Plummer's organisation. The flat nose was a testament to his habit of fighting with his guard down. Hitch maintained he could stop buses with his head (and frequently did).

'So, tell me what you found out about Connelly,' said Plummer. 'Is it right he's moving into drugs?'

'As far as we could find out, he's got no plans to expand in that area, Ray,' Hitch said, sipping his drink.

'He's making bundles out of the money business, isn't he?' Morton added. 'Why should he try that other shit?'

'Because *that other shit* is worth a damned sight more,' Plummer said scornfully.

'Well, we spoke to at least half a dozen members of his firm and none of them knows anything about a shipment of cocaine,' Hitch announced. 'That call must have been someone winding you up.'

'But why?' Plummer wanted to know.

Hitch could only shrug.

'The bit about the warehouse was right,' Plummer continued. 'Connelly's just bought himself a warehouse down by the docks.'

'Maybe his boats unload there, the ones that bring his mags in,' Hitch offered.

Plummer remained unconvinced.

'You spoke to members of his firm,' he said. 'They're hardly likely to tell you what the cunt's planning, are they? Especially if he's planning to take over London with the money he makes from selling that fucking cocaine.' Plummer got to his feet and walked across to the fireplace, staring into the flames.

'There's no reason why he should want to try and "take over",' Hitch said. 'It doesn't make sense, Ray. There's been peace for over three years now. Connelly's not going to fuck it up by starting a drugs war, is he?'

'He might,' Morton offered.

'Oh, shut it, Terry, for fuck's sake,' Hitch said wearily.

'So what are you saying?' Plummer demanded. 'That the call was bollocks? A wind-up? If it was, I'd like to get my hands on the bastard that made it.'

'Forget about it,' Hitch advised, sipping his drink.

The phone rang.

Plummer crossed to it and picked up the receiver.

'Yeah,' he said.

'Ray Plummer.'

'Yeah, who's this?'

'We spoke a few days ago,' said the voice. 'Well, I spoke, you listened.'

Plummer, the receiver still pressed to his ear, turned to look at Hitch.

'You're calling about the cocaine shipment,' he said.

Hitch was on his feet in seconds.

'Well done,' said the voice.

Plummer put his hand over the mouthpiece and jabbed a finger towards the door to his right.

'The phone in the bedroom,' he hissed quietly.

Hitch understood and bolted for the door, picking the receiver up with infinite care so that he too could hear the voice on the other end of the line.

'Are you still interested in the shipment?' the caller wanted to know.

'Maybe,' Plummer said warily.

'What kind of fucking answer is that?'

'I'm interested if it actually exists,' he said.

'It exists all right. Ralph Connelly is going to be spending the money he earns from it pretty soon. Unless you decided you wanted it.'

'What do you get out of this?' Plummer wanted to know.

'That's *my* business. Now, if you're still interested, be here at this time tomorrow. I'll call then.'

The caller put down the phone.

'Fuck!' roared Plummer.

Hitch emerged from the bedroom.

'Recognise the voice?' Plummer wanted to know.

The younger man shook his head.

'If I was you, Ray,' he said, 'I'd wait for that call.'

Forty-five

'They're here, Mr Nicholson.'

The Governor of Whitely heard his secretary's voice over the intercom and glanced up at his wall clock. The delegation was punctual, if nothing else. It was exactly 10.00 a.m.

'Show them in, please,' he said, adjusting his tie and rising to his feet as the door was opened.

The first of the four visitors entered and Nicholson recognised him immediately as Bernard Clinton, the MP. He was followed by his companions. The Governor's secretary left them alone

178

in the room, promising to return in a moment with tea and coffee.

Nicholson emerged from behind his desk slowly, almost reluctantly. He extended a hand and shook that offered by Clinton, who introduced himself then presented his colleagues.

'This is Mr Reginald Fairham,' Clinton said, motioning towards a mousy-looking man in an ill-fitting suit. He was tall and pale and when Nicholson shook his hand he found it was icy cold. 'Mr Fairham is the Chairman of the National Committee for Prison Reform,' Clinton explained.

Nicholson said how glad he was to meet him.

A second man, chubby and losing his hair, was presented by Clinton as Paul Merrick.

'Mr Merrick serves in my office in Parliament. He's been active with me in this issue for the last few years,' the MP announced.

Nicholson looked squarely into the chubby man's eyes, scarcely able to disguise the contempt he felt for such a soft, weak handshake. Merrick needed to lose a couple of stone. His hands felt smooth, like those of a woman or someone who's never done a hard day's work in their life. Nicholson gripped Merrick's hand hard and squeezed with unnecessary force, watching the flicker of pain cross the man's face.

The fourth member of the group was a woman, in her mid-thirties, Nicholson guessed. She was smartly dressed in a grey two-piece suit and posed elegantly on a pair of high heels. Her face was rather pinched, tapering to a pointed chin that gave her features a look of severity not mirrored in her voice.

'Good morning, Mr Nicholson,' she said as she shook hands.

'Miss Anne Hopper is a leading member of the Council for Civil Liberties,' Clinton said, smiling obsequiously.

179

Introductions over, Nicholson motioned for his guests to sit down.

'We appreciate the chance to come to Whitely, Mr Nicholson,' Clinton said. 'Thank you for your co-operation.'

'Why did you choose Whitely?' the Governor asked.

'It is one of the worst examples of overcrowding in any prison in Britain,' Fairham said. 'And it does have one of the worst disciplinary records, too.' He clasped his hands on his knees. 'My organisation has been monitoring it for some time now.'

'Monitoring?' said Nicholson. 'In what way?' He spoke slowly, his gaze never leaving Fairham, who found he could only hold that gaze for a couple of seconds at a time.

'As I said, it has a very bad disciplinary record,' he offered.

'When you have over sixteen hundred violent and dangerous men in one place twenty-four hours a day, three hundred and sixty-five days a year, then the occasional problem *does* arise,' Nicholson said, leaning back in his seat and pressing his fingertips together.

'But the disciplinary record here is worse than at any other prison in the country. How can you explain that?' Fairham persisted.

'Because the class of prisoner is lower,' the Governor said scornfully. 'Perhaps your monitoring system didn't tell you that.'

'I think Mr Fairham means that we all share a concern over the incident that happened here not so long ago,' Clinton said.

'The death of the remand prisoner,' Fairham interjected, as if reminding Nicholson of something he might have forgotten.

'It was unfortunate, I agree,' the Governor said.

'It wouldn't have happened if the prison had been run more efficiently,' Fairham snapped.

'This prison is run *more* efficiently than most,' Nicholson rumbled, his eyes blazing. 'My staff are more highly trained

180

than the majority of officers at other prisons in this country. But no matter how well-trained or well-organised warders are, they can't always anticipate the actions of these . . . men you represent. That killing would have happened in *any* gaol, not only Whitely. My men are trained to *control* prisoners, not to read their minds.'

Fairham swallowed hard and began drumming his fingers distractedly on his knees.

'I don't think anyone is casting aspersions on you or your officers, Mr Nicholson,' Clinton offered. 'What happened was unfortunate, we're all agreed on that.'

'It was also inevitable,' Nicholson said sharply. 'The men in here are unpredictable, violent and dangerous. To some, killing is a way of life, whether you want to face that fact or not. Mr Fairham obviously chooses to ignore it.'

'Do you feel that the killing would not have taken place had overcrowding been less intense?' asked Merrick, pulling a pair of spectacles from his top pocket. He began cleaning them with a handkerchief which, Nicholson noticed, bore his initials.

'The killing would have happened whatever the population of the prison. As I said to you, for some of the men in here it's all they understand.' Nicholson looked at Fairham. 'Most criminals are of low intelligence, as you're probably aware. The difference between right and wrong seems to escape them. Presumably you are aware of the dead man's background?'

'He'd been remanded to appear in court for a driving offence,' Fairham said.

'A driving offence which included being drunk in charge of a vehicle,' Nicholson said. 'A vehicle he lost control of, which ran into a bus queue, killing a six-year-old girl in the process. A little more serious than an expired tax disc, I think you'll agree.'

Fairham didn't speak.

181

'You sound as if you feel his killing was a kind of justice in itself,' said Anne Hopper.

'They say God pays back in other ways, Miss Hopper,' Nicholson said flatly.

A knock on the door broke the heavy silence and a moment later Nicholson's secretary entered with a tray of tea and coffee, which she distributed before leaving once more.

'What attempts are there at segregation between remand prisoners and convicted men here?' Clinton finally asked.

Nicholson sipped his tea thoughtfully.

'Very little,' he said flatly. 'We simply don't have the facilities to cope with the number of remand prisoners sent here.'

'Does that *bother* you, Mr Nicholson?' Fairham wanted to know.

'They're all criminals,' the Governor said.

'No, they're not,' Fairham protested, putting down his cup. 'The men on remand are *awaiting* trial. Some may be acquitted. Yet you insist on placing them with men who have already been convicted of far worse crimes.'

'I don't insist on it,' snapped Nicholson. 'I have no choice. What would be *your* answer to overcrowding?' he said, challengingly.

'Build more prisons,' Fairham answered.

'If you empty a rubbish bin onto the ground, it doesn't mean the rubbish will disappear,' Nicholson said, smiling. 'All you do is re-distribute the rubbish over a wider area.'

'And what is that supposed to mean?' Fairham snorted indignantly.

'If you build more prisons you're doing the same thing,' the Governor said. 'You're not removing the problem, you're just re-distributing the rubbish.'

'I'm not sure I like your analogy,' Fairham said. 'We're speaking about men, not garbage.'

182

'You have your own view,' Nicholson said icily.

'Is that how you view the men in Whitely, Mr Nicholson? As garbage?' Anne Hopper wanted to know. She held his gaze as he looked at her.

'As I said, we all have our own views. Perhaps I'm the wrong one to ask about that.'

'I would have thought you were exactly the one to ask,' Fairham interrupted vehemently. 'You are, after all, in charge of over a thousand men. You are responsible for their welfare.'

'Perhaps you'd be better off asking the families of their victims how *they* feel,' hissed Nicholson, turning his full fury on Fairham. 'There's a man in here who kidnapped and murdered two babies. One of them was less than six months old. He beat them so badly there was hardly a bone left unbroken in either of their bodies. Why don't you speak to the mothers of those babies? Or perhaps Miss Hopper should speak to the women who've been raped by some of the men in here. Or to the husbands of those women. Speak to *them*.' He looked at the woman. 'Do you have any children?'

She shook her head.

'No,' he echoed. 'Then perhaps the prisoners in here who have sexually abused children won't seem quite so odious to you.'

Clinton held up a hand to silence the Governor.

'All right, Mr Nicholson,' he said, smiling ingratiatingly. 'I think we understand your point.'

'Don't patronise me,' he snarled. 'This is *my* prison. Run *my* way. I understand the mentality of the men in here. I see them every day and familiarity doesn't breed contempt so much as disgust in me. When you've lived around men like that for as long as I have, when you've seen at first hand what they're capable of, then you can come here and tell me how to handle my affairs. But for now this is the way things will continue.'

'Mr Nicholson, we didn't come here for a battle,' said Clinton. 'And I'm sure no one doubts your knowledge and ability in this job. We came to see how the prison is run. Perhaps now might be a good time to do that.'

He got to his feet and looked first at his companions and then at Nicholson, who nodded, a slight smile creasing his lips.

'If Mr Fairham will allow me to say one more thing,' he offered, the tone of his voice even, 'we also find overcrowding a problem here but the answer isn't to build more gaols. Before you leave here today, I'll show you how overcrowding can be dealt with once and for all. Not just at Whitely, but at every prison in the country.'

Forty-six

The rumbling of conversation gradually died down as DI Frank Gregson got to his feet.

'All right, keep it down,' he said, raising his voice, looking out at the twenty or so uniformed and plain clothes men seated in the room. The air was thick with cigarette smoke. Beside him, his colleague DS Finn was adding to the pollution, blowing out long streams from his Marlboro.

The babble gradually subsided into near-silence.

Gregson walked across to a blackboard that had a map of the West End stuck to it. There were several red-tipped pins protruding from it and an area of Soho had been ringed in red marker pen. To the left of the map pictures of Paula Wilson, plus the remains of the two dead murderers, were tacked. On the other side of the map there were several pictures which, from a distance, looked like ink blots. They were in fact the blow-ups of the print taken from Paula Wilson's thigh.

'Nine deaths, including two suicides,' Gregson began. 'All within the space of a week. The murders, as far as we can tell, are motiveless; the killers are now dead, burned to a crisp both of them. By their own choice. Nine bodies and no leads. That is the state of play at the moment.' He prodded a picture of Paula Wilson. 'You all know about this woman, how she was killed and where. What we don't know is why and by who. Now Dean Street, where he killed her, isn't exactly a quiet area; someone somewhere must have seen or heard something. And, seeing as no one has come forward with any information about this killing, I suppose we're meant to think that no one saw anything.' He smiled humourlessly. 'That's a load of bollocks.' The smile faded rapidly. 'If they won't come to us then we'll have to go to them. I want you to talk to people.' He looked slowly around the other faces in the room. 'I want pubs, clubs, clip-joints, restaurants and anything else you can think of, checked out. Talk to the staff. Two men have committed suicide within a one-mile radius of each other within a week. We've had a fucking chase through Soho and now a woman's been murdered. Somebody has seen something. Somebody *knows* something. I want that somebody found and I want them talking.'

'Who exactly are we looking for?' asked a plain clothes man in the front row. 'A suspicious character?'

A ripple of laughter ran around the room.

'In fucking Soho?' grunted Gregson. 'You might as well pull in every bastard who works there.'

More laughter.

'Just talk to them, find out what they've seen and heard over the last couple of weeks,' the DI said.

185

'Do you think there's a link between the two killers?' a tall ginger-haired officer asked from near the back of the room.

'It's possible,' the DI said quietly, his gaze still roving around the other men in the room. 'We know it isn't a gang-related thing. Not unless London's been invaded by a bunch of fucking fireaters who haven't quite mastered the trick yet.'

Another ripple of laughter greeted this remark.

'Maybe it's the Irish Fire Brigade,' a voice added and the men laughed even louder.

'All right, all right, enough of the joviality,' said Gregson. He turned towards the map and jabbed at the red-ringed area. 'This area is to be gone over with a fine tooth-comb. You'll each be designated one particular area. We don't want to be tripping over each other. As it is, there'll be more policemen than punters on that patch.' He looked round the room. 'You'll report back to me on a daily basis. I don't care if you think you've got nothing, I want to hear what you know, what you found out.'

'Have either of the dead men been identified yet?' another man asked, puffing on his cigarette.

Gregson shook his head.

'We got a print off the second one from Paula Wilson's body, though.' He pointed to the photo of the print. 'It would seem to be just a matter of time before the man's identified.'

'You seem very sure, Frank,' Finn observed.

'Humour me, eh?' Gregson said wearily.

Should he mention the possible copy-cat overtones of the killings? He decided not to.

'Right,' he continued. 'Let's go. If you move through into the next room you'll find the area you're to work. And, like I said, I want to know everything you hear, what anyone's got to say, from the pimps to the tarts through to the doormen at the clip-joints and the managers of restaurants. Got it?'

186

The men got to their feet and began filing through the door on Gregson's left, muttering to themselves and each other as they went.

'What are you expecting us to find, Frank?' Finn wanted to know.

'Some answers?' he mused, none too convincingly.

'The way you talk, Frank, I'm beginning to wonder if you know something I *don't*,' Finn said.

Gregson didn't answer.

Forty-seven

'What are the nets for?'

Anne Hopper paused beside the rail of landing three and looked over, running her gaze over the wire mesh strung from one catwalk to the other.

'To prevent suicides,' Nicholson explained, standing beside her.

'Are there many attempts at suicide, Mr Nicholson?' Paul Merrick asked.

'No more than usual in a prison this size,' the Governor answered without looking at the other man.

'And how many would be *usual?*' Reginald Fairham wanted to know.

'There are three or four attempted suicides every week,' Nicholson said, his tone emotionless.

'And how many are successful?' Merrick wanted to know.

'Two or three. It's a good ratio for a gaol with a population this size.' Nicholson began walking again, satisfied that his visitors were following him. Behind them Warders Niles and Swain walked slowly and purposefully, occasionally stopping to peer through the observation slots in the cell doors.

The small procession moved on towards a set of metal stairs that led them down to the second landing. Their footsteps echoed on the metal catwalks.

'The nets aren't that successful, then?' Fairham said. 'If you have three suicides a week.'

Nicholson caught the note of sarcasm in the other man's voice but he did not turn, did not look at the visitor.

'It wouldn't matter if we welded steel sheets across the landings,' he said. 'They'd still try and kill themselves. There are plenty of other ways than throwing yourself from a walkway.'

The tone of his voice hardened slightly. 'You might be interested to know, Mr Fairham, that the last prisoner who committed suicide by jumping from a landing also took a prison officer with him.'

Fairham didn't answer.

They continued along the walkway, the members of the delegation peering towards the cells or over the rails every so often.

'How many hours a day are the men locked in?' Clinton asked.

'Twenty-two, sometimes twenty-three. It depends on the circumstances,' Nicholson said.

'One hour outside their cells every day,' snapped Fairham. 'That's hardly sufficient, is it?'

'I said it depended on the circumstances,' Nicholson repeated irritably. 'The higher risk prisoners are locked up for longer. Some of the other men are allowed to work outside in the grounds of the prison, as you will see. Others perform duties in the kitchens, the infirmary or the laundry rooms. Every man is allowed a certain amount of time in the recreation room, too.'

'How many are there in each cell?' Clinton wanted to know.

'Usually three,' Nicholson said.

'Would it be possible to have a look inside one?' asked Anne Hopper.

Nicholson stopped his slow strides and turned to look at her.

'If you wish,' he said and nodded to Swain to unlock the nearest cell.

The warder peered through the observation slot then selected a key from the long chain that dangled from his belt. He opened the door and walked in.

'On your feet,' he snapped, glancing at the two occupants. They were both lying on their bunks, one reading, one scribbling a letter on a notepad.

Mike Robinson looked down from the top bunk and saw Swain standing there.

'Mr Swain, what a pleasure,' he said. 'What can we do for you?'

'You can shut your mouth and get on your bloody feet,' snapped Swain.

'Leave them, warder,' said Anne Hopper, moving past him into the cell.

Both men eyed her approvingly as she entered.

'Sorry to disturb you,' she said, smiling.

'No bother, darling,' Robinson told her, grinning. He swung his legs around so that he was perched on the edge of the bunk. He put his pencil and pad aside. Rod Porter peered at her over the top of his book, glancing at the other visitors.

'Less of your lip, Robinson,' hissed Swain. 'Show a bit of respect.'

Robinson caught sight of Nicholson standing on the landing and his smile faded rapidly. He nodded a greeting to the other three visitors, who crowded into the cell as if they were playing some bizarre game of sardines.

There was a table and two wooden chairs at the far end by the slop buckets. Clinton sat down beside the slop bucket and smiled at the two men. Robinson smiled back. Porter merely regarded the man indifferently, his gaze straying back to the woman.

'These are the visitors you were told about yesterday,' Nicholson informed the two men.

'You said there were usually three to a cell,' Clinton observed.

'That's right,' Nicholson repeated.

'There *were* three of us in here,' said Porter slowly, his gaze flicking from one visitor to the other, but always returning to Anne Hopper. 'Our cell-mate had an accident.'

'Shut it, Porter,' Swain said under his breath.

'No,' said Fairham, raising a hand. 'Let him speak.' He looked at the prisoner. 'What kind of accident?'

'He forgot to test the temperature of his bath water,' Porter said cryptically.

Robinson laughed, looked at Nicholson and then fell silent again.

'I'm not with you,' said Fairham.

'Neither is *he*, any more,' Porter said.

'What was this man's name?' Fairham wanted to know.

'Marsden,' Nicholson said. 'He was in here for sexual crimes against children.'

'He was a fucking ponce,' Porter said venomously.

190

'Watch your language,' snarled Swain.

'He *was*. We all knew it, the screws knew it too. That's why they didn't interfere when he . . . *hurt* himself.' The vaguest hint of a smile creased Porter's lips.

'You called him a ponce,' Clinton said. 'What *is* that?'

Robinson chuckled again.

'You must have got a few in the Houses of Parliament,' he said, smiling.

Porter looked directly at the MP.

'A ponce. A pimp. He lived off little kids,' the prisoner said contemptuously. 'Made them sell themselves. Girls *and* boys. He had kids as young as twelve in his stable when they lifted him. A ponce.' He emphasised the word with disgust.

'I still don't understand what you mean about him having an accident,' Fairham said.

'I told you,' Porter said. 'He didn't test his bath water. He got a bit hot.'

'Where is this man now?' Fairham wanted to know.

'He was taken to the hospital wing, then removed to Buxton General Hospital,' Nicholson said. 'He had been scalded. We found him, at least two of my officers did, in a bath full of boiling water in the shower rooms. When they got to him ninety-eight per cent of his body had been burned. There was nothing we could do for him here, so we had him transferred.'

'How did he get in that state?' Fairham asked, perplexed, his gaze shifting back and forth from Nicholson to Porter.

'He slipped on the soap,' Porter said.

Robinson laughed.

'He always *was* careless,' the other man added.

The realisation finally seemed to hit Fairham. The colour drained from his cheeks.

191

'You mean someone tried to kill him?' he said, his voice low.

'No,' Porter told him, flatly. 'He just had an accident.' He raised his book and continued reading.

The visitors turned and filed out of the room, realising that the conversation had come to an end.

Swain threw the two convicts an angry glance before slamming the door and locking it.

On the landing Nicholson was leaning on the rail.

'A man is nearly murdered in here and your officers knew about it?' snapped Fairham.

Nicholson rounded on him, his eyes blazing.

'My men knew nothing about what was going on,' he hissed.

'But that man said . . .'

'Are you going to take the word of a prisoner over mine?' snarled Nicholson. 'My men knew nothing about it.'

'But you don't deny that it could have been deliberate?' Anne Hopper added.

'Miss Hopper, the man who was injured ran a child prostitution ring,' Nicholson said, his tone a little calmer now. 'He set the children targets every day. If they didn't bring back the amount of money he'd told them to, he beat them with a baseball bat.' The Governor paused, for effect. 'A baseball bat studded with carpet tacks.'

'Oh God,' murmured Merrick.

'God had very little to do with it, Mr Merrick,' Nicholson added. He looked at the visitors. 'What you must understand is that even convicts have a twisted code of ethics that they live by. They have their own rules and their own hierarchy. The gang members, the hit men in here are at the top of their tree. Child molesters are the lowest of the low, even to other criminals.'

'Why?' Anne Hopper asked.

192

Nicholson smiled thinly.

'Even scum have to have *someone* to look down on.'

Forty-eight

The figures moved furtively in the darkness, glad of the protection of night.

As they worked the sound of water slapping against the canal walls was a ceaseless accompaniment to their labours. The wind whipped down the narrow side-streets and alleys, whistling in the wide estuaries. The breezes seemed to skim off the water like stones. The surface was constantly moving, as if some unseen force were continually hurling large rocks into the water at the quayside.

The small boat moored there rocked with each wave. The men on board looked up towards their companions on the quayside, muttering to them to be quicker.

A pile of wooden boxes as tall as a man stood on the quay. Piles just like it had already been loaded onto the boat, carefully stowed in its hold, covered by heavy sheeting and secured.

The last of the boxes were being transferred from the back of the truck now, carried by men who sweated under the effort despite the chill wind that had come with the onset of the night.

Further up the quay, larger boats were anchored. Most of the crews or owners had gone ashore. Only the odd light burned, a warning to any other craft travelling the canals on the coal-black night. The churning water looked as impenetrably gloomy as the night, as if it were a liquid extension of the umbra. Pieces of rotting wood drifted past on the flow. The odd tree branch, too. Even a torn jacket.

When a car passed by the men gave it a cursory glance.

The lorry was unloaded. The last two boxes were lifted on to the small boat, the men who strained under their weight cursing as they completed their task.

One of them paused for a moment, inspecting the lid of the last box. It was loose. Several of the nails had come free. The man drew it to the attention of a companion and, together, they lifted the strut of wood clean. He reached inside, pushing his hand through the layers of packing and into something dark and pungent.

Coffee beans.

The aroma was strong in the chill night air but he dug deeper, finally allowing his hand to close on what he really sought.

He pulled the small plastic box free and laid it on top of the crate, fumbling in his jacket pocket for something.

The plastic box was about seven inches long and five across.

He opened it and looked at the video tape cassette inside.

In his pocket he found a screwdriver and inspected the narrow end as if he were a surgeon about to perform a delicate operation. Then, working swiftly, he undid the six screws that held the cassette together and gently eased the back off.

Nestling between the two spools was a tiny plastic packet, smaller than a thumbnail.

He inspected the plastic bag, satisfied that its contents had not been touched.

The cocaine looked like talcum powder, luminescent in the darkness.

The man quickly replaced the back of the cassette, screwed it in place and shoved it back into its box. This he returned to its position beneath the layer of coffee grounds. The grounds acted as a kind of olfactory barrier should the boat be searched and sniffer dogs be brought on. They couldn't detect the smell of cocaine through the more pungent odour of coffee.

The crate was re-sealed and loaded. The boat was ready to leave now and two members of its small crew began casting off, one of them pushing the boat away from the quayside with a long boat-hook. The current gradually took hold. The Captain decided not to switch on his engines until they were further away; he was content to let the vessel be carried by the tide.

The men watching from the quayside waited only a moment. Their duty was done now, their responsibility discharged. The shipment was someone else's concern. Not theirs.

They, at least, had ensured that the cocaine shipment was safely on its way.

The first leg of the operation was underway.

Forty-nine

The cleaver swung down with incredible power and accuracy, severing the leg with one clean cut.

It sheared through bone and muscle alike, the strident snapping of the femur reverberating inside the room.

Anne Hopper winced as she looked at the remains of the bullock lying on the large wooden worktop in the prison kitchen. As she watched, the tall thin man in the butcher's apron raised the cleaver once again and lopped off another part of the leg.

There were other men in the chill room, all dressed in white overalls. Some of them were spattered with blood from the carcases that hung on a row of meat-hooks nearby.

'The man with the cleaver,' said Reginald Fairham quietly, cupping his hand conspiratorially around his mouth. 'He isn't a prisoner, is he?'

Nicholson turned and looked at the other man contemptuously.

'You maintain that the prisoners here are worthy of trust, don't you, Mr Fairham?' Nicholson said. 'Some of them have to work in the kitchens.'

Fairham swallowed hard as he saw another portion of the carcase cut away by a powerful blow.

'As a matter of fact the man with the cleaver is one of the warders here. He was a master butcher before he joined the service,' Nicholson explained.

Fairham visibly relaxed.

The procession moved through the kitchen, through clouds of steam from several large metal vats of food. Clinton inspected the contents of one of the vats, smiling amiably at the man who was stirring the mass of baked beans. The man looked at Clinton indifferently and peered down into the vat. The MP moved on, rejoining his colleagues.

The procession moved through the prison at a leisurely pace, Nicholson answering the visitors' questions with the minimum of elaboration, constantly struggling to hide his contempt for some of the more idiotic queries they presented him with.

What did he think the effects of overcrowding were?

How many men took advantage of the educational courses?

How were prisoner and warder relationships? Nicholson remained slightly ahead of his group so that they could never quite see the expression of disdain of his face. He led them

196

along corridors and walkways until they came to a double set of metal-barred gates.

The warder on the other side, at a signal from the Governor, pressed a button and the doors slid open with a faint electronic burr.

Nicholson led them through to another solid steel gate. This one was unlocked by a warder with a key. As he pushed it open a powerful gust of wind swept in from outside. Led by the Governor, they stepped out into the exercise yard. It stretched around them in all four directions, empty, enclosed by high wire mesh fences.

'How much exercise do the prisoners get?' Clinton wanted to know.

'An hour a day,' Nicholson said, leading them across the yard.

'It isn't long enough,' Fairham observed, looking round the empty expanse of concrete.

Anne Hopper noticed the chapel.

She pointed towards the graveyard beside it and the markers on the handful of graves.

Nicholson explained what they were. How the men buried there had no families, no other place to lie.

'It's a wonder there aren't more of them,' Fairham said.

'It's a *pity* there aren't more of them,' Nicholson rasped under his breath.

'Mr Nicholson,' Paul Merrick said, brushing loose strands of wispy hair from his face, 'you said you were going to show us some kind of answer to the problems of overcrowding. May I ask when?'

Nicholson glared at him.

'Now, Mr Merrick,' he said, the knot of muscles at the side of his jaw throbbing angrily.

The hospital block was ahead of them.

Nicholson looked up at the grey stone building. It was as dull as the overcast sky. The gaunt edifice appeared to have dropped from the heavens, a lump of the bleak sky fallen to earth inside the prison grounds.

'What's that?' asked Fairham, pointing at a rusted grille set in the concrete close by the wall of the hospital wing. The grille was about a foot square.

'It's one of the vents over the sewer shaft,' Nicholson explained.

'Hardly hygienic, is it?' Fairham noted. 'So close to the hospital.'

'This prison, as you know, is very old,' the Governor explained. 'The whole place is dotted with vents like that. A network of sewer tunnels runs under the prison. It isn't used now and most of it is blocked off. There's no danger to health from the outlets.'

As they neared the entrance to the wing, Nicholson slowed his pace imperceptibly. He looked up one last time at the grey edifice, licking dry lips.

Those inside had been given their instructions.

He just hoped to God they had followed them.

Fifty

It was smaller than a man's thumb nail and Nicholson held it between the thumb and finger of his right hand with surprising delicacy.

The microchip was square and the entire complex structure was encased in smooth plastic. Nicholson laid it on a piece of black velvet that lay on the work top, allowing his visitors to get a better look at the tiny object.

'Is this some kind of joke?' Fairham asked.

'Why should it be?' the Governor asked irritably.

'You promised to show us a way of relieving overcrowding. Is this meant to be *it*?'

'The idea was first perfected in America. A number of states are already using it,' Nicholson declared.

'But that didn't work,' said Fairham.

'Ours is a different system. The microchip is inserted into the gastrocnemius muscle of the prisoner's leg.' He looked at Fairham with scorn. 'The calf muscle, to keep it simple.' He held the other's gaze for a moment then continued. 'The operation takes less than fifteen minutes. It's carried out under local anaesthetic, there is no pain to the prisoner. No side effects.'

'What does it do?' Clinton asked, his eyes fixed on the tiny square.

'Once inside the prisoner's leg it gives off something called a Synch-pulse,' Nicholson said. 'A tiny electrical charge which in turn produces a signal that can be picked up by monitoring equipment here at the prison. It's like a tracking device.'

'What range has it got?' Merrick asked.

'Fifteen miles at the moment,' the Governor told him. 'The modifications that are being made to it will probably increase that range by anything up to thirty miles.'

'And what is the object exactly, Mr Nicholson?' Anne Hopper enquired, looking at the Governor.

'An end to overcrowding, Miss Hopper,' he said. 'The thing you all seem so concerned about.'

'How the hell can that,' Fairham jabbed a finger towards the microchip, 'help with overcrowding?'

'The device is placed in the leg of certain remand prisoners,' Nicholson explained. 'They can then be released from Whitely and monitored on our electronic equipment here. We know where they are twenty-four hours a day.'

'And what if they move outside the range of the tracking device?' Clinton murmured, his eyes still fixed on the device.

'We don't allow that to happen,' Nicholson said. 'The prisoners are picked for the operation according to the severity of their crime. Everything is explained to them, including the fact that if they do travel beyond the range of the device they'll be re-arrested and prosecuted for attempted escape. They usually co-operate. It's in their own interests to do so. Many of them prefer this to being stuck inside for twenty-three hours a day. Some are even working while they're on the outside waiting for their trials.'

'Do I detect a note of compassion in your attitude, Mr Nicholson?' said Fairham, contemptuously. 'You actually sound as if you care about what happens to the men who undergo this operation.'

'It gets them out of *my* hair, Mr Fairham,' the Governor said. 'It means that my officers have fewer prisoners to deal with.'

'How many men has this been tried on so far?' Clinton enquired.

'Ten,' Nicholson said. 'And all of them have been successful.'

'And what is your definition of success, Mr Nicholson?' Anne Hopper wanted to know.

He looked at her impassively.

'Not one of them tried to escape,' he said. 'They all reported to the police station they'd been assigned to and they all went on to stand trial.'

'When is the device removed?' Clinton asked.

200

'As soon as the trial is over.'

Clinton stood back and nodded, looking at the microchip then at Nicholson.

'Well, I must say I'm impressed, Mr Nicholson,' said the MP.

'Me too,' Merrick echoed. 'It seems a great step forward.'

Fairham merely prodded the device with one index finger.

'Who does the operations?' he wanted to know.

'There are a number of doctors involved,' Nicholson told him. 'None resident at the prison.'

'That's a pity,' Anne Hopper intoned. 'It would have been interesting to meet them.'

'The work is still in its infancy, Miss Hopper. They're not too anxious to be put in the limelight just yet,' Nicholson told her.

'Why? In case something goes wrong?' Fairham said, challengingly.

'As I said, the work is still relatively new. Until it's completely perfected we'd rather keep it quiet,' the Governor said, glaring once again at the other man.

'I can understand that,' Clinton said, smiling. 'It seems to be successful though, Mr Nicholson. Full marks to you. We'll be reporting this as very satisfactory progress when we return to Whitehall.'

'Satisfactory?' Fairham snapped. 'This man is using remand prisoners as human guinea pigs and you call that satisfactory?'

'I think you're being a little over-dramatic, Mr Fairham,' Clinton said, smiling patronisingly.

'It is preferable to the alternative of being locked up twenty-three hours out of twenty-four,' Merrick echoed.

Nicholson smiled triumphantly at Fairham.

'What is your view, Miss Hopper?' the Governor wanted to know.

The woman shrugged slightly.

'I suppose I would have to agree with Mr Clinton and Mr Merrick,' she said. 'As long as the patients are volunteers and the risks are explained to them before the operation, I can see no objection myself.'

'You appear to be out-voted again, Mr Fairham,' Nicholson said, smiling.

'I'd like to know a little more about the actual mechanics of the project,' Clinton said. 'How the tracking devices are built, what the operation entails, how the prisoners are monitored. That kind of thing. I will have to make a report to the House, you understand?'

Nicholson nodded, his ingratiating smile spreading.

'Certainly. If you'd like to come back to my office we can discuss it there,' he said, looking at Fairham.

The other man was flushed with anger.

The Governor turned to lead the small procession out.

'We've only seen a small part of the hospital wing,' Fairham observed. 'I'd like to inspect the facilities here before we leave.'

Nicholson retained his air of calm.

'Of course,' he said, leading them towards a door at one end of the room. It opened out into the infirmary. There were half a dozen prisoners in the beds; other men in white overalls moved among them, performing their duties. One was mopping the floor, another dispensing pills. A third man was pushing a trolley, collecting dirty laundry. Patients and workers alike gave the Governor and his visitors only cursory glances. More lingering looks were reserved for Anne Hopper.

A warder stood at one end of the infirmary, standing by a thick metal door.

Nicholson looked towards him, hoping that none of the visitors noticed the look of apprehension on his face.

He stood back as the visitors moved among the men, speaking to them where possible, usually meeting with only perfunctory grunts in answer to their questions. The Governor caught the eye of the warder at the far end of the infirmary and the man nodded almost imperceptibly. A silent answer to an unasked question. The Governor licked his lips, aware that they were once more dry.

Come on, hurry up and get out of here.

One by one the visitors returned to join him.

They're not going to ask.

Fairham looked to the far end of the infirmary.

'What's through there?' he asked, pointing at the door.

'The morgue,' Nicholson said quickly. 'It's where we keep any prisoners who die until they've been identified, or until arrangements can be made for their burial.'

Fairham nodded slowly.

Come on, come on.

'I think we've seen enough now, Mr Nicholson,' Clinton said.

Fairham was still gazing at the door.

The Governor licked his lips again.

'We'll go back to my office, then,' he said.

At last Fairham tore his gaze away and filed out in front of Nicholson. The Governor glanced back at the solitary warder and nodded.

As he walked out he let out a sigh of relief.

He would return here as soon as the delegation was gone. For now, at least, it was still safe.

Fifty-one

Coffee dripped from the bottom of the cup as DI Frank Gregson lifted it to his mouth and took a sip. It was strong. He pulled the lid from one of the other milk cartons and poured in the contents, stirring until the dark colour lightened.

Opposite him DS Stuart Finn was smoking a Marlboro, blowing out streams of smoke, alternately gazing into the depths of his tea cup and glancing out of the window.

The neon lights outside were barely visible through the sheen of condensation coating the inside of the café window. The film of steam combined with the patina of dirt on the glass made them almost opaque. Inside the café there were half a dozen other people. At a table in the corner three young girls sat, smoking and chatting quietly, occasionally glancing across at the two policemen.

Two men sat at a table near the counter, one of them pushing huge forkfuls of food into his mouth, the other sipping at a cup of tea.

Another man sat alone at the table next to them, peering at a magazine. Finn noted that he was tracing a column of names and addresses with the tip of his pen, occasionally ringing one with the biro.

The place smelled of fried food and damp.

Finn stubbed out a cigarette in an already overflowing ash-tray and immediately lit another. He noticed that he was almost out of them and fumbled in his jacket pocket for some change to feed into the cigarette machine. On the radio in the background, a voice announced that it was 9.30.

'It's weird, isn't it?' said Finn. 'How all these places start to look alike after a while.'

Gregson shrugged.

'The cafés, the bars, the clip-joints,' Finn continued. 'In the bookshops, too, there's something familiar about them, every one of them. Even the same punters, it seems.' He chuckled. 'I was flicking through a couple of magazines at that last place.' He smiled. 'More cunts than a meeting of the Arsenal supporters' club.' The DS shook his head, still grinning.

Gregson didn't return the smile. He merely sipped at his strong coffee and ran a hand through his hair.

'Yeah, the places look familiar and the answers are starting to *sound* familiar, too,' he said wearily. 'No, never seen him. Never *heard* anything. Didn't *see* anything.'

'I wonder if any of the other blokes are having better luck.'

'Are you serious? This whole fucking area is sewn up tighter than a nun's crotch,' Gregson grunted.

'Then why are we here?'

'Because it's our job.'

Finn sucked gently on his cigarette and looked across the table at Gregson, who was peering through the window into the street beyond.

'You knew it was going to be like this, Frank,' he said. 'You knew that no one around here was going to help us. Why call a search in the first place?'

'Procedure,' Gregson told him.

'Bullshit,' Finn said, smiling thinly. 'What do you know?'

'I know that we should be asking questions instead of sitting on our arses drinking cups of tea,' the DI told him, pushing his half-empty cup away.

205

'Come on, tell me the truth,' Finn persisted. 'You owe me that. We've been working together long enough. If I had a hunch or an idea about these killings *I'd* tell *you*.'

Gregson smiled thinly.

'The idea I had was crazy,' he said slowly. 'Illogical. Impossible, even. I checked it out. You remember I said to you that the only thing any witnesses could agree on about the first bloke who killed himself was his staring eyes?'

Finn nodded.

'I checked the files, because that rung a bell somewhere. We arrested a bloke called Peter Lawton for a series of armed robberies. Remember me telling you?'

'Yes, I do,' said the DS 'He's banged up, though, isn't he?'

'In Whitely Prison in Derbyshire. Yeah. He has been for the last six years.'

Finn looked vague.

'The second killer, the one who murdered the girl, I checked out his MO because that sounded familiar, too.'

'And?'

'It matched with the MO of a guy called Mathew Bryce who was also arrested over eighteen months ago. He's doing time in Whitely as well. What conclusions can you draw from that?'

Finn shrugged.

'That someone copied them,' he said.

'Or that they both escaped and duplicated the crimes they were originally arrested for.' Gregson smiled when he saw the look on Finn's face. 'See why I didn't mention it before? It's fucking crazy. We know they didn't escape because we would have heard, the whole country would have heard. They're still inside Whitely.' The phrase on both the files he'd read re-surfaced in his mind. *Term being served*. 'But if someone imitated the crimes committed by Lawton and Bryce, what's to stop somebody *else* imitating

206

murders committed by *any* killer locked up in *any* jail in the country?'

'That still doesn't explain why they torched themselves,' Finn observed.

Gregson shrugged.

'On that point,' he said, 'your guess is as good as mine.' The DI got to his feet and headed for the door. The other occupants of the café watched him go. Finn left some money for the tea and coffee on the table, then fed change into the cigarette machine and pulled a packet out. He joined his superior at the door, pulling up the collar of his jacket as they stepped out into the street.

'Where to next?' he said, cupping his hand around the Marlboro he was trying to light.

'Over there,' said Gregson, nodding in the direction of the neon-shrouded building opposite.

The lights formed the word 'Loveshow'.

Fifty-two

'Scotty. Police.'

Zena Murray emphasised the last word with distaste, stepping back to allow the two plain clothes men into Jim Scott's office. Gregson was the first in and he looked across at Scott indifferently as Finn entered, smiling thinly by way of a greeting.

'What can I do for you?' Scott wanted to know. 'The licence is in order, we haven't had any trouble on the premises and, as far as I know, my boss is bunging the back-handers in the right places. So, what can I help you with?'

'A comedian, eh?' said Gregson, flatly. 'Everyone's a fucking comic when the law arrive, aren't they?' The two men locked stares for a moment. 'You're Jim Scott, right? Manager of this . . . place?'

Scott nodded.

'Ray Plummer owns it, doesn't he?' Finn added, looking around the office.

'Actually it's a tax dodge for the Prime Minister,' Scott said smugly. 'What does it matter?'

'Look, Scott, we don't want to *be* here any more than you *want* us to be here,' Gregson told him. 'If I wanted to wade around in shit I'd go for a walk down a sewer. We just want to ask you a few questions and get out. We've already spoken to your staff. The quicker you answer our questions the quicker we'll be out of your hair.'

Scott glanced at each of the policemen in turn, then motioned to the chairs close to his desk.

'Have a seat,' he offered.

'No thanks,' said Gregson, wrinkling his nose.

'It's no problem, I can get it disinfected afterwards,' Scott told him.

Gregson met the other man's gaze and pulled a small photograph from the inside pocket of his jacket. He dropped it on to the desk in front of Scott who picked it up, studying the outlines of Paula Wilson's face.

'That girl was killed a couple of streets away from here the night before last. Have you seen her around here before?' the DI wanted to know.

'We don't get many girls coming in here as spectators,' Scott said, tossing the photo back across the desk.

'She might have come in with a boyfriend. This is supposed to be a show for *couples* to watch too, isn't it?' Gregson observed.

'Never seen her. I'm usually in here. I don't go out front much.'

'This is the nerve centre, is it?' Gregson said, smiling, scornfully. 'Where all the big decisions are taken?'

'I told you, I don't know the girl. I can't help you. Why don't you piss off? And don't forget to shut the door on your way out.' Scott sat down at his desk and turned his attention to the ledger he had before him.

'How many staff have you got here?' Finn asked.

'It varies. Between six and eight,' Scott told him.

'And you're in charge of all of them?' Gregson said with mock respect. 'What it must be to have responsibility, eh?'

Scott glared at the DI.

'I don't remember you showing me any fucking ID,' he snapped.

Both men flipped open the thin leather wallets they carried. Scott gazed at the photos, then at their faces.

'Satisfied?' said Gregson.

Scott nodded.

'Yours is a better likeness,' he said to the DI, a smile flickering on his lips. 'You look a miserable cunt in the picture, too.'

Gregson held his stare for a moment, a smile forming at the corners of his own mouth.

'I'm surprised I don't know you,' he said quietly. 'Geezers like you usually have form, or has Plummer been recruiting *up-market*?'

Scott merely glared at the DI. The heavy atmosphere was finally interrupted by Finn, heading towards the door.

'Come on, Frank,' he said wearily. 'Let's get out of here. He doesn't know anything and we've got other places to check.'

209

The DS actually had his hand on the door handle when it was turned.

He stepped back a pace, smiling broadly as he saw the young woman who stood before him, looking slightly surprised. She returned his smile as she stepped inside the office, glancing across at Scott's desk. Gregson eyed her disinterestedly.

'They're coppers, Carol,' Scott told her. 'Here to ask some questions,' he sneered.

'Another member of your staff?' Finn enquired. He showed Carol his ID as he spoke. She looked at him again but this time there was no smile on her face.

'Questions about what?' she wanted to know.

Never taking his eyes from her, Gregson slipped out the photo of Paula Wilson and quickly explained the reason for his and Finn's presence, enquiring whether or not the face in the monochrome picture rang any bells.

It didn't.

'Happy now?' Scott asked, noticing that Gregson was still gazing at Carol.

Stop staring, you bastard.

'Well, well,' said the DI, smiling thinly. 'Long time no see, eh, Carol?'

Scott glared at the policeman then at Carol.

What the fuck is this?

'How long's it been now?' Gregson continued. 'Two years?'

She looked at him through narrowed eyes.

'How the hell do you know him?' Scott wanted to know, unable to contain his anger.

'We met on a professional basis,' said Gregson, his smile broadening. 'I arrested her for soliciting.' He allowed his gaze to travel slowly up and down her shapely body. 'No wonder

210

you were doing such good business,' he said. 'You still look good.'

Scott clenched his fists until his nails dug into the palms of his hands.

Carol didn't answer. Like some naughty child who's been caught playing a prank she just kept her head low, staring at the floor.

'Maybe I'll see you again,' the DI said as he and Finn reached the door.

'Just get out,' hissed Scott.

They closed the door and were gone.

Scott brought his hand crashing down on the desk top, his face pale with rage, the vein at his temple throbbing.

'Did you recognise him when you walked in?' he demanded.

'Jim, that was in the past,' she said. 'Besides, it's nothing to do with you. It was my problem.'

'How did he catch you? Had you fucked him before he lifted you?' There was a stinging vehemence in Scott's words.

Carol looked angrily at him, turned and headed for the door.

Scott shot out a hand and grabbed her by the shoulder, spinning her round.

'Had you?' he roared.

She struck him hard across the left cheek with the flat of her hand.

'Get off me,' she shouted.

Scott moved a pace towards her, his face stinging from the blow, his eyes bulging wide.

'You don't own me, Jim,' she hissed, her voice faltering slightly as she saw the look of pure rage etched across his features. She opened the office door. 'You don't own me.'

She slammed it behind her and walked away hurriedly, her heart beating madly against her ribs.

Inside the office Scott touched the cheek she had slapped, his breath still coming in gasps.

'Bitch,' he hissed, turning back to his desk. He found the bottle of Southern Comfort and poured himself a large measure. His breathing gradually slowed as he propped himself against one edge of the desk, drinking. Again he touched his cheek, but this time he felt no anger, merely a deep sorrow.

One thought surfaced in his mind.

Would she forgive him?

Outside in the street Finn lit up another cigarette and looked at his watch.

'Where to next?' he said, pulling up the collar of his jacket.

Gregson didn't answer; he was staring at the doorway of 'Loveshow'.

'Frank. I said, where next?' the DS repeated, blowing out a stream of smoke and looking at his companion. 'Hello, is there anyone in there?'

Gregson looked impassively at his colleague.

'Something on your mind?' Finn asked.

'You could say that,' Gregson told him vaguely. He started walking and Finn followed.

'You're fucking weird sometimes, Frank, you know that?' he said. 'Who was that tart, anyway?'

'I said, I arrested her a couple of years ago,' Gregson muttered.

'You were right, she's good-looking. I'm not surprised you remember her.' The DS chuckled.

Gregson merely continued walking.

He remembered her all right.

Fifty-three

Ray Plummer looked at his watch, checking the time against the clock on the marble mantelpiece.

11.24 p.m.

He crossed to his drinks cabinet and poured himself another large measure of whisky, glancing at the phone every few seconds as if willing it to ring.

Perhaps it was a wind-up, he thought. There would be no phone call from the mysterious informant. The whole fucking scheme was somebody pissing him about.

Wasn't it?

He downed what was left in his glass and thought about pouring himself another. He looked at the phone again. What if the caller rang and couldn't be bothered to hold on?

Someone pissing about.

It was a hell of an elaborate plan just for a wind-up.

Could it be true about the twenty million?

He crossed to the drinks cabinet once more and tipped the bottle.

The phone rang.

Plummer spun round, almost dropping the bottle and his glass. Whisky slopped onto his hand as he hurried to pick up the receiver.

'Hello,' he said.

Cool it. Don't let the bastard think you're too interested.

'Ray?' said the voice.

First name terms, now, eh?

'Yes. What have you got for me?'

'Ray, are you okay?'

Plummer frowned.

There was something wrong here.

'Who *is* this?' he said, some of the tension leaving his voice.

'It's Jim Scott. What's wrong?'

Plummer exhaled deeply and gripped the receiver tightly in his hand.

'What the fuck do you want?' he snapped.

'We've had the law round here tonight,' Scott told him. 'That girl who was killed the other night, they've been checking the area.'

'Some girl was killed, was she?' Plummer muttered irritably. 'Jim, I couldn't give a toss if the Queen Mum has been gang banged.' The anger returned to his voice. 'I'm waiting for a very important call. Get off the line, will you?'

'I just thought you should know,' Scott said. 'They spoke to all the staff here. I know everything is covered with the running of the club, but I didn't think you'd be too happy about the Old Bill sticking its nose in.'

'I couldn't care less, get off the fucking line,' shouted Plummer and slammed the receiver down.

He stepped away from the phone, angry with Scott for disturbing him but also angry with himself for being so jumpy. He'd been in the penthouse flat since about nine that evening, trying to watch TV, trying to listen to music but with no success. All he could think about was the impending phone call. *If* it came. John Hitch had seemed convinced that it would and Plummer trusted the instincts of his colleague almost as he trusted his own. And yet.

214

11.36.

Fuck it. No one was calling, he thought.

He's six minutes late. That's all. Six lousy minutes.

He turned his back on the phone.

The strident ringing startled him again, but this time he turned slowly, gazing at the phone.

Plummer finally plucked up the receiver.

'Where the fuck were you?' the voice rasped. 'I said I'd ring at half past. Your phone was engaged.'

'What am I supposed to do, apologise?' Plummer snapped. 'Say what you've got to say.'

'It's on.'

'What's on?'

'The shipment is on its way, you stupid cunt. What do you think I mean?' the voice hissed.

Plummer gripped the receiver tightly.

'Listen . . .'

The caller cut him short.

'No, *you* listen. Perhaps you have a pen and paper with you, or will you be able to remember what I'm going to tell you?'

'Get on with it.'

'The shipment of cocaine will arrive two days from now. It's going to be on board a small boat called *The Sandhopper*. The coke will be in among a load of porn mags and videos, right?'

'Where is it being unloaded?' Plummer wanted to know.

'Chelsea Bridge.'

'What about that warehouse in Tilbury that Connelly bought? You said it was going to be there.'

'I never said that. I told you Connelly had bought a warehouse. I never said for sure that's where the stuff would arrive.'

'Chelsea Bridge,' Plummer murmured, more to himself than the caller.

'Yeah. The drop is scheduled for two in the morning. There'll be a lorry waiting to pick the stuff up. It'll look like a refrigerated lorry carrying beer.'

'How many of Connelly's men are involved?' Plummer wanted to know.

'I'm not sure.'

'How the fuck are they going to get the stuff up the Thames without the river police tumbling them?'

'What am I, an information service? That's your problem. That's all I've got to say now. I won't call again. Things are starting to get dangerous now.'

He hung up.

Plummer replaced the receiver slowly, massaging his chin thoughtfully with his other hand.

He was about to phone John Hitch when there was a knock on the door.

Plummer swallowed hard and froze for long seconds.

The knock came again, harder, more insistent.

He moved stealthily to the bedroom, to the wardrobe close to his bed. There was a small safe in the bottom which he hurriedly opened.

Plummer pulled the Delta Elite 10mm automatic from inside the safe and slid one magazine into the butt. He worked the slide as quietly as he could, chambering a round, then he moved back out into the sitting room towards the door.

The knock came again.

'Yeah, all right, I'm coming,' he called, unlocking the door with infinite slowness. He left the chain on, the words of the caller flashing into his mind:

Things are starting to get dangerous.

Precisely *how* dangerous, Plummer was about to find out.

216

He turned the door handle slowly, the automatic gripped in his fist, held high so that he could swing it down into a firing position if necessary.

He opened the door, allowing it to reach only the length of the chain.

The Delta Elite was ready as he peered through the gap.

His voice was coloured with surprise as he gazed at the newcomer.

'What are *you* doing here?'

Fifty-four

Plummer slid the chain free, allowing the door to open wider.

Carol Jackson stepped inside.

'What's wrong?' Plummer wanted to know, closing the door behind her and slipping the bolts once more. He saw her expression of surprise as she noticed the automatic gripped in his hand. Plummer lowered the weapon, easing the hammer forward and slipping on the safety catch. He laid the pistol down and crossed to the drinks cabinet, pouring glasses of whisky for himself and for Carol. He thought how tired she looked. She took the glass from him and drank.

'Why the gun?' she wanted to know.

'It doesn't matter,' he said. 'Just tell me why you're here.'

'Do I need a reason?' she asked, slipping off her coat and sitting down. She perched on the edge of the sofa, gazing into the mock flames from the gas fire.

Plummer ran a hand over his hair then stood beside her, touching her cheek with the back of his hand. It was an aberrant gesture but she reached up and touched his hand all the same.

'The law were in tonight, then?' he said.

'How do you know?' she asked.

'Scott told me.'

She looked up at him, her eyes filled with surprise and something more.

Fear?

'Scott's been here?'

Plummer explained about the phone call.

'He's going to kill us, Ray,' she said flatly.

It was Plummer's turn to look surprised.

'What the fuck are you talking about?' he gaped.

'I was with him the other night and some of the things he was saying, I know that if he found out about us . . .' She allowed the sentence to trail off.

'I thought you weren't seeing him any more.'

'I was going to finish it, but it's not that easy, Ray.' She recounted the conversation she'd had with Scott, telling Plummer about the gun. 'He'd do it, I know he would.'

'You're overreacting,' Plummer told her.

'I'm scared of him,' she blurted. 'And I think *you* should be, too.'

Plummer took a sip of his drink and wandered across to the window, peering out into the night.

'Mind you, he always was a bit unpredictable,' he murmured. 'You didn't tell him you were seeing me, did you?'

'I'm not stupid, Ray,' she said.

Plummer smiled thinly and rolled the glass between his hands.

'So what do you want me to do about it?' he asked. 'If we stopped seeing each other that would solve the problem, wouldn't it?'

'It's Scott I want to stop seeing, not you,' she told him.

It's your money I want.

'So stop seeing him.'

'I told you, it's not that easy,' she said irritably. 'He won't take no for an answer, I know he won't.'

'Why the fuck did you get involved with him in the first place?' Plummer wanted to know. 'You knew what he was like, didn't you?'

'I knew he thought a lot of me. I didn't think he was so obsessed.'

Plummer laughed.

'That's a bit strong, isn't it?' he chuckled.

'You don't know him, Ray,' she said. 'What I've told you is true. He's dangerous.'

Plummer peered into the bottom of his glass, as if seeking inspiration there.

'If he's dead he's no threat,' Plummer said, looking at her with cold eyes.

Carol looked puzzled.

'Do you want him taken care of? Put to sleep?' Plummer enquired.

'Killed?'

He shrugged.

'Jesus Christ, is that your only answer, Ray? Have him killed? That isn't what I want.'

'It sounds like you think more of him than you're letting on. You either want him out of your life or you don't.'

'I don't want him *killed.*'

'Still feel something for him?' Plummer enquired. 'Or won't your conscience allow it?' He smiled thinly. 'What do you want to do for the rest of your life, Carol? Hang around with a nobody like Scott, knowing you never dare leave him in case the mad fucker tries to kill you? From the sound of it he'd blow you away without a second thought. And he's supposed to love you.'

Carol could feel the tears welling up in her eyes. She wiped them away with the back of one trembling hand.

'What *do* you want?' Plummer continued.

'I want to get away,' she said, her voice cracking. 'From Scott, from that fucking club, from that whole lifestyle.'

'And how do you expect to do that?' he said flatly. 'It's all you know. It's all you *have* known.'

'What about you and me?' she said tearfully. 'Isn't there anything between us?'

Plummer smiled a predatory smile and crossed to the sofa, seating himself beside her. He put down his drink then took her in his arms, holding her tight. He could feel her tears staining his shirt.

'It's okay, sweetheart,' he said quietly. 'We'll take care of it. I said I'd look after you, didn't I?'

She snaked her arms around his neck, pulling him closer. Her body was racked by sobs, muffled as she pressed her head against his chest.

'Don't worry about Scott,' he said, glancing across at the Delta Elite lying on the table. 'I'll take care of everything.'

Before he comes after me.

'I don't want him hurt, Ray. Please,' she insisted, her cheeks tear-stained.

'Don't let him think there's anything wrong,' Plummer told her. 'Carry on seeing him for the time being. Until the time's right.' He looked into her face. 'All right?'

She nodded slowly.

'I don't want him hurt,' she repeated.

Plummer smiled.

'Trust me,' he whispered, pulling her close. His eyes settled on the automatic once again.

The night sky was full of rain clouds, swollen and ready to spill their load on the city below. Clouds which made the blackness all the more impenetrable. A tenebrous gloom which had prevented Plummer from seeing anything except the lights from other buildings nearby and his own reflection in the window of the flat.

Even if he had been aware of the presence, the darkness would have prevented him seeing the man who watched his flat.

Fifty-five

There were rumours of snow on the way and, as Governor Peter Nicholson made his way across the exercise yard of Whitely Prison, he could believe them. The wind was cutting across the open space at great speed, so cold it seemed to penetrate his bones. As he turned a corner it was like being hit in the face by a handful of razor blades.

If it snowed, as was threatened, there was every possibility that Whitely would be cut off. It had happened twice before in his time as Governor. Once, in the winter of 1983, the snow had drifted up to ten feet around the prison walls; teams of prisoners working virtually round the clock had been unable to keep open the single road that linked Whitely with the outside world. No food had got through and the men had been put on half-rations. There had been rumblings about a riot, but Nicholson had received the warnings with little fear. His men were well equipped to deal with any such eventualities. There were small stock-piles of tear gas in the prison to be used in the event of riots or large scale disturbances and Nicholson would have had no compunction about using them.

It transpired that the snow went as quickly as it had come, the road was opened and supplies began getting through regularly again. Possible chaos had been averted.

Two years ago the same thing had happened, but for a shorter time. If anything, though, the more recent incident had proved more damaging. Prisoners, unable to exercise outside in sub-zero temperatures, had been allowed longer in the recreation rooms. Inevitably, men pushed together for long periods of time became edgy and, by the time the prison was freed from the grip of the snow, three men had been knifed (one of whom had lost a kidney) and another had been beaten severely with a pool cue.

Nicholson wondered, if the snow came, what he could expect *this* time.

He glanced to his left and saw the prison chapel, the weather-vane spinning madly in the powerful breeze. The skeletal trees in the graveyard rattled their branches in the wind, bowing almost to touch the ground as the breeze battered them.

Ahead of him was the hospital wing, the familiar grey of the stonework matching the colour of the sky. Nicholson entered, feeling the warmth immediately. He paused by one of the radiators to warm his hands before approaching the doors that led into the infirmary.

Inside, the wind rattled windows in their frames. One or two heads turned to look at him as he strode through, glancing at the occupants of the place.

A man who'd been scalded in the kitchens by cooking oil. Another, who'd been injured in a brawl during exercise, sported fifty-eight stitches from the point of his chin to the corner of his left eye. When he left the infirmary he was due to spend two weeks in solitary. His assailant was already there.

Another man had his leg in plaster, recovering from a broken ankle. He regarded Nicholson coldly as the Governor passed by.

A man in white overalls was busy collecting dirty bed sheets and towels, pushing the excrement – and blood-stained linen into a trolley he was wheeling up and down the ward. He stepped to one side as Nicholson approached him but made sure that he left a sheet soaked with urine dangling from the trolley, hoping that Nicholson would brush against it.

He didn't.

Ahead of him, the guard at the locked door stood up as Nicholson nodded. The warder found the key he sought, unlocked the door and allowed Nicholson through.

The ward beyond was empty but for ten beds, only one of which was occupied.

There were no windows in the walls, the only light being provided by the banks of fluorescents set high in the ceiling. Walls and floors were of the same uniform grey.

The one bed that was occupied was at the far end of the ward. As Nicholson headed towards it his shoes beat out a tattoo on the polished floor.

There was a man standing over the patient looking down at the face completely encased in bandages. The man held a clipboard he was scribbling on. He was tall, his hair grey, his features wrinkled. His cheeks were sunken and the onset of years had given him heavy jowls.

He turned to face Nicholson as the Governor drew closer. Nicholson thought that he looked vaguely pleased to see him; a small smile hovered on his dry lips.

'Can you spare me some time?' said Nicholson.

Dr Robert Dexter nodded.

Fifty-six

The years had not been kind to Robert Dexter. The lines in his face had deepened into clearly defined wrinkles. The flesh of his forehead looked like pastry after someone has drawn a fork across it. He sighed and looked at Nicholson.

'Any progress?' the Governor said, nodding towards the man in the bed.

'I was just about to look,' Dexter said, his voice low and guttural.

With that he reached into the pocket of his white overall and took out a small pair of scissors. He cut the bandages close to the man's chin and began slowly unravelling them, pausing every now and then to lift the man's head. All that was visible was a small gap for his nose; the rest of his head was completely encased in gauze. Dexter continued with his task.

'If that delegation had got inside here the other day, you and *I* would be locked up in here,' said Nicholson.

'Does that bother you?' Dexter said.

'It's a chance we were both prepared to take. We both knew the risks,' Nicholson said.

'What did they think of the electronic tagging idea?' Dexter wanted to know, still unwinding bandages.

'They liked it. Needless to say, I didn't mention our other little venture.'

'You won't be able to keep it secret forever,' Dexter exclaimed. 'Besides, secrecy wasn't my aim. Once the technique has been perfected there'll be no need to hide the truth.'

'And how do you propose to announce your findings, Dexter? By showing the world an example of your work?' He nodded in the direction of the man in the bed. The first layer of bandages was off. Dexter began on the next one.

'When it works, it'll be nothing to be ashamed of. It's what I've been working towards for most of my professional life,' the doctor said defensively.

'The world might applaud your achievement but I doubt if it will condone your methods,' Nicholson said, taking his eyes from the bandaged man to look momentarily at Dexter. 'Brain operations on convicted murderers.' He smiled. 'It'll be interesting to see how the Home Office reacts to that.'

'It was you who allowed me to work here; why do you ridicule me?'

Nicholson held up his hands.

'No offence meant.' He smiled again. 'I'm happy for you to do your work here.'

'It doesn't seem to bother you that it hasn't been altogether successful so far.'

Nicholson shrugged.

'I sometimes wonder if you realise what this work actually means, Nicholson. An end to man's violent tendencies . . . An end by the insertion of a device constructed and perfected by me.'

'Don't lecture me, Dexter.'

'If this work is successful it could mean an end to places like Whitely. An end to violence.'

'You're starting to sound like a refugee from a bad horror film. The role of mad scientist doesn't suit you.'

'What the hell is mad about wanting to stop violence?'

'Because it's a wasted dream,' hissed Nicholson. 'If you believe you can stop violence by your surgery, *you're* crazy. You've seen some of the men in here; you know what they're capable of. How can you hope to stop that with technology? I find the twisted nobility of your scheme rather amusing, all the same,' he added sardonically.

'You don't care whether it works or not, do you?' Dexter said. 'You never have. If the men die as a result of the surgery you don't care.'

'They're murderers. If we still had the death penalty they'd be hanged anyway. *You've* become the executioner, Dexter. All you're doing is carrying out a sentence that the courts no longer have the power to impose. *That's* what I agree with. Not the ethics behind your work.'

'And what about the ones who've survived? It was you who allowed me to release them. If they'd been traced back to here, it would have been your responsibility.'

'We've been fortunate, so far,' the Governor said, looking down at the man lying in the bed.

Dexter was pulling the last layer of bandages away, using the scissors to snip off any loose pieces, exposing the face beneath. Only the bandages around his scalp remained. Slowly Dexter began to loosen those, too.

'What makes you think you can succeed now, when you couldn't all those years before?' Nicholson wanted to know. 'You were using surgery on your patients in the asylum.'

'When I was working in Bishopsgate I was using a different method,' Dexter explained. 'My colleague and I thought we

226

could stop patients' psychotic tendencies by *removing* the parts of the brain responsible for triggering violence. I now know that was wrong.' He pulled more bandages away. 'Inserting the device inside the brain, actually placing it *in* the lateral ventricle ensures that the chemical is evenly spread around the brain.'

He pulled the last piece of bandage away, revealing the bald dome of his subject's head.

There was a thin cut running around the skull, stitched in several places but held, in others, by several aluminium clips fixed to the skull like large staples holding the cranium shut.

'Good morning, Dr Frankenstein,' said Nicholson, smiling.

Dexter didn't appreciate the joke.

He took a scalpel from the pocket of his jacket and slipped the plastic sheath off its sharp blade. Then with infinite care, he loosened two of the clips, sliding the tip of the scalpel into the incision in the scalp.

As he applied pressure to the blade, a portion of the skull about the size of a ten pence piece came free. Beneath, the greyish-white brain was clearly visible, criss-crossed by countless tiny blood vessels. The brain was throbbing rhythmically, looking as if it was trying to well up out of the hole in the scalp. In the centre of the pulsing greyness was a gleaming object only millimetres square.

'When hormone levels in the blood rise, due to anger or aggression, the device releases an artificial chemical which neutralises other bodily fluids like adrenalin,' Dexter explained. 'It's like a warning system. As soon as the patient feels anger, the device releases the chemical, calming him down again.'

'Why is it placed there?' Nicholson wanted to know. 'I thought the mid-brain controlled sight and hearing.'

'It does, but no area of the brain has yet been identified as controlling reactions like reason. Violent men don't usually stop to reason first. The device is located centrally because the chemical can be distributed more quickly through the brain that way. It also makes the operation easier.' He kept his eyes on the pulsing grey matter.

'You said you used to cut away portions of the brain,' Nicholson said.

'That was useless,' Dexter said. 'I might as well have lobotomised the patients. It stopped them reacting violently because it stopped them reacting *at all*.'

Nicholson raised his eyebrows.

'I don't want to create mindless idiots, that's not my goal. It doesn't benefit them *or* me.'

Nicholson was unimpressed. He stepped away from the bed.

'Is he going to die?' he asked, nodding towards the patient, the brain still throbbing gently through the hole in the skull.

'Does it bother you?'

'Not really. No.'

'He's got as much chance as the others had.'

'If it works, Dexter, if he survives, this time we have to be sure before we go any further. We can't afford any more mistakes. *Either* of us.'

Fifty-seven

Pick it up.

Come on, for Christ's sake. Answer the bloody phone.

Jim Scott drummed his fingers on the table and held the receiver to his ear, irritated by the insistent ringing tone that throbbed inside his head.

He pressed down on the cradle, waited a moment then dialled again.

He listened to the hisses and pops of static as the number connected and the phone rang again.

'Come on,' he murmured under his breath, glancing at his watch, wondering where the hell Carol had got to at 9.40 in the morning. Perhaps she'd gone out to get some shopping, he thought. Perhaps she was in the bath.

Perhaps . . .

Perhaps she knew it was him and she deliberately wasn't answering.

How could she know? He rebuked himself for his stupidity. Anger that she wasn't answering now combined with concern and something approaching desperation in his mind. If only she would pick up the receiver. He needed to hear her voice, needed to speak and to hear *her* speak. Most of all he needed to apologise. In his clumsy, fumbling way he needed to say sorry for what had happened at the club the night before. He shouldn't have grabbed her, shouldn't have shouted at her. She was right, he had no hold over her. He didn't own her.

Pick up the fucking phone.

She had left the previous night without speaking to him, without giving him the chance to say how sorry he was. He'd sat up for most of the night brooding about it, wondering what her reaction to him would be, finally deciding that he couldn't wait until the evening to find out.

He put down the phone, sat staring at it for a moment and then dialled once more.

The ringing tone greeted him.

'Shit,' hissed Scott and slammed it down. He got to his feet and pulled on his jacket, heading for the front door.

He *would* speak to her, no matter what.

The journey took him the better part of an hour, due to delays on the Tube, but now, as he walked from the station, he felt a curious mixture of elation and anxiety.

He was going to see Carol. Not just speak to her, but *see* her. He could tell her face to face how sorry he was for the incident of the previous night. As he walked he wondered if he should have bought her flowers. No. It was enough that he should have taken the trouble to visit her and offer his apologies.

What if she wasn't home?

He would wait for her. If she was out he'd sit on her front step and wait until she returned, or he'd walk around and try again later. He would not leave until he'd seen her.

He rounded a corner, passing three children kicking a football back and forth across the road. The ball bounced near Scott and he trapped it with his left foot, then swivelled and hooked it to one of the young boys with his right, smiling to himself.

The boy, no more than ten, looked at Scott and frowned. 'Flash cunt,' he called as the man walked on.

The kids continued their game.

Scott finally reached the house he sought. He knew that Carol occupied the basement flat. A short flight of stone steps led down to the entrance. Scott paused for a moment, looking up at the house. The paintwork on some of its window frames was blistered and peeling like scabrous skin. A pane of glass in one of the ground-floor flats had been broken, replaced hastily with just a sheet of newspaper held in place by masking tape.

There were tiles missing from the roof. Scott wandered down the short set of steps to Carol's door, noticing that there was a pint of milk on the step.

He banged twice and waited.

No answer.

Perhaps she was still in bed.

He banged again. This time, when he received no answer, he moved across to the window and, cupping one hand over his eyes, endeavoured to see inside the flat. Net curtains prevented his attempted intrusion. He could see nothing.

'Can I help you?'

The voice startled him and he spun round, looking up to see a young woman standing there. She was in her early thirties, dressed in a worn leather jacket and faded jeans. She was carrying a bag of shopping that she kept moving from one hand to the other.

'I live upstairs,' she told him.

'I'm looking for Carol Jackson,' he said, noticing that the woman was running appraising eyes over him. 'I'm a friend of hers. I've been ringing all morning but I couldn't get any answer.'

The woman nodded.

'I should have taken her milk in,' she said. 'I usually do if she doesn't come home.'

Scott frowned.

'She's not here, then?' he exclaimed.

'She didn't come home last night,' the woman told him.

Scott gritted his teeth.

'Where is she?' he demanded.

The woman shrugged.

'I take her milk in, I don't ask her for reports,' she said as Scott started up the steps.

He brushed past her.

'Can I give her a message?' the woman asked. 'I'll probably see her later.'

Scott was already stalking off up the road.

'*I'll* see her later,' he called over his shoulder.

The woman shrugged and made her way into the house.

When he reached the end of the street, Scott turned and looked back towards the house.

Where the hell is she?

Could something have happened to her on the way home last night?

Perhaps she never got home.

The ball the three youngsters were kicking about landed near Scott once more.

If she didn't go home, where the fuck did she go?

'Oi, our ball,' shouted one of the kids.

Scott looked at the lad, then at the ball close to his feet. He lashed out at it and sent it flying down the road, away from the trio of kids.

'You bastard,' one of them shouted as he raced after it.

Scott ignored his insult and continued walking, his face set in hard lines.

Where the hell was she?

Fifty-eight

The shutters were still closed, the door firmly locked. It would be another two hours before Les Gourmets opened for business.

Inside the restaurant the tables were bare but for cloths, all immaculately clean. The staff wouldn't arrive to set them for a while yet. Out in the kitchen preparations were already taking place in readiness for the lunch-time trade. The restaurant always did well at lunch-times, situated as it was in Shepherd Market. It was one of five such establishments owned by Ray Plummer.

Now he sat at one of the tables, cradling a glass of white wine in one hand. With the other he gently stroked his hair.

There were five other men with him. They too had drinks. Plummer put down his glass and reached into his inside pocket for the monogrammed cigarette case. He took one and lit it, looking round at his companions.

'Same voice as the other night, Ray?' said John Hitch, flicking his long blond hair over his shoulders.

Plummer nodded.

'And I still couldn't pin the bastard down,' he complained.

'He says the shipment's coming in by boat?' Terry Morton said.

'*The Sandhopper*, it's called,' Plummer told him. He repeated the other details about the shipment of cocaine, as relayed to him by the mysterious informant the previous night. He sat back when he'd finished and sipped his wine.

'Could it be a set-up?' Joe Perry wanted to know. Perry was a thick-set, bull-necked man who looked as if he'd been eased into his suit with a shoe-horn. The material stretched so tightly across his shoulder blades it threatened to rip. His face was smooth, almost feminine; it looked as if it had never felt the touch of a razor.

Plummer shrugged.

'It could be,' he said.

'It could also be bollocks, couldn't it?' Morton interjected. 'I mean, there might not even *be* a shipment of coke.'

233

'Then why bother phoning?' asked Adrian McCann, rubbing a hand over his close-cropped hair. Over his ears it was completely shaved. 'It's a bit fucking elaborate, isn't it?'

'That's what *I* said,' Plummer agreed. He turned to Hitch. 'You heard the geezer the other night, John; he didn't sound like he was joking, did he?'

Hitch shook his head.

'I agree with Joe,' he added. 'It *could* be a set-up.'

'But by who?' Plummer wanted to know, a note of exasperation in his voice. 'We know it's not another organisation in London, especially not Ralph Connelly's firm.'

'Could it be somebody working for Connelly with an axe to grind?' asked Martin Bates, running his finger around the rim of his glass. Bates was in his early twenties, one of Plummer's youngest employees.

Plummer shrugged.

'Who knows? The point is, do we go with it or not? Do we assume there *is* a shipment? And, if there is, do we knock it over?'

'Are you asking for votes, boss?' Hitch said, laughing.

The other men laughed too. Plummer didn't see the joke and glanced irritably at Hitch, waiting until they calmed down.

'Right, let's assume there *is* a shipment of coke,' he continued. 'Let's say that phone call was kosher. The day after next the shipment is meant to be arriving, *if* the information's right. If it *is* right then the coke is hidden among a load of coffee beans. Now the question is, if this is a set-up, we're going to get hit when we try to take the lorry they're transferring the shit to. How do we get round *that*?'

'Take out the lorry first?' offered Joe Perry.

'No,' Hitch said, smiling. 'We hit it before they even take it off the boat.'

Even Plummer smiled.

'Hijack the fucking boat,' Hitch continued. 'Unload it somewhere else down the river. We have our own lorry waiting. Unload it, pack it away and piss off.'

Plummer slapped him on the shoulder.

'That's what we'll do,' he said. 'Take the shipment while it's still on the river.'

'Like pirates,' chuckled Morton.

The other men laughed.

'Ray, there are some other things to consider,' offered McCann. 'Once we've hit Connelly's shipment, he ain't going to be too happy.'

'I wouldn't be if I'd just lost twenty million,' Plummer said humourlessly. 'What are you getting at? You reckon he might come looking for bother?'

'Wouldn't you?' McCann said.

'He's right, Ray,' Hitch interjected. 'A fucking gang war is the last thing we want.'

'What am I, stupid?' Plummer said. 'There's no need for Connelly to know who turned him over. If it's done properly, and I'm not talking about fucking balaclavas and funny accents, there's no reason why he should know who hit him.' He looked at Hitch. 'I'm leaving that side of it to you, John. Like I said, you got about thirty-six hours.'

Hitch nodded.

'If the worst comes to the worst and he *does* find out, what then?' Perry wanted to know.

'A gang war would be as damaging to Connelly as it would to us. He won't want it,' Plummer said with assurance. 'But if he *does*, he can't win. We're stronger and, for twenty million, I'm bloody sure we're going to be better equipped. Connelly will realise that. He's not stupid.'

'So we go with it, then?' Hitch echoed.

235

Plummer nodded. He reached across and touched Hitch's arm.

'John, I want Jim Scott to drive one of the cars,' he said quietly.

Hitch looked puzzled.

'Scott? He runs one of your clubs, doesn't he? I wouldn't have thought he was the right bloke for this kind of operation,' Hitch said.

'I *want* him involved,' Plummer said, his eyes never leaving Hitch. 'He knows how to handle himself. He'll be all right.'

'I'm sure he will. I just don't know why you want him in on it.'

'I've got my reasons,' Plummer said.

Hitch shrugged.

'I'm sure you have,' he said. 'Okay, I'll tell him. If you want him in, that's fair enough, Ray. You're the boss.'

Plummer smiled.

'Yeah, I *am*.'

Fifty-nine

They were watching him. He was certain of it now.

As the tube pulled into Westminster station Trevor Magee looked directly across the compartment and saw his own reflection in the glass. He tried not to look either left or right. As the doors slid open he glanced at the middle-aged couple who got out but then stared straight ahead again.

The doors remained open for a moment but no other passengers got on.

Magee realised that he was alone apart from the other two. And he knew they were watching him.

The two youths, both in their early twenties, one black, one white, had boarded the train at Gloucester Road station. At first they had sat directly opposite him, but as the train travelled through the subterranean tunnel one of them had moved three seats to his left. The other had moved to the right. Both sat on the opposite row of seats and Magee moved uncomfortably under their gaze. He looked up briefly and saw that the black youth was watching him. He was tall, taller than Magee's six feet, dressed in faded jeans and baseball boots which made his feet look enormous. He had one hand in the pocket of a baggy jacket. The other he was tapping on his right thigh, slapping out a rhythm, perhaps the accompaniment to the tuneless refrain he was humming.

His white companion was also staring at Magee. He too wore baggy jeans and baseball boots, and across his T-shirt the words 'Ski-Club' could be clearly seen. His face was pitted and he needed a shave.

Magee was painfully aware that he was alone in the compartment with the youths. He glanced at the map of the Underground on the panel opposite and saw that they were approaching Embankment Station. He decided to get off.

Would they follow him?

Out of the corner of his eye he could see the white youth had draped one leg over a plastic seat arm and was reclining, his gaze never leaving Magee.

He began to consider the worse possible scenario. If they both came at him at once, from opposite sides, how would he deal with them?

He tried to tell himself he was being ridiculous. He was, after all, thirty-six years old, six feet tall and well built. Should they try anything he should be more than capable of dealing with them. But the doubts persisted.

The black youth got to his feet, standing still for a moment, swaying with the motion of the train, gripping one of the rails overhead for support. Then he began walking towards Magee.

The train was slowing slightly; they must be close to the station.

The youth sat down opposite.

Magee clenched both fists in the pockets of his long leather overcoat. The knot of muscles at the side of his jaw pulsed.

He was ready.

The train eased into the station and he got to his feet, heading for the door, pressing the 'DOOR OPEN' button even before it was illuminated. The orange light flared and he jabbed at it. The door slid open and he stepped out onto the platform, walking quickly towards the exit. Once there he paused and glanced behind him.

There was no one following.

He smiled and hurried to the escalator, scuttling up the moving stairway towards street level, finally emerging into the ticket hall. As he passed through he cast one last glance behind him to assure himself he was free of pursuers. Satisfied that he was, he walked out into Villiers Street, into the arms of the night.

A chill wind had come with the onset of darkness and Magee pulled up the collar of his coat as protection against the breeze. Both hands dug firmly in his pockets, he walked along the narrow thoroughfare, the lights of the Strand up ahead of him. A young woman passed close and smiled. Magee returned the gesture, nodding a passing greeting, turning to look at her, appreciating the shapely legs visible below her short skirt.

238

She had not been the first woman to offer him a smile during the past few hours. Magee was a good-looking man, his shoulder-length black hair and chiselled features making him look at least five years younger than his actual age. He had helped one woman with a pushchair and screaming infant on to a bus earlier, and she had gripped his hand tightly in hers as she had said thank you. He had merely smiled and waved to her as the bus pulled away.

You either had it or you didn't, thought Trevor Magee, smiling broadly to himself.

He passed a pub on his right called *The Griffin*, the sound of loud music swelling from inside. For a moment he thought about going in and fumbled in one of his pockets for some change, but he decided against it. He walked on, climbing the flight of stone steps that brought him up into the Strand itself.

To his right there was a McDonalds; behind him the lights of the Charing Cross Hotel glowed in the darkness. To his left was Trafalgar Square.

Magee's smile broadened.

He looked around him, aware of the traffic speeding up and down, of the people who walked past him on the pavement, of people coming out of McDonalds laden with fast food. There was a dustbin outside and an elderly man dressed in a filthy jacket and torn trousers was shuffling towards it. There was a dark stain around the crotch of the trousers; Magee wrinkled his nose at the stench the old man was giving off.

He watched as the tramp sorted through the rubbish, finally pulling out a soft-drinks container. He took off the lid and sniffed the contents, satisfied the liquid was drinkable. He swallowed it down as if parched.

Magee's smile faded to a look of disgust.

239

The tramp tossed the empty cup away and shuffled off in the other direction.

Magee watched him go, pushing his way past pedestrians, finally disappearing down a side street.

The younger man swallowed hard, then turned and walked briskly in the direction of Trafalgar Square.

He had things to do.

Sixty

She rubbed a thin layer of Vaseline over her lips and smiled, satisfied with the extra lubrication. Zena Murray had seen on television that beauty queens used the trick so she figured it would work for her. After all, she had to do a lot of smiling in her business, too. Contestants in a beauty contest had only judges to impress with their looks and stance. Zena had many other, more trenchant critics to impress. The punters were always demanding.

Jim Scott watched as she finished applying the Vaseline, pacing the dressing room as she stood naked before him, slipping on a G-string and a suspender belt.

'And you haven't seen or heard from Carol since last night?' he said agitatedly.

'Scotty, we work together, that's it,' Zena told him, rolling one stocking up her leg.

'She didn't stay with you?'

'There's hardly room in my place for *me*, let alone bloody guests,' Zena told him.

240

Scott sighed.

'She's okay, I bet you,' Zena said, trying to sound reassuring. She looked at Scott, something close to pity in her voice. 'Look, Scotty, you shouldn't worry about her so much. She's got her own life to lead, you know.' *And you won't be part of it for much longer.* 'You'd be better off looking for someone else,' she smiled, her attempts at light banter failing miserably. 'I'm unattached, you know.'

'I don't want anyone else, Zena,' he told her.

She shrugged.

'Just trying to help,' she said. *Help, or soften the blow?*

Scott opened the door.

'When she comes in, tell her I want to see her, will you?' he said, then he was gone.

Zena pulled on another stocking and heard his footsteps echoing away up the corridor.

Scott returned to his office and sat at his desk, glancing at the phone, wondering if he should try calling Carol's flat again. He resisted the temptation, leaning back in his seat, running a hand across his forehead. A confusion of emotions tumbled through his mind: anger, concern, fear. He couldn't seem to settle on one that suited him. It was not knowing where she was that was so unsettling.

Or who she was with?

He pushed the thought to the back of his mind.

She wouldn't do that to him.

Would she?

He got to his feet and crossed to the window of the office. Below the streets were alive with people, all of them bathed in the neon glow that seemed to fill the very air itself with multi-coloured energy.

Who was she with?

Scott gritted his teeth.

241

There couldn't be anyone else. He would know. There would be signs he'd have spotted. He sucked in a deep breath. No. There was a rational explanation for all this and, when Carol arrived, he'd discover what it was.

If she arrived.

He returned to his desk and sat down. Even as he did there was a knock on the door and he was on his feet again instantly. The door opened.

John Hitch walked in, smiling at Scott, who merely exhaled wearily.

'Hello, Jim, I'm glad to see you too,' Hitch said, still smiling.

'Sorry, John,' Scott said. 'I was expecting someone else.'

The two men shook hands and Scott offered the other man a seat which he accepted and a drink which he declined.

'Is Ray with you?' Scott wanted to know.

Hitch shook his head.

'I'm allowed out on my own tonight, Jimmy boy,' Hitch grinned.

'This isn't a social call, is it, mate?' Scott said.

'No. Ray sent me. I've got a job for you.'

Scott looked puzzled.

'Tomorrow night,' Hitch continued. 'We're going to hit a shipment of coke that Ralph Connelly's bringing in.' He laced his fingers on the desk top. 'You're supposed to drive one of the getaway cars.'

'Are you fucking serious?' Scott exclaimed. 'That's not my line of work.'

'I know that. I was as surprised as you, but Ray Plummer wants you in on it.' He sat back in his seat. 'I'm just a messenger, Jim. I do as I'm told, and he told me to include you in this job.'

'Why?'

242

Hitch shrugged.

'Fuck knows. Like I said, I'm just doing what I was told.'

Scott ran a hand through his hair, bewilderment on his face.

'You'll be picked up from here tomorrow night at twelve,' Hitch told him. 'You'll be briefed on what you've got to do. I don't know what else I can say.' He looked almost apologetic.

'I don't like this, John,' Scott told him.

'Maybe not, mate, but you've got no choice.' Hitch got to his feet and crossed to the door.

'You got a shooter?' he asked.

'Beretta 92S. Why?'

Hitch nodded.

'Bring it.'

Sixty-one

The beating of dozens of wings sounded like disembodied applause, receding gradually into the darkness.

Trevor Magee stopped and looked up as the pigeons took off, anxious to avoid him as he made his way across Trafalgar Square. To his right was a hot-dog stand with a number of people gathered around it. From where he stood the pungent smell of frying onion was easily detectable. To his left one of the massive bronze lions that guarded the square had become a meeting place for some teenagers grouped around a ghetto

243

blaster. Music was roaring from it. Magee didn't recognise the tune. Ahead were the fountains and Nelson's Column, jabbing upwards towards the overcast heavens as if threatening to tear the low cloud and release the torrents of rain that seemed to be swelling in them.

Magee walked on, across the square, hands still dug firmly into his pockets. Every so often he would glance over his shoulder.

As far as he could tell no one was following him. His pace remained steady as he walked past the low wall surrounding the fountain.

A man was standing precariously on the wall urinating into the water.

Magee stopped to watch him, his face impassive.

'What the fucking hell are you looking at?' the man slurred, almost falling into the water.

Magee stood his ground a moment longer, then headed towards the stone steps. He took them two at a time, pausing at the top to look back across the square.

He scanned the dark figures moving about in the blackness, saw the odd flash-bulb explode as tourists took pictures of one of the capital's most famous landmarks. Then he crossed the street in front of the National Gallery, glancing up at the massive edifice of the building in the process. There was a man outside, close to one set of steps, selling hot chestnuts, the smell of burning coals and roasting nuts filling Magee's nostrils. The sights of London at night were something to behold but how many people, he wondered, ever noticed the variety of smells?

He continued walking, past a queue of people filing aboard a sight-seeing bus, jostling for the best positions as they reached the open upper deck. Finally he turned into St Martin's Place.

Across the street, on the steps of St Martin-in-the-Fields church, there was movement.

Magee could make out two figures crouched on the steps near the top, quite close to the door of the church.

They were passing a bottle back and forth between them.

As he looked more closely he saw what appeared to be a bundle of rags behind them. On closer inspection the bundle of rags rose and revealed itself to be a woman, filthy dirty, her skin so grimy she was almost invisible in the gloom.

As Magee watched she tottered down the steps and wandered off down Duncannon Street in the direction of the Strand.

He stood watching her, his face set, the muscles in his jaw pulsing angrily.

After what seemed an eternity he moved on, casting a cursory glance across at the two men sitting on the steps outside the church. As he reached Irving Street he paused again, looking behind him.

Still no sign.

Magee quickened his pace, walking up the centre of the wide road, passing restaurants on either side. The people inside them reminded him of goldfish, seated in the windows, bereft of any privacy from prying eyes as they ate. He emerged into Leicester Square, slowing his pace again, glancing once over his shoulder before moving off to his right, past a line of people waiting to enter the Odeon. Two buskers were playing banjos, walking up and down the line, while a dwarf scampered in and out of the waiting cinema-goers with an outstretched hand, cajoling money from the queue.

He was holding a flat cap full of coins. As each woman dropped money into the cap he would kiss her hand before skipping on to the next.

He even looked up at Magee, who merely ignored the little man and walked on, hands still dug deep into his pockets.

A drain had overflowed at the end of the road and water was running down the tarmac. Magee paid it little heed as he continued his nocturnal stroll, looking around him constantly, occasionally slowing down to look over his shoulder or perhaps changing direction quickly, ducking into a group of people.

Just in case.

He could hear shouting up ahead; and there was a large gathering of people around a man who was obviously standing on a box of some kind.

Magee pushed his way carefully through the crowd until he reached the front. The man was dressed in a combat jacket and jeans, and behind him stood two more men, their hair cropped short, dressed in a similar fashion but holding two flags, a Union Jack and a red flag with a cross on it. Another was handing out leaflets with 'THE JESUS ARMY' emblazoned on them. Magee took one, glanced at it and stuffed it into his pocket.

The man on the box was shouting about death and re-birth, Heaven and Hell.

Magee smiled.

He walked on, heading round the square towards the cinema.

To his right he saw another of them.

Man. Woman.

At first he couldn't be sure. As he drew closer he saw that it was a man huddled beneath a thick overcoat, sitting on the pavement watching the crowds go by. In front of him he had a piece of cardboard on which was scrawled: HOMELESS AND HUNGRY.

Magee looked at the cardboard and then at the man who, he guessed, was younger than himself.

Two girls passed by and tossed coins into his small plastic cup.

The man nodded his thanks and watched the girls walk away. Both of them wore short skirts. He smiled approvingly.

Magee glared at him, his hands still deep in his pockets.

He hardly felt the hand on his shoulder.

He spun round, his heart thumping against his ribs.

He had been careless.

'You got a light, please, mate?'

A man stood there with the cigarette held between his lips. When he repeated himself, the words seemed to sink in. Magee nodded and fumbled in his coat pocket for some matches he knew were there. He struck one and cupped his hand around the flame.

'Cheers,' said the man and disappeared back into the throng.

Magee nodded in silent acknowledgement and slipped the matches back into his pocket.

As he withdrew his hand he felt the coldness of the knife and corkscrew against his flesh. He patted them through the material of his overcoat and walked on.

Sixty-two

The light on the telephone was flashing. Someone was trying to reach him. Steve Houghton ignored the red bulb. He finally pushed the phone aside so that he couldn't see the distracting light. That task completed, he returned his attention to the work in front of him.

On his desk there were six files. One of his assistants had worked slowly and laboriously through the records and come up with half-a-dozen prints which looked at least similar to the ones taken from Paula Wilson. Now Houghton reached for the first file and took out the piece of card that bore the fingerprints of a possible match. He looked at the name on the file. George Purnell. Murderer. He'd strangled two children with his bare hands, then called the police to give himself up.

Houghton traced every curve and twist of the prints, comparing them beneath his microscope when he felt it necessary.

He shook his head. No match. Not close enough.

He reached for the second file. William Fisher. Killer of three elderly women he had robbed. Again Houghton began the comparisons.

He paused for a moment, increasing the magnification on the microscope. A number of loops seemed similar. The radial loops were definitely alike. He sat back from the microscope for a moment, then looked again.

Were his eyes playing tricks on him? Perhaps he was tired. They seemed totally different now. Houghton convinced himself he was searching so avidly for the match that he was almost willing himself to find it.

He discarded Fisher's file and reached for another.

Mathew Bryce.

Murderer of a number of young women in a particularly brutal manner.

He slipped Bryce's prints beneath the microscope.

He peered through the lens, frowning slightly.

Maybe . . .

He crossed to the VDU on his other desk and punched in a series of numbers, checking the number on Bryce's file. He pressed in the number, then Bryce's name, his face bathed in a green glow as first figures then images began to appear on the screen. From the two and a half million prints on file those of Mathew Bryce appeared on the screen. First those of the right thumb. Houghton pressed a button and the index finger patterns appeared. He paused and looked through the microscope again, this time at the print taken from Paula Wilson. Then back at the green image on the screen.

'Jesus,' he murmured, looking at the loops and composites on the VDU screen.

There was a hook on the crime print.

Matched by one on the suspect print.

A fork on the crime print, glowing on the screen.

Houghton checked against the one beneath the microscope.

Match.

He knew that he was searching for sixteen points of comparison before he could be sure of positive identification.

The clock on the wall ticked noisily in the silence as he continued his task. The red light on the phone console stopped flashing as whoever sought his attention tired of waiting.

Thirty minutes had passed from his initial inspection to the point where he now marked down another match.

He had fourteen marks of comparison.

It was enough to convince him.

Now it was *his* turn to reach for the phone.

He tried Gregson's office.

Nothing.

Then his home.

His wife said he wasn't back yet.

Houghton asked her to instruct Gregson to call him as soon as he could. Then he put down the phone and glanced once more at the fingerprints beneath the microscope.

Sixty-three

It was the smell that alerted him.

Trevor Magee had passed the small entryway to Long's Court when he noticed it.

The rank odour of sweat and urine made him wince.

Long's Court was silent, a curious contrast to the noisy hustle and bustle of the square just yards away. The smell, coming from the rear of a building, might easily have been the unpleasant odour given off by a dustbin in need of emptying. There were bins in the small yard behind the building, even a large wheeled skip which bore the name BIFFA. But it was, in fact, a bundle of dark clothing that looked as if it had been hurled against the far wall of the darkened yard. A bundle which, as he drew closer, he realised was a person.

From more than a few feet it was impossible to tell even the sex of the figure. Magee moved closer, inside the high stone walls of the yard, walls that effectively cut it off from anyone who might be passing.

He moved into the impenetrable gloom of the yard, one hand slipping inside his left hand pocket. He was standing over the reeking individual now, peering close to get a look at the face.

It was a man. He was yet to reach his thirtieth birthday, Magee thought, but ravaged beyond his years. How long he'd been sleeping rough no one could tell. Magee looked closely at him, trying to focus on the face in the darkness, to pick out his features beneath the grime that covered his face like a second, darker skin.

The smell was almost unbearable; Magee could feel it clogging his nostrils.

He reached into his pocket and slowly pulled the knife free.

It was about eight inches long, double edged and as sharp as a razor.

Magee leant forward and touched the man's shoulder, simultaneously pushing the knife gently up beneath his chin so that the point was just touching flesh.

There was no movement.

'Wake up,' Magee whispered, as if trying to rouse a lover from slumber. His voice was gentle, cajoling. 'Come on, wake up.'

He shook the man more firmly, the knife still poised.

Magee could feel the beginnings of an erection pushing against his trousers. His breath was starting to come in low gasps.

'Wake up.'

The man opened his eyes and blinked myopically, trying to focus. He was suddenly aware of the coldness beneath his chin and his eyes widened in shocked realisation.

Magee smiled.

He drove the blade upwards with one powerful thrust, feeling it puncture skin, rip through muscle and crash into teeth. Gums were cut open and the knife scythed through the man's tongue, momentarily pinning it to the roof of his mouth before severing it. As the man opened his mouth to scream, part of his tongue fell into his lap. Blood gushed from the open orifice. Magee smiled broadly. He struck again, this time bringing the knife

251

down into the top of the man's head, using all his strength to force it through bone that splintered and cracked with a strident shriek.

As Magee tugged it free a large lump of bone came away on the end of the knife. For fleeting seconds, a sticky mass of brain matter welled up through the hole.

The tramp had fallen forward onto his face, his body twitching madly, blood spreading out around his head. Magee ignored the crimson puddles and knelt beside the dying man again, this time rolling him over onto his back. He felt inside his own coat pocket and pulled out the corkscrew.

The tramp's eyes were closed but Magee used his thumb and forefinger to push back the lids. He drove the corkscrew forward, burying it in the man's right eye, shoving down hard on it, twisting it in the socket, ignoring the spouting vitreous liquid that erupted from the riven orb. He felt the point scrape bone and pulled back hard.

Most of the eye came away, torn from the socket. But the corkscrew had burst it like a corpulent balloon and its fluid ran down the tramp's face, clear liquid mingling with blood. Enough of the eye came free to please Magee, though, and he watched as it dangled on the optic nerve.

He rammed the corkscrew into the left eye and pulled again. This time the curled metal merely came away with jellied lumps of vitreous humour sticking to it. He tried again, uncaring that the tramp was motionless by now, the stench of excrement already beginning to permeate the air.

The corkscrew tore the flesh at the side of the man's nose before skewing into his eye again, gouging the torn sphere badly and tearing the lower eyelid. Magee shoved two fingers into the socket, scooping the eye out until it fell onto the concrete. He looked at it for a second then got to his feet and stamped on the eye, hearing it pop beneath his foot. He slipped the knife and the corkscrew back into his pocket and walked away, turning out of the yard and into St Martin's Street again. He walked unhurriedly to the bottom of it and peered down Orange Street.

A taxi was approaching, its yellow light on. Magee raised an arm to stop it, walking round to the driver's side.

The driver looked at him aghast.

'What the fuck happened to you?' he wanted to know.

'I want your cab,' said Magee, tugging at the door.

'Fuck off, I'll . . .'

The driver got no further.

Magee pulled the knife from his pocket and, with a blow combining demonic strength with effortless expertise, slashed open the taxi driver's throat.

Gouts of blood erupted from the wound and hit the windscreen with a loud splash.

The cabbie made a squealing noise and clutched at the ragged edges of the wound as if trying to hold it together, to prevent the blood pouring through his hands.

Magee tore open the driver's door, grabbing the man by the shoulder, hauling him from the cab. He fell heavily onto the road, his eyes bulging wide with fear as he felt his life-blood draining away. As he tried to breathe the chill night air filled the gaping hole in his neck. His body began to spasm.

Magee leapt into the driver's seat and pressed down on the accelerator, heading away from the scene of carnage, his own brow furrowed. He glanced into the rear-view mirror to see if anyone was following.

All he saw was the body of the taxi driver lying in the road, blood spreading out rapidly around him. There was blood all over the windows, too, and Magee had to wipe it away with the sleeve of his coat in order to see through the windscreen. The car was like a mobile abattoir.

He put his foot on the accelerator and the taxi shot forward. He found himself struggling with the wheel, fighting to keep the vehicle under control. As he swung it into Charing Cross Road he nearly collided with another car. The driver sounded his horn furiously as the taxi sped on. Magee paid it little heed. Up ahead the traffic lights were on red but he didn't slow up. The taxi went hurtling across the junction with Cranbourn Street doing sixty.

Hunched over the wheel, Magee smiled.

He was relieved that no one was following him. He didn't want anyone trying to stop him.

Not yet.

Sixty-four

Detective Inspector Frank Gregson tapped agitatedly on the steering wheel as he looked up at the red light, waiting for it to change.

He revved his engine.

Come on. Come on.

He sped away with them still on amber, narrowly avoiding a car coming the other way. The driver banged on his horn but Gregson drove on at speed, unconcerned by the accident he'd almost caused.

He'd spoken to Houghton less than ten minutes ago.

The DI had returned home and been greeted by Julie telling him that the Records Officer had called. Gregson had asked what it was about. Julie had only been able to tell him that it was urgent. Gregson had called immediately and Houghton had explained about the fingerprints and how he was sure he now had positive identification of at least one of the bodies. Gregson had hardly allowed him to finish speaking before telling him he'd be there as soon as he could.

Julie had asked him what was going on but he'd rushed out without telling her, mumbling only that it was important and that he didn't know when he'd be back.

Now he pressed his foot down harder on the accelerator and eased the Ford Scorpio past a car, cutting in ahead of the driver. Gregson glanced at the clock on the dashboard and estimated that he could be at New Scotland Yard in less than thirty minutes, traffic permitting.

Thirty minutes. It seemed like a fucking lifetime.

However, mingling with that frustration was a small feeling of triumph. He'd been right about Bryce. The copy-cat MO theory he'd come up with had born fruit. It should prove so for the first killer as well. He almost smiled to himself.

He had been proved right, but how could it be? The men he had suspected were in prison serving life sentences. No escapes had been reported.

What the fuck was going on?

'Lima 15, come in.'

The metallic voice that rattled out of his radio made him jump.

'Lima 15, do you read me? If you're there, pick it up, Frank.'

He recognised DI Finn's voice.

'Frank, for fuck's sake . . .'

Gregson snatched up the handset.

'Lima 15, I hear you,' he said. 'This better be good.'

'Where are you?' Finn wanted to know.

'On my way to see Houghton, he's identified one of the dead killers.'

'Jesus,' muttered Finn. There was a moment's silence, then the DI spoke again. 'Frank, you'd better tell Barclay to have one of his slabs ready.'

'Why?'

'We've got another one,' Finn told him flatly. 'A murder suicide. Just like the other two. The guy tried to torch himself.'

'What happened?' Gregson demanded, hardly slowing down as he drove.

Finn told him about the murders of the tramp and the taxi-driver. 'He stole the cab, drove it up Charing Cross Road then aimed the fucking thing at the fountains outside Centre Point. The car blew up as soon as it hit the wall.'

'Shit,' hissed Gregson. 'What about the driver?'

'Well, like I said, he was obviously trying to kill himself. The thing is, when the car hit the wall, *he* went through the windscreen. He was thrown clear. They fished him out of the water. He's badly cut up from the broken glass but he's more or less in one piece.'

'Any ID on him?' Gregson wanted to know.

'Nothing. Not even a name tag in his fucking underwear. Just like the other two. The only difference is, this geezer doesn't look like burnt toast.'

'No ID at all?' Gregson repeated. 'Could he have dropped it in the car? You said he was thrown clear. He might have been carrying something, it might be lying around . . .'

Finn cut him short.

'The boys here have been over the area with a fine toothcomb, Frank. I'm telling you. There was no fucking ID. All he had on him was a couple of quid in small change.'

'Where are you now?' Gregson wanted to know.

'I'm still at the scene. We've closed the road off while the boys go over the area. The fire brigade have put out the blaze, thank Christ.'

'Meet me at the Yard in thirty minutes. Stuart, I want a full report on what happened, right?'

'Thirty minutes?'

'Yeah.'

'I'll see you there, over and out.'

The two-way went dead and Gregson replaced it, pressing his foot harder on the accelerator, coaxing more speed from the Scorpio.

Another twenty minutes, he thought, then perhaps at last they might have some answers.

Sixty-five

Why?

The word kept rolling around in his mind like a marble.

Why?

Jim Scott looked at his reflection in the mirror, studying his features.

Why did they need *him* for this job? He sighed. Plummer had insisted that he be involved.

Why? Why? Fucking why?

He slammed his hand down on the top of the dressing table, causing some of the bottles to topple over. An aftershave bottle spilled its contents and Scott inhaled the aroma momentarily before stepping back. He crossed to his bed and sat down.

257

Outside the wind was blowing strongly again, wailing around the block of flats. He heard footsteps passing his door as someone made their way home. There was a thumping noise coming from above that was a record player. He got to his feet, staring up at the ceiling, wondering whether or not he should shout to the owner to turn the volume down.

Better still, go up there and *tell* him.

Scott finally decided to do neither. He wandered out into the kitchen and took a pint of milk from the fridge, supping straight from the bottle.

He wiped his mouth with the back of his hand and walked back into the bedroom.

Why?

Why did they want him on this particular job?

Why couldn't he get in touch with Carol?

Why hadn't she been in to work?

Why hadn't she called him?

Fucking why?

He slammed the milk bottle down on top of the bedside cabinet, pulling the drawer open.

He reached in and took out the Beretta, cradling it in his hand, working the slide. He held the piece up and sighted it, squeezing the trigger, allowing the hammer to fall on an empty chamber. Finally he lowered the weapon and dropped it onto the bed beside him, then fumbled in the drawer again for the box of ammunition.

He began feeding 9mm shells into the magazine.

She could hear him moving about in the sitting room. Carol Jackson rolled onto her back and gazed at the ceiling, aware of the movement from the adjacent room and also of the perspiration that sheathed her body. She ran a finger through the glistening moisture, allowing her hand to trail lower, through her pubic hairs. She felt the wetness of Plummer's semen as it trickled from her. Carol sighed and reached for a tissue from the bedside table.

Plummer called through and asked if she wanted a drink. She called back that she didn't.

For some reason her thoughts turned to Scott. He must be wondering where she was by now. She hadn't been to work for two nights. Carol could imagine his state of mind.

Had he finally realised there was someone else?

If so, what was going through his mind?

She closed her eyes and swallowed hard. If only she'd had the courage to tell him she wanted to end their relationship when the cracks had first started to appear. He would have been disappointed. Upset. Perhaps even angry. But now she feared what he might do.

Would he *really* try to kill her?

She wished she could convince herself that what he'd said had merely been an idle threat. But she knew him too well. There was no avoiding the issue any more. Either he would find out she was seeing Plummer or she would have to tell him.

It was only a matter of time before the truth emerged.

And then?

She exhaled deeply.

Plummer would look after her, wouldn't he? After all, he was her lover.

Carol almost smiled.

Lover.

The word implied some kind of emotional bond and that, she knew, they didn't have. But he thought a lot of her; he seemed to want her around.

If she could move in with him.

The prospect of escaping her job and her flat suddenly seemed to lift her spirits and the threat of Scott was momentarily shrouded.

Move in.

He'd never mentioned it to her and she had not even thought about it until now, but therein lay her escape. Both from Scott and from her lifestyle. Carol sat up, resting her back against the padded headboard. She wasn't escaping. She was running, running from herself as much as her surroundings. She wanted to move in with Plummer, though. Even loveless comfort was preferable to what she had.

She called to Plummer to come back to bed but he didn't answer.

Twenty million pounds.

He concentrated on the figure, held it in his mind, savouring it as a wine expert savours a fine vintage.

Twenty million fucking pounds.

Hitch had arranged details of the job and Plummer felt safe enough with him dealing with it. He hated having to trust anyone, but Hitch was one of the few he did. Plummer poured himself another drink, pulled his monogrammed housecoat more tightly around him and paced the sitting room slowly, glancing around at the expensive furnishings and ornaments which filled the flat.

Carol called him again and he called back that he wouldn't be long. He told her to go to sleep.

Pain in the arse.

He smiled and sipped his drink, glancing across at the phone as he refilled his glass.

There had been no more calls since the informant had rung with the news of the cocaine shipment. Plummer licked his lips and frowned.

Who the hell *was* the informant?

He'd wondered countless times, ever since that first call it had played on his mind.

Set-up?

Wind-up?

They'd soon know.

If it was a member of Connelly's gang it made no sense, yet who else would know about the shipment?

It made no fucking sense at all, but Plummer had his reasons for believing the information. Twenty million reasons.

Carol called to him again.

He smiled and headed for the bedroom.

Sixty-six

'You were right about the killers being linked,' said Phillip Barclay.

Gregson smiled to himself.

'But not just in the way you said,' Barclay continued. 'The MO's they used may have been copies of earlier killings, even this latest one. And the fact that they all burned themselves, or tried to. But there's something else, something more conclusive to link them, but it's more puzzling, too. That device – whatever the hell it is – that I found in Magee was made of the same material I found melted in the other bodies.'

'And I checked his fingerprints against the files on screen at Hendon,' said Steve Houghton. 'There's no doubt about it, the man *is* Trevor Magee.'

'And number one?' asked Finn.

'Going almost solely on your files and his MO, I'd have to say it was Peter Lawton,' the Records Officer told him.

Finn looked at his colleague, then at Houghton.

'Which we know is impossible, right?' he said, almost laughing. 'Lawton and Bryce are banged up.'

'So is Magee,' Gregson told him, flipping open the file. 'According to this.' He jabbed the file with his index finger.

Houghton crossed to the wall behind him and flicked a switch. Panels lit up and he reached for a number of X-ray plates which he attached to the luminescent plastic. They were skull X-rays.

'Now look. These are of Magee,' he said. 'Taken when they brought his body in.'

Barclay pulled a pen from his pocket and prodded part of the first plate. It showed a dark mass close to the front of the skull. On other angles it was also present. 'See it?' he said.

'What is it?' Gregson wanted to know.

'Wait,' Barclay told him. Houghton reached for another set of plates. The shape was far less well defined. 'These are X-rays of Mathew Bryce's skull,' said Barclay, 'at least what was left of it. Unfortunately he'd been burned, but not badly enough for the bone structure to be altered as it was in Lawton's case.' He jabbed his pen at a dark area on Bryce's X-rays too.

'Come on, Phil, what the fuck is it?' Finn muttered, reaching for his cigarettes but deciding not to light one when he saw the look of disapproval on the pathologist's face.

'Both men were suffering from brain tumours,' Barclay said.

'How can you be sure?' Gregson demanded.

Barclay sighed.

'It's on the plates, you can see it,' he said, motioning to the X-rays again. 'And, if you'd care to look at Magee, I haven't replaced the cranial cap yet and you'll *see*

262

the tumour. Come down to the morgue and I'll show you.'

'I'll take your word for it,' Finn said. 'What you're saying is, these three fucking murderers we've got in cold storage have all committed crimes identical to ones committed by Peter Lawton, Mathew Bryce and Trevor Magee, right? Three blokes we *know*, for *sure*, are locked up, doing time in Whitely nick, yeah? Now, you're trying to tell me that this is the *real* Trevor Magee lying downstairs? That the *real* Peter Lawton killed six people and then killed himself on a motorbike less than two weeks ago? That the *real* Mathew Bryce cut up a girl, then torched himself? And tonight the *real* Trevor Magee murdered a tramp and a cabbie and then smashed his car into the Centre Point fountains? You're telling me that blokes we arrested, blokes we stood in court and saw sentenced, blokes we saw driven away in fucking armoured vans, have committed the exact same crimes that they were put away for? *That's* what you're telling me?'

Houghton looked almost helplessly at Gregson.

'It's bollocks,' said Finn angrily. 'Absolute bollocks.' He looked at Gregson. 'You said yourself it was impossible. If *one* of them had escaped from Whitely we'd have known about it, but *three* of the cunts? Do me a favour.' This time he *did* reach for a cigarette and light it up.

Silence.

'Somebody say something, for Christ's sake,' snarled Finn in annoyance. 'Somebody tell me again what all this shit is supposed to mean.'

'Could there be a mistake with the identification?' Gregson said.

'It's possible with Bryce,' Houghton admitted. 'I found fourteen matching characteristics in the ridge patterns of his fingerprints. There should have been sixteen, but I

263

think my figure is conclusive enough. But even if I was wrong about Bryce, it's impossible I could be wrong about Magee. His prints match those on file. His dental records match. His blood type. Everything. Unless he's got a twin identical in every way, then that man is the same one you arrested.'

Finn shook his head.

'I don't fucking believe this,' he said, an incredulous smile on his face. 'It's not possible.'

'Then what's your explanation?' Houghton challenged him.

'You're telling me that you believe three convicted killers just walked out of Whitely prison without anyone noticing and now they've come back here to duplicate their original crimes? Do you believe that? Really?'

'I believe what I see here, Stuart, and this man *is* Trevor Magee,' Houghton said quietly. 'If it helps, I'm as sceptical as you, but the evidence is here.'

'Evidence for what?' Finn snarled. 'That we're all going fucking crazy? They're inside!' He shouted the last two words.

Gregson crossed to the phone and jabbed the button. He asked the switchboard operator to connect him with Whitely Prison and waited.

Finn turned to his colleague.

'Frank, for Christ's sake . . .' he began, but Gregson held up a hand to silence him.

'Hello,' he said finally into the phone. 'My name is Detective Inspector Gregson. I'm calling . . . Yes, Gregson.' He spelt it out. 'I'm calling from New Scotland Yard. I'd like to speak with the Governor please. It's very important.' He sucked in an angry breath. 'Yes, Gregson.' He spelled it out again. Then he waited. The other men watched as he tapped gently on the desk top.

'When will he back?' he said finally. 'Can you get him to call me as soon as possible? It's very urgent. It concerns three of the inmates there.' They saw Gregson's features harden. 'Who *are* you, anyway?' He sighed. 'All right, perhaps you can help me. Their names are Peter Lawton, Mathew Bryce and Trevor Magee. I need to speak to Governor Nicholson about them as soon as possible, do you understand?' The other three saw a flicker on the DI's face. 'Say that again?' He looked across at Finn, a look of bewilderment on his face. He shook his head slowly. 'Can you tell me when?'

'What the fuck is this?' Finn whispered, still watching his superior.

'Thank you,' said Gregson. 'Tell Governor Nicholson to ring me on this number as soon as possible.'

Gregson put down the phone.

'Well?' said Finn.

The DI looked at Houghton.

'Are you *sure* that's Trevor Magee?' he said, the knot of muscles at the side of his jaw pulsing.

Houghton held up his hands.

'Frank, for God's sake,' he sighed. 'If I had children I'd swear on their graves. It *is* Magee. There's no question of it.'

'And you're sure about the others as well?'

Houghton nodded.

'According to that guy I just spoke to,' said Gregson quietly. 'Trevor Magee died six months ago. As a matter of fact he's buried in the same piece of ground as Peter Lawton and Mathew Bryce. They never left Whitely. All three of them are buried there.'

265

Sixty-seven

There was an explosion of blood and the nose seemed to burst.

The coloured man fell backwards, his legs buckling under him, a look of pain on his face.

As he fell the spectators rose, a chorus of shouts and cheers ringing around the arena.

'Good punch,' Ray Plummer shouted approvingly. The coloured boxer looked into the referee's eyes, then watched his fingers; he was raising them one at a time as he counted. His opponent was dancing about in a neutral corner, one eye on his quarry. The other eye had been closed for most of the fight by a left hook that had caused a large amount of swelling both above and below the brow. He was older, pale-skinned and looked too thin to be a welterweight, but the right cross that had put his younger opponent down had belied his looks.

As the referee reached the mandatory eight the black fighter rose quickly to his feet.

'Come on, Robbie!' shouted Plummer, cupping one hand to his mouth.

Beside him Carol watched the modern-day gladiators as they came at each other. She was wearing a tight red dress which showed off her shapely legs. It clung to her so tightly that she wore no underwear beneath. Plummer liked that. He also liked it when he saw other men around the ringside looking at her approvingly. Look all you want, he thought. She's with me.

She ran a hand through her hair and glanced up at the fighters again, one arm linked through Plummer's.

She saw him look at his watch again. He'd been doing it all evening.

'Are you expecting someone?' she asked. 'You keep looking at your watch.'

He shook his head, smiled at her briefly then returned his attention to the fight.

The younger fighter seemed to have recovered from the knockdown. Despite the blood streaming from his nose, he was driving in a series of combinations which looked to have his opponent in trouble.

'Work the body!' one of his cornermen shouted.

'Cover up!' the other fighter's trainer responded.

'Get away from him!' Plummer bellowed, watching gloomily as a body punch brought down his fighter's guard and a thunderous uppercut lifted him off his feet and sent him crashing to the canvas. 'Oh, fuck it,' murmured Plummer, as the referee started counting.

'If he counts until tomorrow night your boy won't get up, Ray,' said the tubby man sitting on Plummer's left.

Plummer nodded and glanced at his watch again.

10.46 p.m.

The referee made a sweeping gesture with his arm over the prostrate figure of the white fighter. It might as well have been the last rites.

Some members of the crowd moved away towards the bar between contests. Others were content to sit and wait, reading their programmes or gazing around. Television cameras were covering the bill and a number of those opposite the prying lenses spent the time waving at the cameras. Two men passed by and looked down at Carol, who crossed her legs, dangling one high-heeled shoe from her toes.

267

She noticed with disgust that there were several droplets of blood on the patent leather. One of the perils of sitting ringside.

Plummer looked at his watch again and sighed.

10.48.

There were still nearly three hours to go.

The other staff had gone home. Jim Scott had locked up. Now he stood in his office drinking from a paper cup, swilling the Southern Comfort around, staring into the liquid.

The knock on the door was at precisely one minute after midnight.

He went upstairs and opened it, allowing John Hitch inside.

'You set?' Hitch asked him.

Scott nodded.

'Show me,' Hitch insisted.

Scott pulled the Beretta from its shoulder holster and handed it to Hitch, who held the weapon for a minute before returning it to its rightful owner.

'You've got good taste, Jim,' he said, smiling, pulling his own pistol into view.

Like Scott's it was a 92S. He holstered it and motioned towards the door.

'Let's go,' he said. 'Car's waiting.'

Scott followed him out.

It was a small boat, less than thirty feet from stem to stern. It moved quietly up the River Thames, hidden by the darkness, only its warning lights visible on the black swirl of the water. *The Sandhopper* moved evenly and unhurriedly through the water.

The river was quiet. Many of the small boats which usually travelled its waters were moored for the night and *The Sand-hopper* passed a number of them as it made its way up river. Lights from the banks reflected off the water like a black mirror. One of the crewmen of the small boat stood looking out at the city all around him, smoking a cigarette and gazing at the myriad lights.

'I can see one of them.'

Martin Bates adjusted the focus on the binoculars, trying to pull into sharper definition the man moving about on the deck.

'Where's the boat now?' John Hitch asked, his voice breaking up slightly on the two-way.

Bates picked up the radio, still holding the binoculars in one hand, following the progress of the boat.

'Just passing Hay's Wharf,' he said.

'Tell Wally to keep his eyes open and let me know when they pass him,' Hitch instructed.

'Will do,' said Bates. He put down the radio for a moment, taking one last look at the boat as it chugged slowly up river. He leant on the car and lit a cigarette, puffing at it before he picked up the radio again.

'Wally, come in, it's Martin. You awake or having a wank?' He smiled to himself.

'I'm awake, you cunt,' a deep Scots voice thundered back.

'They'll be with you in about ten or fifteen minutes, mate,' Bates told him.

'Right,' muttered Wally Connor.

From his own vantage point he moved forward, leaning on the parapet of Blackfriars Bridge, peering down into the murky blackness of the river. Waiting.

Waiting just like the other four men Hitch had positioned at various places along the Thames.

Scott looked at the clock on the dashboard of the Lancia and sighed.

'How much longer?' he said irritably, gazing through the windscreen, out across the Thames. It looked like a swollen black tongue licking its way through the city.

'Not long,' John Hitch told him, looking first at his own watch then at the dashboard clock.

'I'd just like to know why I'm here,' Scott murmured.

'I told you, Scotty, it wasn't my idea. I get paid for doing what I'm told. It's as simple as that.' He looked at his watch again. Then he pulled the Beretta from its holster and worked the slide.

It jammed.

'Shit,' muttered Hitch.

Scott seemed unconcerned by his companion's problem and looked to his right. The four giant chimneys of Battersea Power Station thrust upward into the night sky like the upended legs of a gigantic coffee table. Below them was a pier, accessible by a set of stone steps. The steps were green with mould where the rising tide lapped against them. At the end of the pier another small boat was moored. Scott couldn't see the name painted along one side of it but he'd already been told it was called *The Abbott*. Not that he really cared.

Hitch was still struggling with the Beretta.

'Bloody slide's stuck,' he grunted, pulling back hard on it.

'Why do you need a gun, anyway?' Scott wanted to know. 'You intending to use it?'

'Just call it insurance,' Hitch said, still tugging at the pistol. 'Fuck it,' he snapped finally. 'Give me yours.' He held out one gloved hand.

Scott hesitated.

'Give me yours,' Hitch repeated. 'Come on, you're going to be up here in the car. If things get too complicated, just drive off.' He sat there with his hand still open. 'Let me have your gun, Jim.'

Scott reached slowly inside his jacket then pulled the Beretta free and handed it to Hitch, who gripped the automatic in his fist and checked that the magazine was full, slipping it from the butt. Satisfied that it was, he slammed it back into place and holstered the weapon, sticking his own pistol in the belt of his trousers.

On the dashboard in front of him the radio crackled and he picked it up.

'John, can you hear me?' a voice enquired.

'Yeah, Rob, go ahead,' Hitch replied.

'*The Sandhopper* just passed under the Vauxhall Bridge. Should be with you any time now.'

'Cheers,' said Hitch and snapped off the radio. He pushed open the passenger side door and clambered out, turning to look back at Scott. 'This shouldn't take long,' he said, smiling, the wind ruffling his long blond hair. 'Just sit tight.'

Scott nodded, watching as Hitch scuttled across the road and disappeared out of sight as he began to descend the embankment steps towards the pier.

Scott switched on the radio, heard pop music, twiddled the frequency dial past classical and reggae and finally found a discussion programme. He listened for a moment then switched off again, content with the silence inside the Lancia. He drummed his fingers on the steering wheel and waited.

He couldn't sleep.

He knew he wouldn't be able to and now, as he swung himself out of bed, Ray Plummer wondered why he

271

hadn't just sat in front of the television until the time came.

He pulled on his dressing gown and padded through into the sitting room.

'What's wrong, Ray?' Carol asked, rolling over.

He ignored her enquiry so she hauled herself out, slipped on a long T-shirt and followed him into the other room. She found him standing in front of the fireplace, his eyes fixed on the clock.

'Are you all right?' she wanted to know. 'You've hardly spoken since we got back.'

'I've got something on my mind,' he said sharply, sipping at the drink he cradled in his hand.

'Anything I can help with?'

'No, it's all right,' he said. 'Thanks for asking, though. It's just a little bit of business that's got to be done.'

She knew better than to ask what *kind* of business.

Plummer turned to face her, running appraising eyes over her long slender legs, her nipples taut against the thin material of the T-shirt.

'Get yourself a drink,' he said, nodding towards the cabinet. As she did he glanced at his watch once more.

Nearly time.

Carol crossed to him and slipped one hand inside his dressing gown, stroking his stomach.

'Are you sure I can't help?' she said, smiling a practised smile.

Plummer allowed her to rake her fingernails across his stomach, feeling her probing lower, encircling his penis with her hand. Then he took a step back, a slight smile on his face.

'No,' he said flatly. 'You *can't* help. Not yet.'

Again he looked at his watch.

Sixty-eight

The engine of *The Abbott* sounded deafening in the silence, the loud spluttering replaced rapidly by a rumble as the boat moved away from the pier.

John Hitch wandered towards the cabin, where Terry Morton was steering the boat, peering out over the river.

'How come you know how to drive these fucking things?' Hitch asked, looking for the first sign of their quarry.

'You don't *drive* a boat, you ignorant cunt,' chuckled Morton. 'You pilot it.'

'Whatever,' Hitch shrugged.

'My old man worked the river all his life, doing deliveries, pick-ups. They used to use it like a canal; anything that couldn't be moved easily by land, they'd stick it on a boat. My old man worked the length of it. He had a pleasure boat for about ten years before he died, used to run fucking tourists down to Hampton Court, that sort of stuff.' Morton moved the wheel slightly, bringing the boat around. 'He made a ton of money ripping them off. I used to go along with him a lot of the time.'

'John, check it out, mate,' called Adrian McCann from the small foredeck. 'Coming up on our right.'

Both Hitch and Morton looked and saw the warning lights of a small boat approaching. As yet it was a little over two hundred yards away. Hitch reached for the binoculars and peered through them. He read the name on the side of the boat.

'*The Sandhopper*,' he said, smiling. 'Bingo.'

Morton guided the boat towards the centre of the river, then towards the oncoming *Sandhopper*.

Still peering through the binoculars he could see movement on the other boat: two men looking ahead, one of them pointing towards *The Abbott*.

'They'll signal us to turn aside,' Morton observed.

'How do you know?' Hitch asked.

'Rules of the river,' Morton told him. 'What do you want me to do?'

'Bring us up alongside them,' said Hitch, and glanced across at his companion. 'You set?'

Morton nodded and inclined his head in the direction of an Ithaca Model 37 shotgun on the bench beside him.

Red warning lights were flashing on the bridge of *The Sandhopper* as the two boats drew closer, Morton now angling *The Abbott* so that it was heading directly towards the other craft. Hitch reached inside his jacket and touched the butt of the Beretta he'd taken from Scott.

The two boats were less than one hundred yards away from each other now.

Morton slowed the speed a little, preparing to bring the boat to a halt when he needed to.

Eighty yards.

Adrian McCann stood by the prow of the boat, one thumb hooked into the pocket of his jeans, his other hand gripping the butt of a Uzi sub-machine gun.

Sixty yards.

Hitch could hear shouting from the other boat, though most of the words were indistinct. He saw one man motioning animatedly with his arms, as if to deflect the other boat from its route.

Forty yards.

'Steady now,' Hitch said and Morton slowed up a little more.

Twenty yards.

They seemed to be the only two vessels moving on the dark water; *The Abbott* was almost invisible in the gloom. The red warning lights of *The Sandhopper* glowed like boiling blood in the blackness.

Ten yards.

Hitch could hear the men shouting now, see them gesticulating madly towards *The Abbott* in an effort to divert it from what appeared to be a collision course.

Morton cut the motor.

The boat floated the last few yards until it actually bumped the side of *The Sandhopper*. One of the crew immediately crossed to the side of the smaller boat and pointed a finger angrily at Hitch.

'What the fucking hell are you playing at?' he bellowed. 'You could have sunk us. You haven't even got your lights on . . .'

The sentence trailed off as Hitch pulled the Beretta free and aimed it at the crewman.

'Cut your engines,' shouted Morton, swinging the Ithaca up into view, working the pump action, chambering a round.

McCann stepped forward too, the Uzi held in both hands, the stubby barrel pointed at the deck of *The Sandhopper*.

'All of you get out where I can see you,' shouted Hitch.

'What the fuck *is* this?' the first crewman said. 'Are you the law?'

'No,' said one of his companions, looking at the Uzi. 'They ain't the law.' He lifted his hands into the air in a gesture of surrender.

'All of you,' Hitch shouted, watching as the third man joined his companions on the foredeck. He was the youngest of the trio, in his early twenties, with short black hair. His companions were

275

both in their forties, one of them greying at the temples, a squat, powerfully built man; the other was a tall gangling individual with deep-set eyes which remained fixed on Hitch the whole time.

'Who the fuck are you?' the second man asked as Hitch stepped aboard *The Sandhopper*.

Hitch ignored the question.

'Get the hold open,' he said sharply, pushing the barrel of the pistol towards the tall man's face. 'Do it,' he rasped when the man hesitated.

The younger of the trio looked at McCann and Morton and decided he would be better advised *not* to try and reach the .38 he had jammed into his belt.

The tall man opened the hold and Hitch peered down into it, glancing at dozens of crates all of roughly the same size.

'Bring one out,' he said, watching as the tall man struggled with it, finally dropping it on to the deck. 'Open it,' Hitch told him.

'You're making a mistake,' said the second man.

'You're the one making a fucking mistake,' Morton snapped, raising the Ithaca and pointing it at his head. 'If you open your mouth once more I'll blow your fucking head off. Got it?'

There was a creak of splintering wood as the tall man prized off the lid of the crate. Hitch told him to back off, then moved across. Beneath a layer of foam rubber there was a dark brown carpet of coffee beans. He dug his hand through the aromatic blanket and his fingers closed round an unmistakable shape. He pulled the video-cassette free and gripped it in his free hand, the pistol still trained on the tall man.

Hitch slammed the cassette hard against the crate. Once. Twice. It cracked, then split open.

Yards of video tape spilled onto the deck, along with pieces of broken plastic.

And a small plastic bag full of white powder.

He tore it open, moistened the end of one gloved finger then dipped it in the substance and touched it to his tongue. It felt cold as the powder reached his tastebuds. He smiled thinly and motioned the tall man back.

Morton looked across expectantly.

'We've got it,' said Hitch, smiling. 'Now let's get it loaded and get out of here.'

Sixty-nine

He was beginning to get cramp in his right leg.

Jim Scott massaged his calf for a moment, then pushed open the driver's side door of the Lancia and clambered out. The chill night air hit him like a fist. He recoiled, but the iciness in the breeze freshened his skin and helped to dispel the lethargy he had been feeling sitting in the car. He walked around the vehicle a couple of times, stretching his legs, stopping by the bonnet to squat down on his knees. As he straightened up he heard the joints pop and winced.

The river was silent. From where he stood, Scott could see nothing but the curling black tongue of water cutting through the centre of the city. He crossed the road, pausing on the kerb and looking back towards the Lancia. The two-way radio Hitch had been using was still on the passenger seat. Perhaps Scott should take it with him in case someone tried to make contact.

Fuck it. They knew where he was if they wanted him.

He strode across the road and headed towards the quayside, leaning against the black metal fencing that ran along the embankment. He gazed down river but could see nothing.

Behind him a car passed and he turned to look at the occupants. It was a young couple, who both looked at him for a second before driving on.

The girl was blonde.

A little like Carol?

He rested one foot on the fence and leant forward, hawking loudly, sending a projectile of sputum into the river below.

Where the fuck was she?

Why hadn't she called him? All he wanted to know was if she was all right. Just a phone call would satisfy him.

Would it hell.

He needed to see her, speak to her, touch her. He felt anger and concern in equal measures. It was the uncertainty that was so infuriating, not knowing where she was. His whole life had become a series of unanswered questions in the past few days. First Carol and now this.

This? This fucking job?

He asked himself again why they needed him here. He still could not begin to imagine why, as Hitch had told him, Ray Plummer had specifically asked for *him* to be included. He kicked irritably at the metal fence and then turned and headed back towards the car, hands dug deep into the pockets of his jacket.

Behind him, the river flowed by.

It took just over forty-five minutes to unload the crates (sixteen in all) from *The Sandhopper* to *The Abbott*.

278

Hitch, Morton and McCann stood over the other three men while they transferred the precious cargo, guns trained on them at all times.

'And there's twenty million quid's worth in there?' Morton said quietly, watching as the tall man lowered the last crate into the hold.

'Twenty million quid's worth of coke,' Hitch said.

'That's all of it,' said the tall man, wiping perspiration from his forehead. Beside him, the youngest of the three was trying to pull a splinter from his palm.

Hitch motioned them back onto *The Sandhopper*.

'Thanks for your help, fellas,' he said, smiling. Then, looking across at Morton, 'Start the engine, Terry, we've finished.'

'You're making a fucking big mistake,' said the second man, his teeth clenched in anger. 'When Connelly finds out about this . . .'

The sentence was interrupted abruptly as Hitch fired.

The first bullet hit the man in the chest, staving in the sternum, cracking two ribs and ripping through a lung. Gobbets of pinkish-grey matter exploded from the exit wound below the right shoulder blade. The man pitched backwards, blood spouting from the wound.

'What the fuck . . .' shouted McCann as he saw Hitch turn on the other two men.

The younger of the two ran for the side of the boat, perhaps in an attempt to dive over the side. A last desperate attempt to escape into the murky waters.

The first bullet hit him in the back, severing his spine. He crumpled to the deck, his sphincter muscle giving out. The soft sound of voiding filled the air as he rolled over in agony like a fish out of water.

The tall man fared no better.

279

Hitch shot him in the face, watching as he toppled backwards, most of his bottom jaw blown off by the close-range blast.

Hitch moved swiftly from one body to the other, firing another shot into the head of each man. Into the nape of the neck of the youngest, who was lying on his stomach with part of his spine exposed, the flesh and muscle ripped away by the 9mm bullet.

Hitch jumped back aboard *The Abbott* and slapped Morton on the shoulder.

'Get us away from here,' he said sharply, and the other man guided the smaller boat away, allowing it to pick up speed.

'What the hell did you kill them for?' shouted McCann.

'They saw our faces,' Hitch said flatly. 'They knew we were with Plummer.'

'That's bullshit,' snapped McCann.

'If word of this had got back to Connelly there'd be gang war,' Hitch told him. 'We couldn't have left them alive.'

'Bollocks,' McCann roared. 'You didn't have to kill them.'

Hitch grabbed him by the lapels, pulling him close.

'And what the fuck would *you* have done with them, hot shot? Invited them out for a drink?' Hitch snarled. He pushed his companion away. 'We leave the boat to float there now. By the time somebody finds them there'll be nothing to link us to the killings.'

McCann sighed and banged his fist against the side of the boat.

'Shit,' he murmured. 'Fucking shit.' He let out a long breath then turned to look at Hitch. 'I suppose you're right.'

Hitch nodded.

Morton was already guiding the boat in towards the quay.

Hitch moved closer to the prow.

'What now?' McCann wanted to know.

'I'm getting off here. I've got to let Plummer know it went okay. You carry on down to Putney Bridge, get this lot unloaded. You know what to do with the boat.' He looked at McCann then at Morton. 'Sink it.'

Morton nodded.

Hitch was about six feet from the edge of the pier when he jumped, landing with surprising agility. He brushed dust from his sleeve and headed towards the flight of stone steps that led up to the embankment. The boat was already chugging away towards Putney. Hitch smiled and crossed the road to the Lancia, pulling open the door and sliding into the passenger seat.

'Let's go,' he said.

'I heard some shooting,' Scott told him, starting the engine. 'What was it?'

'Nothing for you to worry about, Scotty,' Hitch told him. 'Just get me to a phone, will you?'

Scott started the engine and drove off.

Hitch fumbled inside his jacket and pulled the Beretta free. He passed it to Scott.

'Take it,' he said sharply.

The driver did as he was instructed, slipping it back inside the holster, feeling the slight warmth in the metal.

'Tell me what happened,' he demanded. 'This fucking gun has been fired.'

'I had to frighten one of them,' Hitch lied. 'Fired above his head.'

Scott looked across at his companion.

'You better be telling me the truth,' he said threateningly, 'or I'll use the fucking thing on you.'

Hitch looked at him and saw the anger in Scott's eyes. He had no doubt at all that Scott meant what he said. He persisted with the lie, nevertheless.

'I had to frighten them, Scotty, I told you,' he said quietly.

'I heard six fucking shots,' Scott said. 'Why so many?'

'Just drive,' Hitch said.

Scott pulled the car over to the kerb, his right hand slipping inside his jacket. He pulled the pistol free and shoved it against Hitch's cheek.

'How many shots did you fire?' he snarled. 'Tell me or I'll blow your fucking head off.' He thumbed back the hammer.

'Six,' Hitch said. He reached inside his jacket and pulled his own pistol free. 'Here, take the mag out of my gun, replace it with the one from yours.'

Scott seemed satisfied by this and slipped the magazine free from his own pistol, jamming in the full one he'd taken from Hitch Beretta. The two men glared at each other for a moment.

'That temper of yours is going to get you into trouble one day, Scotty,' Hitch told him. 'You ever pull that on me again and I'll fucking kill you.'

'You'll have to be quicker than you were a minute ago, then,' Scott hissed and pulled the car away from the kerb.

'Just get me to a phone,' Hitch said irritably.

Scott drove on.

'There.'

Hitch pointed to the pay phone on the corner of the street and Scott brought the Lancia to a halt, watching as his companion walked across to the phone, picked it up and dialled, feeding more money in.

'Ray, it's me,' said Hitch. 'It's done. Yeah, everything. Well, *nearly* everything.' He smiled. 'Scott's going to drop me off. No, didn't need him.' He listened for a moment, glancing round at his companion in the car. 'Right. I'll call you tomorrow.' He replaced the receiver, scooped his change out of the slot and walked back towards the car, clambering into the passenger side.

Scott drove on.

Ten minutes later he dropped Hitch off close by Clapham Junction Station then drove away, heading home. The traffic was light at such an hour. He might make it back by four in the morning, once he'd dumped the car.

Hitch watched the tail lights of the Lancia disappear and headed for the public telephones nearby. He fed more money into the machine, smiling as he dialled.

Seventy

He fumbled with the key, trying to push it into the lock, cursing when it wouldn't turn. Finally the door opened and Scott stepped inside. He closed the door behind him, leaning against it for a moment, catching his breath.

He'd dumped the car a mile away and walked back to his flat, passing less than half a dozen other people along the way. He'd gone over the car with a cloth, wiping fingerprints from the steering wheel and the door handles, then he'd tossed that into the Lancia, locked it and hurled the keys away. Scott stood motionless for long moments, sucking in deep lungfuls of air. His body ached mainly through lack of sleep, he told himself, reluctant to admit he was so unfit that a mile walk had drained him of energy. Finally he wandered through into the kitchen, pulled off his jacket and draped it over the back of a chair. He hastily unfastened the shoulder holster, too, and laid it on the table, then crossed to the fridge, found a can of 7-Up and drank deeply. He carried the can with him into the bathroom where he stripped off his clothes and turned on the shower. He sat on the toilet, watching the spray, waiting for the water to warm up, sipping his drink.

His head was pounding. It had been ever since he'd dropped Hitch off. Scott reached up and massaged his own shoulders as best he could.

He needed someone to do this for him. Someone to soothe away the ache.

Like Carol?

For once he pushed the vision of her to the back of his mind, his thoughts focusing instead on the events of that night. Most particularly on the six shots that Hitch had fired. Six shots just to frighten the crew of *The Sandhopper*? Scott shook his head.

He got to his feet and thrust a hand into the spray, satisfied that it was warm enough. He stepped under it, enjoying the feel of the water on his skin, his eyes closed, still confused about what was going on. About Carol. About what had happened that night. Christ, things were becoming a mess and he could see no way of sorting them out. He *had* to speak to her. Even if it meant sitting on her doorstep until she either came out of her flat or came home from wherever she was.

For all he knew she could be dead.

He opened his eyes, rubbing his face with both hands, increasing the speed of the jets so that the water stung his skin when it struck him.

He didn't even hear the knocking on the door.

The rushing of water from the shower masked every other sound.

The knocking came again, more insistently this time.

Scott ran both hands through his hair, smoothing it back tight against his scalp.

The banging on the door had become more frenzied.

He reached for the soap and began to wash.

There was a thunderous crash as the door was smashed in. It flew back on its hinges and crashed against the wall with an almighty bang.

Scott heard it at last and looked around, fumbling for the taps, trying to turn off the shower.

There was movement in his sitting room, in his kitchen. He heard voices. Then, through a gap in the shower curtain, he saw a dark shape.

What the hell was happening?

The dark shape was coming closer.

Scott steadied himself, waiting until the shape was only a couple of feet from him, then leapt forward, crashing into the intruder.

Both men went hurtling backwards, Scott slamming the newcomer's head against the bathroom cabinet. The mirror shattered and pieces of glass cut into the intruder's neck. Scott grabbed him by the lapels and hauled him to his feet. But now there were others coming into the room.

He saw the uniforms.

The two policemen in the doorway stared in at him, one of them taking a step closer, anxious to rescue their plain clothes colleague from Scott's attack. The man was dazed but managed to shake loose of Scott's grip. He felt the back of his neck and brought his hand around covered in blood.

'Put some fucking clothes on, Scott,' he said angrily. 'You're under arrest.'

'You've got no right to come bursting in here like this,' Scott snarled. 'What's the fucking charge, anyway?'

The plain clothes man looked at him, his eyes narrowed. 'Murder.'

Seventy-one

'I'm here to help you. But I can't do that unless you help *yourself.*'

Brian Hall leant on the edge of the table and looked down at Scott.

Hall was about thirty-five, dressed immaculately in a charcoal-grey Armani suit. He was clean-shaven and his hair combed perfectly. The contrast between the lawyer and Scott was stark. Scott was dressed in jeans and a T-shirt which needed washing. He sported a thick growth of stubble and his eyes were sunken, with dark rings beneath them. He'd managed to grab a couple of hours' sleep in the cell since they'd brought him in, but it was scarcely enough to refresh him. He looked as bad as he felt. Now he cupped both hands around the plastic beaker full of luke-warm coffee and lowered his head, staring into the depths of the brown liquid as if seeking inspiration there.

Hall had arrived at Dalston police station about twenty minutes ago and announced that he was acting for Scott. He'd been shown to the interview room where Scott sat with a uniformed officer close by the door. The room smelt of stale sweat and strong coffee. All it contained were the table and two wooden chairs, one of which Hall now gripped the back of, looking first at the policeman then at Scott.

'Talk to me, Jim,' he said. 'That's what I'm here for. I'm here to help you but I can't do that unless you talk to me. Tell me what happened.' There was a hint of exasperation in his voice.

286

Scott looked up at him and motioned towards the policeman.

'Could I have a few minutes alone with my client, please?' Hall said. The policeman nodded, got to his feet and walked out, closing the door behind him.

'*Now* will you talk to me?' Hall said.

'How did Plummer know I was here?' Scott wanted to know.

'I don't really see what that's got to do with it . . .'

'How?' snarled Scott.

'Word gets round, Jim. Once he heard you'd been arrested it was just a matter of finding out which police station you were being held at,' Hall said. 'He called me, asked me to help you.'

Scott was unimpressed. He lowered his head again, the knot of muscles at the side of his jaw pulsing angrily.

Plummer knew where he was.

'And are you supposed to get me out of here?' he asked sardonically.

'I can't do that,' Hall said, flatly. 'You know that. They won't even post bail with the evidence against you.'

'I didn't kill those blokes,' Scott told him.

'I'm sure you didn't but . . .'

Scott interrupted him, angrily.

'I didn't fucking kill them,' he snarled.

'That's as maybe, but unfortunately the evidence points to the fact that you did.' Hall exhaled deeply. 'The three men were shot with *your* gun. *Your* fingerprints were found on the spent shell cases they found on *The Sandhopper*'s deck. On top of that you've got no alibi for the time of the murders.' Hall walked slowly up and down. 'They've got enough evidence to throw away the key, Jim. My only advice to you is to plead guilty.'

Scott smiled humourlessly.

'Well, thanks for that brilliant piece of help,' he sneered. 'Did Plummer send you here just to tell me that?'

'I don't know what else to say to you. The evidence against you is overwhelming.'

'I didn't kill them.'

'Then who did?'

'John Hitch,' Scott said flatly. 'Hitch killed them with my gun on Plummer's orders. I've been fitted up.'

'That's ridiculous,' Hall said. 'If Plummer was trying to frame you, why send me here to help you?'

'All part of the fucking act. He's done me up like a kipper and I fucking fell for it. That's what annoys me as much as anything. I walked straight into it.' He clenched his fists.

'You say Hitch killed them. You may believe that . . .'

'I *know* it,' Scott snarled.

'All right,' Hall said, raising his own voice. 'You *know* it. *You* know it, but on the evidence against you there isn't a jury in the world that's going to believe you.' He lowered his voice slightly. 'You'll go down for life.'

Seventy-two

She could hear their voices from the sitting room. As Carol Jackson moved about in the kitchen she could hear the steady burble of conversation, punctuated every so often by a laugh.

She cracked eggs into a frying pan and stood over them while they cooked, wincing as hot fat spat at her from the pan. It missed her skin and stained Plummer's monogrammed dressing-gown.

Beneath it, Carol was naked. She had hauled herself out of bed about twenty minutes ago when she'd heard the doorbell. Plummer had told her to make breakfast while he spoke to John Hitch. The blond man had nodded a greeting to her, and Carol had been aware of his appraising gaze. She retreated to the kitchen to cook breakfast but the odd sentence floated to her through the smells of frying bacon and toasting bread. Words and sentences, some of which she found unsettling.

'Scott was arrested . . .'

'Three killed . . .'

'The boat was sunk . . .'

Scott was arrested. She had almost dropped the frying pan when she'd heard that. She wanted to rush into the sitting room and ask why, ask where he'd been taken, but she knew she could not do that. And she wondered why she felt such a sense of despair.

Or was it loss?

Was it despair for Scott or for herself?

You wanted him out of your life; well, now he'll be gone for good.

But that wasn't how she wanted it. She didn't want him hurt.

He won't be hurt, just locked up. Locked away for the rest of his life.

Carol ran a hand through her tousled hair and sighed.

Out of sight, out of mind.

She heard Hitch mention where he'd been taken.

The fat spat at her again and she jumped back in surprise and pain as, this time, it burned her hand. She ran it beneath the cold tap for a moment then dried it and returned to the pan, lowering the heat, scooping the eggs out and onto a plate. She called to Plummer that his breakfast was ready and a moment later he ambled in, followed by Hitch. Both men sat down and

Plummer began eating immediately. Hitch accepted the cup of tea Carol offered him, looking at her as she turned her back on him. He gazed at her shapely legs, exposed as far as her thighs. Carol gave him his tea then sat down at the table next to Plummer, who carried on eating.

'When will it be unloaded?' he wanted to know.

'By the end of the day it'll be hidden. Safe. Then all we have to do is sit on it until the time's right,' Hitch told him. He glanced across at Carol. She self-consciously pulled her dressing-gown more tightly across her breasts.

'And there's no way Connelly can trace the job back to us?' Plummer said, shoving a piece of bacon into his mouth.

'Not without witnesses,' Hitch said, smiling thinly.

Plummer smiled and shook his head.

'Twenty million fucking quid,' he chuckled.

Carol looked at him. She couldn't even begin to imagine that amount of money. The figures were enough to make her head spin.

And Scott? She wanted to ask. Instead she glanced across at Hitch and found his gaze on her again.

'Nice cup of tea,' he said, smiling.

Carol smiled thinly in response and picked at the piece of toast on her plate.

The phone rang.

Plummer got to his feet immediately and walked through into the sitting room to answer it.

'Is that how you keep your figure?' Hitch asked, lowering his voice slightly. 'By not eating much?' He was gazing at her breasts again.

She shrugged.

'What do you mean?'

'You've got a good figure,' he told her, glancing quickly towards the door to make sure Plummer hadn't returned.

'More tea?' Carol asked in an effort to change the subject.

He shook his head, leaning back slightly, watching as she drew one shapely leg up beneath her on the chair.

From the sitting room he could still hear Plummer speaking.

'You used to go out with Jim Scott, didn't you?' Hitch asked.

She nodded slowly.

'I'll bet he'll miss you inside,' said Hitch. 'Only his right hand for company when he used to have *you* to get his rocks off.' Hitch smiled again. 'Are you moving in with Ray, then?'

'It's not really your business, is it?' she said, glaring at him.

He shrugged.

'I just wondered what was going to happen to your little flat if you *did* move out,' he said, his gaze never leaving her. 'Dollis Hill, isn't it?'

'How do *you* know?' she demanded.

'My business to know,' he told her. 'You're mixed up with Ray, Ray's my boss, I have to look out for him. I just did some checking, that's all.' He took a swig from his mug, pushing the empty receptacle towards her. 'I think I *will* have that cup of tea.'

She took the mug and moved across to the worktop, aware of Hitch watching her every move.

'You must have done a thing or two working in that club,' Hitch said, still looking at her. 'I've seen some of the acts.'

She pushed the mug towards him and sat down again, trying to avoid his gaze.

He glanced towards the door, still able to hear Plummer on the phone.

'Did you used to get off on what you were doing?' he enquired. 'I mean, especially with other girls?' He smiled.

291

Carol looked directly at him.

'If all the blokes I knew were like you then I'd be better off with another girl, wouldn't I?' she said scornfully.

Hitch held her gaze until he heard Plummer heading back towards the kitchen. He sat down and prodded his breakfast.

Hitch finished his tea and got to his feet.

'I'd better go,' he said. 'I'll pick you up in an hour, Ray. I've got a couple of things to do.'

'All right, John,' Plummer said. 'Carol, see John out, will you?'

Hitch smiled thinly.

'It's okay, I can manage,' he said, looking again at Carol's breasts. 'See you later, Ray.' He held her stare this time. 'See you around, Carol.' His smile broadened and he walked out. She heard the door close behind him.

'Are you going to work tonight?' Plummer asked.

'I wasn't planning to,' she said, still uneasy about Hitch. 'I thought we could stay in and . . .'

'I've got business to take care of tonight,' he said.

Carol regarded him impassively.

'I'm going to have a bath before Hitch picks me up,' he told her. He waved an expansive hand around the kitchen. 'Tidy this place up a bit, will you?' Then he was gone.

Seventy-three

He'd been dozing in his sitting room when the noise from upstairs woke him.

Dr Robert Dexter sat forward quickly, sucking in a deep breath as he regained his senses. He looked around the large sitting room, catching sight of the clock on the mantelpiece. The hands had crawled around to 1.26 a.m.

Again the noise from upstairs.

Footsteps.

Dexter got to his feet, glancing up at the ceiling. He swallowed hard and headed for the door that opened out into the hall. Outside the wind was blowing strongly. The house stood on top of a low hill, joined to the main road by a narrow driveway flanked on both sides by dwarf conifers. As he moved into the darkened hallway he could see those conifers bowing deferentially to the strong breeze.

Dexter stood at the bottom of the stairs, looking up into the gloom at their head. He reached across to the bank of switches at his right hand and flicked a couple. The darkness at the top of the stairs was dispelled swiftly by bright lights.

He put one foot on the bottom step and prepared to ascend.

The crack came from behind him.

A sharp slap of wood on glass. He spun round to see that a skeletal branch from one of the bushes beneath the hall window had been blown against the pane.

Dexter felt his heart beating a little faster as he began to climb the stairs.

From above him the sounds of movement had all but ceased; only the creak of a solitary floorboard broke the silence now. As he reached the landing he paused, looking around at the five closed doors that faced him.

He knew which one the sounds were coming from.

Dexter sighed and made his way across to the third door, halting outside it.

He found that he was shaking.

After all these years he was still afraid.

Afraid of the occupant of that room, afraid of what he might find, yet, simultaneously, knowing *exactly* what he would find. The same sight would confront him that had confronted him for the past fifteen years.

He stood by the door, listening for movement, and again heard the slow footsteps, pacing back and forth over the carpet. The creak of the one loose board.

Dexter closed his eyes for a moment. Perhaps it would just be best to walk away this time. Go to bed. Go back downstairs.

He heard breathing on the other side, close to the the door. As ever, he was aware that the occupant was listening for him, was perhaps aware even now of his presence there. The time to turn back had passed. He knew he must enter.

Dexter unlocked the door, turned the knob and walked into the room.

His heart was thudding hard against his ribs and he felt the first droplet of perspiration pop onto his forehead.

The occupant of the room was sitting in one corner.

Dexter closed the door behind him.

PART THREE

'Vengeance is mine; I will repay,
saith the Lord.'

Romans 12:19

'In this last and final hour,
You can't hide.
There's nowhere now that you can run . . .'

Black Sabbath

Seventy-four

The door crashed shut, the loud clash of metal on metal reverberating inside the cell.

James Scott stood in the centre of the small room for a moment, looking round, then sat down on the edge of the bottom bunk.

He felt numb, as if his entire body had been pumped full of novocaine. There was a lead weight where his heart should have been. He felt as if every last drop of feeling had been sucked out of him. The past two days had passed quickly, so quickly in fact that the events of those four days were somewhat hazy. And yet still he retained memories of that time. Like splinters in his mind.

The journey to the court. The police had brought a suit he'd requested from his flat and he'd changed into that, shaved and smartened himself up.

The trial.

He had decided, as advised, to plead guilty and proceedings had moved with dizzying speed. The gun had been produced as evidence. Pictures of the dead men had been circulated around the jury. Scott could remember one of the jurors in particular. She had been in her mid-forties, a smart, efficient-looking woman who had hardly taken her eyes off him throughout the trial. And he had seen hatred in those eyes. When sentence had been passed he glanced at her and was sure he could see the trace of a smile on her lips.

Scott had heard little of the judge's summing up or, indeed, of his comments after the life sentence had been passed. Just the odd word here and there, like 'horrendous', 'brutal', 'cold-blooded' or 'dangerous', had filtered through the screen that seemed to have erected itself around him. He felt as if he'd been inside a cell ever since his arrest, imprisoned within his own mind.

He had spent much of the trial gazing around the court room, particularly into the public gallery, but not once did he see Carol.

Bitch.

God, how he needed her now.

If only he could have spoken to her one last time before he'd been taken down. Touched her. Kissed her. But that was not to be. She was gone now, out of his life as surely as if she were dead.

After sentence had been passed he had been taken to the cells, then back to Dalston in a black van. From there he'd been taken in a police van to Whitely by two police officers.

The journey, despite the distance between London and the prison, had taken a surprisingly short time. Or so it seemed to Scott. It was as if time had lost all meaning, as if even that were conspiring to hasten him to this place where he would spend the rest of his life.

The rest of his life.

The finality of the words hit him once more; only now, within the confines of the cell, they had an almost deathly abruptness. He looked around the room, at the bunks, the other small bed on the other side of the cell. At the thick metal door, the wooden table and chairs. The slop buckets. There was one single window set about seven feet up the wall, covered by wire mesh as well as being barred. Freedom was now only something to be glimpsed through steel. Death must be similar to this feeling, he thought.

298

The four walls of the cell might as well be the wooden sides of a coffin. There was no such thing as life within prisons, only day-to-day existence. Passing time. Waiting for the only real release, which would come in the form of death; the actual termination of life, not the living death of captivity.

He had been shown which locker in the room was his and told that one of his cell-mates was on work detail, the other in the exercise yard. Scott didn't really care. He unzipped his bag and took out what few possessions he'd been allowed to bring in to the cell: a small cassette-radio and a few tapes. The towels were prison issue, along with the roll of toilet paper and the clean white T-shirts and underwear. He crossed to his locker and opened it. From the pocket of his overalls he took a photo of Carol. She was smiling out at him, her long blond hair tousled. She was wearing jeans and a denim shirt (which he'd bought her). He looked at that smile.

A mocking smile?

He wanted her badly.

Bitch.

He needed her.

She had betrayed him.

Perhaps she would visit him. He wedged the picture inside the locker door and stood staring at it.

No, she wouldn't visit him.

Perhaps she'd write.

He looked at the photo.

His jaw was clenched tightly, his eyes narrowed.

Why did you betray me?

I love you.

'Fucking bitch,' he snarled and drove his fist against the door, against the photo.

When he looked at it, there was blood oozing from two split knuckles.

Red spots had splashed across the picture. Across her smile.

Fucking bitch.

'I love you,' he breathed softly.

The blood dripped from his gashed hand.

Seventy-five

John Hitch drained what was left in his wine glass and put it down, looking across the table at Carol Jackson, who held his gaze for a moment and then went on eating.

Beside her, Ray Plummer was struggling to wind spaghetti around his fork but it kept falling back into the dish. Cursing, he began cutting it up, pushing the shorter strands onto his spoon.

Les Gourmets was busy, to Plummer's relief. The trade in all his restaurants had been slack over the past couple of weeks, and he was glad to see so many lunchtime diners. The babble of conversation was punctuated by the chink of bottles against glasses. Hitch poured himself another glass of Chablis, raised his eyebrows at Carol expectantly and moved the bottle towards her, but she shook her head, covering her glass with one hand.

As she did he saw the ring on the third finger of her left hand; the large diamond sparkled brightly.

Fuck knows how much that cost, Hitch thought, glancing at the impressive stone.

He afforded himself a quick glance at Plummer, who was still struggling with his spaghetti.

The manager of the restaurant, a short Italian with sad eyes and a pinched face, emerged from the kitchen and chatted briefly with Plummer about the improvement of business.

Hitch kept his eyes on Carol; by this time, she was beginning to feel uneasy under his almost unwavering stare.

The manager disappeared a moment later, leaving them alone again to finish their meal.

'Dozy bloody wop,' muttered Plummer. 'He used to work for Ralph Connelly. Ran one of his clubs in Kensington.'

'If you don't like him, why did you employ him?' Carol wanted to know.

Plummer shrugged.

'When I took over the club from Connelly I agreed to give old Guiseppe there a job,' he explained. 'Just part of the process, sweetheart.' He smiled at Carol. 'It's called diplomacy. We shafted Connelly when we took his shipment of coke but a gang war wouldn't have been any use to either of us. He knew he couldn't win one; I had too much money behind me. So we agreed to compromise with him on certain things, in return for him keeping his nose out of my business.'

'I still don't trust that cunt,' said Hitch. 'He could still try something.'

Plummer shook his head.

'If he was going to do anything, he'd have done it months ago. You worry too much, John.'

'Maybe you're a little too settled, Ray,' Hitch said challengingly. 'You might get over-confident . . .'

Plummer glared at him.

'Are you trying to tell me I've lost my bottle?' he rasped.

'I didn't say that,' Hitch added hastily.

'Then what the fuck are you saying?'

Hitch looked at Carol, then at his colleague.

301

'Well, you and Carol, you're sort of settled now, aren't you?' he said. 'You've got enough money to keep you for the rest of your life. It must be easy to lose your grip. Without even realising it, that's all I'm saying. I'm thinking about *you*.'

'Your concern is touching, Johnny boy,' chuckled Plummer, 'But don't worry about me. Just because Carol's wearing that ring doesn't mean I'm ready to get out my fucking pipe and slippers.' He eyed Hitch malevolently. 'So if *you've* got any ideas . . .' He allowed the sentence to trail off.

'Leave it out, Ray,' Hitch said indignantly, reaching for his glass of wine. He looked round at the other diners. Mostly businessmen. A few couples, laughing and joking, talking animatedly. Fucking yuppies, all of them, thought Hitch, glancing back across the table.

She's got you where she wants you, you silly cunt, he thought, watching as Carol slipped one hand onto Plummer's thigh, stroking gently as he ate. '

Horny little slag.

Carol looked at Hitch and smiled.

A smile of triumph?

He held her gaze, then allowed his own eyes to drop to her breasts, which were pressing against the clinging material of her dress. He could see the outline of her nipples.

Got him right where you want him, haven't you?

She lifted her glass, the light striking the ring, reflecting off the diamond.

To Carol it was a symbol of victory. A hard-earned trophy fought for and suffered for.

She felt she deserved it.

Sometimes she even felt something for Plummer.

302

Sometimes.

It wasn't love, that much she was sure of.

Gratitude, perhaps. Appreciation that he had provided her with the escape route she had so badly sought? She wasn't sure. What was more, she didn't care. She was here now. She was with him. She wore his ring. She shared his penthouse flat.

She looked at Hitch and smiled thinly, wetting her lips slightly with the tip of her tongue.

The gesture was provocative and he knew it.

Little slag.

Beneath the table, his fists were clenched.

Seventy-six

'We spoke on the phone a few days ago.'

Detective Inspector Frank Gregson shook hands with Governor Peter Nicholson, feeling his own strong grip matched. Nicholson motioned for him to sit down.

'I'm sorry I couldn't see you earlier, Inspector,' Nicholson said.

'*Detective* Inspector,' Gregson corrected him. The Governor smiled thinly.

He offered the policeman some tea but he declined.

'What exactly can I do for you, *Detective* Inspector?' Nicholson wanted to know. 'I must say, I was a little surprised by your enquiries.'

Gregson exhaled.

'Well, it's like this. I've been investigating a series of murders in London. In each case the killer imitated an MO used before and then killed himself, committed suicide. It took a while to identify the first two but we've finally managed to do that. The third one there was no mistake with.'

'I don't see what that has to do with this prison.'

'All the killings were committed by men incarcerated here.' Nicholson smiled.

'That's impossible. Are you trying to tell me that some of my prisoners have escaped without me noticing?' He chuckled.

'Do the names Peter Lawton, Mathew Bryce and Trevor Magee mean anything to you? Because if they don't, let me refresh your memory. They were all in here doing life sentences for murder.'

'I appreciate the refresher course, Detective Inspector, but I was familiar with those three men. I'm also familiar with the fact that they are no longer with us. By that I don't mean they've left the prison; I mean they're dead. They died here in Whitely.'

'I'm aware of that,' Gregson said.

'Then why are we having this conversation?'

'Because the three men that I've got in the morgue back at New Scotland Yard are Peter Lawton, Mathew Bryce and Trevor Magee.'

'You realise what you're saying?' Nicholson murmured incredulously.

'I know bloody well what I'm saying,' Gregson snapped, 'and if it's any consolation it sounds as crazy to me as it probably does to you. But the fact is, those three men committed nine murders between them in London less than three weeks ago.'

'Men who looked like Lawton, Bryce and Magee perhaps?'

'No. Not their doubles. Not their fucking twin brothers, either. *Those* men,' rasped Gregson, exasperated.

'It's not possible.'

Gregson got to his feet.

'I know it's not possible but it's happened,' he said angrily. 'Look, we have more than enough forensic evidence to back up their identity. What I'm asking is, could there have been some kind of mistake here, at your end?'

Nicholson pressed his finger-tips together.

'What you mean is, could we, by accident, on three occasions, have released murderers back into society? Could we have let the wrong men go?' His smile faded, to be replaced by a look of anger. 'We might make the odd administrative error, Detective Inspector, but releasing the wrong men doesn't usually fall into that category.'

'Then *you* explain what the hell is going on,' Gregson challenged him. 'Because I feel as if I'm running around in circles looking for answers.'

The two men regarded one another silently across the desk. The silence was finally broken by Nicholson. He got to his feet.

'There's a simple way to settle this,' he said. 'Come with me.'

Together they left the office, walking down the short corridor to a set of steps. Nicholson led the way. At the bottom of the steps was another corridor, a much longer one this time. They finally reached a door which opened into the courtyard at the rear of the building. A blast of cold wind hit them. Gregson pulled up the collar of his jacket.

'What did they supposedly die of?' Gregson wanted to know.

305

'I don't remember exactly, but if you'd like to check their medical files before you leave you're quite welcome to,' the Governor said.

'Thanks, I think I might,' the DI said, following his host towards the church. The weather-vane on top of the small steeple was spinning madly in the wind. A couple of inmates were collecting fallen leaves and stuffing them into black bags. Another man was trimming the grass in the churchyard with a pair of shears, raking the clippings into a sack.

'This way,' said Nicholson, heading up a short path by the church.

Gregson followed. The inmates watched them.

'There,' said Nicholson, pointing at a simple wooden cross.

Gregson peered at the name on it.

MATHEW BRYCE.

'And here,' said Nicholson, pointing at another of the markers.

PETER LAWTON.

Gregson felt the wind whipping around him, felt the chill grow more intense.

There was one more.

TREVOR MAGEE.

Gregson looked at the dates on each one, noting the year and month each man had died. All had expired within the last eighteen months.

'Satisfied?' Nicholson said. 'I don't know who you've got in your morgue back in London, but as you can see they're not the three men you thought they were.'

Gregson jabbed the nine on the phone to get an outside line and pressed the digits he wanted.

He sat on the edge of the bed in his hotel room and waited for the phone to be answered. When it finally was he recognised the voice immediately.

'Stuart, it's me,' he said.

'How's it going, Frank?' DS Finn wanted to know.

'I wish I knew,' Gregson said wearily, and repeated what he'd seen at Whitely. 'The fucking graves are there, no question, no mistakes.'

'The graves are there, fair enough, but there's no mistake about who the three geezers in cold storage *here* are either. What the fuck is going on?'

'I wish I knew. Listen, I need you to check something out for me. Go through some files. I want you to check on any murderers who've been convicted and sent to Whitely in the last three years, got it? I want a list on my desk by the time I get back.'

'When will that be?'

'Tomorrow. Early afternoon, if I can get a train.'

'Okay, Frank.'

'Stuart, just a minute,' Gregson said hurriedly. 'When you check those files there's something specific you should look for. Like I said, I want to know how many murderers have been sent to Whitely in the last three years. More importantly, I want to know how many of those men died there.'

'What have you got, Frank?' Finn asked, quietly.

'Maybe nothing. Just check those files. If you find anything, call me here at the hotel.' He gave him the name and the number of the hotel in Buxton. 'Otherwise I'll see you tomorrow.'

Gregson hung up and sat back on the bed, cradling a glass of whisky in his hand which he'd poured himself from the room's mini-bar.

He felt as if he needed it.

Outside it was beginning to get dark.

307

Seventy-seven

Scott looked up as he heard the key turn in the lock. The heavy iron door swung open and a man stepped into the cell, the door hurriedly closing behind him. The sound of the turning lock seemed deafening.

'Scott, right?' said Mike Robinson, crossing to his own bunk. 'Jim Scott?'

He nodded.

'How do you know my name?' he wanted to know.

Robinson smiled.

'The same way we know what you're in for,' he said. 'There isn't much we *don't* know about in here. At least when it comes to other members of the population.' His smile faded. 'Besides, it pays to know a few things about a bloke you're going to be sharing with, especially when that bloke's topped three other geezers.'

Scott looked at him angrily.

'I didn't kill them,' he said. 'I was set up.'

Robinson crossed to the small washbasin in the corner of the cell and spun the taps.

'Yeah,' he muttered humourlessly. 'You and everybody else in here. We're all innocent, Scott. We were *all* fitted up.' The smile returned.

'It's the truth. I didn't kill those men,' Scott insisted.

'Look, I'm one of your cell mates, not a fucking jury, and it's a bit late to start pleading innocence, isn't it?' Robinson dried his hands on the towel. 'I don't care if you killed three or three hundred. The only thing I care about is that I've got to share a cell with you. So if you cut your toenails don't leave them lying around on the floor, don't make too much noise if you have to use the slop bucket at night and if you're a shit-stabber then I'll tell you now, my arsehole isn't for rent. Right? I don't care how much snout, cash or force you use, my ring-piece is out of fucking bounds and if you try anything I'll cut your heart out.'

Scott looked impassively at him, a slight grin on his face.

'You trying to say I'm queer?' he said quietly.

'No, I'm just telling you that if you *are* then you're going to have a long love affair with your right hand because *I'm* straight and so is Rod. But there's plenty in here who aren't. If you want to find them, good hunting.'

'Who's Rod?'

'Rod Porter. The other bloke in this cell. He's on work detail at the moment.' Robinson swung himself up onto his bunk and pulled a magazine from beneath his pillow.

Scott regarded him impassively for a moment.

'You know enough about *me*,' he said. 'Who are *you*?'

'Mike Robinson.'

Scott extended his hand in greeting.

Robinson regarded it cautiously for a moment, then shook it, feeling the power in the other man's grip. Scott squeezed more tightly, the muscles in his forearm standing out like chords. When he finally released his grip, Robinson's hand felt numb but he managed to hide the discomfort.

'You got life, didn't you?' he said.

Scott nodded.

Jesus, even the words made him shiver.

Life.

'What else do you know about me?' he asked.

309

'In the real world you worked for Ray Plummer,' Robinson told him. 'And just a word of warning on that score. There are a couple of Ralph Connelly's boys in here who weren't too happy when they heard you'd blown away three of their mates.'

'I didn't kill them,' Scott snapped.

'Sorry, I forgot. You're innocent,' Robinson said. 'Whatever the case, watch your back with Connelly's boys. I'll point them out to you when I get the chance.'

Scott nodded.

'You done time before?' Robinson asked.

Scott shook his head.

'What about you?' he wanted to know.

Robinson smiled.

'I've been in and out since I was ten,' he said with something bordering on pride. 'Remand homes, detention centres, borstals and nicks. They're all much the same. It's usually just the screws who are different. The ones here are okay, as far as screws go. It's the Governor who's the *real* cunt.' He described Nicholson briefly, and mentioned particularly his words before the visit of the prison delegation. Scott sat on the edge of his own bed listening intently, hands clasped on his knees.

Robinson was still giving him the low-down on life in Whitely when the key rattled in the door again and it opened to admit Rod Porter. He was wearing a white overall on top of his grey prison issue clothes and he pulled the overall off as soon as he was inside.

Scott noticed there were bloodstains on it.

'Hard day at the office, dear?' chuckled Robinson as Porter crossed to the sink and began splashing his face with water.

He finally turned and looked at Scott.

'Well,' he said. 'I suppose a murderer is better company than a ponce.' He extended his right hand. A token of greeting.

310

Scott shook it.

Brief introductions were made and Porter explained about their last cell-mate, just as he had to the prison delegation.

'There's just one thing, Rod,' Robinson said, still smiling. 'Old Jim here is innocent. He didn't kill those three blokes. He was framed.'

Porter smiled.

'How many fucking times do I have to tell you?' snarled Scott. 'It *wasn't* me who killed them.' There was fury in his eyes.

'The cheque's in the post, I love you and I promise not to come in your mouth,' Porter added. '*They're* the three most common lies, mate. Except inside and you just added the fourth. We're *all* fucking innocent. I don't know why they don't just open the gates and let us all out now.'

'Fuck you,' Scott rasped.

'You don't have to,' said Porter. 'A jury already did that. They fucked me, Mike and you and everyone else in this shithole. There's no virgins in here. The law fucked everybody.'

Robinson chuckled.

'Very philosophical,' he said.

Porter stretched out on his bunk, hands clasped behind his head.

'So what do you think of the hotel?' he said.

Scott shrugged. He felt cold, as if all the warmth had been sucked from his body. He sat down on his own bed, exhaling deeply.

Life.

He nodded in the direction of the balled-up overall Porter had been wearing.

'What's that for?' he wanted to know.

311

'Work detail,' Porter explained. 'Laundry. I collect it and deliver it. It's better than sitting in here every day. Apart from the hospital wing.' He grunted. 'That's where the blood came from. Blood, shit and Christ knows what else. It used to be used as a punishment: they'd make inmates clean up the hospital wing, that sort of thing. Even make them change sheets and empty fucking bedpans.'

'What did anybody do to get that punishment?' Scott wanted to know.

'It was usually if somebody tried to escape,' Porter said.

Escape.

'Has anyone ever managed it?' Scott wanted to know.

'Not since I've been here,' Porter told him. 'A couple of blokes tried to go over the wall about a year ago. Before that, some prat even managed to hide in the boot of one of the warders' cars.' The other two men laughed.

'Somebody did it a while back,' Robinson said. 'Actually got out. They didn't get far, of course, but they managed to get out of the prison itself . . .'

'How?' Scott demanded, cutting him short.

'This place is very old, as you know. Supposedly there's a network of sewer tunnels running under it,' Robinson explained. 'Most of them have probably caved in by now. But one old boy over in B Wing was telling me that it's like a fucking maze down there. Some geezer got down into the tunnels and found his way out.'

'Rather him than me,' Porter muttered. 'That was probably how they found him. Just followed the smell of shit.'

Robinson laughed.

312

Scott *didn't*.

He sat back on his bed, looking around at the confines of the cell.

Life.

He sucked in a deep breath, closing his eyes momentarily.

A vision of Carol filled his mind.

Then Plummer.

He gritted his teeth.

'You all right?' Porter asked.

Scott nodded slowly, opening his eyes.

When he spoke his words were almost inaudible.

'I was just thinking.'

LIFE.

The word screamed inside his brain.

No. *There had to be a way*.

Seventy-eight

The raindrops against the window sounded like a handful of gravel being hurled at the glass by the strong wind. Rivulets of water coursed down the panes, puddling on the sill.

Governor Peter Nicholson watched the rain, hands clasped behind his back, his office lit only by the desk lamp at one corner.

He was looking out over the prison courtyard, watching the sheets of rain falling, the brightness of the observation lights along the prison walls reflecting in his eyes.

The wall clock ticked somnolently in the silence, each movement of the minute hand magnified by the stillness in the office.

It was 10.56 p.m.

'As far as I can see, it's a perfect choice.'

The voice cut through the stillness like sunlight through night.

Nicholson didn't turn, hardly seemed to acknowledge the other voice. He merely shifted position slightly, knotted his fingers more tightly together and continued gazing out of the window.

'No living relatives. There's no family anywhere, as far as I can tell,' said the other voice. 'There's a history of violence, at least that's what the psychological profile says. More recent events would appear to substantiate that supposition.'

Nicholson remained silent.

'I need to be one hundred per cent sure, though,' the voice added.

At last Nicholson turned to face the other occupant of the room.

Dr Robert Dexter ran a hand through his hair and nodded slowly, as if answering his own unasked question.

'How soon do you want to start?' Nicholson asked.

'I think we should leave it a week,' the doctor told him. 'I need to observe. As I said, I have to be one hundred per cent sure.' He exhaled deeply. 'In fact, perhaps we ought to wait longer than that.' He looked questioningly at the Governor. 'You said that policeman had been here.'

'He suspects nothing,' Nicholson said dismissively. 'I showed him the graves.'

'Even so, it might be an idea to stop work for a while. Just until the fuss has blown over.'

'What fuss? I told you, I showed him the graves.'

314

'But you said they'd identified Lawton, Bryce and Magee. What if he *isn't* satisfied with your explanation? He might come back.'

'And find what?' Nicholson leant across the desk and looked closely into Dexter's eyes. 'We've gone too far to turn back now. There's no need to delay the work, let alone stop it altogether. Unless *you're* beginning to have second thoughts.' He smiled scornfully. 'One failure too many, perhaps?'

'They were not failures, Nicholson. It *can* work, I've proved that.'

'So you say, doctor. I'm yet to be convinced.'

'It doesn't matter to you if they die, anyway, does it?'

'Not really, no.'

'I sometimes wonder why you became involved in the first place.'

'You know why.'

'Medical executions,' said Dexter quietly. 'That's what you see them as, isn't it? The ones that don't work.'

'You know my views,' Nicholson said sharply. 'This current situation is all that concerns me at the moment. Will you do it or not?'

'I need a week to observe, as I said.'

Nicholson nodded thoughtfully.

'However, the choice is perfect,' the doctor continued. He picked up the file that lay on the desk and flipped it open. Amid the plethora of papers there was a photo. He picked it up and studied the contours of the face, a slight smile on his lips.

'He'll be a good subject,' Dexter murmured. 'I'll operate as soon as I'm ready.'

He slipped the picture back into the file and closed it, looking once more at the name on the cover:

JAMES SCOTT.

Seventy-nine

Detective Inspector Frank Gregson paced slowly back and forth from one side of his office to the other, his gaze occasionally shifting to the blackboard behind his desk. To the names written on it.

DS Stuart Finn took a long drag on his cigarette and nodded at the board.

'Six murderers have been sent to Whitely in the past three years,' he said. 'I checked it out, just like you asked. Four of them died in there, all in the last eighteen months.' He looked at the blackboard once again.

'Including *our* three men,' Gregson said, finally perching on the edge of his desk. He looked at the last name on the list.

GARY LUCAS.

'It's a hell of a coincidence,' the DI muttered. 'All died there, all buried there.'

'All except Lucas,' Finn told him.

Gregson turned to look at his companion.

'By the terms of his will, Lucas asked if he could be buried near his home, instead of in prison grounds. This burial in unconsecrated ground crap hasn't been enforced since they stopped the death penalty,' Finn went on. 'It's just that none of the other three had any family to protest.'

'Nor had Lucas, had he?'

'No; but, like I said, the terms of his will specified he could be buried outside prison grounds. They planted him in a cemetery in Norwood about three weeks ago.'

Gregson stroked his chin thoughtfully.

'What did the coroner say was the cause of death?' he wanted to know.

Finn blew out another stream of smoke.

'It says cardiac arrest on the death certificate, but a proper autopsy was never carried out,' said the DS. 'The certificate was signed by some geezer called . . .' he consulted his notes, 'Dr Robert Dexter. He's down as resident physician at Whitely. The body was *prepared* there too, you know. They even put him in the coffin and shipped him home instead of leaving it to a local undertaker. Thoughtful, eh?' He took another drag on his cigarette.

'Jesus Christ,' muttered Gregson, his eyes fixed on the name of Lucas.

'Lucas must have fitted in well with the other three there,' Finn observed. 'He killed four people, including an eighty-seven-year-old woman, with a claw hammer before he was caught. Apparently he kept the old girl's left hand in his wardrobe. After he killed her he tried taking her wedding ring and when he couldn't get it he hacked her whole fucking hand off.'

Gregson appeared not to hear this last piece of information. He was already reaching for his phone, jabbing an extension number.

It rang. And rang.

'Where the hell is the boss?' he hissed.

'I should think he's gone home, Frank,' Finn said. 'It is nearly midnight, after all. What do you want him for, anyway?'

Gregson slammed the phone down.

'If I want an exhumation order he'll need to go and see a magistrate. I want Lucas dug up.'

317

'Are you serious?' Finn murmured uncomprehendingly. 'You want to dig Gary Lucas up? Why, for Christ's sake? He's dead.'

'So, apparently, were Lawton, Bryce and Magee.'

'You know they're dead. You saw their graves.'

'Yeah, I did. I also saw the three bodies downstairs in pathology. The ones that were positively identified as those same three men.' Gregson pulled his jacket on.

'Frank, where the fuck are you going?' Finn demanded, standing up as his superior headed for the door.

'I'm going to find out once and for all what the hell is going on,' Gregson told him.

Finn gripped his colleague's arm but the DI shook loose.

'Get off me,' he snapped.

'This is fucking crazy,' Finn blurted.

'If you want to help me, that's great,' Gregson said quietly, his voice soft but his tone and expression full of menace. He pointed at Finn. 'If not, stay out of my way.' The vein at his temple throbbed angrily.

Finn stood there helplessly for a moment, his own breath coming in gasps as he looked into the wild eyes of his superior.

'Where the hell are you going?' he demanded.

'Norwood Cemetery.'

Eighty

The Ford Scorpio came to a screeching halt at the massive wrought-iron gates of the cemetery.

Gregson looked at the huge barriers and banged the wheel angrily.

'You didn't expect them to be open, did you, Frank?' Finn grunted. 'Perhaps you should have called ahead and warned them we were on a zombie hunt. They might have laid on some lights too *and* some fucking shovels.'

'We're going in there,' Gregson snapped, his face hidden by the gloom of the night. He hauled himself out of the car and walked towards the stone wall surrounding the necropolis. The DI looked up at it, estimating the height to be about six feet.

He could climb it easily.

Taking a few steps back he ran at it, gripped the top row of bricks and pulled himself up onto the rampart. Balanced there, he looked into the cemetery. To his right was the chapel of rest; a little to the left of that was a wooden hut he took to be the domain of the cemetery caretaker.

They would find tools in there.

'Come on,' he called to Finn.

'You're fucking mad,' the DS snarled, looking up at him.

In response Gregson merely leapt down from the wall, landing on the gravel drive of the cemetery and rolling over to cushion his fall. The pieces of stone crunched loudly beneath him.

Finn sucked in a deep breath and ran at the wall, springing up and swinging himself over. Cursing quietly, he lowered himself down, dropping the last foot or so to the ground. He set off after Gregson, hearing his own feet crunching gravel as he hurried to catch up with his superior.

A cold breeze whipped across the open space, stirring fresh flowers on a new grave close by. One of the blooms was lifted from its pot and sent tumbling across the grass.

Trees towered over both sides of the driveway, which snaked through the vast graveyard like a mottled tongue. Branches stirred by the wind clattered together like muted applause as Finn finally caught up with his companion.

'Frank . . .' he began.

'We've got to get this door open,' Gregson said, ignoring his colleague. He took a step back and kicked at the doorknob. It came loose. Another similar impact and it gave way, the door flying inwards to crash against the wall. Gregson walked in, squinting in the gloom. 'Give me your lighter,' he said to Finn, who fumbled in his pocket and pressed the Zippo into his superior's palm.

Gregson flicked it on and raised it above his head, the sickly yellow puddle of light spreading out to illuminate the inside of the hut. There was dried mud on the floor and the place smelt damp. Ahead stood a wooden workbench; to the right on the wall there were cupboards. To the left there were tools. Gregson smiled at the shovels, spades, picks and assorted other pieces of hardware.

'Try and find some lights,' he said to Finn, who shook his head and wandered towards the cupboards.

In the darkness he cracked his leg against a wheelbarrow, yelping in pain, then cursing as he rubbed his shin.

Gregson picked up a couple of spades and a pick-axe and turned to see that his companion had discovered a large torch in one of the cupboards.

'Bring that,' he snapped as Finn flicked it on. The beam was powerful and broad. 'We've got to find the grave.'

'I joined the force to uphold the law, not play at fucking Burke and Hare,' snapped Finn.

Gregson smiled thinly and motioned for his companion to lead the way.

'Take this,' he said, handing Finn a spade.

'There must be thousands of people buried in this fucking place,' snarled the DS. 'How the hell are we

320

supposed to find *one* grave? We don't even know where it is.'

They set off along the driveway, feet sinking into the loose chippings.

'If Lucas was only buried three weeks ago, I know which part of the cemetery he'll be in,' Gregson reassured his companion. 'A friend of my father's died about a month ago. He was buried here, too. I came along with my old man. All the new ones are put in the same place. It's not far.'

As they walked Finn shone the torch from side to side, the light picking out graves on either side. Headstones stuck up from the earth like accusatory fingers, many moulded with age. Larger, sepulchral edifices appeared occasionally out of the night; marble reflected the beam of the torch. Some graves had crosses, others were completely unmarked. In many places the grass was overgrown. Great long tufts of it encroached onto the graves, the blades stirred by the strengthening wind.

As the path sloped upwards slightly, both men spotted a secondary track that was little more than a well-worn path carved out by the passage of many weary feet.

'Over there,' Gregson said, indicating the muddy path.

They changed direction. Finn sucked in breath.

'Do you reckon they'll still pay us our police pensions when we're locked up in a nuthouse? Because that's what's going to happen when people find out what we're doing,' he said.

'This is no joke,' hissed Gregson.

'You're fucking right it's not,' snapped Finn. 'Traipsing round a graveyard at one o'clock in the morning isn't my idea of a fun way to pass the time.'

'Give me the torch,' Gregson snapped, taking the light from his companion. He shone it over the headstones, picking out names.

'It's around here somewhere,' he said. 'It has to be.'

'I hope to Christ you're right,' Finn said, pulling up the collar of his jacket against the wind. A tree nearby bowed mockingly, its skeletal branches clacking together.

Gregson noted that most of the graves had fresh flowers on them. He could smell violets as he moved from one plot to another, moving the torch beam steadily over the monuments, careful not to tread on any of the graves. He noted the names, the inscriptions. The ages.

VALERIE SUTTON
BELOVED WIFE – SLEEPING
MARK KELLER –
TAKEN BY GOD
JONATHAN PIKE –
THE LIGHT OF OUR LIFE –
DIED MARCH 8th AGED 11 MONTHS

'This could take all night,' said Finn. Everytime he stepped on a grave he apologised to its occupant, feeling stupid but unable to stop himself.

Gregson kept the torch beam moving steadily.

LOUISE PATEMAN –
OUR DARLING DAUGHTER – AT REST

A metal rosebowl, overturned by the wind, clattered off its plinth and rolled against a headstone.

'Shit,' hissed Finn, spinning round.

COLIN MORRIS –
A SPECIAL HUSBAND – SADLY MISSED

The roses from the bowl were quickly scattered by the wind. The bowl continued to roll back and forth.

Finn reached for his cigarettes.

'Stuart.'

The sound of the voice startled him and he spun round to look at Gregson who was holding the beam on a simple plinth set into the ground. It bore only the name.

'I've found it,' said the DI.

Eighty-one

Gregson propped the torch up on a nearby headstone, ensuring that the beam pointed towards the grave of Gary Lucas. Then he shrugged off his jacket, draped it over a marble cross and gripped one of the shovels, driving the blade into the earth.

'Come on, help me,' he snapped, looking up at Finn.

'This is fucking crazy,' the DS said, shaking his head, watching as Gregson lifted huge clods with the spade. His own breath was coming in short gasps now. He wondered if Gregson had gone insane.

'Dig, for Christ's sake,' the DI snarled. Finally, Finn began to drive his own spade into the moist earth.

'This isn't *right*, Frank,' he said angrily.

Gregson didn't answer, but continued digging, perspiration already beading on his forehead despite the chill wind whipping around them.

The two men hardly spoke as they burrowed deeper into the earth, leaving mounds of dirt on either side of the hole. Finn paused for a moment to catch his breath but Gregson kept up his labours, digging deeper all the time. His shirt was sticking to him now and he was panting like a cart horse but still he persevered, driving the spade into the soil and hurling dark mud away behind him.

They were getting close now, he knew it.

Finn ran a hand through his hair, feeling the slickness of sweat on his face, but one look at Gregson's expression persuaded him to continue digging.

There was a loud scraping sound of metal on wood.

They had reached the coffin.

Gregson immediately scrambled down beside it, scraping earth from the top of the casket with his hands.

'Give me the torch,' he said, snatching it from his companion and shining it on the lid.

'What now?' Finn asked breathlessly.

Gregson reached up over the side of the grave and found the pick axe.

'We open it,' he said flatly.

Finn grabbed him by the shoulders.

'Frank, you can't do this,' he said angrily.

'Why the fuck do you think I dug him up, to admire the craftsmanship of the bloody box? I want to *see* that body.' He pushed his companion away. 'Hold that fucking torch over here,' he rasped, sliding the end of the pick-axe beneath the first of the coffin screws.

Finn wiped sweat from his face and pointed the torch downwards, watching as his colleague exerted all the force he could muster on the other end of the pick.

As the screw came loose, part of the coffin lid broke away.

Gregson drove the pick underneath the lid, prizing upwards until the casket snapped again.

One more screw loose and he'd be able to remove the lid.

He forced the pick between the two edges of wood and pressed down.

Finn's heart was thudding madly against his ribs as he held the light steady over the ghoulish tableau.

The screw came loose with a whine of snapping wood.

Gregson pulled the lid free and tossed it aside.

Finn shone the torch into the coffin.

'Jesus Christ,' he murmured slowly, the colour draining from his cheeks.

Gregson stood beside him, panting, his eyes riveted. He shook his head very slowly.

'What the hell is it?' Finn whispered, his voice cracking, almost lost in the blast of wind that swept across them.

The DI leant forward slightly, still gripping the pick in one hand.

In the bottom of the coffin was a black dustbin bag, its top secured by a piece of thick string.

Nothing else.

No body. No rotting corpse.

Nothing.

Gregson used the pick to tear the plastic open while Finn shone his torch at the bag.

The DI reached in and pulled something out, holding it up.

A brick.

There were a dozen more in the dustbin bag.

'What the fuck is going on?' murmured Finn. 'Where's Lucas?'

Gregson slumped back against the wall of the grave, his eyes closed. Then he dropped the brick back into the weighted coffin.

Finn looked at him, his face pale.

'Where's Lucas?' he asked.

Gregson shook his head.

'I wish I knew.'

Eighty-two

The huge refectory of Whitely Prison was filled with rows of long tables, each of which could seat over fifty men. Above, warders patrolled the catwalks, looking down onto the seething mass of grey-clad men, while other uniformed officers stood on either side of the queue for food. More warders were positioned at every third table, eyes constantly flicking back and forth over the rows of faces as they ate.

The inmates were usually allowed in according to the number of their landing. Each landing would eat in turn, then the refectory would be emptied of mainstream prisoners while the occupants of D Wing were ushered in.

Those in D Wing were kept in permanent solitary for their own protection. They were men guilty of child molestation or abuse, who had either already been threatened or injured by other inmates. These men, twenty-six of them, would be closely guarded even as they ate before being ushered back to their cells to the jeers and threats of the prisoners who were now locked up again.

Jim Scott had come to know these men from D Wing and he felt the same disgust and anger towards them as so many other inmates of Whitely. Twice he had seen men from that wing have boiling water thrown over them by the kitchen workers, the last one just two days earlier. After that, Scott was offered a job on kitchen detail. He accepted mainly because it was preferable to the boredom of being locked inside the cell for twenty-three hours of the day.

He cleaned, peeled potatoes, even helped to cook the vast quantities of food necessary to feed the inmates. He stood at the counter to splash dollops of stew or thick wads of mashed potato onto their plastic trays as each presented it in turn, moving in a slow and well ordered line along the counter, gathering mugs of tea and plastic cutlery at the end before taking their seats.

Scott was ladling soup into the bowl of a prisoner when he looked up and saw a familiar face.

Mike Robinson nodded a greeting to him and held out his bowl. Scott scooped soup from the massive copper container.

'A woman's work is never done, eh?' Robinson chuckled, winking at his cell-mate.

He reached for a bread roll, allowing the man behind him to pass by, obviously not enticed by a bowl of soup that resembled bubbling vomit.

Robinson's smile faded rapidly. He looked first at Scott, then back down the line to where a red-haired man stood, hands thrust deep into the pockets of his overalls.

'Clock the geezer with the red hair,' Robinson said.

Scott looked.

'See him?' Robinson persisted.

Scott nodded.

'His name's Vince Draper. He's one of Ralph Connelly's boys. Remember I warned you there were two of them in here? Watch yourself.' He moved on, noticing one of the warders moving across towards him.

Scott glanced up and saw that the red-haired man was coming closer. He had the plastic tray in his hand now, about three places back.

327

'Fucking cunt,' the words came drifting towards Scott. It was Draper who had spoken them. He was looking directly at Scott.

The warder who had approached Robinson had retreated to a nearby table, out of earshot.

Scott ladled more soup and tried to ignore Draper.

'I knew those three guys you shot, you fucker,' the red-haired man said, drawing closer.

Robinson glanced back to see what was happening.

'Did your girlfriend know you killed them?' Draper said, smiling. 'Did you do it to impress her?'

Scott gritted his teeth.

'You didn't have to kill three blokes to impress her,' Draper continued. 'You could have waved a twenty-quid note in front of her. That would have impressed her. It's good enough to get anyone else a fucking blow job, isn't it?' He laughed quietly.

He was two places away now. Scott gripped the handle of the ladle until his knuckles turned white, pouring the boiling soup into the bowl of the man in front of him.

'I bet she's impressed with Ray Plummer,' Draper said.

Scott glared at him.

'Impressed with his money, his power and his cock,' the red-haired man said. 'She must have had it up her and in her mouth enough times.'

He was level with Scott now.

Scott could feel himself shaking with rage. He glared at Draper.

'Fill it up,' Draper said scornfully, pushing the bowl towards Scott. 'Fill it like Plummer fills your bird's cunt.' He smiled. 'Everyone knows about them. Everyone knows she's fucking him. Everyone knows they made a prick out of you.'

Scott's face darkened; the vein at his temple throbbed. His entire body was quivering.

'Come on, fill the fucking bowl, Scott,' Draper said. 'Just try not to think about your tart with Plummer's dick stuck down her throat. Carol Jackson, isn't it? Carol "I take it anywhere for a tenner" Jackson.' He leant towards Scott. 'Seems like the only dick she's not getting any more is yours.'

Scott struck out, bringing the ladle down with incredible force on the top of Draper's head. The blow split his scalp. Already warders were running towards them, but Scott moved quickly.

He grabbed Draper by the hair and shoved his face downwards into the boiling vat of soup.

The red-haired man struggled madly as the searing fluid stripped flesh from his face and neck.

Scott pushed his head deeper, ignoring the pain in his own hand as the boiling liquid lapped around his wrist.

Others had seen the struggle now and a chorus of shouts and cheers rose from the other prisoners.

Scott, his face contorted madly, drove down with even greater force, dragging Draper off his feet.

The entire vat of soup toppled backwards, spraying up in all directions as the copper container hit the floor, spilling its load over the tiles.

Scott still had hold of Draper's hair. As he pulled the other man upright, he looked into his face. The flesh was red-raw, large portions of it hanging off the muscles where the incredible heat had stripped it away. Slivers of flesh hung like leprous wet tendrils from the blistered mess that had once been Draper's features. The other man was burbling incoherently, his eyes rolling upwards in their sockets, but he remained on his feet, supported by Scott's hand, until finally he felt the thunderous blow from the metal ladle once again. This time it was across his swollen face. His nose was shattered by the impact, blood bursting outwards,

329

spattering his overalls, mixing with the soup and the slivers of skin.

The first of the warders crashed into Scott, knocking him to the ground.

The new clash was greeted by a fresh wave of shouts from the other inmates.

Another warder pinned him down, forcing the ladle from his grip. A third man pulled Draper away, sickened by the hideous sight of his scalded features. Blisters that had already risen on the face were liquescent and close to bursting.

Scott struggled in vain as two more officers dragged him to his feet and hauled him away.

Away from the bloodied image of Draper. Away from the deafening shouts of the other inmates.

Scott found that he too was shouting, screaming his rage not just at his captors and at Draper but at someone else.

At Plummer.

At Carol.

Consumed by rage unlike anything he'd ever experienced, he was dragged bellowing from the refectory.

Up above, on one of the catwalks, Governor Peter Nicholson had seen the entire tableau. He watched as Scott was dragged away, his face impassive.

He stood there for a moment, listening to the cacophony of sound crashing all around him, then walked off.

Eighty-three

To Finn it was as if they'd been sitting there for hours.

The Detective Sergeant fidgeted uncomfortably, his hand moving habitually towards the pack of cigarettes in his jacket pocket, but each time he glanced across the outer office his eyes were met by the sign which proclaimed NO SMOKING in large red letters.

Beside him, DI Gregson kept crossing and uncrossing his legs, occasionally rubbing the palms of his hands over his thighs. Every now and then he would glance at his watch, wondering how much longer they were going to be kept waiting.

The outer office of Police Commissioner Lawrence Sullivan was large and brightly decorated. There was a desk behind which sat Sullivan's secretary, an officious woman in her early forties with long auburn hair and, Finn had noticed, a terrific pair of legs. Gazing constantly at her legs had just about made the wait worthwhile, taking his mind off the task to come. She had already offered the men coffee; the DS had accepted but Gregson had refused. Now Finn was considering whether or not to ask for another cup, even if only to watch her sashay out of the office. His request was interrupted when a buzzer on the intercom sounded and she leant forward to press a button. She answered and got to her feet, approaching the two policemen. They also rose and followed her as she beckoned them.

331

She showed them into the Commissioner's office, then left.

Sullivan was a powerful, bull-necked specimen of a man who looked more like a refugee from a bare-knuckle ring than Commissioner of Police. He was in his mid-forties, his complexion ruddy, his nose flat against his face. His normally piercing eyes were almost hidden by thick eyebrows.

On his desk Gregson saw a number of framed photos. His wife, his children and one that looked strangely incongruous, considering Sullivan's demeanour: it showed the Commissioner cradling his baby son in his arms, feeding him with a bottle. Gregson thought he might have looked more at home using one hand to choke a goat.

The big man was reading a report of some kind when the other two policemen entered and did not look up.

'Sit down,' he said sharply.

They obeyed.

Sullivan glared at them immediately.

'You're lucky I'm not suspending both of you,' he snarled. 'What the bloody hell were you playing at last night? Digging up a man's grave? I should have you locked up.'

'There wasn't time to obtain an exhumation order, sir,' Gregson said.

'Why?' Sullivan roared. 'Was the man you dug up leaving? What was so important it couldn't have waited one more day?'

'If you'll just listen, sir, I'll tell you,' Gregson said, aware of the acid glance Sullivan shot him. The DI waited a moment, wondering if his superior was going to interrupt again. When he didn't, Gregson began, keeping it as brief as he could. He mentioned the three killers, their victims, the suicides. Sullivan didn't move a muscle as he listened, his eyes never leaving Gregson as he talked about his visit to Whitely. How he'd seen the graves of men who, he knew for a fact, were actually dead and in the pathology room at New Scotland Yard itself. About four men who had died in Whitely in three years and now . . .

Sullivan held up a hand to silence him.

'Enough,' he said, rubbing his forehead with one thumb and forefinger. There was a long silence finally broken by the Commissioner himself. 'You *are* aware of what you're saying, Gregson?' he asked. 'You're asking me to believe that three men returned from the dead to re-enact their crimes? You're talking to me about zombies?' He smiled menacingly. 'If you're not out of this office in five seconds I'm going to have you both suspended. You'll be pounding a bloody beat by the end of the month.' The anger had returned to his voice.

'They didn't return from the dead,' Gregson said defiantly. 'Lawton, Bryce and Magee never died in the first place. They each committed suicide after re-enacting their crimes.'

'They were all in prison, you said yourself you saw their graves,' Sullivan reminded him.

'The men who committed those murders recently *were* Lawton, Bryce and Magee. There is no mistake,' the DI insisted. 'As I said, they never died in prison. Their deaths were faked. Just like the death of Gary Lucas. Someone went to a lot of trouble to make out that Lucas died of a heart attack inside Whitely. A weighted coffin was buried in that cemetery at Norwood to make it look convincing.'

'So where's Lucas?' Sullivan asked.

'We don't know yet.'

'And, more importantly, why would anyone want to fake his death? Are you trying to tell me there's some kind of conspiracy going on?' Sullivan got to his feet. 'Four murderers are pronounced dead, headstones are erected for them, and they're still alive? Why would anyone want to do that?' he continued. 'But you're not just implying that their deaths were faked, you're trying to tell me they escaped from Whitely. Four killers over the last three years escape from one of Britain's biggest maximum security prisons and nobody hears about it.' He turned on Gregson angrily. 'For God's sake, man, do you *really* know how ridiculous that sounds?'

'Then *you* explain the weighted coffin, sir,' Gregson said defiantly.

'I don't have to explain it,' Sullivan told him. 'I'm not the one who dug it up. As I said, you're both lucky I'm not suspending you.' He looked at Finn, too, and the DS blenched and lowered his gaze.

'There was no corpse in that coffin,' Gregson said.

'Then it must be buried somewhere else,' Sullivan said dismissively. 'I suggest you find out where. I also suggest you keep these *revelations* to yourself until you have more evidence to back them up.'

'How much more fucking evidence do we need?' snapped the DI.

'More than a *fucking* weighted coffin!' Sullivan bellowed, the two men holding each other's gaze. 'Now get out of here.' He motioned towards the door.

Gregson and Finn rose. The DS was only too happy to leave. His companion hesitated a moment.

'Lucas will kill again, sir, I'm sure of it,' the DI announced.

'Gary Lucas is dead,' Sullivan pronounced with an air of finality.

'No, he isn't,' Gregson said. 'Lucas is alive and I'm going to find him.'

Eighty-four

He could feel his hand throbbing.

Scott sat on the floor of the cell looking at the raw flesh, wincing as he touched it. It was beginning to blister in places, large pustules rising on the pink skin. At the time he'd felt nothing. Even when he'd forced Draper's head into the boiling soup he'd felt no pain. All he'd felt was the furious pleasure of being able to inflict agony on his tormentor. For all he knew Draper could be dead. A slight smile touched Scott's lips. So what if he was? What could they do to him? What more could they threaten him with? He was destined to spend the rest of his life inside; how else could they punish him? *Fuck them.*

Fuck the law.

Fuck Draper.

Fuck Plummer.

Plummer.

He clenched his fists as he thought of his boss. The act of closing his hand causing him pain, but he seemed not to mind it. One of the blisters on his palm burst, spilling its clear fluid over his skin.

Fuck Carol.

That treacherous, lying, spineless little whore.

He closed his eyes and sucked in an angry breath through clenched teeth.

Carol.

He hated her.

The vision of her came into his mind.

He wanted her.

Just to see her would be enough. For a few fleeting seconds.

To touch her.

To kill her.

He whispered her name.

Fucking slag.

The sound of the key in the lock startled him. He looked up to see the door opening, a shape silhouetted in the doorway. The solitary cell was tiny, less than six feet square, containing just a mattress and a slop bucket. Scott banged against the bucket as he hauled himself onto the mattress, trying to see who his visitor was. It was dark inside the cell and the light from the corridor outside dazzled him momentarily, obscuring the features of his visitor. As the door closed the light inside the cell went on. Scott looked up at the man but was none the wiser.

'They'll stick another five years on your sentence for what you did to Draper,' Nicholson told him.

Scott sneered.

'What's five more years on top of life?' he grunted.

'You would have been out in fifteen with good behaviour. Now you'll be an old man when they let you out.'

'What difference does it make to you? Who are you, anyway?'

Nicholson introduced himself.

'And, by the way,' he added, 'it makes no difference to me at all when and *if* you get out. You can rot in here for all *I* care.'

'So why the visit?' Scott wanted to know.

'Do you want to spend the rest of your life in here?'

'That's a fucking stupid question. What do *you* think?'

'I think that you'd settle for another six months in here instead of another twenty years,' Nicholson said cryptically. 'But there are risks.'

Scott looked vague.

'If I told you there was a possibility you could be out of here in six months, would you be interested?'

Six months is too long.

Scott looked wary.

'How?' he demanded.

'Would you be interested?' Nicholson persisted.

'Tell me how.'

Nicholson banged on the door and a warder opened it. He turned to leave.

'Tell me,' snarled Scott, getting to his feet, moving towards the Governor.

'Remember, there are risks,' Nicholson said as he stepped out of the cell. The door was slammed and locked. Scott was left with his face pressed against the metal.

'I don't care about the risks,' he shouted, banging his fist against the steel door. He struck it again, ignoring the pain as more of the blisters burst. Blood began to dribble down his arm. He pounded for long moments.

'I don't care,' he whispered breathlessly, but there was no one to hear his words.

He sank slowly to the floor of the cell and lay there gazing at the ceiling.

Eighty-five

There was always one.

David Lane muttered to himself as he rang the bell and the bus pulled away, passing Kensington Market on the right.

Always one who wanted to sit upstairs. Always one who ensured that he, as conductor, would be forced to climb the bloody stairs. At the beginning of a shift he didn't mind; he'd happily bound up and down the stairs to collect fares. But today he could hardly manage to walk from one end of the bus to the other, let alone up to the top deck. He'd pulled a muscle in his thigh playing football the previous Sunday and it was giving him a lot of pain. He'd thought about calling in sick, but he had actually received a phone call asking if he'd work a double shift as someone *else* had called in to report an illness. Consequently Lane had been working for almost ten hours, with just a break for lunch, and his leg was killing him. He moved among the passengers on the lower deck, cursing the single passenger who had chosen to sit above.

The bus was moving slowly, picking up at nearly every stop as it moved down Kensington Road towards Hyde Park Corner. Just the odd one or two extra passengers but they all, luckily, chose to sit downstairs.

Except the one bloke who'd got on at the earlier stop.

Lane massaged the top of his thigh gently as he waited for an elderly woman to find her bus pass. Perhaps he was getting too old to be dashing about every Sunday morning. He was

338

approaching thirty-three and his wife had told him he should be taking it easier now. But what the hell, he enjoyed playing, despite the fact that he'd picked up half a dozen niggling little knocks since Christmas. And his pub team were doing well in the league; he didn't want to forsake them now. Anyway, thirty-three was hardly an age to think about 'taking things easy'. Plenty of time for that when he got old. He smiled as he thought of his wife's concern. Michelle was always worrying about him. The long hours he worked, how little sleep he sometimes got. His musings were interrupted as the old girl found her bus pass and presented it to him. He smiled and handed it back to her, steadying himself as the bus came to a halt and two passengers got off. He rang the bell and continued collecting fares, making his way to the back of the bus, pausing at the bottom of the stairs. As they passed Hyde Park Corner he began to climb.

The pulled muscle in his thigh stiffened as he moved higher and it was with something akin to relief that he finally reached the top deck.

The man was sitting at the front, gazing out at the lights of London, oblivious to Lane's presence. The conductor moved towards him, using the backs of seats as support as the bus lurched on into Piccadilly.

'Fares, please,' called Lane. But still the man didn't turn, didn't even move to reach for money.

He continued staring out of the front window as if mesmerised by the lights, glancing to his left as they passed the Hard Rock Cafe.

'Fares, please,' Lane repeated more loudly as he drew level with the man.

'Where to, mate?' he asked, shifting his weight onto his other leg.

The man didn't answer.

Perhaps he was deaf, Lane wondered. He was in his mid-thirties, his hair short, his face covered by a dark carpet of stubble. The collar of his jacket was pulled up around his neck and there were holes in the knees of his jeans. *Don't tell me you've got no fucking money.*

'Where do you want to go?' Lane said, more loudly.

The man looked at him, his eyes large, almost bulging in their sockets. Lane could smell the drink on him.

Piss-artist. Great, that was all he needed. He turned the wheel of his ticket machine and cranked out an eighty pence ticket. If this bloke was smashed then he wanted him off at the next stop.

'Eighty pence, please, mate,' Lane said.

The man nodded and reached into his pocket, fumbling beneath his jacket.

'Eighty pence,' he repeated.

He smiled and looked up at the conductor.

'If you've got no money . . .' Lane began.

'I've got no money,' the man said, grinning. 'I got this.'

He pulled the .357 Magnum free and pointed it at Lane.

'Have you got change?' asked Gary Lucas.

Then he fired.

Eighty-six

The roar of the pistol was deafening in such a confined space. The muzzle-flash briefly lit the interior of the bus upper deck as the Magnum spat out its deadly load.

Lucas fired from less than ten inches. The impact of the heavy grain shell bent Lane double at the waist as the bullet tore easily through his abdominal muscles, destroying part of his lower intestine before erupting from his back, tearing away most of one kidney. A sticky flux of viscera spattered the shattered window behind him and he fell backwards. Lucas got to his feet and fired again at the fallen man, the second bullet powering into his face just below the left eye, punching in the cheekbone and staving in the entire left side of his head. The skull seemed to burst as the bullet exited, greyish-pink slops of brain carried in its wake.

Lucas turned and headed for the stairs, noticing that the bus had slowed down slightly.

He reached the running platform in time to see two of the other passengers rising, obviously having heard the shots from above. One of them, a woman in her early twenties, screamed as she saw Lucas raising the gun.

He fired, hitting her in the left shoulder, the bullet shattering her clavicle. Blood spurted into the air as he turned towards the other passengers. There were four of them.

He shot the older woman in the back of the head, watching gleefully as her grey hair turned red, her skull riven by the bullet. She pitched forward, slamming what was left of her head against the seat in front.

The bus veered to one side and Lucas cursed as his next shot missed its target. Instead it smashed through the window at the front, glass spraying in all directions. He fired again, his next shot hitting a man in the chest, caving in his sternum and bursting one lung.

Two passengers were left, a young couple at the front of the bus.

The youth was already advancing towards him, his face pale, while the girl screamed madly.

Lucas squeezed the trigger.

The hammer slammed down on an empty chamber.

Scarcely believing his luck, the youth ran at Lucas, crashing into him, knocking the gun from his hand. They both fell onto the running platform. However, despite his efforts, the youth was slightly built compared to Lucas and the older man fixed his hands around the younger man's neck, lifting his head up. He brought his knee up into the youth's groin and heard the grunt of pain.

His girlfriend was still screaming.

The bus lurched across the road and Lucas realised it was beginning to stop.

He rolled over, hurling the boy from him into the road, then scrambled to his feet, snatching up the .357. He flipped out the cylinder and pushed in fresh cartridges.

The bus had almost come to a halt now, the driver glancing behind him to see the madness on the bus.

The girl screamed once more, even as Lucas fired.

The bullet entered her open mouth, tore through the back of her throat and practically decapitated her as it pulverised sections of spinal cord. She dropped like a stone, blood spraying everywhere.

Lucas immediately turned to the driver and fired off three shots.

The first crashed through the glass partition and exploded from the front windscreen; the second hit the man in the back, squarely between the shoulder blades. The third took off most of the right side of his head. As his body went into spasm, the driver's right foot was forced down onto the accelerator, and suddenly the bus sped forward at incredible speed, crashing into a car and sending another spinning aside.

It flattened the traffic lights at the junction of Piccadilly and Berkeley Street, picking up speed as it roared towards the front of the Ritz Hotel. The blue-uniformed doormen ran fearfully from the oncoming juggernaut, which bore down on the hotel entrance with the dead driver slumped over the wheel.

Lucas shouted in triumph.

Guests and others outside ran in all directions. The sound of screams filled the air.

Then the bus hit concrete.

There was a massive explosion as the vehicle went up, bursting into flames, portions of it flying across the street like massive lumps of shrapnel. Other pieces, propelled by the force of the blast, stove in great sections of the hotel's front. The revolving doors, with two guests inside, disintegrated as the bus engine was sent flying into them. The sound of shattering glass mingled with the deafening roar as the explosion shook Piccadilly. A searing reddish-white ball of fire blossomed out from the riven bus, a thick mushroom cloud of smoke rising from the inferno. Windows not shattered by the impact were forced inwards by the sheer power of the concussion blast.

Immediately cars parked outside the hotel, caught in the detonation, began to burn. A Mercedes exploded with incredible ferocity, part of its roof spinning across the street and smashing through the plate glass windows of a chemist's. It was as if the first blast had set off a chain of smaller eruptions as half a dozen cars disappeared beneath shrieking balls of flame. Those running for cover were lifted off their feet by the shock waves; some were hit by flying glass. There were people lying all over the road and pavements, cars immobile as their drivers scrambled to escape the inferno that had filled the road and engulfed the Ritz.

In the shattered, blazing wreckage of the bus lay Gary Lucas, flames slowly devouring his skin, blistering lips still frozen in what looked like a grin.

Eighty-seven

Scott was waiting when the cell door was opened. He dutifully followed the two warders, walking briskly between them, his eyes occasionally straying to right or left as he heard voices behind the thick steel of the doors.

The trio marched along one of the catwalks around landing C and descended the iron steps carefully.

It felt good to be able to move about again after the cramped conditions of solitary. As the three men reached the exercise yard, Scott sucked in deep breaths of air. The sky above was the colour of wet concrete but he didn't care. Anything was better than the cold, insipid yellow walls of his cell.

Life.

He sucked in another lungful of air, remembering his conversation with Nicholson.

Risks. What kind of risks?

He didn't care. There was a chance of escape, perhaps. A chance to get away from this place. To return to London.

To Plummer.

To Carol.

He marched faster as they drew near the hospital wing. Despite himself, Scott felt a shiver of fear run along his spine.

Was the means of release within that gaunt edifice? And, if so, what form did it take?

Release.

He clung to the word like a dying man clings to life.

The trio entered the building, Scott recoiling from the pungent odour of disinfectant. He was led down a long corridor. At an office door one of his escorts knocked and was told to enter.

Scott waited, glancing at the other warder. He remained impassive. Finally Scott was ushered in, the first warder hesitating inside the door.

'You can leave,' said Dr Robert Dexter.

'He's dangerous,' the warder insisted.

'Wait outside,' Dexter said, and the uniformed man left reluctantly. He waited until the door was closed, then motioned for Scott to be seated.

'Do you know who I am?' Dexter asked.

'Should I?' Scott enquired.

Dexter smiled thinly.

'No, I suppose not.' He introduced himself quickly. 'And you are James Scott.' He had a file open before him. 'A convicted murderer.'

'I didn't kill those men . . .' Scott began.

'That's as maybe, but as far as the law is concerned you're guilty. You're going to spend the rest of your life inside.'

Life.

Dexter looked at the file, even though he already knew the contents well enough.

345

'You lived alone; you have no family. No wife. No children,' he said quietly. 'No one.'

Scott regarded him coldly.

'Nobody to miss you,' Dexter continued.

'Try telling me something I *don't* know,' Scott snapped. 'You seem to know such a lot about me. Who the hell are you? A doctor? Big deal. What's that got to do with me?'

'More than a doctor, Scott. A surgeon. I specialise in disorders of the mind. God alone knows there are enough in this place.' He smiled thinly, but it faded quickly.

'I still don't understand what this has got to do with me,' Scott told him. 'I couldn't give a fuck if you're a brain surgeon or a gynaecologist. Perhaps you'd be better off if you were. There are plenty of cunts in here, most of them wearing uniforms. Why should it matter to me?'

'The same way it mattered to the five men before you. Four of them were released from here. Four convicted murderers, like you, allowed back into society. Most had only served a year or two of their sentence.'

Scott sat forward.

'They were *just* like you,' Dexter continued. 'Alone. They had no one. That's why we chose them. The same way we've chosen you. They knew of the risks and they accepted them.'

'Nicholson said something about risks. What did he mean?' Scott wanted to know.

'The operation always carries a risk . . .'

'What fucking operation?' Scott snapped.

'The insertion, into the forebrain, of a tiny electronic device. Once it's placed there, after a few months you'll be released.'

346

Scott sucked in a deep breath. His mouth felt dry, and when he tried to lick his lips he found that his tongue was also as dry as parchment.

'No one except the Governor, myself and my immediate staff know about this. It's up to you whether or not you decide to go through with the operation, but think about the possibility. Release.'

'What about the law? They'll know I'm gone, that I've escaped.'

'But you won't have escaped, you'll have been *released*. And there'll be no police interference. All the arrangements will be taken care of here.'

Scott stroked his chin thoughtfully.

'You said you experimented on five men, but you said *four* were released. What happened to the other one?'

'He died. There were complications, the risks that Nicholson mentioned.'

'What happened to him?'

'A massive brain tumour developed where the device was implanted. There was nothing I could do to save him, but he'd known about the possibility of failure from the beginning. It was a chance he was willing to take.' Dexter eyed the other man coldly. 'Are *you* willing to take that chance, Scott? Six months at the most and you'll be able to leave here. Six months. Not life.'

Life.

'If I agree, how soon can you operate?' he wanted to know.

'Tomorrow.'

Six months, Scott thought. Six fucking months and then out. Back to London. Back to Plummer.

Back to Carol. The bitch.

Six months.

347

Fuck it. He wouldn't wait that long.

He looked directly at Dexter, his eyes unblinking, his voice even.

'Do it,' he said quietly.

Eighty-eight

'Could there have been a mistake?'

Police Commissioner Lawrence Sullivan looked up from his desk at Phillip Barclay.

The pathologist shook his head.

'The body that was pulled out of the wreckage *was* Gary Lucas,' Barclay confirmed. 'The dental records matched and so did the fingerprints.' The pathologist sighed. 'And, like Lawton, Bryce and Magee I found that Lucas had also been suffering from a massive brain tumour. There was enough left of the head to ascertain that.'

Sunshine was pouring through the windows of Sullivan's office. Gregson could feel the warming rays on his arms as he sat looking at his superior.

Now tell me I'm wrong, you smug bastard, he thought.

'What were the final figures on dead and injured?' Sullivan wanted to know.

DS Finn flipped open his notebook.

'Twelve dead – that includes Lucas – and twenty-four injured,' he announced.

'I suppose you think this supports *your* idea, Gregson?' said the Commissioner.

348

'It seems hard to argue with the facts now, sir, I would have thought,' he said triumphantly.

'The facts, according to you, being that Bryce, Lawton, Magee and Lucas didn't die inside Whitely. Their deaths were, for some unknown reason, faked. Correct?'

'How can you argue with the evidence in front of you, sir?' Gregson wanted to know.

'I can argue with it because *this*,' he held up a blue, bound file, 'is the report of a government committee chaired by an MP called Bernard Clinton. It seems that he and three of his colleagues visited Whitely not long ago to investigate the overcrowding there. He doesn't mention anything unusual. In fact, he compliments the administration there for their work in trying to alleviate overcrowding.' Sullivan dropped the file onto his desk with a thud. 'No mention of anything like a conspiracy. No mention of faking the deaths of murderers, then releasing them.'

'Well, I don't expect he was shown the process, sir,' snarled Gregson.

'What process, for Christ's sake?' Sullivan demanded. 'Four men died in Whitely. Their crimes were imitated . . .'

'The crimes were re-enacted by their original perpetrators,' Gregson interrupted angrily. 'What the fuck is it going to take to make you realise what's going on?'

Finn looked warily at his companion, then at their superior.

'What do you want, Gregson?' Sullivan asked.

'I want exhumation orders for those other three men,' the DI said flatly. 'I want to go into Whitely. I want those graves dug up. I want to see that Lawton, Bryce and Magee are in the coffins they're supposed to be in.'

'You're insane,' Sullivan hissed.

'Just like I was insane to dig up Lucas? If I'm crazy then so is Finn, because he saw that empty coffin. So is Barclay, because

349

he's told you that it's Lucas we've got downstairs, just like it's the others we've got down there keeping him company. I'm beginning to think it's *you* who's crazy, sir. You refuse to believe what's right in front of your nose.'

'There'll be a dismissal notice in front of *your* nose if you ever speak to me like that again, Gregson. Do you understand?' Sullivan rasped. 'I've seen the evidence, I've heard the facts but I can't issue exhumation orders for those other three men.'

'Why *not*?' Gregson asked, exasperated.

'Because this isn't just police business, it's political,' Sullivan said. 'What the hell do you think the Press would make of it? Police officers, digging up graves in a prison to find out whether or not the men supposedly buried there are really dead? There's a Home Office report testifying to the efficiency of Whitely Prison and *you're* trying to tell me there's a conspiracy going on there with the full knowledge of the Governor.'

'At least consider the facts, sir,' Gregson said, leaning forward. 'We have irrefutable proof that the four men lying in the pathology lab. supposedly died anything up to a year before they actually *did*. We know their identities. We know the death of at least one of them was faked. They all duplicated their original crimes, they all committed suicide. Every one of the four was suffering from a massive brain tumour at the time of his death, and every one had been an inmate at Whitely Prison.'

Sullivan exhaled deeply, sitting back in his chair, massaging the bridge of his nose between his thumb and forefinger. He looked at the pictures of his wife and kids on the corner of his desk, reaching across to straighten one of them slightly. When he spoke again his tone was softer.

'Gregson, I *have* considered the facts,' he said. 'But I've also considered something *you* obviously haven't. Namely, the consequences. Have you stopped to think, once, of the ramifications involved if you're right?' He looked at the DI, whose gaze never faltered. 'Christ alone knows, there's enough public concern about what goes on in our prisons at the moment; can you imagine what would happen if you were proved to be right? A conspiracy of officials at one of the country's leading maximum security prisons? As I said, it isn't just a police matter. It's a question of politics, too. Politics and ethics.'

'I'm sure the people that Lucas and the others killed would be impressed if they were alive to hear you, sir,' Gregson said acidly.

'I can't sign those exhumation orders,' the Commissioner said wearily.

'Why not?' snapped Gregson. 'It's our only way of finding out once and for all what's going on. How many more times has this got to happen before you'll agree?'

'Appeals to my conscience won't work,' Sullivan told him.

'I'm not appealing to your conscience, I'm appealing to your common sense.'

There was a heavy silence, finally broken by Sullivan.

'You're so sure you're right,' he began.

'The evidence . . .'

Sullivan cut him short.

'I know all about the bloody evidence,' he interrupted, holding up a hand to silence the DI. 'But just suppose, for one second, that you're wrong.'

'Then I'll resign,' Gregson said flatly.

'You and all the rest of us, too,' Sullivan said, looking around the room. 'You still don't know *why* the murderers are being released again.'

'And the only way I'll do that is by getting inside Whitely and seeing inside those graves,' the DI said.

'You could be wrong,' Sullivan repeated.

'It's a chance I'm willing to take.'

The Commissioner rubbed both hands over his face.

'Well, I'm *not* willing to take that chance,' he said.

Gregson got to his feet angrily.

'That means you won't sign the papers for the magistrate's order?' he rasped.

'Not until I've thought about it more.'

'How much longer is that going to be?' Gregson wanted to know.

'As long as it takes,' Sullivan told him. 'Now get out.'

As the three men filed out of the office Sullivan called to the DI.

'You want an answer?' he said, reflectively. 'You can have one. In forty-eight hours.'

'Forty-eight hours could be too long,' Gregson snapped.

'You don't have a choice. I'll give you my answer then.'

Gregson nodded, closing the office door behind him.

Sullivan turned his chair to face the sun, looking out over London, the beginnings of a headache throbbing at his temples.

Outside, the sun had been obscured by a thick bank of dark clouds.

Sullivan closed his eyes, fingertips pressed together beneath his chin as if he were praying.

It seemed most appropriate.

Eighty-nine

Pain.

Pain like he'd never experienced before.

Jesus, it felt as if his head were going to explode. As if someone were filling it steadily with molten lead, his veins swelling inexorably.

Make it stop.

James Scott tried to open his eyes but even that simple act seemed beyond him. Whatever he did, it brought more pain.

For fuck's sake stop it.

He clenched his fists, the veins on his arms standing out like cords.

It was into one of these bulging veins that the needle had been pushed, puncturing the throbbing vessel as if it were some kind of bloated worm.

Scott hardly felt it. The massive agony that filled his head eclipsed everything else. He groaned softly, the sound muffled. Again he tried to open his eyes and, again, found it impossible. There was only darkness. Was he blind? Sightless and voiceless, only his pain for company? What was happening to him?

'Scott.'

He heard the voice close by. Whispered so close he could feel the breath on his ear.

'Scott. Can you hear me?'

He tried to speak but no sound would come; his throat felt as if it had been scoured with steel wool. He croaked something inaudible, wondering if his ability to speak had gone the way of his sight. *And all the time there was the pain.*

'If you can hear me, move the fingers of your right hand,' the voice said.

Scott tried but couldn't. Paralysis, blindness and an inability to speak. He only needed deafness and he had a full set.

'Move your fingers,' the voice urged.

Again he tried, this time managing it.

Christ, that pain was still there, screaming inside his head.

'Good,' said the voice.

353

Scott moved his lips but still no sound would come. He opened and closed his mouth like a goldfish.

'I've given you 50cc of morphine,' the voice told him. 'That should help the pain quickly.'

Scott was sure his head was going to explode. He was beginning to wish it *would*; at least it would mean an end to this pain.

This unbearable, fucking pain.

He clenched his fists, not realising at first that he'd managed to move his hands.

'That's good,' the voice assured him.

Scott lay still, his breath coming in shallow gasps. He was aware of the pain subsiding slightly; perhaps the morphine was working. His skull still felt as if it were full of boiling steel, but the agony was diminishing by the second. He tried to swallow, but it felt as if someone had filled his mouth and throat with chalk. He could only make a strangled hissing sound.

'Drink,' the voice said and Scott felt the cold edge of a beaker against his lips. Drops of water splashed onto his tongue and down his throat. He gasped.

The pain was still there but it was easing off now.

He was still blind, though.

It took him a moment or two to realise that his eyes and, indeed, most of his head were covered by bandages. More water spilled into his mouth. Some of it ran down his chin, to be wiped away by a gentle hand.

'You can hear me?' the voice said. It was a statement rather than a question.

'Yes,' Scott croaked hoarsely.

'The operation is over. You've been unconscious for ten hours.'

It felt like ten years.

354

'Was it successful?' Scott asked, a renewed stab of pain jolting him.

'You're alive, aren't you?' Dexter said. 'I won't know *how* successful for a while yet.'

'How long is *a while*?'

'You must be patient. All I want you to do now is rest.'

'Take the bandages off my eyes,' Scott said quietly.

Dexter gently cut through the gauze until he revealed the two cotton wool pads covering Scott's eyes. He lifted each one away with a pair of small forceps, noticing how dark the lower lids were.

'Open them slowly,' he instructed.

Scott tried but couldn't.

The pain throbbed inside his head once more.

'I can't,' he hissed.

'Yes you can,' Dexter insisted, reaching for a piece of cotton wool. He soaked it in liquid and gently rubbed Scott's lids. When he tried again he managed to open his eyes. The light caused the pain to intensify and he snapped them shut quickly. After a moment or two, however, he opened them again, the lids unfurling like ancient roller blinds. He could make out Dexter's blurred shape. He blinked to clear his vision, his eyes still narrowed.

The image sharpened.

'Can you see?' Dexter wanted to know.

'Yes,' said Scott, a note of relief in his voice.

'Rest now,' the doctor told him. 'I'll be back to check on you in a couple of hours.' He turned and walked away, his footsteps echoing inside the ward. He disappeared through a door at the end and Scott was left alone.

He looked slowly to his left and right, the movement of his eyes causing him pain but nothing as intolerable as that he'd experienced upon waking. He saw that the ward comprised just six beds; only his was occupied. The windows were large, arched and equipped with shutters that were pulled shut. It was difficult to tell whether it was night or day beyond them. A single light in the ceiling above provided the only source of illumination. Scott stared at it until his eyes hurt and the throbbing pain in his skull began again.

Stop the pain.

As he lay there with his eyes closed it lessened and he let out a sigh of relief.

He was tired; his eyelids felt as if they'd been weighted.

Sleep.

If he slept, though, he had no guarantee the pain would not creep over him again like some malignant invader.

There was always the morphine.

Sleep. Pain. Morphine.

A simple equation.

He closed his eyes.

He slept.

'Scott.'

He heard the voice, perhaps in a dream.

'Scott.'

More insistent now. A hand on his arm.

Get out of my dream.

He opened his eyes.

Pain. Not as bad as before.

He blinked hard, trying to make out the features so close to his own.

'It's me, Porter,' the other man said, his voice low.

Scott recognised his cell-mate.

'What are you doing here?' he said, his throat dry. He reached for the water on the table beside him but couldn't get it. Porter put the beaker in his hand and helped him drink. 'How did you get in here?' Scott persisted.

'Laundry, remember? I was told to bring in some clean sheets, leave them here.' He looked at his cell-mate. 'What the fuck have they done to you?'

'Listen to me.' Scott gripped the other man's wrist with almost unnatural strength for someone in his weakened state. 'I need your help. I've got to get out of here.'

'Out of where?' Porter said scornfully.

'Out of Whitely.'

'You couldn't get out of fucking bed.'

'With your help I can,' Scott hissed, wincing as he felt the stab of pain in his skull.

No, please, not that again.

'Help me, Porter.'

'How?' the other man asked. 'You look as if you're ready for the fucking morgue.'

'I'm not going to any morgue,' Scott snarled, his eyes blazing. 'I'm getting out and you're going to help me. Now listen to me. There isn't much time.'

Porter sat on the edge of the bed as Scott began to speak.

Rain clouds were filling the skies, hastening the onset of evening.

It would be dark in three hours.

Ninety

The needle slid easily into his vein and Scott looked down at it, welcoming the morphine as it was pumped into his system.

Anything to stop the pain.

Dexter swabbed the puncture and fixed a small plaster over it.

'You should be all right for the rest of the night now,' he assured Scott. 'One of the orderlies will be around if the pain gets too bad, but I've told them not to disturb you until the morning.'

Scott sucked in a deep breath.

Dexter reached into his pocket and pulled out a pen-light which he shone first into Scott's left eye then his right, watching the pupils react accordingly. He nodded to himself.

'You should be fine until the morning,' he said. He turned to leave, pausing at the door to take one final look at Scott. He walked out, leaving the patient alone.

Take it easy now. Take your time.

He glanced at the wall clock.

8.36 p.m.

The pain in his head was just a dull ache now, thanks to the morphine. He wondered how long it would stay like that.

Forget the pain.

He closed his eyes.

Silence.

Scott awoke in a stillness broken only by the spattering of rain against the windows. Through the gloom he could see the clock.

11.06 p.m.

He blinked hard, feeling a slight pain in the roof of his skull. He turned his head slowly from side to side; the pain was never very far away. Yellow light spilled beneath the door from the room beyond. He could hear no sounds of movement from the other side of the door.

Scott slowed his breathing and then, with infinite slowness, raised his head from the pillow.

The dull ache remained but did not develop suddenly into the searing pain he had come to know so well. For that, at least, he was grateful. He propped himself up on one elbow and rose a few more inches, swinging his feet out of bed, touching the cold floor with his toes.

He sat upright.

No pain.

Steadying himself, he prepared to stand, aware of the weakness in his legs.

He stood up.

A wave of dizziness hit him; for a moment he thought he was going to collapse. The room spun madly around. He shot out a hand to steady himself, almost knocking over the jug of water on the bedside table. It teetered precariously for a second but remained upright. He leant against the bed, closing his eyes, waiting for the dizziness to pass. He stood up more slowly this time, pressing each of his feet in turn hard onto the floor.

All right, hot-shot. Now let's see you walk.

He took a faltering step, afraid that the dizziness would return, or worse than that, the pain.

Neither happened.

He walked with relative ease towards the door, turned and walked back again. He repeated his movements, still aware of the silence beyond the closed door.

He had to know if there was anyone there.

From what Porter had told him, he knew he had to get into the adjacent room.

Porter.

Scott hoped he'd managed to fulfil *his* part of the plan. Not that it would matter if he had or not, if Scott couldn't get into the next room.

He reached down for the door-knob; his hand rested on it.

If the orderly was there he would want to know why Scott was out of bed.

If he wasn't, he couldn't be far away.

If . . .

Scott glanced down at the door-knob again.

He swallowed hard.

Still silence from the other side.

He hesitated, looking across at the bedside table. To the jug of water.

Scott turned and headed back, sitting on the edge of the bed. He waited a moment then pushed the metal jug. It landed with a loud clang on the floor.

No one came running to see what was happening.

The door didn't open.

Scott got to his feet and crossed to the door, this time turning the knob immediately. He peered out into the room beyond. It was empty but for a small desk and some cupboards round the walls.

On the corner of the desk was a steaming mug of tea.

Scott realised that the orderly who'd left it would be back to claim it.

He had to move fast.

The laundry chute was directly opposite him, a hole in the wall about three feet square.

Scott closed the door behind him and made for the chute, clambering in feet first, feeling the cold metal against his back when the surgical gown opened. He supported his weight against the frame of the chute, aware of the dull ache in his skull.

Please don't let it be a long drop.

He let go of the frame.

His weight carried him faster than he would have liked; in seconds, he found himself coming to the bottom of the chute. He went hurtling off the metal lip and sprawled on a pile of dirty sheets, rolling over once.

He grunted in pain as he hit the bottom and flopped over onto his back, the pain in his head intensifying for a moment.

It was almost pitch black in the laundry room, the only light coming from a furnace that stood in the centre. It was used to burn any linen too soiled to be used again. The small chamber was lit by a hellish red glow from the furnace's mouth.

Scott got to his feet, touching his head tentatively, aware of the stench around him.

The sheets he was lying on were smeared with excrement. Scott grunted and dragged himself upright, wiping the reeking mess from his hands with a clean portion of the sheet. Still, they had served their purpose to break his fall. As he looked around he could hear the low rumble of the furnace. The stone floor beneath his feet was warm.

Scott squinted in the gloom and finally found what he sought.

The laundry cart was there, just as Porter had promised.

Scott crossed quickly to it, rummaging through the dirty linen inside.

He found the prison overall.

Moving swiftly he pulled off the surgical gown and tossed it aside. Climbing into the overalls, he held on to the side of the cart momentarily as he felt a particularly violent stab of pain inside his head.

Not now.

It passed. He continued searching through the cart, ignoring the stench that rose from its contents.

His hand closed over the torch and he pulled it free. Ficking it on, he tested the beam in the gloom of the furnace room.

At the bottom of the cart he found the knife.

It was fully ten inches long; Porter must have taken it from the kitchen. Scott ran his thumb gently along the edge of the blade, feeling its razor sharpness. Satisfied, he slid it into his belt.

The door of the furnace room opened out onto one of the prison's two courtyards. As Scott peered into the night he could see search-lights moving slowly back and forth over the open, cobbled area.

A little to his left was the drain cover, two feet square and rusted. He knew he must remove it.

He stood there for moments, trying to estimate how long he had between the light passing. It was no more than ten seconds.

The beam swept by and Scott hurried across to the cover. He dug his fingers inside and pulled.

It wouldn't shift.

The light was turning, sweeping back towards him.

He pulled at the lid again.

Jesus, it was heavy.

Five seconds before the light returned.

He pulled.

Pain filled his head as he grunted with the effort.

Four seconds.

It moved a fraction.

Three.

Scott dropped the lid again and scurried back inside the furnace room as the light swept by.

362

He watched it disappear in a wide arc then tried the lid for the second time.

It moved a fraction more, the rusty metal scraping against the stone.

Come on. Come on.

The light was beginning its movement back towards him.

Scott lifted, his muscles screaming with the effort, the pain in his head intensifying.

Nine seconds away.

The drain lid was coming away.

Eight.

He lifted it free with a final triumphant grunt and shone the torch down into the black maw below.

Seven.

The powerful beam picked out a rusted metal ladder. Far below, the light reflected on the surface of a stream of filthy water.

Six.

Scott swung himself into the outlet, climbing down the first few steps. Gripping the metal grille in one hand, he hauled it back into place behind him.

Five.

Jesus, the pain.

Four.

The grille dropped into place above him.

Three.

He clambered down the next few rungs as the light swept over. Scott hugged the ladder, his breath coming in gasps. He shone the torch below, surprised how far down the shaft went. The old sewers must be a good seventy or eighty feet below ground. Scott swallowed hard, then began to descend.

Ninety-one

The stench was almost unbearable in the tunnels but Scott pressed on, wading through filthy water that lapped as high as his knees. The walls on either side of him were crumbling, pieces of rotten stone falling away as he touched them. Occasionally his hand encountered patches of the green slime that coated the subterranean passages like putrid mucus. It was like walking through the gangrenous veins of some sleeping giant, paddling in stagnant blood.

Scott realised that the sewer tunnels were so full because of the rain that was still falling. The knowledge hardly made his journey any more palatable, all the same. He would stop every few hundred yards to catch his breath and try to get his bearings. The tunnels usually ran straight, but when he reached the junction of two he had to be sure he was travelling in the right direction; otherwise he would merely double back on himself and end up wandering these cavernous halls until he collapsed.

There was one such junction up ahead.

Scott leant against a wall, feeling the slippery slime soaking through his overall. He ignored the cold and pointed the beam ahead. It cut through the tenebrous blackness, picking out something that glinted dully in the luminosity.

About fifty yards ahead there was a grille, the steel not yet rusted and crumbling like most of the metalwork down there. It must have been recently fitted, he assumed. Behind the grille the tunnel was much narrower. At present Scott could walk without needing to stoop; if he'd been able to get past the grille he would have been forced to crawl, such was the narrowness of the outlet beyond.

He moved off to his right, grunting as he felt a renewed stab of pain inside his head.

He tried to quicken his pace, but the water rushing around his knees prevented that. He fought his way on through the reeking flow.

Again he paused, sucking in deep lungfuls of the vile air, coughing at its rankness. The spasm set off a dull and persistent ache in his skull. He closed his eyes for a moment, touching one hand tentatively to his bandaged head.

When he brought his hand away he noticed, with horror, that there was blood on his fingers.

'Oh God,' he whispered, the sound amplified by the confines of the tunnel.

He must have opened up the wound when he fell from the laundry chute, he guessed. He'd have to be careful to keep it clean. If any of the dirt down in the sewer got into it, God alone knew what would happen.

Scott pushed on, reaching another tunnel junction.

Left, right or straight on?

He shone the torch first one way, then the other.

The right hand tunnel was blocked about twenty feet on by a new stone wall.

He chose to go straight on, trying to get some kind of mental picture of where he was. He guessed he was below D Wing by now. He couldn't be that far from the wall, surely? It felt as if he'd been walking for hours. His body was quivering from the cold and the pain inside his skull was getting worse.

Perhaps it was the cold breeze blowing into his face which . . .

The realisation hit him like a thunderbolt.

Cold breeze blowing into his face.

The breeze had to be coming from up ahead.

He'd passed beneath many outlets above, but had felt no cold air coming through them because of the depth of the tunnels. But now the wind was blowing *into* him. He *must* be heading in the right direction. He pushed on, his throat dry, his head throbbing but the thought of escape now giving him added energy.

Escape.

It had a beautiful ring to it.

He even managed a smile.

Ahead of him there was a loud splash.

Then another.

Something had dropped into the water.

Scott shone the torch around and it picked out two pinpricks of yellow light.

Eyes.

Staring back at him.

There was another splash, closer this time.

He felt something nudge his leg.

There were rats in the water.

The knowledge brought with it a stark and quite irrational terror that he found difficult to shake off. He moved forward more slowly now.

Close by him a furry shape scuttled along the low ledge that ran alongside the flowing effluent.

Scott moved away, his hand sliding into more of the noxious slime that coated the walls.

He moved as quickly as he could, the cold breeze now strong in his face.

Ahead, less than twenty feet away, he saw the grille.

Beyond it he could smell grass.

366

He tried to run, to reach the barrier more quickly, gripping it with both hands when he finally did. He could see through, out into the darkness of the night. He could see trees swaying, silhouetted against the swollen clouds that filled the sky. The stream of filth was now hardly over his boot tops. He tugged at the grille.

It remained firmly in place.

He tried again.

Still no luck. It was stuck fast, secured by six heavy screws which fixed it to the wall.

Scott pulled the knife from his belt and placed the blunt edge in one of the grooves on the screw-head. He turned it, putting all his strength into it, his teeth clenched.

He closed his eyes as he felt that all-too-familiar pain inside his skull.

The screw began to come free.

He turned it, twisting it the last quarter of an inch with his fingers. He dropped it into the water and set about the second one. Then the third.

Despite the cold wind he could feel the perspiration on his face as he worked to remove the screws.

The last one came free and he tugged the grille away from the wall, hardly feeling the pain as the steel cut into the palm of his hand. He tossed it aside and blundered out into the fresh air, almost slipping on the muddy ground. He breathed in the air. Clean air. Untainted by the stench of captivity.

The air that came with freedom.

He wondered if revenge would smell the same.

A brief image of Plummer flashed into his mind.

Then Carol.

He set off across the open ground towards the trees. Beyond it there was a road.

He would be well away before first light.

367

Free.

He ignored the pain in his head as best he could, but as he ran across the muddy ground a thought occurred to him.

The effects of the morphine were beginning to wear off.

And when it did, the pain would return.

Pain unlike anything he'd ever felt before.

Scott looked back over his shoulder, as if fearing he was being followed.

The prison seemed to be a part of the night itself, the huge walls apparently hewn from the solid blackness.

He ran on.

He knew what he must do now.

Ninety-two

The pain was returning.

Unchecked by pain-killers, it filled his skull more intensely as each moment passed.

Scott fell against a tree and leant there, slumped and dishevelled, trying to get his breath, trying to think about something other than the excruciating agony that was lancing through his head. He put both hands to his temples and felt the bandages there. He fancied he could feel his cranium swelling with each beat of his heart.

He had reached the road now. Looking back in the direction of Whitely, he could see that the prison had all but disappeared in the tenebrous blackness of night. Rain was falling heavily now, the cold droplets beating onto his head. He stumbled onto the tarmac and began walking, not even sure which direction he was heading. Scott didn't know how far the nearest town was but, he surmised, there must be a house of some kind in the vicinity. It was farming land around the prison. Surely there would be somewhere for him to seek shelter. He flicked off the torch and jammed it into his belt along with the long-bladed knife, using both hands to wipe the rain from his face as he walked. Every step seemed an effort. And, with each contact he made with the ground, that searing pain would spear through his skull, making him wince, once almost making him topple over.

Make it stop.

He leant against one of the trees at the roadside, hoping the pain would subside. Then he pressed on, turning a bend in the road.

To his left, across a dark field, he saw some lights.

A house.

Just ahead of him was a wooden gate that opened onto an unguarded dirt track. Scott assumed it led to the house. He could see rain falling in the puddles that had formed in the ruts of the track. As he tried to edge his way forward, avoiding the worst of the mud, one foot slipped in the slimy ooze and he sank up to his ankle in the clinging muck.

Cursing, he shook himself loose and prepared to trudge on towards the beckoning lights.

The approach of car headlamps made him duck back into the bushes.

The car, he guessed, was about a hundred yards off, its lights cutting a swathe through the gloom as it drew nearer.

It was moving slowly, the driver obviously taking care in the treacherous conditions.

Scott, his head throbbing, remained hidden in the sodden bushes.

If only he could stop it . . .

He touched the hilt of the carving knife almost unconsciously.

The car was less than fifty yards away now; soon the headlamps would pick him out.

He moved quickly, walking out into the road, lying down on the wet tarmac. It was an old trick but it was all he could think of.

He lay on his side, facing away from the car whose engine was now audible. His left arm was stretched out beneath his head, his right resting on his hip, close to the knife.

The pain filled his head as he lay there, rain beating against his pale face.

The car rounded the corner, its lights picking out his immobile form. He heard the driver slam on the brakes, the slight squeal of rubber as the car came to a slippery halt on the greasy surface. He lay there, rain soaking through his overalls, waiting.

Waiting.

The car was still where it had stopped, its lights bathing Scott in a cold white glow.

This wasn't right. The driver should have leapt out of his car. Instead, Scott could only assume that the man was still sitting behind the wheel wondering what to do.

Come on. Come on.

He heard a door open, heard a woman's voice in the background saying something about being careful. Then he heard a man's voice too.

There were two of them in the car, perhaps more; he couldn't see from the position he was in.

He heard footsteps coming closer, hesitant and unsure.

His right hand slipped a couple of inches so that it was touching the hilt of the knife.

The footsteps came nearer. A shadow fell over him, the driver silhouetted in the powerful headlamps.

'I think he's alive,' the man called, moving nearer.

He could hear the engine of the car idling.

The man could only be a few feet from him now.

Scott heard more footsteps. Drawing closer.

Closer.

The man knelt beside him; Scott could even hear him breathing. He felt a hand on his shoulder, turning him gently on to his back.

'Oh Christ,' murmured the man, noticing Scott's prison uniform, spotted as it was with blood and excrement, reeking of filth.

Scott's eyes snapped open and he found himself gazing into the terrified features of a man roughly his own age.

Scott struck out with his left hand, catching the man full in the face with a punch that broke his nose. He fell backwards, cracking his head on the concrete of the road, opening a gash on the back of his skull that immediately began oozing blood.

Scott was up in a second, hurdling the prone man, heading for the car.

He saw and heard the woman scream as she locked the passenger side door, then leant over to secure the driver's side of the Renault.

Scott grabbed the handle and tugged, managing to beat her to it.

She screamed again and tried to back away from him, but he grabbed her by the hair and pulled her across the driver's seat, hurling her from the car into the wet bushes at the roadside. One of her high heels came off and she scraped her face on the branches as she fell, blood running from a cut on her cheek.

Scott slid behind the wheel, jamming the car into gear.

The man was rising, coming towards the car again, blood streaming from his nose.

371

Scott floored the accelerator and the car roared forward like a bullet.

It slammed into the man, hurling him into the air and sideways into the bushes where he landed on his back close to his companion, who screamed again as Scott roared away, exhaust fumes filling the air, mingling with the acrid stench of burned rubber.

The Renault hurtled off down the road, leaving the woman to crawl over to her injured companion.

Scott could see her in his rear-view mirror, sobbing helplessly as she sought to revive the man who, for all Scott knew, could have been dead. Come to think of it, the speed the car had been travelling when it hit him probably *would* have killed him. Scott took one more look in the rear-view mirror but the former occupants of the car were nowhere to be seen.

He put his foot down.

He knew he had to get out of this prison uniform and into some normal clothes. The journey back to London was going to be difficult enough without advertising where he'd just come from.

Back to London.

He gripped the wheel tightly.

Back to London.

He guessed it would take him about five or six hours. He should be there before morning.

Back to Plummer.

His head was throbbing mightily now, but there was a fearful determination etched on his face.

Back to Carol.

He glanced at his own reflection in the rear-view mirror and saw the bandages that covered the top of his head and most of his forehead. He slowed, stopped and tore most of them off, leaving just the one that covered the wound of his operation.

The dashboard clock said 2.06 a.m.

The pain seemed to be getting worse.

Scott gripped the wheel more tightly. He must get out of these overalls.

But before that, there was something else he must do.

Ninety-three

There were two Scania trucks parked in the car park of the petrol station. Apart from the two juggernauts, Scott could see no other vehicles.

He drove past them once, trying to see into the cabins, but there was no sign of their drivers. He winced as the pain struck him again, even more forcefully, like a physical blow. The Renault went out of control momentarily but he brought it into line and drove on, slowing down as he reached the covered area that formed a canopy leading up to the door of the service station entrance.

There was one figure in red overalls inside the building. A man in his early twenties. Scott could see that he was reading a newspaper.

Scott parked the Renault around the corner and sat behind the wheel for a moment, waiting for the pain inside his head to diminish.

It didn't.

On shaking legs he forced himself out of the car, ensuring that the knife was hidden as he approached the double doors that led into the service area. Like many along motorways it sold not just books, papers and magazines but also food, drink and even clothing. Scott could see several pairs of jeans hanging up inside, as well as some shirts.

He approached the double doors and pulled at one.

They were locked.

The young man in the red overalls looked up and ran appraising eyes over Scott.

'Use the night window,' he called, indicating the small hatch where he sat.

Cursing under his breath, Scott ambled along to the window, reaching behind him once to touch the hilt of the carving knife.

The young man was looking intently at him, or, more to the point, at his clothes. The grey, blood-flecked, reeking prison overalls made Scott ridiculously conspicuous. He may as well have worn a day-glo sign on his chest proclaiming 'Escaped Convict'.

'What do you want?' the young man asked, his eyes constantly drawn to Scott's overalls.

'I need to use your toilet,' he said.

'We lock it at night. I'll have to give you the key,' the young man told him.

Scott nodded, watching as he retrieved a bunch of keys from the counter.

'I need some things too,' Scott said. 'I want to come inside.'

'Sorry, but it's company policy. This place has been robbed too often in the past year or so. You tell me what you want and I'll get it for you.'

Scott gritted his teeth, both in pain and also frustration. Even if he could get the jeans, the shirt and the pain-killers he wanted, how the hell was he going to pay for them?

374

'The keys for the toilet,' said the young man, extending his hand, the keys lying on his palm.

Scott stepped back slightly, forcing the young man to extend his hand through the narrow gap at the bottom of the cash window.

'Take them,' said the attendant warily.

Scott looked deeply into his eyes, his own bloodshot orbs blazing with intent.

He moved so quickly the youth had no chance to pull away.

Scott grabbed his arm just above the wrist, simultaneously yanking the youth forward, slamming his face into the glass with such force that it dazed him. Then, with his free hand, he pulled the knife from his belt and brought it down with terrifying force onto the young man's outstretched wrist.

The blow severed the hand with one cut.

The appendage fell to the ground, blood spurting from the torn arteries, jetting onto the forecourt as Scott held his victim up against the glass, gripping on above the stump of the wrist that was spewing crimson violently into the air. He jerked the boy forward again and again, each time slamming his head against the thick glass, until he also opened up a hairline cut along his scalp. The glass was smeared with crimson.

Scott continued to hang on to the handless arm, tugging with such force that it seemed he must rip the youth's arm from its socket. He allowed him to lean back a few inches then pulled savagely on the arm, forcing the young man's head against the glass with sickening and powerful force.

A crack appeared in the glass.

Then another.

The fingers of the severed hand at Scott's feet were jerking as if in time to the blows of the boy's head against the glass, which had now spider-webbed. Crimson poured down the attendant's

375

face; Scott fancied he could see bone gleaming whitely through the pulped and torn flesh on his face and forehead. He finally let go of his victim's arm, allowing the body to sag to the floor. Then he gripped the hilt of the knife in his fist and drove it hard against the splintered glass.

It broke immediately, pieces of glass flying inwards, showering the prone body of the attendant.

Scott looked around, then pulled himself up into the frame of the small window. It was a tight squeeze. He groaned as he tried to pull himself through, yelping in pain as he cut his calf on a chunk of broken glass. Blood began to soak through the overalls as he fell into the motorway shop, sprawling onto the unconscious attendant.

Scott struggled to his feet and hurried over to the rack of jeans and shirts. He pulled half a dozen pairs off the hangers, grabbed an arm full of shirts. Then he hurried back behind the counter, picking up a large bottle of lemonade, his eyes scanning the shelves for pain-killers. He stuffed packets of aspirin, paracetomol and any other pill he could find into his pocket. He grabbed two tins of Elastoplast. Then, carrying his haul, he clambered back over the unconscious attendant and out of the broken window, dropping two pairs of the jeans in the process. One pair fell across the pulped face of the attendant, hiding his terrible injuries. Blood began to soak through the denim.

Scott fell onto the concrete of the forecourt and sprinted for the Renault, cursing as he looked down to see blood from his torn calf seeping through the material of his overalls. He tossed the jeans and shirts into the back of the car, slid behind the wheel and drove off, struggling one-handed to free some paracetamol from their container. He shook two out and pushed them into his mouth, chewing them dry, almost gagging at the bitter taste. Then he swallowed another two, washing them down with a swig from the lemonade bottle.

In a short while he would pull in somewhere and change into a pair of jeans and a shirt. It would give him a little more camouflage for his journey.

He gripped the wheel tightly, closing his eyes momentarily against the pain.

On the opposite carriageway a police car hurtled past him, lights flashing.

Scott drove on, past a sign which proclaimed: LONDON 143 MILES.

He looked at his watch, wincing once again at the unbearable pain inside his head. He swallowed two more tablets, wondering how long they would take to work. *If* indeed they did.

He drove on.

Ninety-four

The cell door crashed open, slamming back against the wall, the impact reverberating round the small room.

Mike Robinson blinked hard, shocked from sleep by the sound and, now, by rough hands on him, pulling him from the top bunk.

Beneath him, Rod Porter was also being pulled from the warmth of his bunk, hurled across the room by the first of the warders who had barged into the cell.

'What the fuck is *this*?' snarled Porter but, as he turned, he was struck hard across the face with a baton. The hardwood

377

split his cheek and he fell to the ground, blood pouring from the gash.

Robinson was thrown against the wall, a fist driven into his stomach, knocking the wind from him. Through pain-misted eyes he saw his locker torn open and its contents scattered, saw the bunks being overturned, saw the small cupboard that had housed James Scott's belongings ripped open. The photograph of the blonde woman Scott had spoken of (Robinson couldn't remember her name) fluttered to the floor where it was trodden on in the melée.

Then another blow to the stomach sent him crashing to the ground, where he was allowed to lie for only brief seconds before being dragged to his feet behind Porter. Both men were dragged on to the landing.

Other prisoners, woken by the noise, were shouting and banging against their doors, not knowing what the early morning disturbance was. As warders passed by cell doors they smashed their batons against them by way of warning, but this only served to inflame the inhabitants further. The cacophony of noise rose to deafening proportions as Robinson and Porter were dragged along the landing towards the stairs, almost hurled down them by their captors.

'What the fuck is going on?' shouted Robinson at one of the men pulling him.

'Shut it,' the warder hissed, driving a punch into his kidneys, almost throwing him down the metal steps behind Porter.

The noise from the other cells filled the prison.

'How could he have got away?'

Governor Peter Nicholson glared at Dexter, his eyes unblinking.

378

'I wish I knew,' Dexter said. 'He would have been weak from the operation. In pain. I can't understand how he managed it.'

'Well, he won't get far,' Nicholson said, an air of conviction in his voice.

'I can't see how he'll survive so soon after the operation,' Dexter added.

'I don't care if they bring him back dead but I want him back here.'

'You never *did* care, did you? It never bothered you whether the men who were operated on lived or died.'

'That isn't what's at stake here, Dexter,' Nicholson hissed. 'No one has ever escaped from a prison where I've been Governor and I don't intend to let Scott be the first.'

'Your pride doesn't matter any more, Nicholson. The man is already out. He got away, that's the point. He *did* escape.'

'We'll find him. He'll be brought back. I want to know how he did it.'

There was a knock on the office door and Nicholson called for the visitor to enter.

The door opened and Warder Paul Swain entered, supporting Porter. The other two men in the room saw the blood pouring down the convict's face.

Nicholson nodded and Swain threw the man down.

Robinson followed, landing heavily on his arm.

'Get up,' snapped Swain, kicking Robinson hard at the base of the spine.

The office door slammed shut behind them.

'Don't tell me I won't get away with this,' Nicholson said, a slight smile on his lips, his gaze flicking back and forth from one inmate to the other. 'You can report this to the prison authorities if you like, but you'll never prove it happened. No matter what we do to you.'

379

'What do you want from us?' Robinson said.

'You were cell-mates with Scott; I want to know how he got out. I want to know if he talked about escaping. I want to know if you helped him.'

Porter eyed the Governor coldly, a slight smile on his face.

Nicholson saw it, took a step forward and struck Porter hard across the face, splitting his bottom lip. He fell backwards into the arms of Swain, who drove a fist into his kidneys then let him drop to the ground.

'For God's sake, stop it,' Dexter said.

'You keep out of this,' Nicholson roared. 'This is *my* prison and this is *my* affair.'

'You've lost him, Nicholson,' Porter said, sucking in a painful breath. 'He's long gone by now and *you* won't find him.'

'Did you help him escape?' the Governor rasped.

Porter spat blood, then clambered to his feet.

'Yeah, I gave him a leg up over the fucking wall,' he said.

Swain hit him hard across the small of the back with his baton.

Porter doubled up, falling to the floor once more.

'This will put another five years on your sentences,' Nicholson snarled. 'Both of you.'

'We don't know where he's gone,' Robinson protested angrily.

'Five years,' Nicholson spat. 'And I'll make it five years of hell.'

'Fuck you,' rasped Robinson and hawked loudly, propelling a gob of mucus into the Governor's face.

It hung there like a tear, trickling slowly down his cheek until Nicholson wiped it away.

Swain struck Robinson across the shoulder with his baton, then the shoulder blades, both blows almost cracking bone. Then the warder turned and opened the office door. Two of his colleagues, jackets already removed and sleeves rolled up, walked in.

'Take these men to solitary,' Nicholson said. 'See if they feel more like talking there.' He nodded, watching as the two men were dragged away.

'You can't do this,' Dexter protested as the office door slammed shut behind them.

'I've told you before,' Nicholson snarled, 'this is *my* prison and I can do what I like. Now, if you're not a solution to this problem then you're a part of it, so get out of here.'

Dexter turned to leave.

'I'll find him, Dexter,' said the Governor. 'And if he's not dead when he's brought back, he will be by the time I've finished with him.'

Ninety-five

'I don't like having to trust other people, Gregson.' Police Commissioner Lawrence Sullivan held the pieces of paper in his large hands, shuffling them like playing cards. 'I warned you before, you'd better be right, otherwise I'll have you back pounding a beat quicker than you can imagine.'

DI Gregson looked on indifferently.

'I told you, if I'm wrong, I'll resign,' he said flatly.

Sullivan got to his feet, the three pieces of paper in his hand.

'These,' he said, brandishing the papers before him, 'could be the key to what's been going on, or they could mean an end to your career *and* mine. I hope you realise what a bloody risk I'm taking. Not only do I dislike having to trust other people, I also hate gambles. And this, to me, is a gamble.'

'There's too much evidence . . .'

Sullivan cut him short.

'I know, you've told me that before. Well, after considering it all, I tend to agree with your theory that things at Whitely are, shall we say, a little irregular. But while there's the slightest element of doubt I don't like it. A conspiracy is one hell of an accusation, Gregson. Like I said, you'd better be right.' He sat down at his desk, the exhumation orders laid out in front of him.

'Are you going to pass them, sir?' Gregson asked, looking at his superior.

'They're already signed,' said Sullivan. He handed them to Gregson.

'A helicopter will take you, Finn and two other men to Whitely. It'll pick you up in an hour. It shouldn't take more than about fifty minutes to get there.' He exhaled deeply. 'Gregson, I want a full report on what you do or don't find up there, do you understand? An investigation of this kind makes me accountable to the Government as well as to our own people and the prison authorities.'

Gregson nodded.

'Do *you* think I'm right, sir?' he finally asked, quietly.

'Would it matter one way or the other?'

'Not really. I'm just curious as to what made you decide to get these.' He held up the exhumation orders.

'You seemed to have a pretty strong case to support your argument and if there *is* some kind of conspiracy going on at Whitely, then it should be exposed. Or perhaps, for once in

382

my life, I decided to gamble.' He looked at Gregson. 'But there's a lot on this bet. More than I think you either care or realise.' They exchanged glances once more then Gregson turned to leave.

'A full report,' Sullivan reminded him as he left. The door closed and the Commissioner was left alone in his office. He sat back in his seat, hands clasped together beneath his chin, gazing out of his window at the overcast sky.

'I got them,' Gregson said triumphantly, holding the ex-humation orders in front of him.

'Now what?' Finn asked him.

Gregson explained about the helicopter, the impending journey to Whitely.

'I doubt if they're going to be very helpful up there,' the DS observed.

'I couldn't give a fuck,' rasped Gregson. 'They don't have to be helpful. The only thing that matters is, with these exhumation orders they can't stop us.'

Ninety-six

He'd slept in the back of the car on a side-road, the merciful oblivion he sought interrupted so often by the pain in his head. Finally, after two disturbed hours, Scott had decided to drive on. He'd discarded his prison overalls in favour of one of the shirts and a pair of the jeans but he still wore his prison boots.

He'd washed his face and hands in the rain and he'd fixed a small bandage over the surgical dressing with Elastoplast. The wound in his calf had stopped bleeding, but it hurt; every time he pushed his foot down on the clutch, fresh blood seeped out.

The pain inside his head was less insistent. That was the handfuls of pain-killers he'd taken, he told himself. But it was still there, ever-present as he drove, glancing around him, wincing in the early morning sunlight that streamed through the windscreen.

He was well inside the outskirts of London now, heading for his own flat in Brent. If only he could reach it, the flat would provide a haven at least for a couple of precious hours. Providing the police hadn't already covered it, waiting for him to go there. No, surely they wouldn't expect him to head back to London so soon. *Would they*? He was convinced his escape must have been discovered by now, but he'd seen precious little in the way of police pursuit. Not as yet, anyway.

He decided to return to his flat; he would take the chance. Besides, there were things there he needed. A change of clothes, for one. And after that?

He gripped the wheel tightly, wincing at the pain that filled his head.

Plummer.

Scott ran one index finger tentatively over his forehead.

Carol.

She wouldn't be expecting him back, either.

The bitch.

How surprised they would be to see him.

Scott almost smiled. He glanced down at the passenger seat, at the pile of shirts and jeans there.

And the carving knife that lay hidden beneath.

This time he *did* smile.

As he glanced ahead once more he saw the police car.

It was travelling slowly up the other side of the road towards him; there was just one man in it.

Scott gripped the wheel, a reflex action brought about by a combination of pain and panic.

Should he pull in to the side of the road until the police car had gone?

It was getting closer. He knew he must make up his mind quickly.

He drove on, his eyes fixed firmly on the road as he by-passed the vehicle. Its driver offered him only a cursory glance. Scott watched the car in his rear-view mirror, saw it turn a corner and disappear from sight. He exhaled deeply, checking his mirror again to ensure that the police car hadn't turned to follow him. Satisfied that it hadn't he drove on, drawing nearer to his flat.

He saw no police cars parked outside; no officers waiting for him, at least none in uniform. They'd be plain clothes, he thought, angry with himself. The cars would be unmarked. There was an old Capri parked outside the block of flats where he lived, but it had no occupant. Scott looked around. A group of school-children were making their way noisily across the road in front of him, one of them slapping the bonnet of the Renault as he passed. Scott ignored the children, his eyes flicking back and forth as he drove past the block, satisfied that he was safe. He parked the car behind the Capri and climbed out, walking briskly across to the main doors, the knife tucked inside his jeans, covered by the folds of his shirt.

He would have to use the knife to get into his flat as he had no keys.

Wearily he began to climb the stairs. He felt the blade cold against his flesh.

The razor-sharp blade.

He thought of Carol.

The knife.
Plummer.
He continued to climb.

Ninety-seven

'Down there.'

The pilot tapped Gregson's shoulder and directed his attention towards the ground.

Through the cockpit windows of the helicopter the DI could see the shape of Whitely Prison standing darkly against the moorland that surrounded it.

He nodded as the pilot said something else, his voice metallic through the headset the policeman wore. The noise of the rotor blades filled the small cockpit as the twin-engined Lynx cruised smoothly towards its destination. Gregson checked his watch, noting that it had taken less than an hour to reach the prison from London. He glanced behind him to the rear seats, where Finn and two other plain clothes men sat. One of them, a tall man in his early forties called Clifford, was looking distinctly queasy. The other, Sherman, was looking out of the side window, watching the countryside rising up to meet them as the Lynx swept lower.

Finn was tapping his fingertips against his knees, waiting for the helicopter to land. He didn't like flying at the best of times and the Lynx, as far as he was concerned, offered even less protection in the air than an aircraft. He was looking forward to getting his feet back on firm ground.

386

One glance at Clifford told him the tall man felt the same way.

'You okay?' Gregson said, raising his voice above the roar of the rotors.

Finn nodded.

'Where do you want me to drop her?' the pilot interrupted, tapping Gregson's arm once again.

The DI scanned the prison below and stroked his chin thoughtfully. From their present height the huge Victorian structure looked like a model. He could see figures moving about within the grounds, some doubtless able to see the approaching chopper and wondering about its presence.

'Land in the exercise yard,' Gregson answered, pointing. 'There.'

The pilot nodded and the Lynx went into a swift descent which caused Finn to hold his stomach. The uncomfortable feeling he always experienced upon landing, his ears popping, seemed to intensify in the small aerial vehicle. Clifford thought he was going to be sick. Sherman felt like an extra from *Apocalypse Now*. He smiled at his own joke.

Gregson looked down as the Lynx descended, scanning the prison, wondering if Nicholson had seen them coming, wondering what the Governor was thinking as he saw the helicopter dropping gently out of the sky. The DI almost unconsciously touched the exhumation orders inside his jacket pocket. He felt a curious kind of exhilaration as the Lynx went lower, an excitement at the thought of finally finding an answer to the riddle of the killers. If there were answers, they were here at Whitely. He was sure of it.

The helicopter wavered slightly as the pilot prepared to set down. A strong gust of wind caught it and one of the skids bumped the concrete of the exercise yard but it re-adjusted and gently touched down. The pilot immediately switched off the rotors and Gregson and his companions hurriedly unstrapped themselves, the DI pushing open the passenger door.

'Keep your heads down,' the pilot yelled as the rotors continued to carve a pattern through the air. 'What do you want *me* to do?'

'Wait here for us,' Gregson told him, cupping one hand to his mouth to make himself heard over the dying engines.

The pilot raised one thumb in an attitude of acknowledgement, watching as the other three men clambered out and hurried away from the helicopter.

Two warders were approaching them, bewildered by the sudden, unannounced arrival of the Lynx. Before either of them could speak Gregson had taken his ID out and was holding it out in front of him for inspection.

'I want to see Governor Nicholson,' he snapped. '*Now.*'

Ninety-eight

What if they were waiting inside for him?

The corridor was deserted, just as the stairs had been during his tortuous climb. Maybe they were waiting in the flat itself.

Scott hesitated a few paces away, the thought turning over and over in his mind. He reached for the knife and pulled it from his belt, inserting it in the door frame close to the lock.

He had to take the chance.

Scott moved the knife gently but firmly and the lock finally slipped.

He stood close to the door, listening for any sounds of movement. Satisfied that there were none, he pushed the door open and stepped inside the flat, closing the door quickly behind him.

The place smelt damp. Cupboards were open and furniture lay overturned, the way it had been the day they arrested him. Scott stood looking around for long moments, pressing one hand to his temple as a particularly vehement stab of pain lanced through his brain. He gritted his teeth, thought for a second he was going to pass out. When it cleared, he moved into the bedroom. There he pulled open his wardrobe. His clothes were still there, at least. He tried the bedside cabinet.

The Beretta was gone.

He slammed the drawer shut, realising that the police had obviously kept it. Bastards. He sat down on the edge of the bed, acutely aware not only of the pain from his head and his leg but of his weariness, of the stench he was giving off. He decided a shower would remedy both those problems and stumbled through into the bathroom, spinning the cold tap and scooping water to swallow two more aspirins. Then he turned on the shower and pulled off the shirt and jeans he'd been wearing, finally standing naked.

Scott turned to the bathroom mirror and looked at his reflection. His skin was pale, his eyes sunken through pain and lack of sleep but it was the bandage to which he addressed his attention. With infinite slowness he began to peel it off, finally dropping it onto the floor. There was a piece of gauze on his forehead, held in place by two pieces of surgical tape. Carefully, the noise of the shower filling the room now, Scott removed them, pulling the encrusted gauze pad free.

The wound in his skull was less than two inches long, running from just below his hairline, diagonally towards his right eyebrow. The wound was caked with congealed blood and the dark stitches stood out even more vividly against the paleness of his flesh. He looked more closely, the breath sticking in his throat.

The wound was pulsing gently.

As he put his forefinger to it, he noticed that his hand was shaking.

The wound throbbed rhythmically, like a small heart, but the steady beat was not that of his pulse.

It bumped gently to its own tempo.

Scott swallowed hard, closing his eyes as a fresh wave of pain hit him.

Make it stop.

He moistened a piece of cotton wool and cleaned some of the dried blood from around the wound. The pain was intense. He rubbed both hands across his face and stepped beneath the shower, allowing the streams of water to wash the accumulated filth from him. He closed his eyes briefly, then looked down at the cut on his calf. It was deep and had bled profusely but he could attend to it himself. Besides, it was only a dull ache compared to the excruciating agony inside his skull. He washed quickly, seeing blood swirl around the plug-hole as he stepped out, switched off the shower and began to dry himself.

He found some bandages in one of the bathroom cabinets and hastily wound one around his calf, securing it with a stout bow. The wound on his forehead, he discovered, could be covered by a large plaster. Careful not to press too hard on the wound, he affixed it, leaning on the sink for support. He swallowed more aspirin and found, to his joy, that the pain was subsiding. He splashed his face with cold water and dried it carefully, satisfied the plaster was in place. Then he wandered back into the bedroom and slipped on a shirt, a fresh pair of jeans and a pair of cowboy boots.

He slid the knife down the side of one boot.

He crossed to the phone, checking that it was still connected.

He dialled Carol's number and waited.

Waited.

Nothing.

Three times he tried it. Three times he was greeted by the ringing tone.

Finally he pressed down on the cradle, listening to the monotonous buzz of the dial tone for a moment before punching new digits.

Ray Plummer's phone rang.

And rang.

And was picked up.

'Hello.'

He recognised the voice immediately.

'Hello. Who is this?' Carol Jackson wanted to know.

Scott gripped the receiver in his fist then, with a loud roar, slammed it down, the force of the impact shattering the plastic phone in two. He picked it up and hurled it across the room.

Fucking slag.

Dirty fucking slag.

He got to his feet, pulling on the leather jacket he'd taken from the wardrobe, and headed for the door.

The knife bumped against his leg as he walked.

The drive to Plummer's flat would take him less than an hour, he guessed.

But first, he had other tasks to perform.

Ninety-nine

He had seen the helicopter land, seen the four men disembark.

Now Governor Peter Nicholson heard the commotion outside his office, the raised voices of his secretary and of a man. A man who, seconds later, barged into the office, pushing Nicholson's secretary aside.

'What the hell is going on here?' the Governor asked.

'I might ask you the same thing,' Gregson snapped, followed into the room by Finn, Sherman and Clifford.

'I tried to stop them, Mr Nicholson,' the secretary protested, 'but they . . .'

'It's all right,' Nicholson said, waving her away. When the door was shut he turned on the invading policemen. 'How dare you come barging in here like this? I want to know what's going on.'

'So do we, that's why we're here,' Gregson said. 'In case you've forgotten, my name is Detective Inspector Gregson . . .'

'I remember your last visit,' Nicholson told him scornfully.

'Good, then you'll remember what it was about. Well, this time I'm not leaving until I get the answers I want.'

Nicholson smiled.

'And what answers are those?' he said.

'I'm going to find out what's going on in this bloody prison. I'm going to find out how four convicted murderers, supposedly locked up here, could re-appear in London and re-enact their crimes. I'm going to find out what your game is, Nicholson.'

'Get out of here now before I call your superiors,' the Governor said angrily, turning his back on the policemen.

'My superiors know I'm here and they know *why*,' Gregson announced.

The colour drained from Nicholson's face and he remained with his back to the DI, hiding his expression.

'Do they know what you're accusing myself and some of my staff of?' he said, some of the bravado gone from his voice.

'Cut the bullshit, Nicholson, we haven't got all day. We've got work to do,' Gregson hissed.

Nicholson turned to face him.

'Perhaps you should reconsider what you're doing before it's too late.'

'It's already too late, too late for *you*.'

'And what, exactly, are you proposing to do?'

'I'm going to open the graves of Peter Lawton, Mathew Bryce and Trevor Magee.'

'You can't do that,' Nicholson said quietly, the steel gone from his voice.

'Why not? We've already opened the grave of Gary Lucas,' Gregson told him, leaning forward on the desk. 'And do you know what we found? Nothing. Fuck all. No corpse. Just a bag of bricks. Lucas never died, did he? Just like Lawton, Bryce and Magee never died. You faked their deaths to cover up what you'd done to them here. Then you released them.'

Nicholson shook his head.

'You're insane,' he snarled.

'Maybe I am, but I'm also *right*.'

'You can't open the graves,' Nicholson said defiantly. 'I won't allow it.'

'You have no choice,' Gregson said triumphantly. He reached into his jacket pocket and pulled out the three exhumation orders, hurling them down in front of Nicholson. 'You can read them if you want to, but the most important thing is the signature at the bottom. Look at it.'

Nicholson picked up one of the documents with his thumb and forefinger, as if he were handling some kind of contagious material. He saw the sweeping hand of Commissioner Lawrence Sullivan on the order and the signature of a well-known judge.

'Do you still want to argue with me?' Gregson said.

Nicholson merely glared at the policeman.

'The records we had on Lucas say that his body was *prepared* by your resident doctor,' the DI said. 'Someone called . . .'

'Dexter. Dr Robert Dexter,' Finn interjected.

'I want to speak to him, too,' Gregson insisted. 'No autopsy was carried out on Lucas, according to the records. Did Dexter *prepare* the other three, as well?'

Nicholson nodded.

'Was he the one who experimented on them?'

'What are you talking about?' Nicholson snapped.

'There's nowhere to run *now*, Nicholson. We know it all. We have the bodies back at New Scotland Yard. We know the men were all suffering from massive brain tumours, possibly triggered by some kind of brain surgery. Surgery performed by Dexter. Where is he?'

'In the hospital wing.'

'Get him. Now.'

Nicholson's hand hovered over the phone.

'And then?' he asked.

Gregson smiled thinly.

'We've got some digging to do.'

One hundred

Scott could see the CLOSED sign on the door of Les Gourmets as he pulled up across the street from it. He parked the Renault and sat behind the wheel for a moment, his head resting against the steering wheel.

Stop this fucking pain.

He swallowed hard and opened his eyes, squinting at first to clear the mist of pain that seemed to have clouded his vision. A cobbled walkway ran alongside the restaurant and led to the back entrance. Scott swung himself out of the car and crossed the street. The walkway was wide enough for a small delivery truck and Scott noticed that there was a dark red Rover Sterling parked there.

He recognised the car; it belonged to Terry Morton.

As Scott moved towards the rear of the restaurant he saw two men in shirt-sleeves carrying large metal bins to a skip in the back yard of the eatery, emptying waste into the receptacle. He paused for a moment, his hand slipping down to touch the hilt of the knife. He pulled it free and slipped it into the back of his belt, hiding it beneath his jacket.

Scott moved closer as the men finished their task. He could hear the clanking of pots and pans inside the kitchen at the rear and there were several excitable voices being raised within. He peered around the corner and noticed that the door to the kitchen was open.

He assumed that Morton was inside.

He edged towards the back door, cursing as he slipped in a mess of spilled potato peelings. He walked on, into the kitchen of the restaurant. Several curious heads turned to look at him.

'Can I help you?' one of the staff asked, wiping his hands on a tea-towel.

'I work for Mr Plummer,' Scott said, regarding the man coldly. 'I noticed one of my friends is here. I saw his car parked round the side. Where is he?'

The man seemed to relax.

'Mr Morton is through there in the restaurant with Mr Perry,' he told Scott. 'Shall I tell them you're here?'

Scott shook his head.

'No, I'll surprise them,' he said, pushing past the man, who watched as he stepped through the macramé streamers that separated the kitchen from the dining area.

It was dull inside the restaurant, despite the daylight outside. The shutters were only half-open.

Morton and Perry were sitting at a table close to the window, a bottle of wine between them. Perry was glancing at a newspaper.

Scott took a couple of steps towards them.

It was Morton who saw him first.

'Jesus Christ,' he murmured.

'Not quite,' said Scott softly, a thin smile on his face.

'You're supposed to be banged up,' Morton told him, as if imparting information only *he* was aware of.

'Yeah, well, there's been a change of plan,' Scott told him.

'You look like shit, Jim,' Perry said, putting down his paper. 'What happened?'

'It's a long story. Where's Plummer?'

The two men looked at each other, then back at Scott.

'Why?' Morton asked.

'I want to talk to him. We've got some business to discuss. About twenty years' worth.' Scott moved closer.

Perry's hand moved to the inside of his jacket.

'Back off, Jim,' he said, his hand touching the butt of the .357 inside his jacket.

'Fuck you,' rasped Scott and moved the last few paces towards them with lightning speed.

He pulled the knife free as Perry went for the pistol.

Scott brought the knife round in a wide arc, the powerful backhand swing catching Perry across the face, slicing through his cheek and shearing off bone. A flap of skin fluttered uselessly. Perry shrieked in pain, blood spouting from the wound. He fell backwards off the chair, the gun falling from his hand.

Scott kicked it away from him, driving his weight against the table at the same time, knocking Morton back against the window.

Perry made a grab for the pistol but Scott kicked him hard in the side of the face, shattering his left cheek bone. Then he himself snatched up the .357, aware of shouts from behind him as the terrified staff watched the struggle.

Scott swung round, bringing the pistol to bear on Morton, who was reaching for his own gun.

'You fucking . . .'

The words were drowned by the massive discharge of the .357, the sound amplified within the confines of the deserted restaurant. Scott was blinded momentarily by the searing muzzle-flashes as he fired three times.

The first bullet missed, shattering the window behind Morton, but the second two struck home. One tore through his chest to the left of the sternum, exploded a lung and erupted from his back, carrying blood and portions of bone with it.

The other heavy-grain slug caught him in the stomach, doubling him up as it macerated a large portion of the duodenum and pulverised the liver on its deadly course. Morton was hurled backwards by the impact, blood jetting from the wounds, his own pistol falling to the floor.

He pitched forward, crashing into the table, spilling the bottle of wine, sending it flying. Scott stepped back and looked down at Perry, who was still trying to crawl away.

Scott shot him once in the back of the head, the bullet blasting away a sizeable portion of his skull, exposing his brain. He lay in a spreading pool of blood, his body twitching spasmodically.

Moving quickly now, Scott snatched up the pistol Morton had dropped, jamming the Smith and Wesson 459 automatic into his belt. He then rifled through the dead man's pockets and found his car keys. These he dropped into his own pocket before straightening up and moving across to Perry.

Scott found two full quick-loaders in the man's jacket. Each one carried six hollow-point .357 rounds. He pocketed those, too, then hurried towards the rear of the restaurant, where the staff who hadn't bolted in panic at the sound of gunfire were standing paralysed with fear. At one of the stoves a gas flame leaped high beneath a large copper pot. Scott's eyes narrowed.

'Get out!' he shouted at the staff. 'All of you, get out of here, now.' The sight of the .357 and the tone of Scott's voice combined to accelerate the evacuation. He crossed to the gas flame and stuck a balled-up tea towel in it, watching as the material ignited. He tossed it inside the dining area, then threw another after it, watching with delight as flames began to lick at chairs and tables, began to ignite table cloths. Fire spread rapidly, greedy tongues of it flaring wildly inside the room. Scott looked through the curtain of flames to the bodies of Morton and Perry, then turned and headed out into the yard and around the corner to the waiting Rover. He unlocked it and clambered in, sliding behind the wheel.

He stepped on the accelerator and the car sped away past the front of the restaurant.

Smoke and flames were already belching through the shattered front window.

Another few minutes and the entire building would be an inferno.

One hundred and one

All three of the coffins were empty.

They lay beside the graves, as if forced up from the dark earth, now discarded by it.

Empty.

Gregson moved slowly between them, not quite ready to believe the evidence of his own eyes but aware of the twinge of triumph deep within him.

The wind, blowing across the cemetery, ruffled his hair as he stood looking at the boxes. Beside him Sherman, Clifford, Finn and the two warders who had helped to disinter the caskets also looked on.

Nicholson and Dexter said nothing.

'There was a reason for it,' said Dexter finally.

Nicholson looked contemptuously at him.

'I'm not interested in your reasons,' Gregson told him.

'It was to *help* the men,' Dexter protested.

'What about the public, you bastard,' snapped the DI. 'You released murderers back into society, knowing they'd kill again.'

'No,' Dexter protested. 'The experiments would have worked. Their violent tendencies *would* have been cured.'

'Well they *weren't*, were they? You're as guilty of murder as the men who actually pulled the triggers or used the knives.'

'They got what they deserved,' said Nicholson. 'They died. Died as they would have done thirty years ago. We did the country a favour by experimenting on men like Bryce and Magee. What else would they have done? Sat here for the rest of their miserable lives feeding on taxpayers' food, clothed by the state, protected.'

'Well, it's over now, Nicholson,' said the DI. 'You're both under arrest.'

'It isn't over,' the Governor told him flatly.

'What the hell do you mean?'

'A man escaped from here last night. Another man we'd experimented on.'

Gregson's expression changed to one of shock.

'Who was he?' he demanded.

'He can't have got far,' Dexter said, dejectedly. 'I only operated . . .'

'Who was he?' Gregson roared.

'His name was James Scott,' Nicholson said.

Finn and Gregson looked at each other.

'How long's he been gone?' the DI wanted to know.

400

'We can't be sure,' Dexter said. 'Probably since late last night.'

'Jesus Christ,' murmured Gregson. He looked at Finn. 'Stuart, you take care of things here. I've got to get back to London as quickly as possible.'

'You think Scott will head back there?' the DS said.

'It's the only place he knows,' Gregson said, stepping over an empty coffin. 'I'll put out an alert to all units to watch for him. If he got a car he's probably there by now.' He looked at Dexter. 'Have you any idea what you've done?' he snarled.

'All I wanted to do was help them,' Dexter said quietly.

Finn pushed him and Nicholson away, nodding in the direction of the graves.

'Fill those in,' he said.

Gregson ran off across the cemetery, almost slipping on the mud in his haste. He sprinted across the exercise yard towards the waiting helicopter, wrenching the passenger side door open. The pilot hurriedly stubbed out his cigarette and looked in surprise as the DI scrambled into the other seat.

'Get us back to London as fast as you can,' Gregson told him. 'Move.'

He was already strapping himself in as the pilot switched on the motor and the rotors began to turn, carving an arc through the air as they rotated with increasing speed. The power built up rapidly.

Gregson clenched his fists together, his emotions a curious mixture of elation and foreboding. Elation that his theory had been proved correct. And foreboding at what Scott might do or, indeed, might have already done.

As the Lynx rose into the air he found that his hands were shaking.

One hundred and two

'I don't want to kill you, Rick. But I will if I have to.'

Rick Calder froze when he heard the voice. He felt the colour drain from his face, felt his bowels loosen as the barrel was prodded into the small of his back.

'Open it up,' James Scott told him, watching as Calder turned the key in the lock that secured one of the two metal grilles at the front entrance of 'Loveshow'. Calder hooked his fingers beneath the sliding screen of metal and pushed upwards.

'I thought you were inside,' he said quietly. His hands shook as he tried to find the key to open the door.

'Yeah, you and everybody else,' Scott told him, prodding him a little harder with the 459. 'Come on, get a fucking move on.' He looked to his right and left, satisfied that the gun he held was hidden from the view of any passers-by.

Calder finally found the right key and unlocked the door, stumbling inside as Scott pushed him through the entrance and slammed the door behind them. He winced as he felt that all-too-familiar pain inside his head, throbbing and pulsing. His brain seemed to be swelling, trying to burst through his skull.

'How the fuck did you get here?' Calder wanted to know, turning to face the other man, seeing the automatic levelled at him.

'It doesn't matter,' Scott told him.

'Jim, I didn't have anything to do with this,' Calder blurted. 'I don't know what you want with me. I haven't done anything to you.'

Scott thought Calder was going to start weeping.

'I know you haven't,' he said flatly. 'It isn't you I want,' he continued.

'So what are you doing here? Did you escape? How did you get out?' Calder's words were almost incoherent, they were spoken so quickly.

'Rick, just shut it, will you?' snapped Scott, taking a pace towards him. 'Give me the keys.'

Calder handed them over without hesitation.

'Take them, do what you want. Just don't hurt me, please,' Calder babbled, his eyes flicking from Scott's face to the barrel of the Smith and Wesson. 'I'll help if you want, just don't hurt me.'

'Rick, shut up will you,' Scott said wearily.

'I'll shut up, I'll shut up. Whatever you want, Jim. I'll shut up. Don't hurt me, though. I won't say anything else but . . .'

'For fuck's sake,' hissed Scott, taking another step towards Calder, whose eyes widened in terror. 'Shut up!' he roared.

He struck Calder on the temple with the butt of the pistol, the sound of metal on bone making a sickening thud. Calder dropped like a stone and lay still. Scott leant back against the wall, his breath coming in gasps. There was an ugly cut on Calder's temple, and already the area around it was beginning to darken. A thin trickle of mucus dribbled from his mouth.

Scott gritted his teeth.

Stop this fucking pain.

He sucked in several deep breaths, his hands pressed to his temples, his eyes closed.

He stood there for several seconds, finally taking one last glance down at the prone figure of Calder. Then Scott made his way downstairs.

He slapped on lights as he reached the bottom of the flight. Everything was how he'd last seen it. The bed in the centre of the room, the old chairs and sofas. The fading pictures on the peeling walls. He walked through towards his office, past the changing room, selecting the key to his office. He walked in, looking round.

Scott exhaled wearily and walked across to his desk.

With a shout of anger he overturned it, then snatched up the chair, swinging it wildly around his head, smashing the light bulb as he lashed out. The chair shattered and he was left holding just one of the legs. Brandishing it like a club, he headed back into the other room. There he smashed the nearest picture on the wall, overturned chairs and sofas. He picked up one of the small coffee tables and hurled it across the room, watching as it broke against the far wall. Scott's breath was coming in gasps now as he moved towards the small bar.

He stuck out his hand and, with one movement, swept the bottles from the shelves. They landed on the floor, glass shattering, contents spilling everywhere. He picked up one bottle and hurled it across the room, watching it smash against the far wall. Then another. And another. The place was filled with the sound of breaking glass. He hurled the bottles at the pictures, at the bed, at the walls. When there were no bottles left he ripped the shelves from their brackets, wielding one like a staff, breaking it across the bar top.

Scott picked up a handful of match books. He struck one match and held it close to the others, watching them ignite, then he dropped the flaming bundle to the floor.

The alcohol that had been spilled there ignited

immediately, flames leaping up around his feet. He moved away from the bar and lit more matches, tossing them onto the bed, the sofas. All went up with a loud whump. Flames began to take hold now, scorching their way across the floor in the wake of the spilled drink. Like the tentacles of some fiery octopus the flames shot out in all directions, incinerating everything they touched.

Satisfied that the fire had taken hold, Scott headed for the stairs, thick smoke already swirling around him.

As he reached the top of the stairs he noticed that Calder had regained consciousness. He was sitting up, tentatively touching the spot where Scott had hit him.

As he saw the other man he cowered back against the wall.

'Jim, please . . .' he began.

'If I was you, I'd get out of here, Rick,' Scott told him and headed for the door.

Thick black smoke was already beginning to fill the stairwell behind him.

'Oh Jesus,' murmured Calder, seeing the noxious clouds coming from below.

Scott pushed the door and stepped out on to the pavement, striding across to the Rover which was parked across the street. He slid behind the wheel and started the engine, noticing that, as Calder bolted from the building, the smoke billowed out of the door after him.

The flames had taken a grip. They would work their way up the stairs, destroying everything.

Scott watched for a moment longer then started the engine. As he shifted position slightly he could feel the two pistols jammed into his belt. They had a reassuring bulkiness to them. In one pocket he had the two quick-loaders, in the other a couple of spare magazines for the automatic.

He took one last look at 'Loveshow', smoke now belching from its door, and drove off.

One hundred and three

'How much further?'

DI Frank Gregson looked at his watch then at the pilot, who adjusted his microphone before speaking.

'Another twenty or thirty miles,' the pilot told him.

Gregson muttered something under his breath and looked out of the side window, watching the cars on the motorway below speeding along. The journey had seemed to take an eternity, although he realised they had been in the air less than forty-five minutes. Already the outskirts of London were appearing below them; the areas of greenery they had passed over when first leaving Whitely were now giving way to more densely populated conurbations.

The steady drone of the rotor blades continued and the maddening sensation of little or no speed only served to exacerbate the policeman's impatience. Again he checked his watch.

He'd called through to New Scotland Yard within minutes of leaving Whitely, to tell them that Scott was loose and probably back in the capital. He had also said that the man was possibly armed and extremely dangerous. Gregson had asked for armed squads to aid in the hunt for the fugitive. The radio had been conspicuously quiet, apart from the pilot picking up flying instructions. Despite Gregson's insistence that someone get back to him with a progress report, nothing had disturbed the airwaves yet.

He glanced at the radio and thought about calling again.

Had Scott been caught yet?

Had he been cornered?

Gregson wondered if he might even have been shot.

But no information had been forthcoming. No pieces of knowledge for him. Christ, he felt helpless.

'Tango Zebra, come in.'

The metallic voice over the radio seemed to startle Gregson.

The pilot flicked a switch on his control panel.

'Tango Zebra, I hear you, over,' he said.

'I want to speak to Detective Inspector Gregson,' the voice said.

Gregson tapped his microphone and the pilot nodded.

'Gregson here. What have you got?' he said.

'James Scott has been sighted in two places.'

'Where? How long ago?'

'He killed two men at a restaurant called Les Gourmets about an hour ago. The men are believed to be Terry Morton and Joe Perry.'

'What do you mean, believed to be?' Gregson snapped.

'After he killed them he set fire to the place. The bodies were quite badly burned. He also wrecked and burned the place where he used to work, a clip-joint called "Loveshow". Both places, as you probably know, were owned by Ray Plummer. Morton and Perry worked for Plummer. It seems like Scott's on a little crusade.'

'When was he last seen?' the DI demanded.

'About forty minutes ago. He's driving a stolen Rover Sterling which belonged to one of the men he killed.'

Gregson chewed his bottom lip thoughtfully for a moment.

'Tango Zebra, can you hear me?' the voice said, insistently.

'Don't try to take Scott alive, do you understand?' the DI said.

Silence from the other end.

'Did you hear what I said? *Don't* try to take him alive. Is that understood?'

'Understood.'

The Lynx was descending now, the shapes and outlines of the buildings below becoming more discernible.

'If you see Scott,' he said, 'Shoot to kill. Over and out.' He switched off his microphone.

The pilot looked across at him, saw the expression on his face and decided to say nothing.

Below them Gregson could see the Thames, winding through the city like a dirty ribbon.

It wouldn't be long now.

One hundred and four

The black police transit van stood with its back doors open, two uniformed men waiting.

DS Stuart Finn shielded the flame of his lighter as he tried to light the Marlboro he'd just taken from the pack. The wind was blowing strongly now; twice the lighter flame was extinguished. Cursing, Finn stuck to his task, drawing gratefully on the cigarette at last. He looked up to see Governor Nicholson being led out of the main building by two of his warders.

The irony of the situation was inescapable. The two men looked bewildered, embarrassed almost as they led the older man towards the waiting transit. He allowed Finn only a cursory glance as he passed, clambering up into the back of the van and sitting down on one of the benches. A uniformed policeman joined him.

Finn watched as Dexter was also led towards the van. He had taken off his lab coat and now wore just a pair of plain brown trousers and a brown jacket. His shirt was undone at the collar. Finn thought how weary he looked. His face was pale and drawn, his eyes sunken and lifeless.

He was scanning the exercise yard as he walked, noting that there were a couple of unmarked police cars nearby as well as an official one besides, of course, the transit in which he was about to take his place with Nicholson.

The plain clothes men who occupied the unmarked cars were standing around chatting, two with their hands dug in their pockets, collars turned up against the icy wind cutting across the open courtyard.

Inside the van, Nicholson looked out and saw Dexter approaching. So this was how it was to end, he thought. The irony of the situation was not lost on him. He glanced up at one of the windows of B Wing to see an inmate staring down.

The two men would be held at the nearest police station until charges could be formally brought against them. What exactly those charges were, Finn wasn't sure as yet.

Conspiracy. But conspiracy to do what?

Pervert the course of justice?

What did the rule book say about brain operations on convicted murderers? Where were the clauses on experimentation and release of those same murderers?

That, he was relieved to think, was not his problem. His only problem was getting these two men to the nearest police

409

station. He took another drag on his cigarette and patted the side of the the transit.

He'd ensured that the coffins had been reburied before they left. It was rather an empty gesture, considering they'd been without occupants, but Finn had a curious feeling of respect and dread for graves and he felt it only right that the cemetery be restored to its former state before he and his colleagues departed.

Dexter was slowing down, looking at the transit.

Perhaps the realisation was finally hitting him, Finn thought.

The doctor looked at the black vehicle and seemed to swoon. He took a step backwards.

Finn frowned, moved forward to help the older man.

Dexter ran at him and crashed into him, the power of the impact unexpected enough to send Finn toppling. He spun round in time to see Dexter running towards the nearest of the unmarked cars.

The drivers were standing about twenty feet away. They hadn't seen what had happened.

Dexter was already behind the wheel of the black Sierra.

'Stop him!' Finn bellowed, now chasing after the doctor. Dexter had started the engine, oblivious to the plain clothes and uniformed men running at him from all directions.

The closest of the officers actually managed to get a hand inside the car through the open side window. His fist closed around Dexter's collar, but the doctor stepped on the accelerator and the car shot forward, dragging the policeman. With one hand Dexter hammered at the vice-like grip, speeding up as he approached the open prison gates. He braked hard and the jolting impact caused the policeman to lose his hold. He somersaulted, landing heavily on the concrete.

410

Dexter drove on, glancing in the rear-view mirror, seeing that Finn had clambered into the blue Citroën and was following. The marked car was also in pursuit.

Dexter roared through the open gates and felt the car skid on the slippery track, but he regained control and drove on, flooring the accelerator, the needle on the speedometer touching ninety.

Behind him the Citroën and the police car followed, Finn hunched low over the wheel.

The Sierra reached the road and Dexter wrestled with the wheel, guiding the vehicle to the right. It skidded madly on the road but he kept it under control, noticing that Finn was closing the gap on him.

The police car had cut across in an attempt to head him off but Dexter saw what was happening and sent the Sierra speeding towards a ridge ahead. A wire fence separated the road from the field beyond, the bank sloping up like a ramp.

Dexter gripped the wheel and drove straight at the fence, crashing through it, the Sierra hurtling up the low bank. It was moving at such a speed that all four wheels left the ground and the vehicle seemed to hang in mid-air, suspended as if on invisible wires, for long seconds before slamming down with a bone-jarring crash.

The car skidded again, great geezers of mud spraying up behind it, but Dexter, his face covered by a thin sheen of sweat, kept control and sped on across the field.

Finn, his face set in an attitude of concentration, followed. The Citroën hit the bank and hurtled through the air, banging down in the muddy field.

The police car wasn't so lucky.

The driver, either because of misjudgement or fear, eased up his speed and the car hit the bank. But instead of sailing through the air, it nose-dived into the mud, the rear end toppling over until the entire vehicle crashed onto its roof, metal buckling under the impact.

Finn saw in his rear-view mirror that the other car had come to grief but he was more concerned with the Sierra now, roaring away from him across the field.

Surely, he thought, Dexter would have had more chance of outrunning him on an ordinary road. The muddy field could only slow him down.

What the hell was he playing at?

The cars roared on.

One hundred and five

How easy it would be to turn the gun on himself. To push the barrel of the .357 into his mouth and squeeze the trigger.

End the pain forever.

So simple.

Scott sat behind the wheel of the Rover, his head spinning, his vision clouding. And all the time there was the pain, gnawing away at him like some parasite feeding off his brain.

Take the gun and bite down on the barrel, taste the gun oil and the metal, then fire.

He could picture his own head exploding as he fired. Could feel the blissful oblivion. Could see himself at peace.

Could . . .

Fuck it.

No. He would not die yet. He refused to give up now. He had come too far, gone through too much to get to where he was now.

He gazed across the road towards the block of luxury flats where Ray Plummer lived. The one at the top. The penthouse flat. The pinnacle.

What had Cagney said in that film? 'Made it, Ma, Top of the World.' And then . . .

Scott pulled the Smith and Wesson from his belt, worked the slide and chambered a round. Then he jammed the pistol back into his belt and reached for the .357, flipping out the cylinder, checking that every chamber was filled with its deadly hollow-tipped load.

He was satisfied.

So it had come to this. His quest was almost over. He felt like some kind of medieval adventurer, some searcher after a lost treasure who could see that prize just yards away.

His prize was revenge.

It had kept him alive so far. Now he needed to claim that prize.

Scott swung himself out of the car, leaning against it for a moment as a fresh wave of pain hit him.

Keep me alert.

Stop the pain. Just for a while.

If he'd believed in God he might well have whispered a prayer.

Stop the pain.

He began walking, heading towards the entrance to the small block of flats.

Just for a while.

Just until . . .

He walked with his head down, gazing at the floor, only looking up as he reached the opposite pavement.

Had he looked up he might well have seen Ray Plummer watching him from the top window.

Scott reached the main entrance and slipped inside, pausing as he looked first towards the lift, then the stairs.

Which way to approach the penthouse?

If he took the lift he would be a sitting target as soon as the doors slid open. At least the stairs offered a modicum of cover.

He began to ascend.

Scott moved slowly, to minimise the sound of his footsteps. As he reached the second landing he pulled the 459 from his belt.

The doors on the other landings were closed, shut tightly like the eyes of witnesses to an accident who don't wish to see the carnage.

He reached the third landing.

One more left and he would have reached the penthouse.

He paused.

One floor above him, crouching at the top of the stairs, was John Hitch.

He had the Beretta 92S loaded and ready.

He listened as Scott ascended.

One hundred and six

'Get out of the fucking way.'

DI Frank Gregson banged the steering wheel furiously and roared at the car in front of him.

The learner who was driving the car had stalled at traffic lights and was now endeavouring to get the vehicle restarted as traffic built up behind.

Gregson glanced up and saw that the lights were about to change to red.

He would be stuck.

'Come on, come on,' he snarled.

The car in front remained stationary.

The lights were on amber.

Gregson reversed a few feet, almost bumping the radiator grille of an Audi behind him, whose driver now shouted at *him*. He then swung the Ford Scorpio around the back of the learner and, as the lights changed to red, shot across the junction, beating the oncoming stream of vehicles, ignoring the chorus of indignant hooter blasts that accompanied his move.

He floored the accelerator and drove on, swerving to avoid some pedestrians who had stepped out into the road.

The car sped on towards Kensington Road.

Gregson didn't know if he would be in time; he could only try and reach Ray Plummer's flat before Jim Scott.

The helicopter had landed back at New Scotland Yard less than twenty minutes ago. Gregson had gone straight to the armoury and checked out a Taurus PT-92 automatic and three magazines of 9mm ammunition. He'd been told that Commissioner Sullivan wanted to see him but he'd ignored the order, saying he must get to Plummer.

Scott, he already knew, had destroyed one of Plummer's restaurants and one of his clip-joints. It seemed only logical that he should now go after the man himself.

Gregson tried to coax more speed from the Scorpio, but ahead of him, coming into Kensington High Street, the traffic was slowing down again.

He had called once already for armed back-up, given the

address of Plummer's flat.

Would he be too late?

There had been no answer yet.

He snatched up the radio, banging the hooter with his free hand as a car turned left ahead of him without indicating, causing him to brake hard.

'This is Lima 15, do you read me?' he rasped.

'Lima 15, go ahead.'

'I asked for back-up, *armed* back-up to some flats in Kensington. Where the hell is it?'

Silence for a moment, just the hiss of static.

'What address was that, Lima 15?' he was asked.

Gregson gave the address again.

'What the fuck are you playing at there? I need those men fast. Do you understand?' he added angrily.

'Affirmative, Lima 15. A unit is on its way . . .'

Gregson snapped off the handset and replaced it, speeding on, cursing again when the traffic came to a standstill. He glanced to his right and left, thought about guiding the car up onto the pavement. No, too many fucking pedestrians about.

He looked at his watch again.

Something told him he was too late.

One hundred and seven

The step creaked under his weight.

Scott paused a moment, thinking how loud the sound seemed in the silence of the stairway.

416

He was about five steps from the top now, ducked low, the Smith and Wesson automatic gripped in his fist.

He prepared to move again.

Another creak.

From ahead of him this time.

A sound not of *his* making.

Scott looked up, saw a shadow. A dark shape crouched there.

He moved down a step.

There was more movement ahead, above.

John Hitch took a couple of steps towards the head of the stairs, the Beretta gripped in his hands.

Scott raised his own pistol simultaneously. There was a thunderous roar as both men fired. The stairway was lit by muzzle flashes so brilliant they could have blinded. The walls shook as the roar of the automatics bounced around, amplified in the stairwell.

Scott felt a bullet blast through his shoulder, blood and portions of bone spraying the wall behind as he fell backwards, but he managed to get off three shots of his own.

One blasted a huge chunk of plaster from the wall, another hit the step Hitch was standing on. The third caught the man in the right shin. The bullet shattered his tibia, the strident cracking of bone audible even above the monstrous discharges of the pistols. A part of the bone tore through the skin and also through the material of Hitch's trousers. He shrieked in pain and dropped to the ground as Scott tried to force his way back up the stairs. His left shoulder was already beginning to go numb but he forced himself to keep a grip on the 459, firing again.

Another bullet hit Hitch in the forearm, but it passed through the muscle without touching bone.

He shot Scott in the stomach.

417

Scott felt as if he'd been punched by a red-hot fist. The air was knocked from him and the impact almost lifted him from his feet but he remained upright, blood running freely from the wound. The bullet exited through his side, taking muscle with it, spraying the bannister and stairs with blood, but Scott was lucky. No vital organs had been touched by the 9mm slug.

Scott fired twice at his prone foe, who was now trying to drag himself away from the top of the stairs.

The first bullet caught him in the left side of the chest, smashing two ribs as it blasted its way through, punching an exit hole the size of a fist and almost throwing Hitch against the far wall, which was sprayed with crimson and gobbets of lung tissue.

The second shot hit him, more by luck than judgement, in the hollow of the throat, blasting two cervical vertebrae to powder as it exploded from the back of his neck.

His head flopped back uselessly, his eyes rolling upwards in their sockets.

Death was instantaneous and Scott heard the soft hiss as the sphincter muscle relaxed. He smelt the excrement, saw a dark stain spreading rapidly across the front of Hitch's trousers.

Scott stumbled to the top of the stairs, the stench of blood and cordite strong in his nostrils.

He had pain now, but it was everywhere.

His head. His shoulder. His stomach.

He coughed and tasted blood in his mouth. A thick crimson foam dribbled over his lips; streamers of bloodied mucus hung from his mouth. He spat, wiping his mouth with the back of his hand.

As he reached the top of the stairs, stepping over the body of Hitch, he could see the door to Plummer's apartment.

He moved slowly towards it, ejecting one magazine from the automatic. Scott rammed another in and worked the slide.

He moved closer to the door.

The fucking pain . . .

He thought he was going to faint.

Not yet.

He was outside the door now.

Not yet.

There was a spy-hole in the door.

He threw himself to one side as a fusillade of bullets tore through the wood, blasting huge holes in it.

Scott landed heavily on his injured side, more blood filled his mouth. He swivelled round, hauling himself upright, and crawled towards the door.

Silence had descended again; only his own wheezing breath was audible in the desolate solitude. Curtains of smoke wafted around, grey-blue smoke flecked with tiny cinders and pieces of wood that settled like dirty snow on the carpet.

He dragged himself upright, smearing blood against the wall. Then he stood beside the bullet-blasted door, steadying himself.

He gritted his teeth.

Now. It was time.

Scott swung his foot at the door with incredible force and it flew open, slamming back against the wall.

He dashed in, firing wildly to cover his entrance.

Bullets raked the apartment; ornaments were hit, blasted into oblivion.

Scott kept his finger pumping the trigger, firing all fifteen of the bullets until the slide flew back, signalling the pistol was empty.

He saw Ray Plummer standing to his left, in the entrance to the bedroom.

Carol was behind him, her face blank, drained of colour.

Scott turned on Plummer, realising that his gun was empty.

Plummer held a 10mm Delta Elite on him.

Scott opened his mouth to roar his rage but the sound was lost beneath the thunderous blast of the Delta.

The bullet hit Scott in the chest, punctured a lung and exploded from his back, chipping the bottom of his left scapula, tearing an exit hole large enough to get two hands in. Portions of greyish-red lung tissue and pulverised bone erupted from the wound.

Scott was lifted, as if by some invisible hand, and sent sprawling over the sofa, blood spraying out behind him.

He crashed into a coffee table, the impact almost making him black out. Then he rolled onto his stomach, his mouth open, his eyelids flickering.

He heard Carol call his name, heard Plummer tell her to shut up.

Footsteps came close.

Through pain-misted eyes he saw Plummer looking down at him, the 10mm levelled.

Scott was lying on his right hand, his fingers within reach of the .357. He felt his shaking digits touch the wood of the stock.

'You should have stayed away,' sneered Plummer. 'Stayed in prison. You came a long fucking way to die.' He aimed the pistol at Scott's head.

Scott rolled onto his back, the .357 now in his hand. He fired upwards, twice.

The first bullet blasted Plummer's nose off, obliterating the fleshy appendage, which dissolved in an explosion of blood.

He screamed in agony but the sound was cut short as the second hollow tip bullet hit him below the chin, tearing upwards into his head, through his brain and finally bursting from the top of his skull, lifting him off his feet.

His head looked as if someone had placed an explosive charge inside it. The entire cranial cavity seemed to detonate, blood and brain spattering the ceiling, spraying everything within a foot or so.

His wig was blown clear, flying off to one side like a flattened cat.

Plummer tottered for interminable seconds, his bald dome open to the air, portions of his brain hanging from the riven cavity, blood jetting madly into the air. Then he fell forward across the sofa, his body sliding to the floor, crimson spreading in a pool around him.

Carol could only stand mesmerised. Her body shook, her nostrils were filled with the smell of cordite and death, her eyes had been blinded by the muzzle flashes, her ears rang from the thunderous discharges.

She looked at Scott, then at Plummer.

Scott. Plummer.

Scott.

She moved towards him, noticed that his chest was rising and falling slowly. She could hear a soft, wet sound. It was Scott's breath wheezing through the hole in his lung. The place was drenched with blood – floor, ceiling, walls.

She felt the warmth beneath her bare feet, felt a jellied lump of matter between her toes and almost vomited when she saw it was part of Plummer's brain. She stepped back and looked down at Scott once again.

He was lying on his back, his eyes half-open.

Carol swallowed hard as she saw the wounds, the one in his chest gaping, a portion of bone shining through the pulped flesh and the bright blood.

She knelt beside him, ignoring the blood that had soaked into the carpet around him.

'Jim,' she whispered, touching his cheek with the back of her hand.

He could see the tears in her eyes.

'Oh God, Jim, I'm sorry,' she breathed. 'I'm so sorry.'

He tried to breathe but couldn't.

421

Tried to speak. Couldn't.

Blood ran over his lips and down his chin.

'Jim,' she repeated, touching his face once more, stroking it as a lover might touch a partner.

His eyes narrowed too.

Fucking bitch.

'I'm sorry,' she said again.

You betrayed me.

His own eyes were moist now, both from pain and emotion.

And fear?

He could almost feel death touching him.

'I didn't want this to happen,' she told him, still stroking his face. 'I'm so sorry.'

Tears were coursing down her cheeks.

She lowered her head, as if in prayer, her hands resting on her thighs.

Scott raised the .357 and pointed it at her head.

Carol had her eyes closed now.

Bitch.

He thumbed back the hammer.

It was then that she looked up.

The roar of the single shot was deafening.

One hundred and eight

The sound of the discharge reverberated inside the apartment for what seemed like an eternity.

It mingled with Carol's scream.

She had seen Scott lift the gun and point it at her, their eyes locked for precious seconds, then she had seen his head burst as the 9mm bullet had hit it, pulverising his forehead.

Frank Gregson stood in the doorway, the Taurus automatic still aimed at Scott, as if he feared the man would move again.

Carol looked at Scott, then at the policeman.

Tears were still coursing down her cheeks.

'He would have killed you,' Gregson said, walking into the room, glancing at Plummer's body. 'Just like he killed the others.' He looked at Plummer once more. 'He was a madman. He wanted revenge.' Gregson nudged Plummer's body with the toe of his shoe. 'He did me a favour, though. Getting rid of Plummer.' The DI smiled. 'I just didn't want *you* to get hurt.'

'What difference would it have made to you?' she wanted to know.

'A lot of difference,' he said, his smile fading. 'I care what happens to you very much. I have done ever since I first arrested you.' He sat down on the edge of the chair, looking down at her. 'That's why I called you.'

Carol looked vague.

'What are you talking about?' she wanted to know.

'The phone calls,' he said. 'I called you at your home, at work, even here.'

'Oh God,' she murmured.

'I hated to think of you with men like Plummer and Scott,' he said. 'You deserved better than that. I wanted you to know I was watching you. I wouldn't have let anything happen to you.'

'You were the anonymous caller,' she blurted, everything now beginning to drop into place with appalling clarity.

'I didn't just ring you,' he said. 'Who do you think tipped Plummer off about that cocaine shipment?'

'But why?' she wanted to know.

'Plummer was too powerful. The gangs in London had taken over,' Gregson said angrily. 'They were running things. Men like Plummer and Connelly. Scum. Criminals and fucking murderers.' He spat out the words vehemently. 'I wanted a gang war, I wanted them to wipe each other out. To save *us* the trouble of trying to arrest them. Getting them to court on charges we knew would never stick. That's what we've been doing for years. The police are fighting a losing battle against men like Plummer and Connelly. I knew the only way was to use force but *I* can't do that, my *responsibility to the community* says I can't. I couldn't stop them. So I realised I'd have to make *them* stop each other. Kill each other. Wipe each other off the face of the fucking earth. That's why I tipped Plummer off about Connelly's shipment; I knew he'd take it because he was greedy. I knew if he took it Connelly would never stand for it. I knew there would be war, and there would have been. *I* would have won. The fucking *law* would have won for a change.' He sucked in a deep breath. 'Well, now it's all over. Now you're not tied to him anymore. You're free.'

'Am I supposed to thank you?' she said softly.

'Perhaps,' he said, smiling thinly.

'Why did you have to do this to Jim?' she wanted to know.

'Plummer set him up, not me.'

'And if Plummer *hadn't*?'

Gregson shrugged.

'Then I'd have got rid of him some other way,' he said.

'You're insane,' she said quietly.

'The whole fucking world is insane,' he said wearily.

'What about me? What happens to me now? You've told me everything. I know about you and what you've done.

424

You're the evil one. You would have let dozens of men kill each other. You let Scott die for no reason. And I know it all.'

'Who's going to believe you?' he said, smiling.

'No one,' she said quietly.

'You're mine when I want you now,' Gregson told her. 'And there isn't a thing you can do about it.' He smiled.

'No,' she said. 'I suppose you're right. No one's going to believe me, are they?'

'You're mine, Carol,' he said mockingly.

'I don't have a choice, do I?'

'No,' he told her.

She picked up the .357 lying nearby, steadied herself and fired twice.

Both bullets hit Gregson in the chest. As he fell she got to her feet and put two more into him.

The hammer finally slammed down on an empty chamber.

Carol continued to pull the trigger, looking down at the motionless, bloodied corpse of the policeman.

'All right, drop it.'

The voice boomed through the flat as the first of the armed policemen entered, pistols trained on Carol. She smiled thinly and dropped the gun.

'Jesus Christ,' one of the men murmured, looking round at the carnage.

Carol felt strong hands grab her. She felt lifeless, unable to move; only her eyes, it seemed, were functioning. She looked down at Gregson then at Scott.

Words drifted to her through a haze that seemed to have enveloped her brain. It was as if she were watching herself from outside, through other eyes. The words continued:

'. . . four dead . . .'

'. . . Maybe she killed them all . . .'

'. . . Tell his wife . . .' Two of the men were kneeling beside Gregson, checking for any signs of life.

One of them looked up at Carol. This time, the words did seem to penetrate the haze.

'Shooting a policeman,' he said angrily. 'You'll get life for this.'

Carol looked across at Scott's dead body.

'You'll get life for this,' she heard again as she was ushered out of the room.

'. . . life . . .'

She smiled thinly.

One hundred and nine

The needle on the petrol gauge was touching empty, Finn noticed with alarm. Nevertheless he kept his foot pressed down on the accelerator of the Citroën, glancing up ahead to see, to his relief, that Dexter too was slowing down.

There was a road of a kind up ahead, a badly tarmacked track that separated the fields from a large house built of dark stone.

Dexter was guiding the Sierra up the short driveway of this house.

Finn saw the doctor clamber out of the car and head for the front door, letting himself in, slamming the door behind him.

Finn screeched up the drive behind him and stood on the brakes. He ran to the front door and banged on it several times, shouting Dexter's name. When there was no answer

426

he turned and looked into the Sierra, noticing that Dexter had left the keys hanging from the ignition. Finn pulled open the door and dropped the keys into his pocket, then made his way slowly to the side of the house.

He found a pathway leading down the side of the building, its entrance guarded by a carefully cut arch of privet. Finn pushed open the gate and walked through, moving briskly around to the back.

The large house towered above the DS as he peered through windows into the kitchen then, moving along, into what he took to be a study of some kind. As he passed the kitchen door he tried the handle but found that it was locked. A long, immaculately kept garden stretched out behind the house.

He saw several objects lying on the lawn.

Toys.

There was a doll and a small yellow ball. A skipping rope.

Finn picked up the doll, looking into its lifeless eyes for a moment, then dropped it back onto the grass and headed back towards the kitchen door.

There were panels of glass in it.

He broke one with his elbow then reached through and turned the key in the lock, stepping inside.

He called Dexter's name as he moved through towards the sitting room.

'Give it up, Dexter,' he shouted. 'There's nowhere else to run now.' He moved through the sitting room. 'If it isn't me it'll be someone else. I've only got to make one call and this place will be swarming with uniforms in less than five minutes.'

He moved out into the hall.

'Don't make things any worse,' he called. 'Chuck it in, now.'

A sound above him.

Finn looked up towards the landing.

The stairs were directly ahead of him. To his left was the door of the study, to the right the front door.

Finn wondered why Dexter hadn't just continued driving in the first place, why . . .

Another noise from upstairs.

. . . Why not escape? Why come here?

He began to climb the stairs, one hand trailing along the bannister.

Why come here?

He was half-way up the stairs now, glancing around, his eyes always returning to the head of the flight.

Another ten steps and he'd be there.

He could hear the sound of his blood roaring in his ears.

'Dexter,' he called.

Silence.

'There's no way out,' he continued.

Movement.

As Finn reached the top of the stairs, Dexter appeared from one of the rooms.

He had a double-barrelled shotgun levelled at the policeman.

'That's no answer,' Finn said, his eyes drawn to the yawning barrels of the Purdey. 'If you kill me, you make it even worse for yourself.'

Besides which, I don't want to die, you fucking maniac.

'This gun has been in my family for three generations,' Dexter told him conversationally.

'Why don't you just put it down, then we'll talk,' Finn said, wondering if his skin looked as pale and cold as it felt.

'The experiments at the prison, they would have worked,' Dexter said. 'They *had* worked.'

'There's a lot of dead people who are lying around to contradict that argument, Dexter.'

428

'It *did* work. It *can* work,' he insisted. 'I *made* it work.'

He snapped his fingers, the barrel still aimed at Finn.

The DS heard movement from behind Dexter, from the room he had his back to.

'Come out,' Dexter said, turning his head slightly, his eyes never leaving Finn.

A figure moved onto the landing beside him.

'Oh dear Christ,' murmured Finn, his eyes widening as he studied the features of the newcomer.

It was a woman; at least he thought it was. The short hair made it difficult to tell at first, and the voluminous nightdress managed to conceal any shape convincingly. Perhaps she had once been pretty. Finn could only guess. If she had, those days were long gone. The skin was the colour of rancid butter and hardly an inch of flesh on the face was not disfigured by scars, welts or stitches. The forehead had been worst affected, the hair shaved back almost to the top of the head, criss-crossed by stitching, bruises and half-healed wounds, some of which had scabbed over. Others were only purple knots where skin had begun to form but had been picked away.

Finn shook his head.

'Jesus Christ,' he muttered under his breath. 'What is it?'

'There was a car accident,' Dexter explained. 'In January 1976. At times it seems as if it was only yesterday, other times it seems like centuries ago. She was taken to hospital, but they couldn't do anything for her. The brain damage was massive. I worked in an asylum then. They brought her there to see if I could help. I think they would have been happy if she'd just been locked away, but I didn't want that.'

Finn noticed that the figure next to Dexter was holding a doll like the one that lay on the lawn outside. She was prodding the glass eyes.

'I knew I could do something. They said she was violent. The brain damage had caused some kind of psychosis. My colleague and I experimented on her. Her and a number of others. The others died, but she responded. I've looked after her ever since, here at this house.'

Finn was breathing deeply, his gaze moving from the figure then back to the shotgun.

'You would have been kinder letting her die,' he said, his voice a hoarse whisper.

'No,' Dexter said, shaking his head. 'I wouldn't let her die. Never.' There was a note of anger in his voice as he looked at the policeman. 'Not my own daughter.'

Finn swallowed hard.

The woman smiled at Dexter, streams of mucus running from her mouth, hanging from her lips like thick, elongated tears.

'*Daddy,*' she slurred.

Finn clenched his teeth together until his jaws ached.

'When I'm gone there'll be no one to care for her,' Dexter said. 'No one.'

'*Daddy,*' she whined in a metallic voice.

'I won't leave her,' the doctor said.

With that he spun round, aiming the shotgun at his daughter's head.

'No!' roared Finn.

The sound was lost beneath the blast as Dexter fired.

She dropped like a stone, the doll falling from her grasp. Blood spattered the walls behind. Finn saw fragments of brain and bone dripping from the ceiling.

He lunged towards Dexter, who spun the shotgun in his grasp, bit down hard on the barrels he'd stuck in his mouth and pulled the other trigger.

The top of his head erupted like a bloody volcano as the blast carried most of his skull away.

430

He fell backwards, sprawled across the legs of his daughter, the Purdey falling with a thump.

'Oh Jesus,' Finn murmured, holding one hand to his mouth, gazing at each body in turn. The air smelt of death.

The DS picked up the doll the girl had dropped.

Girl? Woman? God alone knew how old she was. And God had long ago tired of watching over *this* particular wretch.

Finn held the doll in his hands, looking into its cold eyes, then dropped it.

As it hit the floor he heard a whirring sound followed by one word, a metallic whine:

'*Daddy.*'

He turned and walked away, heading for the stairs, for the phone.

The word echoed in his ears. In his mind.

'*Daddy.*'

He who considers more deeply knows that, whatever his acts and judgements may be, he is always wrong . . .

Nietzsche

You can't win. You can't break even and you can't even get out of the game.

Ginsberg's Law